Discovering Elizabeth

A Novel By

Lisa D. Piper

Copyright © 2006 by Lisa D. Piper

All rights reserved. No part of this book may be reproduced in any form without permission in writing from the author or publisher.

The character names and each character's experiences in this book are fictional. Any similarity between the names and characterizations of these individuals and real people is unintended and purely coincidental.

Scripture texts used in this work, unless otherwise indicated, are taken from the KJV.

Published by PraiseHim Publishing
www.praisehimpublishing.com

Printed in the United States of America

ISBN 0-9721453-0-3

Library of Congress Control Number: 2006902252

Printed in the United States by Morris Publishing
3212 East Highway 30
Kearney, NE 68847
1-800-650-7888

For my Mother

my friend, my encourager and my hero

Acknowledgements

Every writer needs a supportive team, and I live with three people that encourage and inspire me. Thank you, Dennis, you are a dream husband! And, thank you, Kyle and Kirstie, for loving my stories...and requesting them over and over again. No one has encouraged your mother as a writer more than you.

Thank you, Joanne Jones, Cassandra Minton, Stephanie & Richard Dakin, Lisa Beyes, Mary Ellen Henry, Darlene & Darrell Dakin, Lou Goff, Sharon Wright, Marilyn Snyder, and Sandy Fowler for helping to review and edit *Discovering Elizabeth*. Your words of encouragement and instruction have been a blessing to me.

I want to take a moment to acknowledge three educators that influenced my passion for writing and instilled courage in me to share my work with others. Thank you Jeanette Larkin (3rd grade), Hular Barrow (high school) and Anne Pruitt (college).

When I began writing, I wanted to write in a way that would both astound and confound the reader. Thankfully, I gave up trying to purposely write books of theological revelation and began to write within the gifting that God has given to me. My hope is that you will enjoy meeting my imaginary friends. I hope you laugh, I hope you feel love and I hope you have fun as you get to know Elizabeth and her friends.

Thank you, Jesus, for giving me the desires of my heart. Thank you for saving me from myself. Thank you for taking this novel out of my heart and putting it into print. I love you. You are greater than my imagination.

*As the story of *Discovering Elizabeth* unfolds, you will meet a wonderful character named Homer. I love his warmth, work ethic, wit and orneriness. Although this character was created before I met Jerry Lynn, there's no man that best fits Homer's profile like my beloved friend, Jerry. Jerry passed away one month prior to the printing of this novel. He was a hard working man who worked in the body of Christ for over 30 years. I want to say thank you to the Lynn family. Thank you for sharing Jerry Lynn. His presence in my life has made the difference.

Chapter ONE

"Thou he fall, he shall not be utterly cast down: for the Lord upholdeth him with his hand" Psalms 37:24

    Elizabeth Anne Pennington moved swiftly to find the object that produced the loud, blaring blast. After knocking her clock off the nightstand, she finally hit the button that would allow her ten more minutes of sleeping pleasure. As she snuggled into her pillow, the sound of a familiar verse echoed in her head, "Great is the Lord. He is Greatly to be Praised.[1]" Smiling, she rolled over and immediately realized she would have to figure out how to escape the twisted blankets that had wrapped around her during the night. Before struggling to be free from her grandmother's homemade quilt, she lay back and whispered a quick prayer. "Good morning, Lord. Thanks for this day and thanks getting me through it."

As Elizabeth padded into the restroom, she grumbled when she noticed her reflection in the hallway mirror. "Oh no. It's going to take a lot of work for this to qualify as a good hair day." Her thick blonde hair was a mess: evidence of a night of restless sleep. Slumber usually engulfed her but last night had been different. Dread for what must happen when she returned to work spilled into her dreams. She thought about the words that had woken her. Somehow she would find the strength to battle another Monday morning at Wright and Wingold.

---

[1] Psalm 145:3a NKJV

Lisa D. Piper

Elizabeth stepped into the shower. She had washed her long blonde hair the evening before but decided that a second washing would be necessary in order to regain control of her rebellious golden locks. The young executive had enough natural curl to make her hair look in disarray if she didn't start the morning taming it. Mousse, hair spray and a blow dryer would be used to bring order to the resistant strands. Elizabeth reached across the counter to retrieve the can of hair spray but instead of retrieving it; she knocked it off the counter. As the falling can knocked the open jar of loose powder to the floor, Elizabeth became more than frustrated. She bent down to pick up the can but dropped it two more times before she was able to pick it up and begin cleaning up the powdery mess. She groaned deeply as she wiped the powder. The mess was formed when it mingled with water left on the floor from where she had not taken the time to dry herself properly because of the Monday morning rush. Her patience was tested as the telephone began to ring.

"Hello?" Elizabeth looked at her watch as the caller, her assistant Jillian, asked her what time she would be arriving to work. Elizabeth replied, "I'll be in at eight o'clock."

She realized her error but not before Jillian's pinched voice muffled, "Elizabeth, it's now ten after eight. You cannot be here at eight. You already missed it. Mr. Bester came in this morning and wanted to talk with you. I didn't know what to say to him. There is trouble here and I really need you. What's going on? I can't handle this alone!"

Gaping at her watch, Elizabeth stammered, "I don't know how this happened." She mentally reviewed the events of the morning. "I must have pressed the "snooze" button more times than I meant to, not to mention my hair and powder disaster."

Jillian paused then asked, "What?"

"Never mind. I'll be there in twenty minutes. I'll just have to put my make-up on when I get there. See you in a bit." Elizabeth stood with her hands resting on her hips. The morning's frustrations left her dreading the rest of the day. Due to her tardiness, she would only have a short amount of time to speak with Jillian. As she gathered her

Discovering Elizabeth

things, she tried to remember everything Rebecca had told her the night before.

Her trusted friend, who also served as the administrative assistant of Wright and Wingold's CEO, had said that Jillian was spreading rumors. Elizabeth hoped that Rebecca would be proven wrong. Rebecca had said that Jillian was repeating everything Elizabeth had said to her in trust with the addition of a word here and there. There had been a few times since Elizabeth had worked with Jillian that she suspected her to be playing the role of a busybody. Even so, she had much difficulty believing the allegations. Jillian had been a great help to Elizabeth. She was prompt, dependable and competent. Her keen eye for detail and tenacity for perfection had been a great help to her. As Jillian's immediate supervisor, it was Elizabeth's responsibility to speak with her. She hoped she could get it over with before her afternoon meeting.

With one last look in the mirror, Elizabeth rolled her eyes in disdain at the circles under her eyes and the rebellious locks of gold that were foreshadowing the beginning of her Monday morning trials. She picked up her purse, cosmetic bag, brief case and glass of milk then headed for her own personal battlefield.

After a twenty-minute drive through morning traffic, Elizabeth was feeling rushed to get to her office. She trudged up the four flights of stairs that led to her office. She normally took the elevator; but on this day, she didn't want to risk the possibility that someone might see her before her face was cosmetically constructed. As Elizabeth began the ascent on the third flight of stairs, she lowered her head and placed all of her strength into lugging her baggage. Elizabeth never saw the busy man reading the content of a file while descending the same staircase. Elizabeth and Ray Morgan collided in a fashion that could have been described as an unceremonial head butt. Elizabeth gasped in pain as she groped for the flying cosmetic bag, purse and brief case. The entire contents of what Ray Morgan had been carrying began a spiraling descent to the bottom floor. Ray held his newly lacerated eye as he leapt in what proved to be a futile attempt to retrieve the airborne documents. With what seemed like slow motion, Elizabeth and Ray ceased the arm waving frenzy of trying to retrieve their belongings and began to look at each other.

Ray held his eye as he said painfully, "I'm so sorry Ms. Pennington, are you all right? I wasn't watching where I was going. Are you okay?"

Lisa D. Piper

Elizabeth wanted to cry, shout or just sneer at the man. She wanted to scream, "Does everything look okay?" Before she could belt out any accusations, her composure returned. As she looked at the president of Wright and Wingold, she realized with embarrassing dismay that she had no make-up on and that depending on the force of the cosmetic bags fall, she might not have any make-up left to cover her now reddened complexion. Elizabeth lowered her head and whispered, "No, Mr. Morgan, I'm fine. My head hurts, but I think I'm okay. Are you? I mean…we hit pretty hard. I wasn't watching where I was going either. I'm very sorry, Sir."

Ray looked at Elizabeth as if checking to make sure she was truly okay. While rubbing his head, he looked down at the newly created mess then said, "Let me get these papers picked up then we can go down the stairs and check to see what kind of wreckage is waiting for us at the bottom."

Elizabeth protested, "Don't worry with it. I'll go down and make sure no one was caught in the crossfire while I get my things. Again, I'm sorry." Elizabeth bounded down the stairs where a young man from the custodial staff pointed at the littered carpet strewn with cosmetics and the contents of her brief case. She quickly gathered her belongings then bolted for the nearest ladies room.

Once inside, she quickly threw everything into her brief case then groped for her cell phone. As she dialed the number, she was doubtful that her friend would be home. Impatiently, she waited for Gabrielle to pick up while she inspected the knot forming on her head. Elizabeth muttered, "Oh please be home Gabby, please be home."

"Hello?"

"Gabby! I'm so glad you made it home! This is Liz." As she finished her greeting, wet tears coursed down her face.

Gabrielle Storm raised a perfectly arched eyebrow. "Elizabeth? What's wrong? Are you crying?"

Elizabeth wasn't sure she could respond as the lump in her throat worsened. "Gabby, I'm having an awful day, just awful."

Gabrielle quietly smiled then said, "Well, I kind of figured you had started the morning out right when I got here this morning and found what I thought to be the remains of the bath room."

Discovering Elizabeth

Elizabeth sniffed. "Oh, I'm sorry about the powder. I didn't have time to do a good job cleaning it up." Elizabeth cried. "I also broke the spray nozzle on your hair spray. I'll get a new bottle today. Oh Gab, I'm so embarrassed." Elizabeth explained to her friend and roommate what had happened in the few minutes she had been at work. "I managed to break your stuff, arrive to work late, shock the boss with my appearance and give him a black eye. The presentation I worked so hard on over the weekend is in shambles."

Gabrielle listened with concern as her friend gave an account of the crazy turn of events. During Gabrielle's comforting words of wisdom, Elizabeth turned to look in the mirror. Gabrielle heard her friend gasp aloud then begin to giggle pitifully. The change in Elizabeth's emotional state concerned Gabrielle so she questioned, "Liz, what are you doing? Why are you laughing?"

"Gabby, my problems didn't end in the stairwell. I just turned to look into the mirror and realized that I must have gotten dressed faster than usual. Please remind me from now on to look into the mirror before I go anywhere."

Gabrielle asked, "Why's that?"

Elizabeth wiped away her tears as she grinned. "Because I just ran into the president of the company with my right shoulder pad blowing in the wind. It's sticking out like a bowl on top of my shoulder and I never noticed it until now."

Gabrielle had difficulty conjuring up the picture Elizabeth had described. Elizabeth didn't go to work until she was picture perfect. Her hair would have been neatly pulled back in a no-nonsense fashion. Her clothes were pressed and completely coordinated. Elizabeth didn't look the executive part at home, but when she worked she was the epitome of professional. Elizabeth continued to giggle every few seconds until Gabrielle joined in. She gave her friend one last piece of encouragement. "Liz, put in your shoulder pad, get your things together and go be an executive. Act like nothing has happened and perhaps no one will guess that you have been a little, um…off beat this morning."

Elizabeth grinned. "A little off beat? I think that I left the band and began a whole new sheet of music. Thanks for listening Gab."

Lisa D. Piper

"You're welcome. If you have any more troubles, let me know. I'll leave the phone on the hook just in case. I'm going to get a few minutes of shut-eye." Gabrielle hung up the phone then said a prayer for her friend.

Elizabeth quickly applied her make-up while trying to comb her hair in a way that would not reveal the hard knot forming on the top of her head.

Ray Morgan had picked up his belongings then walked quickly toward the conference room where he would apologize for being late to the important client. As he walked past the employee break room on the second floor, his right eye made contact with a woman whom he knew to work in the accounting department. The woman looked almost pompous. He recognized the smile of satisfaction. Ray's eyebrows began to rise as he heard the woman expound in a voice loud enough for him to hear. The mousy looking woman threw her hands toward the ceiling as she snarled, "Who knows where that woman is! She is always late and so undependable. I phoned her this morning to remind her to come to work. All she had to say was that she was having a bad hair day. I told her that if I were in her position, I wouldn't lose track of time when I had early appointments with important clientele. If I were in charge, this wouldn't happen!" After this declaration, Ray noticed that the exchange in voices became quieter: almost as if the entire scene had been for his own benefit. He shuddered inside as he realized his company had its own busybody. Ray walked on to the meeting room, temporarily forgetting what he had just witnessed.

A satisfied Jillian clucked her tongue as she walked out of the break area; never knowing that she hadn't been successful in her quest to tear down Elizabeth Anne Pennington's reputation with the chief.

Elizabeth walked into her office to find that Jillian was gone. A note on her desk said she had taken a break. Elizabeth sat down to check her voice mail while turning on her computer. As always, Jillian had left up-to-the-minute notes on things she thought Elizabeth would need to be reminded of for the day. As Elizabeth looked over the tasks that needed to be completed, she whispered a heartfelt prayer. "Oh Lord, thank you for Jillian. I don't know what I would do without her." Elizabeth had just finished her thanksgiving when a jubilant Jillian waltzed into the office. Elizabeth smiled and greeted her helper and

Discovering Elizabeth

friend. "My, my Ms. Hunter, you look absolutely glowing today. I take it that you had a better weekend than I did."

Jillian sat down and replied, "Yes I did and I'm having an absolutely wonderful morning. You know, sometimes one can make goals and plans that never seem to materialize. Today is different. I think things are going to turn out as I anticipated for you and me!"

Elizabeth applauded. "Wow! What optimism!" Elizabeth teased her assistant, "Have you changed your coffee? If so, pass the cup around!" Elizabeth gave a brilliant smile to her exuberant co-worker. Jillian was very astute, especially when it came to the nuances of those with whom she worked. She had no doubt that Elizabeth was truly happy for her. Jillian had noticed that when Elizabeth was touched emotionally, her ocean blue eyes took on the depth of a midnight blue. There were those who were in awe of the change, but the love in Elizabeth's eyes made Jillian want to lash out at her.

Jillian decided to react to her boss in a playful manner. "Well, Elizabeth, I think it's just evidence of a good day. The coffee is very tasty this morning since yours truly perked it." Jillian stood to hand some files to Elizabeth as she pointed to the top file. "Don't forget to get with Mr. Bester. I told him Friday that you would get with him first thing this morning."

Elizabeth touched the folder, "Jillian, I wish you hadn't done that. Why did you tell him that I would get with him first thing today? The figures aren't going to be ready until I get some information from supply. That could take until this afternoon."

Jillian put out her hand to stop Elizabeth from questioning. "Don't worry about it. When he came in, I told him that something unexpected had happened. I told him that you are personally seeing to his account. I told him how important his business is to us and that none of us want to make any mistakes by hurrying the process." Jillian left out the part where she had sighed after telling Mr. Bester about his importance. Jillian admitted to Mr. Bester that she had no idea of where Elizabeth could be and complained that Elizabeth never let her know what she was doing when she left the office.

Elizabeth thanked Jillian for taking care of the situation after the two reviewed the plans for the day. After several meetings and the completion of a cost analysis report, Elizabeth and Jillian decided to go to lunch. The restaurant of choice, The Yummy House, was only a couple of blocks from the Wright and Wingold building. Two elderly sisters made homemade bread for the sandwiches at the Yummy House. As Jillian entered the door to their favorite luncheon spot, she breathed in deeply. "Elizabeth, it always smells like a combination of baking bread and fresh brownies in here."

"I could live in this place." Elizabeth gave an appreciative nod. "That's why I love coming here! I feel the stress leaving me now, I just need to inhale the yeast aromatherapy."

A cheerful waitress took their order and within minutes the food arrived. Jillian and Elizabeth blessed their meal then began the process of savoring and devouring every bite of sourdough bread which had been dubbed by the locals as "yummy dough."

The familiar waitress refilled their drinking glasses. Jillian looked up quickly as if she had just remembered something. "Elizabeth, guess what! I saw Mr. Morgan today and I think something is up with the commanding officer!"

Elizabeth paused as she swallowed the last bite of her turkey sandwich. The sound of the name of her morning assailant brought back a flood of unwanted memories. "What do you mean Jill?"

Jillian leaned in, "Well, I saw him this morning and he didn't look so good."

Elizabeth shifted uncomfortably. She wasn't sure she wanted to hear what came next. Surely Ray hadn't broadcasted the staircase mishap. Jillian pleaded, "Come on, aren't you going to ask me why?"

"Okay, why didn't he look so good?"

"Because it looks as if someone tagged him in the left eye!"

"What? What did you say?"

Jillian said impatiently, "It looks like someone gave him a big shiner, or at least it will in a few hours. He went by the break room this morning. That's where I saw him. I bet one of those girls downstairs did it." Jillian began to laugh. "I guess he couldn't take a verbal no for an answer. He's a womanizer you know. He's a looker and I think he believes every girl downstairs would fight for the chance to be involved with him."

Discovering Elizabeth

Elizabeth sat in shock as she watched Jillian do exactly what Rebecca had said. She wasn't sure if she should just tell Jillian that she didn't want to hear the gossip, particularly about the president of the company. Instead, she began defending his position, "Jillian you're jumping to conclusions. There's no way to know what happened to him. He could've bumped into someone. Please don't tell anyone else what you've just told me. I would hate for this to get back to Mr. Morgan." Elizabeth wasn't sure why she didn't want to inform her friend of what had really happened to the CEO but something inside of her wanted to keep it from Jillian's ready-to-hear-gossip ears.

Jillian waved her hand toward her boss as if she were dismissing the matter. "Oh Elizabeth, I wouldn't tell anyone but you. I just thought you should know in case he tries something with you. I'm looking out for you. I know that you're a little naive when it comes to the male persuasion. I've seen his kind before. Face it; you're one of the most attractive women in this building. It's just a matter of time before the inevitable happens. You're going to have a run-in with the big man."

Elizabeth almost grinned at the pun while Jillian rushed onward. "He would make quite a catch and he knows it. He would have to know it or he wouldn't be so forward with all of the women. I'm not blind. I've noticed that he's very good looking." Jillian's appearance took on a whimsical glow as she continued; "I've noticed that his wavy brown hair is getting a tinge of gray in it too. Sophie says that he just happens to be one of those men who look better with a little gray hair. Some of the girls have told me that when they look at him, it's all they can do to keep from drowning in those clear, slanted hazel eyes. And those cheekbones…"

"Hold on a minute Jillian. I don't want to hear anymore of this." Confusion registered on Jillian's face as she received an unwanted response from Elizabeth. "Jillian, you're a married woman and I hope it's not someone in my department who's spending this much time analyzing the boss! Evidently, too much damaging talk is going on about this subject or you wouldn't appear to know so much about it."

Jillian studied Elizabeth before she retorted, "What has gotten into you today? Okay, I'm sorry, but I think you should know that there is someone in the department who would love the opportunity to go out with Ray."

Elizabeth sighed.

Jillian hurried, "No, I'm telling you the truth. Sophie is a good friend of mine and I wouldn't tell you anything I wouldn't tell her I told you. She's the one, she's crazy about him."

Elizabeth stared at the woman who sat adjacent to her. Elizabeth couldn't believe that Jillian was sharing such private information with her about Sophie. Sophie had been Jillian's friend for a long time. "Jillian, you might want to talk with Sophie the next time she comments on Mr. Morgan. It's not a good idea to mention her interest in the boss and please tell her to consider the affects her comments might have on those who might hear her. It just isn't wise."

Jillian agreed, "Sure, I'll speak with her. I guess she shouldn't be saying such things, especially while she's on the clock." Jillian mumbled about how unproductive Sophie could be then stood to her feet. "Are you ready? I know we have a long day ahead of us."

Elizabeth sighed, "I know, I just hope it gets better. I'm ready to go. When we get back, I need you to come by my office. We need to talk about something in private. It should take about twenty minutes or so."

Jillian nodded while each woman withdrew enough money from her wallet to cover the expense of the meal. Elizabeth and Jillian walked to their building in silence. The pretty spring day on Savannah Boulevard didn't portray the weight that both women felt. It was a lovely day and both women would have loved to spend the day outside the building. As they neared their destination, Elizabeth began to feel apprehensive. How could she approach the subject with Jillian? Would Jillian be receptive or take her comments as an accusation? Elizabeth's heart began to pound. Her stomach felt as if it had been tied into a knot. Elizabeth berated herself. She knew that if she wanted to be an effective supervisor, she would just have to go through with the morning interview with Jillian.

When Jillian entered her office, Elizabeth quickly prayed a prayer for wisdom. She told Jillian what had been said and asked for her thoughts on the allegations. Jillian glared at Elizabeth as she thought of how she could divert the attention she was getting for her wayward actions to someone or something else. Jillian quickly tried to think of a way out of the uncomfortable conversation. Elizabeth's kind yet intense eyes didn't waver from Jillian's glare. Elizabeth's intent was to get the truth out of Jillian, which proved to be an impossible task. Elizabeth restated her questions then said, "Jillian, you're a valuable

Discovering Elizabeth

team member. I need to know if you've said what I've been told you said."

Jillian loathed the woman in front of her. Elizabeth had never confronted Jillian in this manner. Jillian regretted the slip of her tongue. She had been so enthralled with her tale of deception that she hadn't thought that her tall tales would finally get back to Elizabeth. Jillian quickly tried to figure out who could have been the nark. Jillian hastily thought through her strategy. The "victim" charade always worked and this would be a time for one of her greatest performances.

Jillian conjured up a look of despair as she began her response to her boss. "Elizabeth, I'm hurt. I'm not angry at whoever told you these awful things. I'm not angry because you have come to me with this." Jillian began to sob. The quiet sobs turned into a stream of tears requiring her to remove her glasses. She wiped at her drab brown eyes that Elizabeth noticed matched her mousy brown hair. She looked up at Elizabeth whose face was visibly beginning to reveal that her position was softening. "Elizabeth, I'm hurt because you would think I would do such a thing. You have believed these lies without even asking me about them. Did you once even think about me and how I would feel hearing them from my boss…my friend? You know I try to do a good job for the company. I pour my heart into it." Jillian paused for effect then slowly shook her head while burying her eyes into a tissue. "We went to lunch and you never said anything. We come back here…and you're down my throat. What kind of answer are you wanting?"

Elizabeth looked down at her helper, her friend, and her assistant of three years. There were times that Jillian anticipated business needs before they occurred. Her intuition had saved the company a lot of money and had saved Elizabeth a lot of time. She saw that Jillian's eyes were red from crying. As Jillian lowered her head to avoid her boss's gaze, Elizabeth noted that Jillian's petite frame looked so fragile with her tiny legs curled up under her as she wept. Jillian's plain brown hair now covered her face, falling slightly past her shoulders. Elizabeth weighed her words before she responded to the unexpected outburst.

She thought she might say something to cause Jillian to refocus on the subject of the reported gossip. She could assure Jillian of her commitment to her and vow to never bring it up again. At this point, Elizabeth wished she had some type of managerial handbook to give her some advice. Elizabeth wondered at what she could say to assure

Jillian that she wasn't questioning her commitment to the company or her loyalty to her supervisor. Jillian always seemed to tear up during conflict of any kind, but this façade of torrential tears caused Elizabeth to question her own judgment of the woman's character.

Somewhere between friendship and work duties, Elizabeth's judgment became altered. Later, she would see that she should have told Jillian that the question was about her behavior and nothing else. Elizabeth tried very hard to separate her friendship and working relationship with those close to her. Without ever realizing it, the lines had been crossed and she found it difficult to take just a business position with her friend/subordinate.

Elizabeth couldn't ignore the information Rebecca had given her. She had to admit that she was naïve when it came to dealing with anyone who would purposefully negate the truth or seek to harm someone's reputation. Although naïve, she wasn't ignorant to the smirks on the faces of those with whom she worked after they exited Jillian's office. On more than one occasion, Elizabeth had decided that whatever the secret joke had been, everyone knew it but her. Elizabeth had refused to jump to conclusions and had chosen to believe that her assistant was up to nothing but good.

A sob from Jillian brought Elizabeth's thoughts to the present. Elizabeth allowed her eyes to soften with compassion for the woman sitting before her. "Jillian, I'm not accusing you of anything, please understand this. I'm responsible for the effective operation of this department. If I'm given a report that one of the persons I supervise may be endangering the reputation of our company, I have no choice but to take it seriously. The success of the business and the satisfaction of our clientele are dependent upon our behavior and business ethics. It is a requirement that we do business with integrity and treat one another with the same respect we desire for ourselves. You know what I think of your work. I've often told you how much I appreciate your effort. I can't imagine running this department without you. I don't mean to offend you, but I do need your cooperation. Did you or did you not tell Rebecca during Monday's luncheon that I told a potential client that our president, Ray, has a vicious temper? Did you say that he is known for outbursts of anger that often end with Ray tearing whatever he has in his hands to shreds even if it is a highly sensitive document? Did you say that he has screamed blatantly at me?"

Discovering Elizabeth

Jillian's eyes widened as she stood to her feet. Her slender hand brushed through her hair while she breathed a deep sigh before responding. "Elizabeth, I did talk to Rebecca. I told her that I'm concerned about you. Maybe she took it the wrong way, but do you remember when you came to the office and said you had just seen Ray? You said that he wasn't happy about our budget performance and that he would like to shred every budget report he could find. While you were saying this to me, Mrs. Richards walked in the door and wanted to see you. I left the room to give you privacy. I did tell Rebecca what had happened. I told her that you were upset and that I wished Ray wouldn't get so angry. We do our best in this department. You're the best supervisor that Mr. Morgan has. I don't want anyone thinking otherwise." Jillian hiccupped with a new sob as she finished her seasoned confession.

Elizabeth sighed, "Jillian, where did you come up with the conclusion that Ray was angry? I had jokingly told you that he was tired of looking at all of the budgets. He was teasing me with my hard work when he said he wanted to shred it. Jillian, even if you thought he was 'in the wrong'; it wasn't appropriate to discuss it with anyone at a luncheon or anywhere else. Did anyone else hear what you said?"

Jillian sighed with an inner relief, knowing that she had yet another victory of saving her own reputation with the boss. Jillian opened her eyes until they were slightly wider than normal then puckered her lips for effect as she said, "Elizabeth, no one heard me say that. I simply misunderstood and was concerned about you. You're my friend as well as my boss, you know. I can't help it if Rebecca took what I said the wrong way, too. Now I know what I shouldn't have done and can make sure this kind of thing doesn't happen again."

Elizabeth looked at Jillian's somber smile then replied, "Okay Jillian, but please keep this conversation between us. There's been enough talk about this subject, alright?"

"Done." Jillian threw a smile toward Elizabeth then exited through the office door.

Elizabeth suddenly felt as if she should've redirected Jillian's focus before she left. Somehow, the fact that Jillian still viewed Rebecca as the one who had some part in misconstruing what Elizabeth had said was disturbing. Elizabeth muttered to herself, "Lord, please help me to be a good leader. I know you heard what just went on so you can see I need help."

Elizabeth rubbed her temples as soon as Jillian was out of view. Her need for a break outweighed her desire to move to her next task on the agenda. The confusion of the day had drained her. Elizabeth left her office and slowly walked through the corridors of the modern looking building. She wasn't sure of her destination but it would be somewhere where there would be no questions to answer, appropriate responses to be made or responsibilities to tend. Had Elizabeth opted to take the elevator to the basement floor, she would have seen an animated conversation between Jillian Hunter and Sophie McKlaun. While Elizabeth walked through the hallways trying to find relief from the stress of the morning, her assistant delivered a speech of a victim's plight to anyone who would listen.

Elizabeth mused at the bustle of activity throughout the corridors of Wright and Wingold. As she weaved her way through the cubicles and filing cabinets, she didn't think about where she was going. While wondering aimlessly, her mind relaxed and her headache seemed to dissipate. Gabby had once told her that she could find solace and strength in the wisdom of Scripture. She wished she could remember the verse Gabby quoted every time Elizabeth tried to complain about something from work. Thinking positively wasn't an easy thing to do.

Elizabeth tried to mumble the verse as a reminder of what she should be doing. "Oh, think! Umm...Whatever is good and pure and holy and of a good report, if there is anything worthy enough to think about, think on this[2]. Well, that'll have to do it. Gabby would be disappointed that I can't remember," Elizabeth whispered.

Elizabeth thought about the last couple of years of her life. She had been promoted to Wright and Wingold's VP of accounting without having had a lot of supervisory experience. Her figures, numbers and equations had never once given her as much difficulty as flesh and blood. Elizabeth mumbled, "Good thoughts, I will not think of this right now, I will think good thoughts." She rolled her eyes as she admonished herself. "I need a vacation." Before Elizabeth could look up to do a check on where she had wandered, her foot hit the leg of a chair. Her arms began a flailing motion as she tried to regain her

---

[2] Phil. 4:8

Discovering Elizabeth

balance. If she fell to the left she would be on carpet but if she fell to the right, she would fall on the executive lounge tile. The flailing helped and in a moment she was standing upright on her feet. As soon as she knew she would not fall she glanced around to make sure there were no observers to witness her near mishap.

No one seemed to be around so she allowed a soft giggle to escape her lips as she thought of how she must have appeared; waving her arms back and forth to keep from taking the Wright and Wingold carpet plunge! A noise from close by stifled her musing. Elizabeth felt someone watching her. Turning very slowly and frowning greatly, she realized who had witnessed her mishap. There in the corner of the employee lounge was Ray Morgan. He was looking in her direction with a slight grin on his tan face. Elizabeth steeled herself while begging her body to cooperate with her wishes. At any minute, Elizabeth knew that the evidence of hot embarrassment would creep up her neck and spread to her face.

Ray turned his head toward the vending machine after Elizabeth returned his smile with a look of reproof. To her horror, she couldn't help but notice that even though Ray now looked to be concentrating on a choice of beverage: he still looked amused. Elizabeth said the first thing that came to her mind, "Hi Ray, I'm just looking for something so don't mind me."

She wanted to withdraw her dumb statement as she silently begged, "Please don't respond, Ray, oh please don't ask!"

Ray asked on cue, "Looking for what?"

Elizabeth was mortified. She opened her mouth to confess but instead of confessing, the most idiotic lie came out her mouth. "I was looking for safety hazards."

Ray looked at her with confusion. "Safety hazards?"

Elizabeth explained, "You know, sometimes there are loose tiles that no one notices until it's too late. I was just checking." In total humiliation Elizabeth turned and darted out of the room. As she walked down the hallway, she groaned. "Safety hazards? What am I doing? What am I saying? Why, oh why did I have to say that? I could've just acknowledged that I almost fell. He would never have given it another thought. He's probably wondering why I would do such a thing. He probably thinks I'm a walking safety hazard." As she tried to justify her actions she said to herself, "Okay, Okay, he has said before that safety is everyone's business. Maybe he'll think I was just listening to his advice." Elizabeth then thought that if she tried hard enough she could find the humor in the situation. She couldn't. What she needed to do was make a call to Gabby. That would help.

"Gabrielle? Oh Gabby, please don't be asleep!" Elizabeth's voice rang through the answering machine in the little house on Lily Avenue where she and Gabrielle had lived for five years.

A sleepy Gabrielle answered the phone. "Yes Liz, I'm here, what's wrong?" Gabrielle worked as a corporate auditor, often traveling for days at a time, and was a professional of professionals. She had finished an assignment in New York then flown back home in the morning hours. Gabrielle yawned as she tried to focus then repeated, "Liz, what's up? Are you okay?"

Elizabeth quietly blurted, "Gab, I'm having a horrible day. So stressful, in fact, that I decided to walk out my frustrations so I walked to the employee lounge...no, I fell into the employee lounge. Gabby, my boss saw the whole thing. Yes, he's the one I ran into this morning." Elizabeth began to cry as she tried to finish the story.

Gabrielle wasn't fully awake. "What else happened Liz...don't leave me hanging!"

Elizabeth held her stomach as she finished the story. "Gab, I told Ray that I was looking for safety hazards. I thought the excuse was stupid but now I know how ignorant it truly was. I was on carpet when I stumbled and it was a flat out lie. It was a lie Gab, I'm so embarrassed!"

At first, there was silence. Gabrielle awoke fully as she began to smile. The mental picture of Elizabeth falling all over the place made her giggle. Before long, Elizabeth too began to laugh through her tears. Gabrielle was sure the usually composed Elizabeth Pennington hadn't taken lightly to looking "out of control" but it seemed as if maybe the Lord was trying to teach her something." As the two laughed together, Elizabeth's laugh was hearty and full. Gabrielle recited, "Truly laughter is like a good medicine[3]." Her friend agreed.

---

[3] Pro. 17:22

Discovering Elizabeth

Elizabeth hung up the phone after telling her friend she would see her later. She returned to the tasks that were still waiting for her with renewed vitality. As her heart began to act normally, Elizabeth said aloud, "This is a day you've made Lord, I want to be glad in it." The declaration brought a smile to her lips as she ended her speech with, "God, I don't know how to do this job again today, let's get through this thing together."

Lisa D. Piper

Chapter TWO

"The words of a wise man 's mouth are gracious, but the lips of a fool shall swallow him up." Ecclesiastes 10:12 NIV

"Ray Morgan! You ole coot, what are you doing?"

Ray looked up from his desk to see the Wright and Wingold custodial manager standing in his doorway. "Listen up, Homer, don't talk like that where someone might hear you. I'm the president you know, and no one is supposed to know that I'm of the "coot" variety!"

Homer smiled and replied, "Okay, boss, but you just remember one thing. I worked with you when you were knee high to a grasshopper, boy, and promotion doesn't come from the east or the west…"

"It comes from the Lord[2]." Ray finished Homer's sentence for him with a smile of warmth for his friend. "Listen here, Homer, I was sixteen when I came to work here as an environmental engineer-hardly the size of a grasshopper!"

The elderly gentleman stroked his imaginary whiskers then raised an eyebrow as he disputed the younger man's words. "Ray, call it like it was. Environment engineer, humph! The fanciest I can muster is custodial janitor and not just plain ole janitor! I've been doing this for over forty years young man and I say you were short like a grasshopper. You were short until I got you to try my Annie's greens and cornbread! That's what put the meat on them there bones!"

With a grunt of mock dismay Ray stood to his full six foot four inches. Homer didn't have to look up at the tall man. He could never

---

[2] Psalm 75:6

have been accused of being a little old man with his own six foot two inch frame. Ray conceded, "Well, Homer, thank Annie for me. I probably should've stopped eating those greens a couple of inches ago." Ray walked over to Homer and unashamedly placed his arm on the older man's shoulder. "Homer, for an ole coot you are the best. What kind of orneriness has brought you to this part of the building today? Don't misunderstand, I'm delighted to see you but I know there's a reason. What is it?"

Homer confessed, "Okay, okay! Annie wants you to come over for lunch after church Sunday. Do you think you can make it?"

"Sure, just make sure she doesn't fix greens and cornbread. If your suspicions are true, I might not be able to fit into that Corvette I've been eyeing in your driveway!"

"Watch it boy! That Corvette is what keeps me looking youthful. As far as the fixin's go, Annie wouldn't tell me what she's concocting. But, do I love her cookin' enough to be anticipating the first morsel?"

Both of the men grinned and mischievously answered Homer's question together, "YES WE DO!"

Homer turned to leave while he mumbled something about Ray getting there on time to avoid any eating delays. Ray returned to his desk to begin the task of fitting eleven hours worth of work into an eight-hour workday. He knew very well that he'd have to work long hours to get everything accomplished. As he opened the book that contained his plans for the day, he read his daily devotional. The words couldn't have been truer. "A merry heart does good like a medicine[2]." Ray silently gave thanks for Homer and asked God to watch over his friend and his wife.

The busy Monday morning set the tone of the week. By the time the weekend arrived, Elizabeth was more than ready to hang up her calculator and keyboard. Saturday came and went without a lot of commotion. Elizabeth and Gabrielle cleaned the house from top to bottom and caught up with what had happened in each other's lives over the last week. Both were more tired than they had thought when they awoke Sunday morning to find that they were once more…late. Elizabeth caused a longer delay as everything that could possibly go wrong with her Sunday outfit did.

Discovering Elizabeth

The roommates arrived at the church only three minutes past eleven. They both stared at the two large entrance doors. Neither Elizabeth nor Gabrielle wanted to be the first one to enter. Elizabeth motioned for her friend to walk through the door first. Gabrielle motioned for Elizabeth to go ahead and take the lead. The embarrassment of trying to find a seat while everyone else was seated was something both women had experienced enough times to not want to do it again. Gabrielle quietly admonished Elizabeth, "Liz, it's your fault we're late. You should go in first! If I were the one who made us late, I would do it!" Gabrielle smiled the sweetest smile she could with the hope that Elizabeth would give in. Gabrielle had been the culprit who had made the pair late the previous Sunday. Gabrielle had just delivered the same speech Elizabeth had given to her to make Gabrielle walk through the intimidating doors first on that occasion.

Elizabeth groaned then opened the large door as if she were going in. Before Gabrielle knew what had happened, Elizabeth pulled the door open then stepped aside-causing Gabrielle to be the first person anyone inside would see. All heads turned toward Gabby as she was forced to either step through the door or stand gazing at the crowd. As Elizabeth followed her friend into the church, she shuddered as she thought of the tongue-lashing she would get once they were out of the sight of others. Elizabeth noticed that Gabrielle was standing erect and her steps were mechanical. A giggle almost escaped Elizabeth's lips as she realized she had truly taken her friend by surprise.

Pastor Matthews greeted Gabrielle from the pulpit. He then turned to look directly at Elizabeth and greeted her. Both women discreetly stepped into an obscure seat while making no eye contact with one another. They knew that if their eyes met; neither would be able to keep her composure. As humiliated as Gabrielle might feel, her sense of humor would require her to want to giggle uncontrollably. Pastor Matthews knowingly glanced at the tardy parishioners then asked for the praise and worship team to congregate at the front of the church. Neither girl missed the glint of laughter in his eyes. No, they didn't fool the man of God. He knew what Elizabeth had done to her friend. Without a doubt, Pastor Matthews would be speaking to them after service.

As the singing began, Gabrielle silently thanked the Lord for her friend. Gabrielle still wanted to scold Elizabeth for her childish spontaneity, but she would forgive her. Most of their classmates during school had believed that God was an impersonal being who was good for the occasional difficulty. Elizabeth had been different from those who had said they knew God. Gabrielle was drawn to her the first day of grade school. She had seen Elizabeth bless her food without fail through twelve years of public education. Gabrielle loved the spontaneity and prankster side of her friend even though Gabrielle was usually the target.

Only Gabrielle knew that it was nearly impossible to get to the real Elizabeth. She was professional and almost somber when she went to work. When she came home she was carefree and bubbly most of the time. Gabrielle didn't consider her friend to be a hypocrite. She had learned that there were many facets to her. She had been Elizabeth's prayer partner for as long as she could remember praying. During prayer time, Elizabeth became complete. Gabrielle never told anyone how Elizabeth lamented over the lives of her family and those with whom she worked. She knew that she had a personal relationship with the same God Gabrielle loved and knew. As Gabrielle watched her friend walk to the front of the building where she would begin to sing- she was once again humbled for God to have blessed her with such a friend. Elizabeth's soprano voice rang out as Gabrielle watched her raise her hands in worship. Gabrielle smiled at her friend.

After the enjoyable service, Elizabeth and Gabrielle prepared to leave. As they were gathering their things a familiar voice from behind them said, "Hello, Liz. Hello, Gabby. Bless you both."

Elizabeth and Gabrielle whirled around to find a smiling clergyman. Elizabeth stammered, "Uh, hi, Pastor, how are you today?"

As Pastor Matthews shook both women's hands he smiled a friendly smile as he said, "I'm doing wonderfully!" After a short pause he continued, "You know, girls, when you all were teenagers, I became familiar with certain aspects of your personalities and behaviors."

"Yes," both girls answered as they anticipated the unveiling of their unceremonial entrance by a man who was too wise and astute not to know what Elizabeth had done.

Pastor Matthews adjusted his glasses as he stated matter of factly, "I have to tell you that I'm so thankful for you both." When both girls looked surprised he finished his statement. "You've both turned out to be so successful. You're both independent and so talented. I don't

Discovering Elizabeth

know of any women who are as well thought of by the children as you two. You're both quite the role models." Pastor Matthews smiled one last time then turned to leave. Over his shoulder he called out, "See you tonight, ladies! God bless you both. I'm praying for you!"

Silence. The message had been delivered with great love and warmth. As the women stood in the aisle, thinking of their influence on the children, Gabrielle quoted Proverbs 12:1, "Whoever loves instruction loves knowledge, but he who hates correction is stupid."

Elizabeth smiled. "Well said, my friend. I really want to love instruction, but it makes me feel really bad. Oh well, I Guess I would rather feel stupid than be stupid. I still feel like a kid…I never thought about being a role model. I guess he's noticed that our timeliness isn't the greatest example, huh?"

As Elizabeth and Gabrielle ate lunch after the morning service, they decided to become more involved in the activities of the church. Both admitted to having slid into some mediocrity where the Word was concerned. Erratic church attendance and a decrease in prayer time was probably the reason they didn't feel as strong in their faith as they once did, the women concluded as they finished their meal. Elizabeth told Gabrielle how she used to wake up with joy and singing in her heart and that lately, the music rarely woke her up. Elizabeth admitted to Gabrielle that she felt she had almost forgotten the commitment she had made to the Lord as a child as the busyness of life had taken over. What the two women didn't know was that very soon both of their lives would take a turn that neither expected.

Annie Mae Foster slapped the bronzed hand as it crept from around the edge of the table to retrieve a delectable from the tray in front of her. The owner of the hand hurriedly took the opportunity of the slap distraction and quickly grabbed a chocolate chip cookie then ran for his life to the living room where an old man was waiting for his share of the stolen goodie. While the two men gulped down the homemade secret recipe morsel, the culinary artist shouted, "The next time you two try those kind of shenanigans, I'm gonna tar ya both! You'd do well to keep your mitts outta my kitchen until ya get an invitation!" Although the command sounded fierce, both men knew that Annie Mae was grinning from ear to ear. She loved to cook and loved the satisfaction of providing a good meal for those she loved.

Lisa D. Piper

Ray Morgan had been a fan of Annie Mae's cooking since the time he could eat solid food. Annie was very fond of the man who had helped her through the years when no one else would want to fool with an elderly woman. When Ray was a child, the other children played together while Ray sat on the Foster's front porch listening to Homer Foster telling stories of the old days. Ray had willingly helped with the chores and with the exception of her childhood sweetheart; Ray was her favorite male in the world.

From her spotless kitchen, Annie looked over at Ray and couldn't help but wonder how long it had been since he had had a good home cooked meal. She worried about him and wondered if he was really taking care of himself as Homer insisted he was. As the president of Wright and Wingold, a manufacturer of cleaning products and services, Annie Mae knew that he had worries, and she knew that he wouldn't share his own worries with anyone except Homer. Ray had always been quiet about his own affairs; preferring to show concern for others rather than revealing his own needs. She thought of his continuous hurt from years gone by. "Oh, that boy," she thought, "When will he ever get over the past?" Annie continued to think about her guest as she finished garnishing the entrée of the day, roasted chicken with special herbs that Homer called Annie Mae spices. "Oh, Lord," Annie prayed as she finished the meal, "Keep your hand upon him. You've made my Ray a fine man, make his joy in you complete."

Annie enjoyed the smiles at her table as Homer and Ray helped themselves to double helpings of Sunday's meal.

Homer and Ray sat back in their respective living room chairs while letting out dual moans. "Sin," Homer groaned, "Sin, that's what it is."

"Oh Homer, don't start that again. I'm miserable enough without you reciting the same old lecture." Ray leaned back into the recliner with his right arm draped over his stomach.

"Son, I know it's hard to take. Shucks, I'm guilty of it myself! I always say I'm not going to fall into that old trap again and then, well, Annie serves it up, and I just can't help myself."

"Homer, are you blaming Annie for your own weakness?" Ray lifted his head from its resting place to glare at his friend.

"Well, she's not 100% to blame, but she does deserve a degree of it," Homer retorted mischievously.

Discovering Elizabeth

"I heard that!" came the reply from one Annie Mae Foster. Annie Mae had removed her cooking apron. A flowery "everyday" apron hung over a dress that had to be outdated but looked so grandmotherly. Ray and Homer knew they were in trouble as Annie bellowed, "Now look here, you scalawags, there was no one offering to do the dishes nor help in any way! You have the nerve to come in here and blame your over indulgence on a helpless little old lady who didn't coerce nor persuade you to eat three helpings of green beans and new potatoes! I suggest you look to your own selves if you need someone to blame for your discomfort!"

Both Ray and Homer began laughing hysterically while Annie sat down with pretended disgust. Homer was the first to address his lovely wife of 47 years. "Now, sweetheart, you know we fellers have gotta blame someone. We can't go blaming ourselves for a thick middle. My clothing seems to be gettin' tighter by the moment! You ought not to include me in the scalawag remark, Love, you know that, Ray, here is the real scalawag! Just look at that shiner he has on that eye! Did I tell you that a girl did that?" Homer chuckled and threw the remote control at Ray.

Ray's quick thinking kept him from getting a blow to the head as a result of Homer's poor aim. Ray stood to his feet then turned to his friend. "Now look here, Homer, don't go making up to her now! You are the one who said to let her do the dishes or we both might be skinned. I might be a scalawag, but I think you're the one who's going to be suffering from supper deprivation tonight! Ray concluded his argument by throwing the sweetest smile towards Annie while Homer protested that he had no idea of what Ray was talking.

Annie looked at Ray and said, "Boy, you and Homer are both in trouble, so don't go trying that handsome smile and twinkling eyes on me. I have lived with Homer for too many years to know when I'm being shanghaied and you have tried that sweet little grin on me one too many times. Yes, it still works, but you need to know that I know what you're doing. Now get into that kitchen and cut a piece of pie to take with you. I knew that you would be leaving soon so I left a plate wrapped in foil on the stove. Take that and have a good supper tonight. If I didn't know the Lord was keeping up with you, I'd worry myself sick."

Lisa D. Piper

"Yes, ma'am," Ray replied as he saluted Homer. "You know, Homer, Ms. Annie here says she's a helpless old lady. Looks to me like she knows how to tell a man what to do!"

Annie smiled at Ray then motioned for him to stop his foolishness and get on with what she had told him to do. After several minutes, Ray returned to the living room and announced that he had the meal she had prepared for him and needed to get back to town. Ray bent down to hug Annie Mae while she said; "I'll see you later dear. Take care of yourself and come back and visit soon." While giving Annie a swift kiss on her weathered cheek, Ray could smell the mixture of baby powder and Irish Summer. The familiar scent caused him to remember days when he had sat in her lap while she read to him. As he turned to leave he said, "Listen, Annie, if you need anything, call me. And if this geezer here gives you any problems, you let me know. I know where he works!" Annie stifled a giggle when Ray winked at her as Homer threw up his hands. "Thanks for the meal. I've been to the finest restaurants in town, and none of them compare to you and your cooking!"

Ray leaned over and patted Homer on the arm then gave him an affectionate squeeze. Homer patted Ray on the back and said, "Watch it ya young whipper snapper. God gave you those strong hands for workin' not for causin' undo pain to the elderly!" Homer laughed at his own sarcasm as he walked Ray to the door.

Monday morning brought new challenges and trials for Elizabeth. She decided to leave for work earlier than usual. Sleep had evaded her most of the night, leaving her feeling apprehensive about the day. Upon arrival, Elizabeth mechanically walked to the break room to find a cup of hot coffee. As she was about to enter the room, she heard two muffled yet high-pitched voices. She didn't think she would be intruding but as she walked around the corner to enter the room she heard her assistant questioning Elizabeth's commitment to the company.

Jillian was quick to pretend that nothing had been said when she realized that her subject had just entered the room. "Good morning, Elizabeth, how are you this morning?" Jillian asked cheerfully.

Elizabeth was puzzled. Jillian didn't look guilty of saying or doing anything wrong. Elizabeth looked at the owner of the other voice she had heard. Trish Stanley, a sales associate, stood with her mouth agape

Discovering Elizabeth

as if she had experienced some sort of shock at the appearance of Jillian's boss. Elizabeth's doubt about the incident overrode her desire to confront the two women as she opted to greet the women as if nothing had happened, just in case she had been mistaken. "Good morning, Jillian. Good morning, Trish."

Jillian giggled nervously then threw her hand into the air. "I'm so glad you're here, Ms. Pennington! I have the most marvelous news! I was just telling Trish about my new trinket." Jillian offered her hand to Elizabeth for inspection. Wrapped around Jillian's tiny wrist was a diamond bracelet. "Isn't it just lovely? I figured I deserved it; so when it went on sale, I talked Arnold into buying it for me. He is such a good boy, isn't he?"

Elizabeth hated it when Jillian referred to her husband as a boy or a puppet. The woman loathed her husband by her own admission. Whatever their personal problems, Elizabeth didn't appreciate hearing personal details of the life of her assistant. Jillian had improved in her choice of conversation topics since the day Elizabeth had pulled her aside and pinpointed subjects considered taboo for the office. As Elizabeth looked at the delicate bracelet, Jillian beamed with pride. Elizabeth demonstrated her appreciation of the fine jewelry by telling Jillian how pretty it looked then quickly poured a cup of coffee and exited the room. Her doubt about what the two women were discussing was diminished as she heard Trish giggle and whisper, "I thought you had bit the big one sister! Either Elizabeth is just like you say or she is plain dumb."

Elizabeth paused until she heard Jillian's response. "Shhhh, she might hear you, Trish." As Elizabeth walked away her heart ached as she heard Jillian whisper, "It could be a toss-up with her; I would bet on the plain dumb." She had heard enough of the petty conversation. Three years ago, she would have walked to her office; closed the door, and wept. That was three years ago.

Elizabeth straightened her back then turned swiftly. Her mind was working quickly to produce a plan of immediate action. As she re-entered the break room, the smiles that Jillian and Trish wore became frowns. Her smile was kind but firm as she began to uncover the break room gossip for what it was. "Ms. Hunter and Ms. Braxton, I'm appalled at what I have just heard." Jillian opened her mouth to protest as Elizabeth continued, "Please don't bother to explain what you meant by saying I'm plain dumb. Our company, as you know, has a policy on gossip so I think I'll get the support of human resources in saying that disciplinary action will be taken if this happens again. Please consider this as a verbal warning to you both."

Trish was silent and obviously embarrassed as she nodded her head. Jillian looked unaffected with the exception of the single tear that ran down her left cheek. Elizabeth wasn't sure, but Jillian's eyes looked as if they were mocking her. After standing for a moment in the silence, Elizabeth said good-bye then left. She walked away quickly, not wanting to hear any conversation that might come from the break room. She hoped that the two women would heed what had been said to them and not continue their malicious conversation.

The morning confrontation became the focus of Elizabeth's day. Her immediate supervisor, Fred Sabine, wasn't in his office and Elizabeth felt as if she must share what had happened with someone. She knew that the two women could easily distort what Elizabeth had said. Since no third party had been available to witness what had happened, Elizabeth decided to go to the next link in the chain of command, Ray Morgan, CEO.

She hesitated before she knocked on Ray's office door. She raised her fist to knock then decided not to proceed. Elizabeth's fist hung in the air as her indecision mounted. Ray's secretary, Rebecca, wasn't at her desk. Elizabeth knew that Ray had an open door policy but she wasn't sure how open. The tension in Elizabeth's stomach rose to her throat as she decided to forget the idea of sharing her concerns with Ray. Before she could flee, the door opened. Ray had his back turned as if he were looking at something on his desk while exiting the room. Elizabeth was so stunned to see him that she didn't move, causing him to walk right into her.

"Oh, excuse me, Ms. Pennington," Ray stammered as he regained his equilibrium. "Again, I apologize for running into you...literally." Light danced in his eyes as he recalled the last time he had bumped into her. Her eyes had looked so big and innocent. Ray looked down as he explained the reason for his impromptu bump, "Uh, I was just trying to figure out how to make the new intercom system work. I was going to see if Rebecca had returned yet...but I guess she hasn't." Ray leaned in toward her as if sharing a secret, "Don't tell anyone, but she is the electronic genius of this office."

Discovering Elizabeth

Elizabeth laughed, "I know."

Ray looked at Elizabeth with a raised brow. "You know? Has she told you what kind of a klutz I am around electronic gadgets?"

Elizabeth shook her head. "No, you spilled the beans yourself. I've known Rebecca for a while. Actually, we went to school together so I know of what she is capable."

Ray chuckled. "Is that a fact? I'm glad I didn't go to school around here. I think that you two could have been a dangerous pair."

Elizabeth agreed, "You think right. Listen, Ray, if you don't have time to talk, I can come back some other time." Elizabeth looked at her watch as she continued; "It's about lunch time now. I'll talk to you later, okay?" Elizabeth turned to go without waiting for a response.

A puzzled look creased Ray's handsome face. "Elizabeth, I never said I didn't have time for you. Please come in and we can discuss whatever is bothering you."

Elizabeth hesitated as Rebecca entered the office. Rebecca's arms were full of food and soft drinks. Elizabeth lifted part of Rebecca's load from her and helped her carry it to a small table. Rebecca smiled at her friend, "Thanks Liz." The fumbling administrative assistant looked at her boss apologetically, "Hi Ray, I'm sorry I'm late. Traffic was really hectic and while I was ordering, I ran into an old friend. I'm going to go downstairs and have coffee with her if you don't mind."

Ray began looking through one of the bags. "Go ahead, feed me then leave. Aren't you going to eat your share?"

Rebecca shrugged her shoulders, "No, I'm not hungry. I ate a couple of fries and it kind of made me sick at my stomach. I'm still not one hundred percent over the virus I had last week."

Ray looked up quickly, "I'm sorry, Rebecca, if you weren't feeling well why didn't you say something."

Rebecca shrugged, "Oh, I'm feeling fine; my stomach is just not used to having your beloved greasy spoon appetite."

Ray laughed. "Call it what you will but you can't deny that it's most tasty." Ray held up his bag then motioned for Elizabeth. "Elizabeth, why don't you stay and eat with me since I'm being stood up by my faithful assistant here. We can talk about whatever it was you came here to discuss."

Elizabeth didn't have time to respond. Rebecca clapped her hands together while pushing a white bag with darkening blotches on it toward Elizabeth. "That's a great idea! Thanks, Liz, I was about to feel guilty for running out on him."

A delighted Rebecca grabbed her purse then left the president of the company to introduce what she called, "cholesterol in its raw element," to his accounting executive.

Elizabeth realized that her mouth was gaping. She grabbed the drinks Rebecca left then followed her boss to a small conference table in his office. Elizabeth watched him bless his food then prepare to eat. The man was precise in every movement he made. As she watched him she thought that he would be a man who would eat his sandwich the same way every time. Her own assumptions about Ray Morgan caused her to smile. Ray chose that moment to look up. He caught his breath when he saw the smile and the way she was observing him.

He had never seen such smiling eyes before and he wondered why he hadn't noticed that about her before now. As he pondered her beauty he couldn't help but wonder at the shade of her blue eyes. Ray smiled at himself for even noticing such a thing. Elizabeth had worked for him for a while. He had noticed that she was very lovely, but she always looked very somber to him. With the exception of the collision in the stairwell, he had never spoken to her without Fred being present before. His curiosity about why she was smiling made him ask, "What in the world are you thinking, Ms. Pennington?"

"Why?" Elizabeth tried to stop smiling but could not.

"Because you're making me nervous. Are you amused with me or at me?" He placed his sandwich on a napkin while he awaited her answer.

Elizabeth decided to be truthful. "I was wondering if you always eat your sandwiches outside in."

"What?"

"I was wondering if you always eat around the outside of your sandwich then the middle." Elizabeth grinned. She wished she could slip into her "accountant look," but could not.

Discovering Elizabeth

Ray looked down at his sandwich, which now looked as if someone had cut a perfect circle around the outside and left the middle. "Of course I do. How do you expect me to eat it?"

"The right way."

Ray feigned offense. "And what may I ask is the right way, Ms. Pennington?"

Elizabeth held her sandwich up for him to inspect. "You are supposed to start on one side and eat your way through to the other side."

He sat in silence until Elizabeth thought she had just ruined her reputation permanently. Finally, he lowered his voice and said, "Elizabeth, you've been holed up in your office with too many figures for way too long. Everyone knows a sandwich is supposed to be eaten in a clockwise fashion."

Elizabeth held up her sandwich in defiance. "That, Mr. Morgan, is a matter of opinion."

Elizabeth and Ray looked serious for as long as they could before their eyes met and laughter rung through the office. For some reason, the unusual bantering between the two broke the ice helping Elizabeth forget her initial reservations about speaking with him.

After finishing his burger and fries, Ray leaned back in his chair and decided to dive into what he thought Elizabeth was thinking. "So, Jillian is giving you problems is she?"

She was still chewing her last french fry. The potato suddenly tasted as if she had a mouthful of sawdust. Unable to chew or swallow, she stared at him as if he had just asked her about problems on Venus.

"So it is Jillian, right?" Ray looked half-amused and half-perplexed at Elizabeth's reaction to his question. He couldn't help but wonder what the woman was thinking.

Elizabeth swallowed the gravel with one painstaking swallow while praying she wouldn't choke. She took a drink of soda then stammered, "Well, y-yes, it's about Jillian. How did you know?"

"I'm the president of Wright and Wingold. It's my job to notice potential problems before they arise. Let me put it this way; I have noticed your assistant."

"Oh." Elizabeth was more than embarrassed. The thought that Ray Morgan could already know of her trials had never occurred to her. Her mind reeled as she wondered if he thought she was a part of the problem or if she was handling things with Jillian poorly. Elizabeth's features became very serious.

"Elizabeth, please talk to me. I'm here for you to use as a sounding board and as a resource for help. You and I haven't spoken about this kind of thing before so let me tell you how to get some resolution here. Be honest and frank with me. I want to know what has you concerned. Please don't worry about what I might think of you or your supervisory skills. If you hold back, this thing isn't going to be resolved. If it doesn't get resolved, you're going to be more affected than you know."

Elizabeth was attentive as she asked, "What do you mean?"

She hadn't expected to feel comfortable with him. A smile betrayed her amusement as she guessed at what he was trying to convey. "Okay, you're saying that if this isn't taken care of, it will be really bad. Or, you could be saying that it has gone on so long that something major is going to be required to resolve it? I have to tell you that I want to do the right thing. This situation with Jillian has been challenging, I just don't know what to do about it, Mr. Morgan."

"Call me Ray, Ms. Pennington." Ray smiled as he fumbled with cleaning the luncheon mess. "I know what you mean about doing the right thing. Experience is what you need and is what you're getting. While conflict and challenges don't always feel good, they're really good for you." He glanced at Elizabeth as she grimaced. "Don't look at me as if I said something in a foreign language. The more you deal with hateful, manipulative, mean individuals, the more adept you'll become at handling those whose lot in life is to test the very depths of your patience."

"Elizabeth, there are some old proverbs that lend wisdom about characters like Jillian. One says, 'They do not sleep unless that they have done evil; And their sleep is taken away unless they make someone fall for they eat of the bread of wickedness and drink the wine of violence.' You see, you're not the only one to have ever met the one who tests your very being."

Elizabeth stared at the man whom she thought she knew. She had read the words he had just quoted the night before. Ray had never said

Discovering Elizabeth

it, but Elizabeth knew he was quoting scripture. "That's Proverbs four, right?"

"Umm, yes, uh, I guess you're right." Ray suddenly looked uncomfortable. "Well then, you understand that this is an ancient problem. The passage in Proverbs goes on to say that those who do wickedly don't know what makes them stumble because they're in darkness. Elizabeth, she will stumble. If Jillian doesn't change her attitude, her future isn't bright. As her supervisor, it's your responsibility to lead her into professional development. If she's doing something that you know will cause her to "stumble," you must run interference."

Elizabeth opened her mouth to protest but Ray held up his hand to signal that he wanted to finish his statement. "Jillian may or may not know better. Even so, you're her supervisor, and it's important that she succeed. This company can't succeed if your assistant doesn't. You can't succeed unless Jillian succeeds and vice versa. Like it or not, we all need each other. I need for every employee to succeed. The worst mistake any leader can make is not realizing that it takes everyone's success to make a business work. Now, I can't make someone a success if they don't want to be. A leader, however, should be able to provide an environment and atmosphere where each person can flourish if they choose to. Since you're her supervisor, the ball is in your court. Elizabeth, if you don't pinpoint where she needs to improve or help her to see it, she probably won't fix it. If that happens, she'll eventually be fired, to put it bluntly. You're doing a dishonor to her by not guiding her by giving her clear-cut expectations. I'm not pointing the finger, just trying to help you get focused. While you're working on this project, don't forget to let her know when she does a good job. Observe her reactions and discern what works and what doesn't. Then, if she refuses to change and doesn't want to work as a part of this team, we'll address it. Let's try to do our best to give her every opportunity before it comes to that."

Ray looked at Elizabeth with friendly eyes as he thought about how he should proceed. She couldn't argue with the wisdom of his words. She knew that for too long she had let Jillian's behavior blind her. Her thoughts weren't focused on the Jillian challenge as her curiosity about the man in charge of Wright and Wingold increased. She looked at his cool hazel eyes that neither mocked nor accused her.

Lisa D. Piper

Ray took the last drink of his soda then stood to discard the container. Elizabeth never knew that Ray couldn't stand the way she was looking at him any longer. He pushed unwanted thoughts out of his mind and asked, "Elizabeth, may I tell you a story?"

"A story?" Elizabeth questioned.

"Yes, one of my favorites."

"Sure." She took a good look at Ray for what seemed to be the first time. She noticed that his shoulders were broad and no one could have accused him of being even average in height. He wore black pants with a white dress shirt. His tie was neither too loud nor too drab and as he stood near her chair, a faint smell of cologne teased her nostrils. Ray interrupted her uncustomary survey as he began the story.

She smiled as the businessman before her began the story the way her mother used to begin bedtime tales. He cleared his throat, smiled at Elizabeth and then began the narrative. "Once upon a time there was a king who had several sons. This king like most kings was very busy. He was a good king who loved his country and his people. This king had a son who was extremely good looking. As a matter of fact, the people often told him that he was more handsome than any other young man in the kingdom." Ray grinned before taking a step toward Elizabeth to sit down beside her.

Ray made sure that he had her attention before he continued. "From the top of the prince's head to the sole of his feet, there wasn't one blemish on him. His raven hair was thick and grew long. The son grew, married and had children. As was custom, the people of the kingdom would go to the king if they needed to have a legal matter resolved.

The lofty son began to get up early in the morning so that he could meet the people before they entered the kingdom. When a person who needed to speak with the king about a dispute would try to enter the gates, the son would befriend them and ask what had brought them to the palace. The son would smile at the caller; listen to the complaint and let the commoner know that he was correct in his side of the dispute. The prince would then sigh and tell the caller that there was no one to hear his side of the story because the king was too busy to listen. The prince would end the conversation by telling the visitor that if the prince were made the king then the people could go to him with their disputes and he would guarantee that justice would be done.

Discovering Elizabeth

The prince did this for a while and eventually; the people began to desire that the prince replace the king. While trying to overtake the throne, the prince tried to have his father killed. The son took over the kingdom while the king fled for his life." Ray shook his head sadly then added, "After a lot of pain and suffering the king eventually reclaimed the kingdom but the prince was killed[5]."

"How was he killed?" The story and the storyteller mesmerized Elizabeth.

"One of the king's men took a sword and thrust it through the prince's heart." Ray waited for her response.

Elizabeth didn't like the sad story but commented, "The king must have been glad that he could get his throne back after all the son had done to him."

"Not so. The father still loved his son even though the son had humiliated him publicly and overthrown his kingdom. Before his son was killed, the king had given an order that no one was to kill him. When the king found out that his rebellious son had been killed anyway, he wept and was very grieved. The king lamented and declared that he wished he had died himself instead of his son."

Elizabeth was shocked. "You are kidding me?"

"No, this is a real story. Elizabeth, the son had been standing at the gate lying to the people and taking over the kingdom for years and years before he actually did it. There are no records that the king ever interfered with what the son was doing. The king loved his son, and he should have. Nevertheless, when you love someone you sometimes have to say things to them and interfere in situations just because it is your job to do so. The king could have possibly spared his son his untimely death had he intervened earlier and perhaps the son could have obtained the throne in a more honest manner.

I've learned from this piece of history that where the heart of the people is, so is their support. Elizabeth, be good and honest to your team. Always listen to them and make it a priority to get to know them. You need to be wise so that you'll know how to deal with those who resemble the prince I told you about. Jillian is trying to undermine what you say and do for her own gain just like this prince. Ignoring the

---

[5] II Sam. 15-18

situation will bring you heartache in the future and could cost you your career."

After allowing the implication of the story to settle in her mind, Elizabeth stood to her feet and prepared to leave the room. "Ray, you have given me a lot to think about. I just hope I haven't waited too long to address the situation with Jillian. I walked in on her as she was cutting me down to another worker this morning. I let her know that I knew what she was doing but I'm not so sure I handled it correctly. Thank you for sharing your story with me. It seems that I've heard something like it before, but I cannot place it."

Ray looked at her petite hand as she extended it to him for a formal handshake. He noticed that she wore only one ring on her right hand. The ruby was brilliant and clear. As Ray stepped toward Elizabeth to take her hand, the unthinkable happened. His foot caught on the leg of the chair Elizabeth had been sitting in. Her eyes widened as the six foot four man stumbled toward her. He groped for her hand to regain his balance. This gesture turned out to be less than an ideal means to an end. His unexpected grab for balance pulled Elizabeth into him as they both landed on the carpeted floor. Elizabeth landed on the back of Ray's feet. She quickly scrambled to get up without even thinking about whether or not she had been injured. In her haste to stand to her feet and in Ray's haste to do the same, the pair wallowed about in a heap for several seconds before coordinating their efforts to leave the carpet. No words were shared as the embarrassment both felt spoke volumes. Elizabeth picked up her sandwich wrapper then quickly left Ray standing in his office, alone. Ray hadn't moved from the spot where she left him until he heard a light knock on the door. Silently, he prayed that the woman hadn't returned. Relief replaced anxiety as Homer peaked around the door holding a basket covered with a red checked table linen.

"Howdy, Son." Homer Foster lightheartedly called. After getting no response, Homer restated his greeting. "Howdy."

"Oh, hello my friend." Ray finally moved from his stance and moved toward the door.

Homer studied Ray then snickered. "Son, does that look on your face have anything to do with a young blonde beauty running down the hallway?"

Discovering Elizabeth

"She's running?" Ray asked in disbelief.

"Well, more like a fast walk I guess. She's holding her leg and limping, but she's going pretty fast I'd say."

Ray was mortified. "Oh no! I never asked her if she was all right. She never really gave me time to, but I still..."

Homer grinned before trying to ease the tension. "What ya do? Did ya kick her?"

"What? No, I did not!"

"Heh, heh, heh, I'm just trying to get to the bottom of the situation, boss. After all, I'm the environmental manager and I can't have any violence in the environment." Homer's humor was getting him nowhere so he decided on a different approach. "Boy, wipe that look off your face and look what I brought for you."

Ray almost smiled. "I'm sorry Homer, I didn't mean to snap at you. What do you have? Is it the usual?"

Homer opened the basket then sniffed the air. "It smells like enough home cooking to last you for about a week."

"Homer, Annie doesn't have to keep pampering me like this. She's so sweet but I wish she wouldn't worry over me." Ray finally gave Homer a grin and added, "I'm not sure what she's doing with you. You'd think that I could've talked her into running away with me by now to be my own personal chef. Surely she's had enough of you, you ole coot, after all these years!"

Homer made a fist then held it up to Ray. After a couple of seconds, Homer was in the finest boxer's form he could manage. Rotating his fists in the air, Homer demanded, "Put up your dukes, boy, them's fightin' words!" Ray stood tall as he prepared to take a friendly swat from his good friend when he heard a noise.

Neither Ray nor Homer had realized that a visitor had entered the room right before Homer's attempt to spar with the CEO. The senior vice president, Fred Sabino, was standing in the doorway with his mouth pursed into a line. Fred's distaste for the "hired help" was evident on his face as he stood with his hands planted on his hips. Fred's voice was elevated as he spat out, "What's going on in here, janitor?" Fred placed an emphasis on the word janitor as Homer turned to look at him with his "dukes" still in the air.

Homer didn't hesitate as he punched into the air and said, "Well, I guess you could say that nothing is up, sir. I was just going to teach this boy a lesson..."

Fred interrupted, looking as tall and proud as he could without standing on the tip of his toes. Ray knew that Fred was about to make a fool of himself. "Fred, you have no idea to whom you're talking. I'll take care of this."

Homer spoke up and said, "Mr. Morgan, I apologize if I was a bit out of line."

Ray rolled his eyes and said, "Homer, don't start that again, hold on just a minute."

Fred didn't see the elderly man grin mischievously and he didn't take his eyes off of Ray. He couldn't believe how Ray was handling the evident insubordination of the elderly man. As Fred almost glared at his boss, Homer walked to the door then said, "It won't happen again, sirs. I guess my temper got the best of me." Homer tipped his hat as he said, "Have a good day, gentlemen." Ray knew that Homer was having the time of his life as he watched him disappear.

As soon as Homer had time to get to the elevator, Fred questioned his boss. "Ray, I don't mean to question how you just handled the situation with that man, but I just have to. If you let the hired help talk to you like that just one time, you'll have everyone talking to you as if you were just an employee. What were you thinking, sir?"

Ray silently walked over to his desk then slowly turned to look at Fred. "I was thinking that you interrupted a conversation of which you knew nothing about and began making inappropriate assumptions. Fred, we've talked about this before. Your opinion is welcome and even wanted, but this isn't a militant operation. Come on Fred; loosen up! That man isn't a bug on a wall nor is he overly capable of causing me harm. He is a vital part of this organization. You aren't going to be an effective representative of the values of this company until you realize that every person is important. You also need to be able to show each person, no matter what they do, that they're valuable. I'm disappointed at the manner in which you spoke to Homer. If I had a problem with him, I would've said so. Fred, if you speak to another

Discovering Elizabeth

employee in a condescending manner again, you'll no longer be employed, is that clear?" Their eyes met and locked as Ray waited for the man's response.

Fred had listened to Ray with more than a little disappointment. He had expected gratitude from his superior for saving him from the wiry old man. Fred wasn't getting what he deserved, in his own opinion.

Knowing that the wrong answer would end his career, he grudgingly nodded in agreement. His pride wanted him to blurt out, "Ray, I'm a blasted Senior Vice President for Wright and Wingold! You don't have to keep evaluating everything I do, and I would think that you would stand beside me before you would take up for someone who knows nothing about the real thing we do here!" Fred fought the wounded pride that wanted to proclaim his true thoughts. Instead, Fred said, "Okay, Ray. I apologize if I made a fool of myself. I'll apologize to...what did you say his name is? Homer? Okay, I'll apologize to Homer first thing." Fred turned to leave as Ray sat down at his desk while picking up the phone to dial the custodial department.

"Hello? May I speak with Homer?" Ray became impatient as he waited for the man.

Homer lost his southern drawl as he spoke properly into the phone, "Hello, you have reached Homer Foster. How may I help you?"

"Homer? This is Ray. How long did you laugh?"

Homer feigned innocence. "I don't know what you mean, Mr. Morgan."

"Like wild fire you don't!"

Homer allowed silence to settle into the conversation before he quietly begged. "Don't tell Annie on me, Ray."

"Ha! You just wait!" Ray didn't know what it was about Homer Foster, but he couldn't help but be cheerful while bantering with him. "How about inviting me over for dinner tonight?"

"Done. Just promise to keep your mouth closed. Oh, and make sure to eat some of those snacks before you come over because Annie will ask you if you ate anything from the basket."

"Alright, Homer." Ray changed his speech to match the slang that Homer used when he was in a comfortable setting. "Now, git back to work before I fire ya myself!" Ray hung up the phone as Homer's laughter rang out. As Homer hung up the receiver he began to scratch his chin. While humor helped him to deal with people like Fred, he didn't doubt for one minute that Ray had already handled the situation. Homer knew Ray well enough to know that he would be able to see that having a man like Fred around his operation could be detrimental to the effectiveness of the company.

The CEO completed all of the necessary tasks for the day then told Rebecca he was calling it an evening. Rebecca couldn't hide her amazement. Her boss never left early. She noticed that Ray's bruise was almost gone as she smiled at him while waving good-bye. As she thought back to the day when he came in with a puffy eye, she still wondered what had happened to him. As she looked down at her keyboard she wondered what time it must be. She was looking forward to leaving a little early as well. Elizabeth and Gabrielle had asked her out for supper. The night was sure to be full of fun if it was anything like the other evenings she had spent with "just the girls."

Chapter THREE

"Who can find a virtuous woman? For her price is far above rubies." Pro. 31:10.

Rebecca arrived at the little house owned by an excited redhead and an impatient blonde. Nestled between two large maple trees, the house spoke of character and charm. The lawn was immaculate and could have been the subject for any gardening magazine. Rebecca felt peaceful as she slowly made her way to the oak door. Squealing with delight, Elizabeth and Gabrielle answered her knock and began to chatter with anticipation of an evening filled with girl stuff. Gabrielle offered their visitor a cola while Elizabeth finished getting ready.

Rebecca looked at the two women who were clad in blue jeans and casual shirts. "I'm glad I didn't dress up! What's on the menu for this evening?"

Elizabeth smiled mischievously then said, "We have decided that we don't want to cook!"

"What?" Rebecca placed her hand on her brow then threw herself onto the couch in a Cleopatra pose. "You're not going to feed me?"

"Cut out the theatrics! I didn't say we're not going to eat. I said that Gab and I aren't going to cook. You should be glad about that!" Elizabeth finished her explanation then stood to her feet to retrieve her purse and keys.

Lisa D. Piper

"Liz, where are we going?" Gabrielle asked as Elizabeth crossed her arms.

"We're going out! I just don't know where we're going. If I asked either of you where you wanted to go we'd spend an hour taking turns saying wherever the other one wants to go. It's possible that we could spend the entire evening being indecisive and I just want to go. I've had a stressful day and I want to de-stress, period." Elizabeth ushered the girls out of the house toward Gabrielle's car. "Can we take your car, Gab? Mine's in the shop!"

Gabrielle laughed, "Yeah right! Your pile of rust is in the garage. You just want to be riding in style tonight and I don't blame you!"

Elizabeth rolled her eyes as she motioned toward her friend's car. "Sure thing, Gab. Why would three women want to ride in my Taurus when we can ride in the Glow Mobile."

Gabrielle rose to the bait. "I'll have you know that this color was the most popular hue available when I purchased this high quality automobile. You would do well to remember that, Little Miss Goody Two Shoes. You're just jealous that I get all of the attention when we're in my little baby here." Gabrielle ran her hand across the dashboard of her yellow jeep.

Elizabeth and Rebecca laughed aloud. Elizabeth shook her head. "Okay, Gab, I concede that you do get more attention. Now, can we just go?"

Gabrielle grinned at her friends then started the car as she shouted, "Look out town! The girls are out and the caffeine is doing its thing!"

As Gabrielle drove through town, memories of their childhood became the topic of conversation. The women hadn't realized how long they had been riding until Rebecca shouted, "You guys! We're only 10 minutes from Henry's Shoreside Shanty! Let's go see if Henry is in. Maybe we can take a walk on the beach like we used to. Perhaps we can do some wading and play shell hide and seek!"

Gabrielle slapped the steering wheel. "Great idea! We haven't played that game since we were what? Ten or twelve years old? I'm game, what about you, Liz?"

Elizabeth shook her hair in the cool wind, "Count me in ole chap! A cool breeze and the sound of lapping waves definitely has a de-stress

Discovering Elizabeth

appeal to it." Elizabeth clucked her tongue purposely. "As a matter of fact, I do believe that I'm the Queen of the Shells from days gone by. I was undefeated if I recall."

Gabrielle and Rebecca glared at Elizabeth. Simultaneously Gabrielle and Rebecca shouted, "You were not! I'm the queen!"

Each woman began to proclaim to be the monarch. The argument continued until Gabrielle pulled into Henry's parking lot. The three childhood friends locked their doors then headed into the building where they would sit down famished and get up complaining that they should've worn elastic waistbands.

The waitress had just finished delivering three plates of fresh seafood when Gabrielle led the prayer of thanksgiving for their food and friendship. After three hearty Amen's, the women were ready to feast. Talking ceased for a moment while they relished the familiar tastes.

Gabrielle finished her last shrimp then turned to Rebecca to ask if she remembered when Gabrielle's parents took them to Henry's to eat for Rebecca's tenth birthday.

Rebecca dropped her fork. "Don't go there, Gabby! I don't want to talk about it." Rebecca's eyes sparkled as memories of her much awaited birthday flooded her mind.

"Talk about what?" Elizabeth asked.

Gabrielle turned to Elizabeth and began to tell a story she had never shared with anyone. "Do you remember Jimmy Jackstone?"

Elizabeth nodded that she did. Elizabeth turned to look at Rebecca's reddened complexion. "Rebecca? No! You didn't!"

Rebecca dropped her head. "I did. I've never told anyone." Rebecca lifted her head then poked Gabrielle in the arm. "That's until big mouth over here had to bring it up."

"Come on, Rebecca, spill the beans!" Elizabeth goaded her friend.

"I can't tell you. I don't think I can stand to relive it. It's been twenty years and I'm still mortified!"

"I'll tell you!" Gabrielle chirped.

Lisa D. Piper

Rebecca groaned. "I was afraid of that! Tread lightly, Gab! My heart is still wounded over that one."

All three girls giggled as Gabrielle began to tell the story to her best friend. "As you know, our Rebecca has an imagination that surpasses that of any three year old." Rebecca rolled her eyes at the familiar remark from one of her dearest childhood companions. "Rebecca had convinced me and apparently herself, that Jimmy Jackstone wasn't really completely too old for us! Jimmy must have been around fifteen at the time. We had read in a teen magazine that all a girl needed to do to attract a boy was pucker her lips while raising her left eyebrow ever so slightly. The article also gave several pick-up lines that could be used to lure the unsuspecting male." Gabrielle began to giggle. Her laugh was infectious and the other two joined in.

After Gabrielle regained her composure enough to continue, Rebecca covered her red face with her delicate hands. "Jimmy was sitting a couple of tables from us. When her parents weren't looking, we gave him our best facial imitation of what we thought had to be alluring. We knew that we were doing what the article had suggested correctly because he kept looking at us. We were thrilled to get the attention and giddy with infatuation as he succumbed to "the look." Eventually, Rebecca's mom and dad told us that it was time to go. Rebecca acted as if a crumb were in her eye." Gabrielle stopped her storytelling and looked at Rebecca. "By the way, Rebecca, that was ingenious. A crumb?"

Rebecca blushed, "I know, I know. I was ten and it made sense. Just finish your awful tale."

Gabrielle sat at the edge of her seat and finished reminiscing, "Anyway, she told her mom to go on to the car while she and I went to the rest room to flush out the crumb. Her unsuspecting mom and dad exited the building never knowing what we had planned. I think Jimmy had been eating with his dad and when his dad got up to pay the bill, Jimmy was left alone to finish his sandwich. We sauntered over to his table with our backs to the cash register so his dad couldn't see. Rebecca had rehearsed the line we had agreed upon. We both puckered or basically pooched out our lips and raised our eyebrows repeatedly while Rebecca cooed, 'What's shakin'?"

Elizabeth wished she hadn't chosen that moment to take a drink of her cola. Between coughs she asked, "Did he return the enthusiasm?"

Discovering Elizabeth

Rebecca grinned sarcastically and retorted, "You don't see him with me now do you? I never became Rebecca Jackstone!"

Elizabeth held her sides as she laughed with her friends. "That's probably a good thing though. I'm not so sure you would've been a good mate for Jimmy."

Rebecca grimaced. "I don't think I had anything to worry about after that day. I think he was afraid of us."

Before Rebecca or Elizabeth had time to pick up the bills that lay on the table, Gabrielle hurriedly grabbed the three green stubs. She paid the bill with two protesting females behind her. Neither Elizabeth nor Rebecca saw the smile that played on the lips of their friend as she looked at the beautiful shells outlining the check-out counter; reminding her of a time in their past. As Gabrielle walked out of the door of Henry's Shoreside Shanty she squealed out a question that caused the hair to rise on the arms of her friends. "Who's the Queen?"

The childhood game took on new life as Elizabeth and Rebecca stood to attention and answered, "I am!"

"I'm the queen!" Elizabeth protested.

Rebecca placed her hands on her hips and argued, "No, you are not. If you'll remember correctly, I was the reigning queen. You my friend were the runner up."

Elizabeth turned to Gabrielle. "Gabrielle, you remember that I was queen, don't you? Tell her who was queen!"

Gabrielle flicked a stray hair from her shoulder before squatting down in the sand outside of Henry's. Elizabeth and Rebecca jumped back as Gabrielle startled them by jumping into the air with a sandy shell in hand while screaming, "I was the queen and I hereby defend my title!" Gabrielle turned swiftly and began her sprint toward the wooden bridge that separated Henry's parking lot from the long sandy beach.

Two women followed the redhead across the gritty sand in a run that revealed the competitive nature of the women and the youth that was hidden from the business world.

Lisa D. Piper

Ray arrived at the Foster residence on time. He looked forward to a homemade dinner by his favorite cook and anticipated the moment that Homer and Annie would retreat to the porch for an after dinner lemonade. Homer would recite stories that Ray had long ago memorized. Ray knocked on the door and was quickly ushered into the coziest home he'd ever entered. Ray breathed in deeply as the aroma of Annie's baking filled the room. He looked around the living room where Homer was setting up a worn out checkerboard.

"This house feels like home," Ray said quietly as he took inventory of all the familiar furnishings. The hard wood floor looked as beautiful as the day it had been laid, with the exception of the one blemish Ray knew was hidden behind the door under the upright corner lamp.

Ray could not resist the urge to make sure it was still there and looked to see if he could find it. As he tipped the lamp to the right, Homer cleared his throat and mumbled, "To the left a little."

Ray was startled into grinning like the youngster Homer sometimes accused him of being. He tipped the lamp to the left until he could see the rough notch of exposed wood. Old guilt washed over his handsome features as he regretted the day that he had permanently marred his favorite couple's flooring. Although Ray wished he had never hammered the first nail into the shiny surface, he found comfort in seeing a mark that proved he was once a creative little boy instead of a creative, starchy businessman.

Homer interrupted Ray's memories by motioning for him to sit down for a duel of wits. Ray took the seat across from his checker rival then asked, "Why didn't you ever get it fixed or do something more to camouflage it?"

Homer moved his game piece as he mumbled, "Cause Annie's proud of it that's why."

"Proud of it? Are you serious?"

"For once, I'm serious. She calls it a nick of love. Every once in a while I see her tip that lamp to the left then grin as if I don't know what she's a thinkin'. You were so small when you began to think you were her keeper. You weren't bigger than a minnow when you took that hammer to her prize possession." Homer watched his opponent as Ray made his first move. "I'll never forget that swat you got for doing what you thought was a good deed!" Homer laughed aloud.

Discovering Elizabeth

"A swat? Is that what you call it?" Ray repositioned himself in the chair as he recalled the "swat" he received from his beloved mama for not asking to destroy the Foster's hardwood before taking the hammer to it.

"Heh, heh, heh, my condolences, son. You didn't get anything like what my mama gave to me. Just look at you now boy! You're a fine upstanding citizen who wouldn't harm another man's property for anything." Homer's eyes were ablaze as he teased the younger man.

"The only difference between us, Homer, is that you probably deserved every whipping you ever got! I, on the other hand, had pure motives for trying to destroy your home!" Ray took the opportunity to jump Homer's game piece with a hoot of triumph.

"Now look what you've gone and done! You're interruptin' my concentration. Now, give the expert a moment to plan a strategy then you won't be so cotton pickin' happy, you little whippersnapper."

"Come on, Homer, don't start the name calling or I'll have to call the reverend."

Homer looked up from the board and grinned. "Go ahead and tell the reverend. He called me an old cheater last week. I'd like to hear what he has to say about name calling!"

Ray fell back with laughter. "He's found you out has he? I like that man more all the time."

Homer grinned. "Yeah, I do too. He's not half bad at the checkerboard either. I'll bet he could beat you!"

Annie Mae Foster walked into the room to scold her husband. "Homer, leave the boy alone! Our meal is ready." Annie watched Homer and Ray race to the dining room. Annie cleared her throat as a gentle reminder for the men to mind their manners. With the slightest reproof from the cook, both men pulled out a chair and motioned for the woman who had made hundreds of meals for them to sit down.

After sitting down at the head of the table, Homer motioned for Ray to give thanks for the food that they were about to devour. "Lord, thank you for this delicious food. Thank you for this wonderful couple; they are such a blessing to me. Please bless them as they've blessed others." Ray paused for a moment. His heart was full of things he wanted to say but could not. He summed up his thoughts with the closing of his

Lisa D. Piper

prayer. "Lord, surround Homer and Annie with your divine protection and grace. May their joy be full, in Jesus' name. Amen." When Ray looked up from his prayer, Homer and Annie looked at Ray as if they had seen a miracle and couldn't believe it. Ray had said his thanksgiving with such fervency and faith that Annie beamed with joy. There was a time when Annie had longed to hear Ray pray with hope. She wasn't, however, sure what had happened but there was a change in the voice of the young man she thought of as her own. No one else would have ever noticed it, but no one knew Ray like Homer and Annie did.

Homer was the first to pick up his fork to sample the beginning of what was to become a very memorable meal. Homer began reminiscing about a place and a time that Ray had never known but had imagined since he was a scraggly little boy.

After pouring three tall glasses of Homer's homemade lemonade, the threesome visited the back porch overlooking the most beautiful view Ray could ever remember seeing. The breeze was just right and the smell of the ocean was as relaxing as the old porch swing. Homer giggled as he brought up the subject of the scarred floor with his wife. "Ray checked to see if his handiwork was still under the lamp a few minutes ago. He wanted to know why we didn't have it fixed."

Annie leaned her head on the shoulder of her husband as she watched Ray fidget. "Ray, I would never have it fixed. When you inherit this old place, I expect you to not fix it. Do you hear me?"

Ray wanted to protest the insinuation that Homer and Annie would one day leave their home to him. He knew that any argument would be futile so he consented. "Okay, I give you my word."

"Good!" Annie seldom began the time of story telling but began to reminisce as she thought about the episode so many years earlier. "Ray, I'll never forget the sound of that hammer hitting the floor. Your mama and I thought that someone was trying to break in the door. When we rushed out of the kitchen to find you with Homer's hammer and an old rusty nail sticking out of my shiny floor, I thought she was going to faint." Annie's laughter prohibited her from finishing the story.

Discovering Elizabeth

Ray began to grin sheepishly as the elderly woman lost her serious temperament to a fleeting memory. "Ms. Annie, I promise you that I had only the best intentions in mind when I master minded the idea."

"I know. I thought your poor mama would fall over when you told her that the reason you were trying to erect a mailbox in the living room was because you were afraid that I would get run over by a car while crossing the street. You were always such a sweet boy. You were sometimes unpredictable, but sweet."

Before Homer could tease Ray about being sweet, a distant sound caused him to whisper, "Listen, Annie."

As Homer and Annie looked out over the railing on their porch, three friends chased each other down the beach as fast as their feet would go in ankle deep sand. Anyone listening to the woman in the lead would have mistaken her for a school-aged child and that's just what Homer, Annie and Ray did.

The three professional women had romped and chased one another until they discovered that they were on a part of the beach they hadn't been in years. Beautiful houses lined the beach. Many of them were visibly unoccupied. Rebecca, Elizabeth and Gabrielle were nearly out of breath as the competition of the game gave them courage to continue. Without warning, Elizabeth looked down at her feet to retrieve a hard object protruding from the sand. To her delight, she took off running wildly while shouting, "Whoopee!" The other girls turned toward the spot where Elizabeth had been standing in time to see her raise a shell that was larger than the one Rebecca held to her chest. As Elizabeth belted out, "I'm the Queen!" the other two women floundered to begin the adrenaline-pumping chase across the moon lit beach. Elizabeth used the burst of adrenaline to run wildly away from the shoreline. Gabrielle and Rebecca screamed loudly while threatening to catch her. The chase had just begun when an elderly gentleman from a porch swing pointed at them.

Homer squinted his eyes and said, "What in tarnation?"

"Homer, Listen! Listen for a minute and think!" Annie's face lit up as she looked at her husband with a look of hope. "Oh, Homer, do you think it's the girls?"

Homer listened and then stammered, "Well, I'll be!" His keen memory took him back to a time when he and Annie would sit on the porch swing watching three pigtailed girls run all over the beach in a dream world all their own. And now, he was watching three very dirty women run all over the beach in a dream world that had been imagined years ago.

Ray became worried at the sounds moving closer to the house. "Who's making all that noise?"

Annie smiled, "I think it's our past visiting us, Son. Three little girls used to come to the beach and chase each other for hours about twenty years ago or so. They would chase each other and have the biggest time without noticing that another person even existed. We couldn't help but enjoy the camaraderie back then and it looks like they remember the fun too."

With that explanation, Ray could hear someone scream what sounded like, "QUEEN!" He wrinkled his brow as he thought back to years ago and remembered Annie telling his mother about the antics of the threesome.

"It's them Annie! How many people run up and down the sand screaming that?" Homer leaned over the railing to watch Gabrielle and Rebecca chase the flying blonde. "I wonder if they remember?"

Annie looked over the railing and said, "I don't know. You can ask."

"Ask what?" Ray wondered.

"Homer used to holler at the girls back then and invite them over. We would serve his ice-cold lemonade to them. The girls would drink the lemonade and leave us with smudged glasses from their dirty little hands.

Homer didn't hesitate as Annie finished her explanation. "Hey you girls out there! What in tarnation is a goin' on? Do I need to call the police?"

Rebecca, Elizabeth and Gabrielle froze. In what looked like a simultaneous, mechanical move, they looked up to the large house where an elderly gentleman held up a tall glass.

Homer burst into laughter as he squeezed his wife. "Look at 'em Annie Mae, it still works!"

One at a time, each perspiring female closed her mouth, as they realized who had yelled at them. All three began to smile and walk

Discovering Elizabeth

toward their caller. Gabrielle snickered and whispered, "Surely... that can't be that old man in that house?"

Homer shouted, "That'll be enough of that 'old' talk! Come here so I can take a good look at ya! Are you thirsty?"

Rebecca shouted, "Why you know we are! I don't remember play being this much work."

Ray recognized the voice of his secretary. As the voices of the women were fast approaching the stairs that led to the porch, Ray jumped up and volunteered to pour three glasses of ice-cold lemonade.

Annie opened the porch gate and hugged each of the women as they entered the familiar back porch. "My, oh my, you've grown. Look, Homer, aren't they just beautiful!" Annie pursed her lips as she had done when scolding the girls years earlier. "What are you all doing out in the dark without your parents?"

Excuses remembered from days that only existed in their memories began to roll from the tongues of the dirty threesome. After laughing at their own lame excuses for being out on the beach without their parents, Gabrielle called out to Homer and said, "Thanks for not calling the cops...again."

Elizabeth agreed. "Yes, I'm glad too. The last thing you ever said to us was that if you caught us out without our parents again after dark that you were going to have the sheriff come cart us away."

Homer grinned. "I think I said that every time I saw you." Homer continued to grin as he looked at Rebecca.

Annie laughed, "You did, Homer. You were full of hot air."

Homer wrapped his arm around his bride. "I won't call the police tonight ladies. We'll have fresh lemonade for you in just a few minutes. Annie and I have talked about you all through the years and wondered what happened to you. Do you live near here and are you married? Do you have children?" Homer stopped asking his tirade of questions when Annie poked him in the ribs with her finger.

Rebecca had been silent. She recognized the voice of the man as she stared at him in disbelief. "Homer...Homer from housekeeping? Is that you?"

Homer squinted and grinned sheepishly, "Rebecca? Is that you?"

Lisa D. Piper

Rebecca walked over to where Homer was standing to give him a quick nudge! "You sure do look different." Rebecca looked down at herself. "I guess I do too, don't I?"

Homer laughed. "Yes, I guess you do. I didn't even know you had long hair. You need to leave it down once in awhile." Homer picked up the hand of his wife to hold it. "I guess you've never seen me without the blue uniform and hat, huh? This is wonderful!"

Rebecca snickered. "Yeah! This is wonderful if you can keep a secret Homer. I wouldn't want Ray to see me like this."

Elizabeth gasped. "I got it! You're Homer the cleaning guy!"

Homer bowed as he admitted, "In the flesh!"

Annie looked at the three and asked if they had ever gotten married and if they had had children.

As Ray stood inside the back door he could hear Elizabeth say, "No, I'm not married and I don't have any children." Rebecca and Gabrielle nodded their heads to show that they too weren't married.

Homer chuckled before asking, "So, who's the queen?"

Homer wasn't disappointed as he received the answer he knew was sure to come. Each of the women declared that she was truly the reigning queen. Elizabeth's voice rose to a higher pitch than the others did as she raised her right hand to the air, revealing her prized shell. Elizabeth curtsied while presenting her find to the couple as she bellowed, "Mr. and Mrs. Homer, may I show you the token with which I'm inaugurated! I'm the Queen!"

Elizabeth could hear ice clinking against glass as the door that led into the house opened. As she turned to see what had made the clinking noises, Elizabeth was aghast as the realization that Wright and Wingold's CEO was standing in front of her holding three large glasses of lemonade.

"Hello, ladies! Having fun?" Ray suppressed the urge to laugh as three jaws gaped. He'd heard the entire conversation from inside the house. He was not, however, prepared for the scene that awaited him. Three very dirty, very disheveled women gaped at him as if they'd never seen him before. Each woman had rolled her pant legs above her knees to keep from getting wet. The cuffs of the pants were wet and

Discovering Elizabeth

packed with sand. Ray would never have been able to imagine what he was seeing with his own eyes if someone else had told him about it. Rebecca and Elizabeth were always so prim and proper at work. Two of his company's brightest stood before him looking as if they were survivors from a shipwreck.

Elizabeth refused to be intimidated, as Ray looked the three of them over with apparent amusement. Later, she would wish she hadn't said it but she had inhaled too much fresh air for one night and cast off all restraint. Elizabeth rose to her full height of five feet ten inches, tilted her head back and said, "What's the matter? Haven't you ever seen...a queen before?"

Ray was quick to respond as he bowed to Elizabeth with as much humility as he could produce. "Beg your pardon, majesty, I didn't recognize you, Queen Elizabeth." Elizabeth's eyes danced as she held out her dirt smudged hand for his royal endearment.

Ray took Elizabeth's hand into his and gently turned it over. He then planted the smallest of kisses right on her sandy palm. The others began to laugh at the game they were playing. Only Ray noticed that Elizabeth had become very still. She didn't smile or frown. Several moments passed before she realized that Ray still held her hand. Elizabeth had no idea what was wrong with her. A friendly game had just turned on her. She quickly walked to the railing to look out over the beach from the porch view. She looked to the ocean as if she were looking for something, while the others became re-acquainted with the Foster family.

After convincing herself that she was sane, Elizabeth turned around and looked to the now vacant spot where she and Ray had been standing. A quick sound of someone rushing brought her back to the present. Elizabeth thought, "The shell! Where's the shell!" She had placed it on the top of the railing while she looked at the moonlight dancing off of the deep blue ocean. Rebecca had noticed that Elizabeth had left the shell on the railing. She and Gabrielle sprinted toward the prize but were disappointed as Elizabeth quickly stepped back to the railing and grabbed her shell. Elizabeth thrust the shell into the air and squealed, "THE QUEEN!" Without a second thought, she bounded down the stairs and ran through her kingdom. An auburn haired auditor and a dark haired VIP secretary followed her in hot pursuit.

Lisa D. Piper

After much running and play, the women were too tired to walk back to the car. They weren't sure how they ended up lying on the sand looking up at the stars. All three of the queen candidates lay underneath the heavens looking at the masterpiece of their Creator. Quietness had hovered over them until Elizabeth asked, "You guys, do you ever think about how you'll end up? I mean, do you think about marriage, children, your role in church; you know...that kind of stuff?"

Gabrielle sighed, "Yes, I wonder about it." Her auburn hair was gritty with salt. "I've been praying for a Godly husband. When I find the man God has for me, it will be forever. I would love to have a house full of children. And, as far as the church goes, well, I have no idea of any calling on my life. I love serving God, but I don't feel like I have anything to offer the body of Christ. I've always heard that everyone has a talent, a gift, a calling or something. I don't know what I've got. When I was little, I dreamed of being a missionary. That kind of ministry just isn't what I can do now that I'm in the corporate world. I guess I'll have to wait it out and see what God has in mind for my future."

Elizabeth shifted to one side so that she could see the faces of her tired friends. "I have the same thoughts about myself. Lately though, I feel as if something is about to happen. I have to admit that I've been kind of afraid. How do I know what the will of God is? I don't even know if I know how to find out anymore. I know He's faithful and that's about all I know."

Gabrielle mused, "Well said. That's what children do you know. God wants us to be like children. They don't know anything, they just trust. That's what I want to do. Doesn't the Bible say that His strength is made perfect in our weakness?[6]"

"I believe it does." Elizabeth continued, "You know, God is the one who has placed me where I am today. I don't have one valid complaint about anything. I'm so blessed. I want to share these blessings with someone. Not just someone, but the one God has for me." Elizabeth's comment was barely louder than the incoming waves as she fought back the emotion that voicing her heart's desire had produced.

Rebecca's disbelief was apparent in her words and tone as she questioned her friend, "Liz, is that you over there? I thought I'd never

---

[6] 2 Cor. 12:9

Discovering Elizabeth

hear you say anything about wanting a mate. Not after... well, what I mean is that I've always thought you were kind of like a permanent loner when it comes to the male gender."

Elizabeth glanced at her friend then responded warmly, "I know. I'm surprised with myself. I don't ever remember thinking about this until now. As a matter of fact, I don't think I wanted it until right this moment. Maybe it's the stress at work. I'm dealing with a difficult employee right now and I'm not sure I'm handling it just right. Then there is, um, well, this person I keep running into who has tried to help me."

"Tell me more, Ms. Pennington." Gabrielle shot up from her sand blanket. "I don't think you've shared this with me."

"Sorry, Gab. It's just that every time I see him I end up looking like an idiot. It's just too embarrassing to talk about."

Gabrielle and Rebecca wanted to ask her what she was talking about but both of the women knew her too well. One unsolicited inquiry would cause Elizabeth to close the conversation and neither would be able to revisit the subject for a long while. It was best to allow Elizabeth to talk about her personal life, as she felt comfortable doing so.

With great fatigue, Elizabeth, Gabrielle and Rebecca stood up and tried to shake the grit out of their clothes. All three agreed that they had more fun on this outing than they remembered having as children. Just like when they were children, the night brought about deep slumber caused from the feverish play. The morning would bring the realization that none of them were children any longer.

Lisa D. Piper

Chapter FOUR

"Be of good courage, and he shall strengthen your heart, all ye that hope in the Lord." Psalms 31:24

"Oh help me, Lord!" The cry from the bedroom was painful.

Elizabeth pulled the covers away from her head so that she could figure out who or what was making the awful groaning sounds. "Ohhhhh!" Elizabeth cried out as she moved to look toward the sound coming from the other bedroom. Every muscle in Elizabeth's body had wound itself tightly around her bones sometime in the night. Moving would be a painful endeavor for the reigning queen.

With much effort, Elizabeth and Gabrielle began to prepare for work. Their movements were slow and neither of them felt like making the effort that conversation would demand.

Elizabeth drove to work then thanked God for elevators all the way to the fourth floor. She winced as she stepped from the elevator as her calf muscle rebelled at the movement. Jillian met Elizabeth with a dozen questions centering around the latest problems that had risen in the first minutes of Friday morning operations. Jillian questioned Elizabeth about the change in her physical state of health from Thursday afternoon to wincing with pain on Friday morning. She told Jillian that she would fill her in on the details later.

Jillian eyed Elizabeth as she limped toward the coffeepot. "Don't forget you have an eight-thirty meeting with all of the department heads in the Brooklyn Conference Room." Jillian reminded her boss,

Lisa D. Piper

"Don't be late! Mr. Morgan doesn't like it! I heard him say so." Elizabeth turned toward Jillian to look at her facial expression. Jillian misunderstood Elizabeth's movement to be an invitation to inform Elizabeth of what she had heard about Mr. Morgan. Jillian lowered her voice while leaning in toward Elizabeth and said, "I'm supposed to keep it confidential, but I have it in good faith that Mr. Morgan verbally sliced and diced his secretary right in front of the other department heads during that meeting when you were out of town."

The phrase, "Be honest and do what is right and wise," echoed in Elizabeth's mind. Elizabeth said a quick prayer, "God, I don't know how to handle this. What she's saying has to be a farce, but what do I say and how do I say it?" Elizabeth made eye contact with Jillian. Jillian had been smiling as if she were too glad to pass on the latest news about the supervisor's boss. Elizabeth looked at her assistant and asked, "Jillian, where did you hear that?"

"What?"

"Where did you hear that Mr. Morgan had verbally reprimanded Rebecca in front of others?"

"Elizabeth, I'm sorry but I can't say. I said I wouldn't say anything. I don't want to get anyone in trouble, so just forget I mentioned it." Jillian turned to place a folder into the nearest filing cabinet.

Elizabeth wasn't sure where the question came from but it was asked before she knew it. She looked at her assistant and asked, "Jillian, do you realize that you were trying to gossip just now?"

"Gossiping? I most certainly was not! I said that I'm not supposed to say who gave me this reliable information. I take my promises very seriously and I promised I wouldn't reveal my source. I just thought you needed to know. I wouldn't have wanted you to be one of his unsuspecting victims. I told you because I trust you."

Elizabeth paused and then continued, "Jillian, you've just told me that someone in this building is spreading damaging information about our CEO. You say that this person doesn't want their name revealed and asked you not to repeat what was said. Are you telling me that another department head has been gossiping about Mr. Morgan?" Elizabeth's tone wasn't accusatory but firm. She waited patiently in the sudden silence for a response from her assistant.

Discovering Elizabeth

"No, That's not what I said." Jillian was visibly shaken. "I never said that a department head said it. I never said it was gossip; and I never said that the information is damaging."

Elizabeth responded pointedly, "Jillian, if a department head didn't say it, then that means a non-department head said it. And since there were only department heads in the meeting along with Mr. Morgan's secretary, then it's gossip; because it is hearsay. Whoever told you didn't hear it first hand, nor did you. Is that correct?"

Jillian threw her hands into the air and said, "Forget it. Forget I said anything. I know when I'm not appreciated and when I'm being set up."

Elizabeth stepped out to walk toward Jillian but hesitated as her sore muscles rebelled at the sudden movement. Elizabeth reached for the desk to steady her balance then swiveled to sit down in the office chair nearest the desk. When Elizabeth looked up, Jillian was gone. Elizabeth sighed. She would finish the tiresome conversation after the meeting. Regardless of what Jillian had said, Elizabeth didn't want to be late for the morning meeting. And, since she was moving a little slower than usual, she left immediately and walked toward the conference room.

Two other department heads were already seated when Elizabeth walked through the conference room door. Elizabeth was wearing a sleek white pantsuit. No one in the office was used to seeing Elizabeth dress in light colors. For once, comfort was of the utmost importance and nothing was more comfortable then her white suit. When Elizabeth took longer than usual to go from a standing position to a sitting position, eyebrows raised but no one mentioned it. She wasn't sure how she had abused so many muscles in her arms during her beach excursion, but she knew she had. Every movement was excruciating.

As Fred, the Senior Vice President, stood to pour some coffee from a table in the corner, he motioned towards Elizabeth to see if she wanted a cup of the steaming liquid. "No thanks, Fred." Elizabeth smiled.

Elizabeth struggled to stifle a moan of agony as she began to remember that she was about to come face to face with the man who had seen her behave like a nine-year-old. Elizabeth hoped with all her might that Ray had forgotten the episode. She had revealed her carefree nature to someone with whom she worked and the thought of rejection

Lisa D. Piper

frightened her. Sure, Ray hadn't acted shocked at her display the evening before, but she was sure he had been caught off guard. As Elizabeth waited for the members of the team to arrive, apprehension engulfed her sore body. Perhaps it was because she was the youngest executive ever hired at Wright and Wingold. Perhaps it was because she didn't want her private world exposed for all to see. Hopefully, Ray would understand her position and would behave as if nothing had happened. Elizabeth hoped with all of her heart that Ray had somehow contracted twenty-four hour amnesia. Elizabeth's thoughts were interrupted by the creak of a door. The door opened but several moments passed before anyone stepped through it.

Rebecca slowly shuffled to the chair where she would take minutes for the morning meeting. Ray walked behind her carrying her brief case and tape recorder. Elizabeth groaned within herself. Ray had definitely not forgotten.

The other executives took their seats while Ray helped Rebecca prepare for the meeting. After making sure there was nothing else she needed, he turned and sat in his chair at the head of the table. "Good morning, everyone!" As Ray greeted the group, Rebecca glanced toward Elizabeth. Their eyes met but no words were shared. Elizabeth knew when Rebecca looked at her that she wanted to release a mischievous smile, but would not. Neither had ever let anyone in the office know that they were childhood friends. The mutual decision to keep their private lives outside of their work environment had benefited them until now. The plan had been concocted to avoid confusion and to protect their relationship from any conflicts that might arise from their positions in the company. Elizabeth thought that perhaps someone might wonder why both women were creeping along, but no one said anything.

As Ray Morgan settled into his chair, the manager of human resources glanced up from his task of analyzing the agenda long enough to murmur, "Good morning."

The only other greeting came from the manager of custodial services. Homer Foster said, "Good morning, Mr. Morgan. How are you today?"

Ray picked up his agenda. He smiled, then said, "Fine, Mr. Foster, and how are you this lovely morning?"

Discovering Elizabeth

Fred Sabino impatiently looked from Ray to Homer. Homer had never been invited to a department head business meeting as long as Fred could remember. Fred didn't hide his dissatisfaction with the presence of the man who, in his opinion, was incompetent. Fred could see no reason to include him in such important matters.

Ray began speaking about some changes in the company and leadership as the meeting began. Ray announced that he would like to begin including the custodial manager in every department head meeting. Homer smiled with pride as the others looked at Ray as if he had gotten the idea from too many days spent in the sun. Ray was patient as he realized that his news wasn't meeting the approval of his team. Ray encouraged those around the conference table; "Mr. Foster has been with our company for more years than most of us combined. He has led his department into being one of the greatest in the company. There isn't another firm that can boast of the cleanliness and professionalism that our firm has. And since we are in the cleaning business, I think that says a lot about us. After thinking about this, I think that we all could benefit from the experience and wisdom of one of our finest. Homer can be a valuable resource to any of you needing leadership help or advice. The stress of today's job market can be overwhelming. I think that if you utilize this priceless resource, your department will benefit from it." Ray didn't add that Homer had attended many meetings before Ray took over the company. It was Ray's insistence that caused Homer to relent and begin attending the meetings once more.

After making the unpopular announcement, Ray began the business meeting by asking Elizabeth to give an overview of what the budget compliance had looked like for the last quarter. Elizabeth had reviewed the numbers so many times that she was able to give the information and answer questions without hesitation. Ray would have thought that Elizabeth would avoid direct eye contact him. To his relief Elizabeth acted no differently than she would have acted before he served her Homer's lemonade. She met his eyes with a coolness he had gotten used to since she had worked for the company. She looked at each person in the room one at a time while she spoke with the confidence of a winning politician.

As Elizabeth concluded her report, she looked into Ray's eyes one last time. Ray would have missed it if he hadn't been looking directly at her. Ray Morgan finally saw the evidence that Elizabeth was uncomfortable or maybe even emotional. Elizabeth's blue eyes had turned a midnight blue. Ray couldn't figure out how her eyes had changed so intensely. He was positive that he had never noticed such a change in her features as he did at that moment. As he realized that Elizabeth was definitely affected by seeing him again, Elizabeth cleared her throat. She had finished speaking while he gazed at her. She didn't flinch as she looked back at him while waiting for his response to what she had shared with the group.

He didn't comment on the report; instead, he glanced briefly at his agenda then began to speak on the next topic for discussion.

After the terse meeting, Elizabeth began to wonder if she had handled the situation with Jillian properly. She began feeling like she had overreacted. Maybe she hadn't interpreted what Jillian had been saying properly...maybe she hadn't really been listening to understand. As she thought about the story that Ray had told her, she realized that she wanted everyone in her department to succeed. She didn't want to give any impression to her staff that her desire was to build herself up to make others look bad. As Elizabeth re-analyzed her motives for dissatisfaction in Jillian's behavior, frustration began to mount.

Elizabeth had been extraverted during her formative years and hadn't lacked confidence in most areas. The new emotion of being in a type of emotional whirlwind was disarming to the young accountant. As Elizabeth walked out of the conference room, she felt an urgent need to pray. As she walked toward the elevator, she prayed, "Father, I need you. You have always paid for what you have ordered. Your Word says that promotion does not come from the East or the West[7], but from you. I need you. I need your wisdom and your understanding. You have placed me in this job. You're ordering my life. You said that the footsteps of the righteous are ordered. I know I'm not perfect, but I know that you are mine and I am yours. Please help me. This feeling of being out of control doesn't feel good at all. In Jesus name I pray. Amen."

Elizabeth had just finished her prayer when she thought about the one person in the company who had years and years of experience in dealing with difficult situations, according to Ray Morgan. She would've never guessed that her childhood lemonade supplier was the

---

[7] Pslam 75:6

Discovering Elizabeth

friendly custodial manager at Wright and Wingold. Elizabeth wondered how Homer could afford such a fine home on ocean front property on a janitor's salary. Although, she thought, he is the manager and has several years of time built up in the company. Elizabeth's thoughts changed to how she would tell her problems to the elderly man. She had never visited the custodial department. She had overheard Homer tell Ray after the meeting that he was going to the office to catch up on some paperwork. Homer had said that he needed to order some cleaning supplies before tomorrow. Without a second thought, Elizabeth began walking toward the custodial department where she found Homer sitting behind a large oak desk. She hesitated momentarily then knocked softly on the door facing.

Homer hadn't expected anyone to take Ray's comments seriously. He was surprised to see Elizabeth Pennington standing outside his door. Homer smiled then stood to his feet while motioning for his visitor to sit down on an elegant deep blue chair near his desk. Elizabeth noticed that Homer's office was immaculate. She became curious about her host as she realized that she knew absolutely nothing about the man even though they worked in the same building.

Certificates and awards were displayed on a beautiful oak bookshelf. The display was tactful and incredible. Another shelf closer to his desk held custodial manuals of every kind. A computer was stationed on a small credenza behind the magnificent desk where he had been writing on an order form. Homer could tell that Elizabeth was bewildered by what she was seeing. Homer Foster wasn't a prideful man; in fact, the humility with which he carried his great wisdom was more than admirable. When some of the employees in the company had snubbed him because of his position, Homer merely laughed it off. In his opinion, they were fools and didn't know it, and that was the worst kind, he reasoned.

When Fred Sabino, the Senior Vice President, became obnoxious and called him, "the hired help", Homer didn't become defensive. Instead, he spent time praying for Fred. He knew that Fred's attitude was a result of Fred's own weaknesses. Homer understood that as long as Fred couldn't see that his attitude, prejudices and narrow-mindedness affected his effectiveness as a manager, he would never be half the leader that Ray had become. Homer also knew that Fred wanted Ray's position and he also knew that Fred's days in the company were short if he didn't get a grip and stop making a fool of himself.

Homer cleared his throat and recited his favorite scripture. "The fear of the Lord is the beginning of knowledge. But fools despise wisdom and instruction."

"What?" Elizabeth stammered.

Homer laughed. "That's Proverbs 1 and 7, Miss."

"Yes, I know. But why'd you say that?" Elizabeth winced at the pain as she shifted in her seat.

"Well, I'm mostly not sure why." Homer chuckled. "I assume that you need a listening ear or some advice? I hope it's not of the medical kind because my only advice would be to not run on the beach for hours at a time when you aren't used to it."

The smile that Homer saw the evening before crept onto Elizabeth's pretty face. "You're a day late, sir. I wish you would've told me that yesterday." As Homer laughed Elizabeth continued, "Mr. Foster..."

"Homer."

"Homer. I've come to get some advice, I guess. I'm at the end of my rope." Elizabeth crossed her legs as she groaned slightly as she told Homer of her trials with Jillian.

Homer scratched his chin thoughtfully and said, "I guess you're feeling like you aren't in control of the situation?"

"Control?" Elizabeth gasped.

"Yes, Control." Homer repeated. "What can you change, Elizabeth?"

"What do you mean?"

"What is it that you have control over right now?" Homer was patient as he awaited her answer.

Elizabeth thought about the whole week that preceded her desire to speak with the wise elderly man. "I seem to only be able to control what I do myself. I have an element of control over the environment in my office and about most decisions for the accounting department."

Homer smiled warmly at the inquisitive manager. "That about sums it up. You have control over yourself. You should have control over the

Discovering Elizabeth

things in which you are responsible for also. So what happens when you begin to worry about controlling others or circumstances beyond your control?"

"Uh...I feel like I'm out of control because I am! Is that right?"

Homer clapped his hands together. "Okay, That's correct. Now tell me what you don't have control over."

Homer carefully watched Elizabeth as she decided. She opened her mouth once to speak but closed it again. Finally she replied, "I guess I don't have control over the behavior and responses of others. How's that?"

"Wonderful. Hang in there with me, we're almost there!" Homer laughed with Elizabeth as she released some of the tension that had been building while trying to figure out what Homer was up to.

"Now let me ask you just a couple more questions. Elizabeth, can you physically stop Jillian from gossiping and damaging the reputation of others?"

"No, I don't think so."

"Then why are you trying?"

"I'm not trying to change her, I'm trying...I'm trying... Oh, I don't know what I'm doing, Homer."

"If you're struggling with her, then you're trying to physically stop her. You're frustrated and feel out of control because you are. What could you do that is within your control?" Homer sat still while Elizabeth's mind worked.

"I have control or say so in what type of environment I allow. I can control how I respond to her and set an example for others. I can guide and influence her and do what I say I'll do. There are all kinds of things I can do." Elizabeth reminded Homer of his Annie when she smiled.

"You have it! Focus on what you can do instead of what you can't! If you'll begin to think like that, there's nothing you won't be able to accomplish. If you run out of things you can do, ask some of your team members. Your team will surely have some ideas of things they can do. The answer's out there, a lot of times it takes a group or committee to figure it out, but there's an answer."

Lisa D. Piper

Elizabeth laughed. "That's way too simple! You're not going to believe this Homer, but I think you are on to something."

Homer looked up sheepishly as he teased, "Ms. Pennington, I didn't warrant this gray hair for nothing. I've done my share of worrying about absolutely everything and nothing! There's even a gray hair up there for worrying about whether or not anyone would actually take Ray up on his advice to come see me."

Elizabeth shrugged, "Why? Why would you worry about that?"

Homer grinned once more. "Even an old man needs to know he has some value, Elizabeth."

Elizabeth stood to her feet. "Well, don't you worry. I'll be back and you can share all of your trade secrets with me anytime." Elizabeth turned to go after shaking Homer's hand. As she opened the door to exit, Elizabeth peered back into the room and whispered. "Thank you, Homer. I feel better already!"

By the time Elizabeth returned to her office, Jillian was on her lunch break. She was grateful for the extra time she would have to think about what needed to be said to Jillian. She decided to go through the mail her assistant had left on her desk. She had sifted through most of the stack of letters, invoices and junk mail before she received the telephone call that would change her plans for the day. Ray asked Elizabeth to come to his office. The sound of his voice hinted of a problem as he asked for the Peters' file. Elizabeth picked up the file then walked toward the office where her patience and interpersonal skills would be utilized to calm the fretting client. It was difficult for Elizabeth to feel as confident as she would have liked as she forced her body to move one leg in front of the other. She purposely straightened her back, lifted her head, and then marched forward as if she were in perfect physical form.

Rebecca attempted to get up to greet Elizabeth when she walked into her office but thought better of it when her muscles reminded her that they still ached. "Hi, Liz." Rebecca lowered her voice and said, "I'm praying for you. Go show them what you're made of!"

Elizabeth quickly thanked Rebecca for her thoughts and then said wryly, "I'm beginning to think that I better find out what I'm made of before I show it to anyone!"

Discovering Elizabeth

Elizabeth's comment confused Rebecca. Elizabeth was the most confident person she knew. Nothing seemed to be able to get under her skin. Rebecca watched her friend as she tapped on Ray's door before entering.

What Rebecca didn't know was that her friend's hard shell wasn't as rigid as it appeared. Elizabeth prayed for the favor of the Lord daily. She believed that God was the one who had everything under control...even when she didn't feel it.

When Elizabeth entered Ray's office, he stood up to acknowledge her presence. Fred Sabino, however, did not. Fred sat in the small sitting area in Ray's office where informal business was conducted. Adjacent to Fred's chair sat a woman who looked very angry. A man Elizabeth assumed to be the woman's husband sat quietly in the chair next to her. Fred's lips were pursed as he used his facial expressions to make sure that Elizabeth knew he wasn't happy about something. Elizabeth ignored his unspoken rhetoric and offered her hand to the client. "Good afternoon, Mr. and Mrs. Peters."

"Humph!" came the reply. Mr. Peters shook Elizabeth's hand while Mrs. Peters glared at her.

"Elizabeth," Ray began, "Mr. and Mrs. Peters are here because they feel as if they've been overcharged for cleaning services for their hotel chain. We were hoping that you would be able to investigate the matter and give us some kind of explanation for any possible discrepancy in the billing." Ray held Elizabeth's gaze for a moment. His eyes were kind, but Elizabeth didn't mistake his intent. He wanted some type of resolution and was serious about it.

"Okay, it would be my pleasure to look into the matter. I need to know what portion of the billing is being questioned and for what properties." Elizabeth waited for Mrs. Peters to speak.

Elizabeth prayed for perseverance as Mrs. Peters began to complain. "Ms. Pennington, are you saying you do not know what the problem is? I'll tell you what it is. Do you want to know what the real problem is little lady?"

Before anyone could respond, Elizabeth calmly answered, "Yes, I would like to know."

Lisa D. Piper

Mrs. Peters didn't hesitate. "Ms. Pennington, we've been using Wright and Wingold services for more years than I'll admit. But this is the first time for these kinds of shenanigans! We were overcharged on a property that doesn't belong to us on an account we do not have! I know that you may be thinking that this is a little matter and that these things happen all of the time but I don't consider it to be little. Who's responsible for this incompetence, and what's going to be done to alleviate our little problem? We'll not pay this bill and I'll not tolerate any negative publicity due to this. I'll not tolerate it. Do you understand? Do you know who we are?" Mrs. Peters looked directly at Elizabeth with more than a little contempt. Mr. Peters sat in his chair without saying a word. Elizabeth noticed that he looked uncomfortable. He didn't look directly at anyone; including his wife.

The community considered the family to be wealthy with contacts in high places. Elizabeth thought about what Homer had told her. She wasn't dealing with a challenging employee but surely an irate consumer could be no different. She thought quickly as Mrs. Peters continued to express her frustrations. Ray was pleased with Elizabeth's response to the obnoxious woman. He moved to request that Mrs. Peters not speak to Elizabeth in such a manner when he decided to wait. Ray decided to allow Elizabeth time to defuse the situation. He wasn't sure why he thought she would consider his interference a sign that she was incompetent, but he was sure she would interpret any premature input from him negatively.

Elizabeth sat down on the chair adjacent to their client. Her height and directness sometimes intimidated some of the most confident people, and for the situation at hand she didn't want to intimidate the angry woman. Elizabeth looked Mrs. Peters in the eye while she talked in cool, non-threatening tones. She didn't want to sound disturbed or condescending as she leaned in slightly without getting into the woman's personal space, "Mrs. Peters, if I understand what you're saying correctly, your invoice isn't correct according to your records. You believe that you have been overcharged for a service you didn't use. I can see how that would be upsetting. Mr. and Mrs. Peters, I'll follow up on this right away and see what I can do to remedy the situation."

Mrs. Peters wouldn't be deterred from her own frustrations, "You will find that there is an error. I'll have you know that we pay our bills. I don't want talk going around that we came in here to try and get out

Discovering Elizabeth

of a bill we owe. I just want this taken care of and quickly. We don't owe this money and we're not paying it and that's final! If you even think about contacting a collection agency I'll personally see to it that you no longer work in this city." Mrs. Peters clucked her tongue as if she were used to giving orders and having them obeyed.

Before Mrs. Peters could begin her endless chatter about how she felt about the situation, Elizabeth interjected by saying, "I'm responsible for the accounting department. I would be more than happy to look at your invoice and resolve the matter. I apologize for any inconvenience this has caused for you and your husband. No one has plans to turn this into anyone. I'll look into the matter and have the information ready for you no later than Thursday. I'd like to have it sooner but this may take some time."

Mrs. Peters seemed to be pleased with Elizabeth's response but said, "I'll give you until Thursday, but please be assured, I want this resolved. Will you look into this yourself or have your staff to do it? I would prefer that you handle it yourself."

Elizabeth thought of the work that awaited her and sighed inwardly. The problem shouldn't take too long to fix but her busy schedule weighed heavily on her. Had Elizabeth been the client, a simple phone call would have been sufficient for such an inquiry. She wondered why a prominent family would take the time to personally visit them over a billing error. Elizabeth agreed to handle the inquiry personally knowing that her planned weekend had just been re-planned. Elizabeth looked toward the desk and said, "Ray, Fred, is this okay with you?"

Fred frowned, as he demanded, "Make sure you have it done by Thursday."

Ray looked at Fred, and for a moment, Elizabeth thought she saw something shadow Ray's face. Ray turned to Elizabeth and said, "Elizabeth, that's fine. Thank you for taking care of this."

The couple stood to leave. Elizabeth followed. As they were leaving, Elizabeth heard Ray ask Fred to remain in his office.

Behind closed doors stood two men and neither one smiled. Ray had spoken with Fred and coached him about his mannerisms. Fred had used the condescending tone Ray had asked him not to use with their team one too many times. Ray was unhappy that Fred acted so harshly in front of their client. He motioned for Fred to sit down.

Lisa D. Piper

Fred didn't sit. He placed his hands on his hips and said, "What, Ray? What is it now?"

Fred had never spoken to Ray with a tone of insolence. Ray remained calm while his voice was low and deliberate. "Fred, I treat you with respect. I speak to you with respect. The tone you're using right now is not acceptable. I expect to be treated with the same consideration as I have given to you; furthermore, I expect you to treat all of our staff with the same discretion."

Fred threw his hands into the air then walked toward the chair that Ray had originally motioned for him to sit in. He didn't look at his boss as he asked, "Ray, what do you need with me?"

"Fred, I need for you to be successful."

"What? Ray, don't play games with me."

Ray looked at Fred with disbelief then allowed the concern that he had for the senior vice president to overshadow the fact that Fred's mannerisms were beginning to perturb him. "Fred, I've spoken with you about how people perceive what you say. Your role in this firm is an important one but you just embarrassed yourself. Elizabeth was trying to find a resolution to a little problem that's been blown out of proportion. We don't even know whether her department made an error or not. You gave your disapproval of her in front of the client. You bullied her and didn't offer any support whatsoever. Fred, a team is supportive of its members. One member of an effective team doesn't try to take another member down in front of others."

"Ray, it's obvious that someone in her department made a mistake. I was being assertive to let her know that it needed to be fixed. I wanted Mr. and Mrs. Peters to know that the leadership of this firm wouldn't tolerate procrastination." Fred crossed his arms and sat back in his chair as if he had made a statement with which Ray could not argue.

Tired of dealing with the irrational man, Ray demanded, "Fred, we don't know anything. You've jumped to a conclusion. Only a fool answers a matter before he hears it! We don't know why or how the alleged error happened. We can't afford to jump to conclusions. I'm sure that Elizabeth feels that you think she's in error and I'm sure the client thinks the same thing." Fred opened his mouth to speak, but Ray held his hand up. "Fred, I'm not finished. I'll not tolerate a member of the leadership team acting irresponsibly. You are one of the most

Discovering Elizabeth

brilliant men in the business world today. You have the potential to add so much value to the services we provide yet you consistently seek to tear the team down."

Fred interrupted, "So what are you saying? Are you saying that if I don't bow down to the employees and the likes of all of the Homer Fosters, and Elizabeth Penningtons of this world, that I'm going to lose my job? Is that what you're saying? Please, don't tell me that you'd lose sleep over the feelings of a two-bit janitor and an accountant that wouldn't know a number on a calculator from a hole in the ground. Ray, I'm tired of bending over backwards to please you. You didn't like the way I looked at Homer, so I made a point to be nice to him. If you want to talk about all of the little 'wisdom talks' we've had then let's do that. I'm the senior vice president of Wright and Wingold for crying out loud! Does that not account for anything? I despise being given lectures for simply acting like a VIP! Last month your secretary didn't like the way I asked her to dictate memos, today I act...how did you put it, irresponsible? Take your pick, Ray. Choose your right hand man or continue this 'all wise' philosophical rhetoric with someone else. I don't have the time for it!"

Ray could've been angry when Fred belittled Homer, but Homer taught him long ago, that it wasn't Homer who made Fred miserable. It wasn't even Elizabeth or Ray. Fred was miserable of his own choosing and was too blind to see it. A scripture came to Ray's mind. He had underlined Proverbs 16:18 just that very morning. He thought quickly over the words, "Pride goes before destruction, And a haughty spirit before a fall."

Ray stood up and simply said, "Fred, I first came to work for this firm as a janitor when I was sixteen. The very man that you berate and dishonor by your snide remarks taught me most of what I know. As a junior janitor, Homer would teach me a new skill as often as he could. He would do this in the morning and then give me the rest of the day to develop the new skill. Homer would spend the last few minutes of each day watching me perform the task he had shown me earlier that day. During the entire process, he took down notes. He would give me a pat on the back at the end of the day and tell me how well I had done. When I would arrive for work the next day, he would sit down with me and I would review his notes. Homer would write everything I could do to improve my new skill from what he had seen me doing the evening before. He would do this until I had the skill perfected. After I took the job that I have now, Homer said that he knew I would be successful. He told me something I have never forgotten. He said that when a person takes instruction from another person he can achieve anything. Had I rejected his wisdom and become belligerent because it was embarrassing or because I thought I knew it already, I wouldn't be the CEO of this company. Fred, until you get to the place that you can take instruction and correction and apply it to your occupation, then I have to say that I'll have to hire someone who can."

Fred's bluff had been called. He lunged for his briefcase then stiffly walked toward the door. As he exited he turned around and said in a loud voice, "Ray, you might believe all of that garbage that you are trying to sell me. Well, I don't want any part of it. You can take your principles, and your self-improvement plan and shove it down someone else's throat." Fred walked out of the door for the last time.

Ray rubbed his head then sat down in front of his desk. As he paused to collect his thoughts, his eyes found his daily devotional book. The little book was opened to a page that read, "Proverbs 9:8,9~Do not correct a scoffer, lest he hate you; Rebuke a wise man, and he will love you. Give instruction to a wise man, and he will be still wiser; Teach a just man and he will increase in learning." Ray looked toward the ceiling and said, "Well said, Solomon."

While Ray sat in his office thinking about what he could have done to prevent the events that had just occurred, he had to admit that he should have taken care of the problems with Fred long before it had ever got to this point.

He thought about Elizabeth's situation and how he had advised her of things he wasn't even doing himself. He had seen the inquisitive looks Homer had given him when Fred began to behave less than professional in front of others. His friend hadn't judged him but Ray knew that Homer was a little disappointed that he had allowed the situation go on and on.

Ray wondered if he wasn't just getting burned out from all of the years of customer and personnel problems. In his earlier years of leadership, he would've let Fred go in half the time it had taken to make Fred angry enough to just quit on his own. Ray ran his hand through his hair in frustration as he wondered what he had to have been thinking to allow Fred to so freely destroy what he had worked so hard to build.

Discovering Elizabeth

Ray made a decision that anything worth doing was worth doing the right way. He wouldn't help to tear down his company by enabling another morale wrecker like Fred.

Little did he know that in another area of the building, another fire was raging and his head accountant was the kindling. Like Ray, Elizabeth was about to learn lessons in leadership that weren't taught in any university. Jillian Hunter would prove to be more cunning and deceptive than Fred.

Lisa D. Piper

Chapter FIVE

"A fool's mouth is his destruction, and his lips are the snare of his soul.."
Proverbs 18:7

The animated voice was unmistakable as Elizabeth heard it proclaim, "What could she say? She knew I spoke the truth. You know me Sophie, I just call it like I see it."

Elizabeth's first instinct was to turn around and act like she never heard the petty conversation between the two women who were supposed to be working. Her second thought was to address the situation before another word was said and that's what she did.

"Hello, Sophie. Good Afternoon, Jillian." As Elizabeth greeted the two women, it was as if time stood still. Sophie and Jillian slowly turned in visible horror. It didn't take long for Jillian to regain her composure as a smile crept onto her face.

"Hello Elizabeth. What brings you down here?" Jillian didn't want to act as if she'd been caught just in case Elizabeth hadn't heard what had been said. Elizabeth's eyes still appeared to have the same gentle quality as usual but Jillian noticed that the color of the woman's eyes had deepened into a dark stormy blue.

"I came down to get some files. Are you on break?" Elizabeth asked.

"Uh, well, actually, I too came down to get a file and decided to stop for a moment to speak with Sophie." As Jillian spoke, Sophie was visibly shaken and confused. Sophie knew that Elizabeth had heard every detail of their conversation. She had seen someone approach but had assumed it was one of the other girls. From what Jillian had said of

Elizabeth, Sophie expected her to become angry and scream obscenities at her assistant, but she didn't.

"Jillian, I need to speak with you." As she followed Elizabeth to a more private area, Elizabeth turned and said, "Sophie, I'd like to speak with you in just a minute."

Sophie nodded then swallowed with difficulty. Her heart began to pound. She wasn't good at making pretenses. She loved to gossip, but once cornered, she would buckle under the pressure of her guilty conscience. Jillian knew it and tried to quickly figure out a way to get to Sophie before Elizabeth had a chance to speak with her.

Elizabeth's tone was low but direct. " Would you please explain what I just heard? Are you repeating things that aren't so?"

Jillian's facial features were bland. Elizabeth couldn't tell whether Jillian was being affected by the question or if she had any emotion at all. Jillian didn't respond until Elizabeth repeated the question. Her blank expression didn't falter as she simply said, "I don't know what you're talking about."

Elizabeth couldn't believe Jillian was going to pretend as if she hadn't done anything wrong. "Jillian, I've told you often enough that I appreciate all that you do. You are capable, quick, and have added value to our department; however, I cannot work with someone who can't be trusted. I'm uncertain as to why you would've fabricated our conversations, but I'll tell you I'm going to have to talk to Fred about this to decide what needs to be done."

Jillian crossed her arms as she demanded, "Fred, why Fred? You're just trying to make me look like the bad one in this. I won't stand around and let you talk to the senior vice president about me while everyone else is doing worse than I am. I try to do my job and this is how you repay me! You say that I'm appreciated but I have yet to see the evidence of that."

Elizabeth tried her best to remain calm as she replied, "Jillian, Fred is my direct supervisor. It's my responsibility to report any occurrences of this type to him, especially when it affects more than one department. Jillian, I'm not telling him because what you said was derogatory about me. I'm telling him this because your actions are not acceptable and the fact that you are refusing to be accountable for what you've done really concerns me. I'll need to see you sometime Monday

Discovering Elizabeth

after I speak with Fred." Elizabeth hoped that by the time Monday arrived, she could make some sense out of the situation and perhaps Jillian would have had time to think about her actions.

Jillian nodded with defiance as she turned to leave. Jillian decided that her number one priority would be to get to Fred before Elizabeth could tell her story. The deceptive woman was to be disappointed when she went to Fred's office to find that he had already left the building.

Elizabeth walked back to where a nervous Sophie fidgeted with her paperwork. "Sophie, could I have a word with you, please?"

Sophie nodded, "Yes, Ma'am. H-How can I help you?" Sophie closed her eyes tightly as she anticipated a quick termination. To her surprise, Elizabeth's questions were asked with kindness; and the eyes Sophie looked into were deeper than the ocean. Sophie knew that she couldn't lie to this woman.

"Sophie, when I walked up to your desk earlier, were you and Jillian speaking about a conversation she and I had supposedly had earlier?"

Sophie bit on her thin upper lip. She thought she could deny the charge, but how could she? Jillian may have already confessed to what had been said so what choice did she have? With this last thought, Sophie admitted, "Ms. Pennington, I apologize. Yes, the conversation was about you and Jillian. Please forgive me." Sophie resisted the urge, to repeat her apology over and over again.

"Why?"

Sophie shifted in her swivel chair and stammered, "I d-don't know w-what you mean...Why?"

Elizabeth repeated her question, "Why were you talking about me?"

"Well, let's see." Sophie thought for a moment then said, "Uh, I don't know why. When Jillian came down to my desk, she looked upset. I asked her what was wrong and she said she, uh, well, she said that she had had enough of, umm...you." Sophie quickly begged, "Oh Elizabeth, please don't get me fired! Please don't fire Jillian. She was just upset at what you had told her and she didn't mean to say those things to you. She just doesn't know how to take someone who is demanding, that's all." Sophie rambled on, "Elizabeth, I don't mean that you aren't a good boss. Jillian just hasn't had to work with anyone without supervisory experience like you before."

Lisa D. Piper

Elizabeth couldn't understand why Jillian would deliberately lie, or how Sophie could believe Jillian's accusations. She pointedly spoke in soft tones, "Sophie, have I ever been manipulative, mean or unfair to you?"

Sophie's smug look turned to one of confusion as she thought. Finally she said, "No, I don't think so."

"Sophie, that's because I don't make it a practice of being those things. I'm not sure what you've heard or perceived you've heard, but I'm not a big bad wolf. I will tell you that I expect professionalism out of those with whom I work. I also expect to be treated with the same respect everyone else wants. If I ever treat you unfairly, I want you to come tell me. If someone is gossiping about any person in our team, then you need to be able to either walk away or let the person know that you are not interested in participating in gossip. The quickest way to stop this madness in these offices is for everyone to stop listening."

Sophie became ashamed of her own actions as Elizabeth spoke with passion. Sophie couldn't be sure but she thought she detected some pain in those dark oceanic eyes. Sophie wasn't sure why she did it or what had provoked her to do it, but she looked straight into Elizabeth's eyes and made a promise she hoped she could keep. "Ms. Pennington, what you're asking me to do will be difficult; however, I give you my word that I'll try to do what you have asked. I'm so sorry if I have assumed something about you. I just never thought about it as participating in gossip."

Elizabeth smiled and hoped that Sophie was telling the truth. Before she could get her hopes too high, Sophie asked, "Ms. Pennington, don't come down too hard on Jillian. She means well, she's just...well she's just jealous, that's all. She doesn't mean to hurt others with her tales. Most of the time her stories are funny!"

Elizabeth wanted to ask Sophie why she would even listen to Jillian if she knew that what she said was not the complete truth. She decided to leave a word picture with Sophie so that she would understand the importance of doing what Elizabeth asked. "I want to leave you with a thought before I go back to my office." After pausing for to make sure Sophie was listening, she continued, "If you saw a little boy throwing rocks at a little girl while his friends stood around laughing as he whirled the stones at her, would you say that all of the boys were tormenting the girl, or just one?"

Discovering Elizabeth

As Elizabeth walked away, a tear slid down Sophie's face. She knew all too well how it felt to have boys and girls shout out names in mockery in a small town school. Sophie's genuine remorse over what had been done to Elizabeth engulfed her. A desire to keep her word was stronger than her desire to continue in vain gossip. Nothing Jillian had said could have prepared Sophie for the emotion she would feel after one conversation with "the boss."

By the time Elizabeth returned to her own office, Jillian was gone. She was almost relieved. Work was all she could see and it was work that needed her attention now. She groaned and turned to the folder she had just laid on her desk.

Elizabeth was determined to solve the mystery of the Peters' account before Monday. As she mentally planned all she would have to do, her stomach reminded her that she hadn't eaten lunch. Elizabeth sat down in her leather chair and placed her head in her hands. She rubbed her temples and prayed, "Oh, God. I need you. Thank you for giving me such joy with my friends last night and thank you for my sore back to remind me how much fun I had and how awesome you are. Lord, I feel just like how I imagined the ocean to feel last night as it rumbled up onto the shore, only to drift back out again. I'm not complaining. You gave me this job and I believe you'll give me the wisdom to do it. Just please; help me to keep my eyes on you and off my circumstances. And Lord, help me learn how to deal with Jillian and Sophie. I know that you love them. I'm trying hard to remember that even though I'm having very strong anti-love feelings about them. Help me to love them no matter what they do, in Jesus' name I pray, Thank you."

Elizabeth decided that before she could dive into the work that would probably keep her busy through the weekend, she would need to get something to eat. She picked up the telephone and dialed her home number. It rang three times before Gabby answered. "Gabby, do you want to go get a bite to eat? I'm going to have to work late. Also, I'll need to cancel our plans for tomorrow. I've got something really important to complete. I've had a really difficult day and could use some friendly conversation right now."

Gabrielle was disappointed about the change in their weekend plans but said, "Sure, I can be there in about 30 minutes. I will forewarn you though; I've not been in a friendly mood today. I found muscles where no muscles have been before! Count me out for any more trips to the beach any time soon. Do you want to meet at Louie's Pizza?"

Elizabeth agreed, "That sounds good. I would settle for anything edible. I'm hungry."

Gabrielle was sitting in a booth next to the window when Elizabeth arrived. As she slid into the seat, Gabby tapped her watch. Elizabeth protested, "I know, I know, I just thought that since it would take you longer to get here than it would take me, I'd have some time to check my email. I got caught up in it and lost track of the time. I'm sorry."

Gabrielle mocked indignation and said, "Well, Ms. Pennington, the next time you interrupt my busy evening to ask me to come sit by myself, I may not be inclined to come."

Elizabeth threw up her hands and lowered her voice until only her friend could hear, "Busy evening? I'm only 10 minutes late."

Gabrielle grinned, "Of course I had a busy evening planned." Tapping her long burgundy nails on the table, she raised one eyebrow then said, "Do you think these babies get long and shapely by themselves?" Gabrielle raised her hand to reveal a slim, perfectly manicured hand.

"No date, huh?"

"No." Gabby pushed a strand of her auburn hair behind her ear. "I don't want to hear any teasing from you, Ms. Pennington. I don't see you breaking a date to work tonight, do I?"

Elizabeth stiffened with mock hurt then said, "As if I would want one. It's been so long since I had a real date that if someone asked me, I would probably be so shocked that he would soon retract his offer."

Gabby grinned at her lovely friend then picked up her leather handbag to sift through the contents as if she were looking for something. Finally, she produced a colored pamphlet that read, "Christian Singles Convention and Retreat." Gabby placed the brochure in front of her friend and said, "Liz, I know that you may not even want to consider this..."

"You are exactly right! I'm not that desperate!"

"Liz, this has nothing to do with being desperate! This is a Christian Fellowship meeting that will take place in Pensacola, Florida! Let me

Discovering Elizabeth

show you why we need to go." Gabrielle unfolded the paper and pointed to the information and read, "The evenings will be spent in glorious corporate praise and worship. Guest speakers will present each evening's message. Several classes targeted toward the single person will be available during the day. Some classes available will be: 'Finding Your Mate...the Way God Intended'...'God's Plan for Your Family'...'Becoming Totally Committed to a Life of Serving God'...'Stress! Don't Sweat It' and Liz there are a lot more classes that I think we could use. This'll be one full week of getting our lives prioritized and learning more about what God wants for us. This isn't so that we can go find a mate. It's about learning how to find the right one and also about living a successful Christian life as a single woman."

Elizabeth was silent. She looked at the picture on the back of the brochure. A wave crashing onto the white sandy beach reminded Elizabeth of her prayer. Gabrielle said wistfully, "Oh, Liz, Don't you sometimes feel like you have just washed up onto the shore and you've been so tossed in the tides that you just can't seem to get a grip about what you even want anymore?"

"Yes, I do feel like that."

"That's why I'm asking you to go to this. Come on, let's make plans to go?"

Elizabeth surprised Gabrielle as she said, "Okay, let's go." Gabrielle had thought that she would need to beg and plead and present the ten reasons why they should go to this outing for Elizabeth to agree to the trip.

"You'll go?" Gabby asked with her mouth gaping open.

"Gabby, I've been praying for God to just do something in my life. This isn't what I would have chosen, and perhaps that's why He decided to do it. If I don't take this opportunity, I fear I might be missing the answer to my prayers."

"Great!" exclaimed a jubilant Gabrielle. "I'll send in our reservations and fees. I'll also get hotel accommodation information and make those plans as well, if you don't mind."

"Help yourself. I can see that your mind is already busy with plans and preparations. I bet that you'll already have a list of what we need

Lisa D. Piper

to take with us by the time I get home this afternoon!" Elizabeth poked at her friend's arm as she teased her. "By the way, when is this supposed to happen?"

"In one month." Before Elizabeth could respond, Gabby held up her hand and said, "No, you don't! I know that you can get off for this. It has been months and months since you have had any time off. You have made a commitment and you cannot break it. Take off for a week, or I'll be forced to go to the CEO of your company myself and declare unfair treatment of one Elizabeth Pennington."

Elizabeth lowered her eyes. Gabrielle's astute perception of why her friend had just reacted oddly at the mention of the CEO made her curious. "Elizabeth Pennington, do you have something to tell me about the handsome Ray Morgan?"

Elizabeth fidgeted and said, "Uh, no I don't. It's just that, well, he makes me nervous." When Elizabeth saw that Gabrielle was again strumming her nails on the table, she knew that Gabby wouldn't let the subject lie dormant until Elizabeth had given some type of explanation. "Okay, okay, he just confuses me, that's all. I've heard terrible things about him and every time I see him, he's doing something thoughtful or speaking about Scripture without really alluding to that fact that he's doing it. I guess I don't know him and I don't know anything about him that is truly horrible. From what I have seen he is pleasant, but Jillian says otherwise."

Gabrielle raised an eyebrow and asked, "What does that woman have to say about the fearless leader?"

"What do you mean by 'that woman'?" Elizabeth was at the verge of defending Jillian when she realized that this wouldn't be a wise thing to do with her friend.

"Liz, I know you may not want to hear this, but I'm telling you that there's something very wrong with your assistant. When she looks at me my stomach just crawls, if a crawling stomach were possible that is."

"You don't even know her. There may be some truth to what you're thinking though. I've had two run-ins with her today. During our first interlude I snapped at her and during the second one, well, during the second one I don't know what I was. I'm so tired of dealing with her. She is fun to be around most of the time and so competent at what she

Discovering Elizabeth

does. I really am becoming confused about it all." Elizabeth twisted a stray curl near her shoulder while she waited for her friend to respond.

"I'm not sure how I can help, but I'd like to try. I've had my share of working with difficult peers and employees, maybe I could offer some advice?" Gabrielle's warm pat on the arm made Elizabeth want to cry. Instead she blurted out the happenings of the day to her friend.

"Wow! You have had a day! You don't need a week off, you need a couple of them." Liz smiled at Gabby's attempt to show that she was trying to understand the situation. Gabrielle then said, "Liz, why is it that you became upset at Jillian this morning? According to what you have told me, she has gossiped about the chief lots of times before, but when she began to do it this morning, you became upset."

Elizabeth pondered the question and then said, "Well, I'm not sure why. Remember what I said a while ago? I said that I thought Ray was really awful, and I had based all of my opinion of him on what I had heard from Jillian. I guess that as I began to realize that he isn't really a big ogre waiting to squash the little employee bugs with his heel, I became angry with myself for believing the garbage I've been told. That's why I'm so frustrated with that woman!"

Gabrielle selected her words wisely. "Elizabeth, you may not want to hear this, but I have to be honest with you for your own good. I'm about to pour some salt into your wounds. Do you want to hear it or should I keep my opinion to myself?"

Elizabeth put her head in her hands and shook it back and forth. "Okay. I hate this, Gabby, but go ahead, I probably need it."

"Good! First I'm going to quote Proverbs 12:1, "Whoso loveth instruction loveth knowledge: but he that hateth reproof is brutish." You're a good woman for listening to this and I think you'll be the better for it. Here we go! My friend, the truth of the matter is this: You trained Jillian to gossip."

"What?" Elizabeth flung her hands into the air.

"Now, wait a minute! Listen to me before you decide to argue the point!" Gabrielle smiled at her friend and softened her voice as if the gesture would help to soften the blow. "I mean that whatever you allow to go on becomes the norm for the office. If you listen to gossip, you're teaching your staff that it's okay to carry tales. If you make it known that you'll not listen to gossip, the expectation is clear, and everyone will know that it isn't okay to talk about others. When you do this, the gossip will cease. You can't feed into this sin and expect everything to flow as if God is blessing it, because I tell you that He isn't.

Gabrielle trudged onward, "King David spoke about those who set traps for others. David had the wisdom to know that those who set traps for others eventually fall into their own netting. Elizabeth, there's nothing ahead for Jillian but calamity, and for you to have known that she was carrying tales about others and not have done anything about it until now is a disappointment. That girl has no idea that what she's doing will eventually entrap her, or at least I would think she would have no idea. As her supervisor, it's your responsibility to teach her what is and what isn't acceptable. I know that you probably didn't realize the severity of allowing this to go on, but you've got to do something about it. It isn't right for you to suddenly change your expectations on her when she was only doing what had been okay to do since you two have worked together. Now, that doesn't mean that you need to continue to allow her to spread gossip, but at least tell her about what you expect first." Gabrielle patted her friend's hand. "Oh, Liz, I know you're going through a tough situation. I don't envy you, but the good thing is that you'll grow from this and become an even better supervisor because of it."

Elizabeth was silently considering her friend's words when she asked, "How do you know so much about this? What made you remember all of those Scriptures?"

"I've walked through this fire already. I was scorched, but I lived through it. You will too, my friend."

"Gabby, what do I do now? What happens if I make the expectations clear and she continues to undermine me and gossip about others?"

"Oh, that's easy. Proverbs 22:10."

"What is Proverbs 22:10?"

Gabrielle took a sip of her cola and said, "Cast out the scorner, and contention shall go out; yeah, strife and reproach shall cease."

The rest of the meal was spent in deep thought. Elizabeth enjoyed the company of her friend even though they didn't continue to talk.

Discovering Elizabeth

Gabrielle was content to sit in silent support of her friend while she sorted through her own emotions.

Elizabeth was determined to have all of the answers for her client's problems before the next business day. As she sat among a mound of papers she didn't hear the corridor door open and then close. She had lost track of the time as she sifted through each file. The plot of the faulty invoice began to develop. Elizabeth felt as if she was some sort of a sleuth and actually enjoyed the investigative skills she was acquiring as she uncovered the needed information.

Ray Morgan stood at the door for a few moments before he spoke. He watched as Elizabeth's eyes combed the pages of whatever she was reading. He smiled as he noticed that she apparently wasn't expecting anyone else to come into the office on a late Friday night. She had paper everywhere. At some point, she had removed her make-up, replaced her contacts with glasses, and swapped her starchy business suit for a pair of hot pink overalls. Ray shuffled his foot as he thought on how to approach her. He wasn't used to speaking to Elizabeth during "off" hours, and didn't know how to begin a conversation. As he was deciding if he should give her a formal greeting or walk up and sit on the side of the desk and say hello, Elizabeth seemed to sense that someone was watching her.

Her first clue that someone was in the office came from her peripheral vision. Her heart began to pound and her mind began racing through all of the scenarios that could happen and what she should do. Ray made a mistake by choosing that moment to take a step toward Elizabeth's desk.

"Huuuuuuu Yahhhhhh!!!" Elizabeth steadied herself into what she hoped would be interpreted as a defensive stance. As she lifted her hands to give the intruder a quick chop, Ray ducked only to be struck in the side of the neck by one tall accountant. Before Elizabeth saw whom she had struck, she began her sprint out of the office. As she scrambled to the doorway, she trembled as she realized she had just assaulted the boss. She looked around hastily and wished she could crawl into the nearest hole and take up residence.

Elizabeth turned toward him and winced as Ray held his neck in pain. He halfway grinned and said, "I'm not sure who you are and what you've done with our Ms. Pennington, but you can put her back right now. She may have caused me pain before, but not with such violent intentions." As Ray began to laugh, Elizabeth glared at him.

She forgot the compassion she had been about to show him as he teased her. "What do you mean coming in here at this time of night? How was I to know that you weren't an intruder? I could've been killed!"

"Elizabeth, I had no idea that you were still here. The coffee pot in my office broke down and someone told me the other day that there was an extra one in here. That's all I was doing. I promise that I had no intention of scaring you." A gleam appeared in Ray's eye as he held out his hand in a friendly gesture and asked, "Could I once more be forgiven for not making my presence known in a better manner? I'm sorry."

Ray couldn't suppress the smile that he had tried to hide. Elizabeth noted that when he smiled he looked years younger. He had a most handsome grin. She returned his gesture and smiled while waving toward the break room. "Have at the coffee pot."

Ray found the pot then started to walk out of the door. Glancing back, he noticed that Elizabeth looked fatigued. "Ms. Pennington, if you get a bit sleepy before you decide to hang up the towel tonight, venture up to my office and I'll share a cup of hot java with you." Ray gave Elizabeth a boyish grin and added, "I promise not to run into you if you promise not to clobber me."

Elizabeth was so mesmerized by the unexpected playful side of her boss that she didn't become embarrassed at his reference to their turbulent and sometimes painful-yet brief encounters. He stood and just smiled at her before she responded. She realized that she was supposed to be answering him but had been too engrossed in trying to figure him out to have heard the question. She murmured, "Okay."

"Great! I'll have it ready in a few minutes. Come on up when you get ready."

"What?" Before he could hear her question he left with the coffee pot in hand. After a few minutes Elizabeth figured out that he had been asking her to join him for a cup of coffee. She sighed. She didn't need this distraction. She sat down to look back over the invoice in question and yawned. She looked down at her watch and noticed it was midnight. Her eyelids felt heavy, but she willed herself to remain

Discovering Elizabeth

focused. After several attempts at fighting fatigue, she decided to wash her face then go get a cup of coffee.

The cool water caused her to take in a deep breath. As she looked in the mirror she asked herself, "What am I thinking?" Elizabeth answered, "I guess I'm thinking that I need some caffeine, and since I have no coffee I'll go mooch some off of the boss." She was engrossed in her thoughts when she realized that Ray hadn't told her why he was at work so late. He seemed to be full of surprises. According to Jillian, he spent every Friday evening boozing it up and flirting with new conquests. Elizabeth became angry with herself as she realized how much gossip and poison she had swallowed from Jillian. When Jillian had told her about Ray's wayward lifestyle, Elizabeth remembered thinking that it might not be the truth. So if she didn't believe it, why did she continue to remember parts of the conversation? Elizabeth took one last look at herself in the mirror. She pointed at herself and said, "Girl, you will not beat yourself up over this. You've learned from it. You've got to clean up the mess you created, so get over it!"

"Helloooo?" Elizabeth peered around the corner and found the guilty culprit. Someone had left crumbs on Rebecca's desk and she was sure that it had not been Rebecca. "There you are Mr. Sweet Tooth! May I ask what you're doing?"

Ray looked up and grinned more mischievously than any ten-year-old could have done. "You may ask, but I do not know that you will understand it. Homer taught me how to dunk a doughnut properly."

"I'm not sure I want to understand it." Elizabeth walked over to the coffee pot and poured a cup of the steamy black brew. She didn't know if it was because they were both out of business attire, but she felt like she could just be herself. Exhaustion may have kept her from reverting to any formality. She sat down on a cushioned chair and crossed her legs while hugging the hot cup of coffee.

As Ray perfected the art of dunking his doughnuts, he motioned to the container of pastries on his desk. "Do you have a sweet tooth tonight? I know I don't need to be eating this stuff, but I thought I'd indulge."

Elizabeth smiled. "Did you happen to eat one of these at Rebecca's desk?" Elizabeth grabbed a chocolate covered Bavarian cream puff. As she bit into the sweet, she closed her eyes and tilted her head back. "This is marvelous. Where did you get it?"

"My Annie made it. And yes, I did eat one at Rebecca's desk. I came in to work on her computer and had to have a snack. I take it that I left the evidence? I'll need to clean that up before she sees it."

"Annie? I didn't know that you're married."

"Married?" Ray coughed and quickly took a drink of coffee. He cleared his throat and said, "No, I'm not married. Please, don't think that! You know…Homer's Annie. She's my Annie when she cooks and she worries over me like a mother hen. She made them because she said that I need some meat on my bones." Ray laughed, "I'd say she's trying to fatten me up!"

"Oh." Elizabeth slowly took anther bite and declared, "I would like for her to be my Annie. This is the best." Both of them sat in silence while they ate and drank. Elizabeth finally said, "You sounded like you have some kind of phobia of marriage the way you answered my question about Annie being your wife. It may be forward of me to ask, but have you been married?"

Ray stopped chewing and looked at her. "Well, yes I guess that is straight forward so I'll give you a straight forward emphatic, Nope."

At first, Elizabeth just grinned, but before long, she was stifling the loudest clap of laughter that the office walls had heard in a while. When Ray cocked his head to one side to put her on "eye surveillance," she lost all reserved composure. Maybe it was the lack of sleep, perhaps it was the caffeine, but whatever it was she suddenly felt overjoyed.

Ray couldn't believe what he was seeing. Within the last 48 hours, he had seen the woman's hair full of sand and had seen her playing like a child. He had just gotten used to the fact that she was not the starchy businesswoman he had first thought, when she showed up for work acting like the first lady of accounting. He knew that she had to be as sore as Rebecca, but she just sat there in the meeting with her back erect and her emotions intact. There was a moment when Ray had thought about asking her to go retrieve a file to see how she was moving. He had resisted the urge to satisfy his curiosity. And now, here she was, sitting in the loudest pink outfit he had ever seen, holding her sides and laughing like he was the greatest comic ever. Ray began

Discovering Elizabeth

to laugh with Elizabeth. The laughter broke the ice and Elizabeth Pennington and Ray Morgan found that they enjoyed each other's company.

Ray told Elizabeth about the time that he had made his first pot of coffee for his father. Between bellows of laughter Ray said, "I gave life to that liquid that day. It was so stout that it picked my dad's cup up and hurled it into the living room."

"You think that's bad?" Elizabeth wiped her eyes and said, "Do you know what kind of coffee I made for my father when he had his boss over for a football game one night? I was ten years old and didn't know anything about making coffee, but I had made chocolate milk with a mix. To impress Dad, I decided to take him some fresh coffee. He smiled with pride when I brought the coffee. My dad began hollering at me after he took one drink. I didn't know that I had to let the water drain through the crushed beans. But let me tell you one thing I learned that night; it's not a good idea to boil water and then stir coffee grounds into the cup. My dad was so embarrassed. I was happy when I found out his boss hadn't taken a drink. He had looked up after my dad had taken a drink and pointed out that Dad had a 'grounds' mustache. I can tell you that I had trouble living that down."

By the time Elizabeth and Ray finished talking, sipping, and eating, the clock had displayed 3:00AM. Elizabeth gasped as she saw the time. "Oh No! I didn't call Gabby and I bet she is worried. She would have tried to call my office to check on me, I'm sure. May I use your phone?"

"Sure, help yourself." Ray stretched his legs out on the couch where he had been sitting for the last hour.

Elizabeth went to the phone and dialed home. "Gabby?" Elizabeth held the phone out from her ear then said, "Okay, okay, I know I should have called. I have been busy. Work? Of course I'm at work. Listen, I'll be home shortly, I just didn't want you to worry."

By the time Elizabeth had finished her conversation, Ray Morgan looked to be sound asleep on the couch. Elizabeth placed her paper cup in the garbage can then turned to leave. For some reason, she was drawn to the couch where Ray was sleeping. She would be embarrassed if he caught her but she just had to get a really good look at him while he wasn't peering at her with those penetrating eyes. As she studied his face she couldn't help but fight the desire to push a piece of a stray hair back into place. After several minutes of examining the details of his features, she decided that she needed to leave. Right before she turned to go, a pair of drowsy hazel eyes met hers.

Ray thought he was dreaming. He smiled a lazy smile then reached up to touch a piece of stray hair. Just before he found that he couldn't reach her, he let his hand drop and mumbled, "Hi, pretty lady," then turned over to continue his slumber.

Elizabeth's mouth dropped open. She turned and left the office. Elizabeth mused over the sleep talker and smiled to herself. Gabrielle always accused Elizabeth of talking, mumbling and gabbing in her sleep. Perhaps, Ray was a disoriented sleeper too. Elizabeth didn't know that Ray hadn't been able to rest in days. He had decided to go into work as a means of keeping his sanity. The stress of dealing with his former VP and then with his resignation had taken its toll. All of the laughter and good-natured fun had relaxed Ray Morgan in spite of the affects of the caffeine laced with doughnut crumbs.

Elizabeth decided to go home and return to work as early as possible the next day. She found that she didn't go to sleep as readily as the man who was sprawled across a brown leather sofa on the penthouse floor of the Wright and Wingold building.

Chapter SIX

"There is a friend who is closer than a brother."
Proverbs 18:24

"Make it go away!" Gabrielle gently shook her friend as Elizabeth declared once again that she didn't want whatever someone or something was giving her. "I told you that I don't want it! Make it go away!"

"Elizabeth!" Gabrielle finally managed to startle her friend enough to get her awake. "Come on, Liz, roll over and shut your mouth. I'm trying to sleep here, and all you have done since you have gotten home is argue and reject someone giving you something. I'm trying to be patient, but I have my limitations too you know."

Gabrielle knew that she might as well have been talking to the wall. Elizabeth looked at her, she even made eye contact, but Gabrielle knew that the woman had no idea what she was saying. Gabrielle often poked fun at what she called Elizabeth's "night time comprehension problem." It didn't take long for Gabrielle to give up on quieting her roommate. She decided to shut all of the doors between the two bedrooms and then place her own head under a plump pillow.

8 a.m. came too quickly for Gabrielle. When she awoke, Elizabeth was in the process of gulping down a bagel and orange juice. "Good morning, Roomie!"

Gabrielle shuffled to the table and sat down. She didn't want to hear the cheery woman so early in the morning. Gabrielle stared straight ahead trying to wake as she said, "Elizabeth, I'm going to hurt you if you don't just shut-up!"

Elizabeth turned toward her friend and tried to look sorry. "Did I talk again?"

"Yes."

"All night?"

"All morning, actually."

Elizabeth stammered, "Did I say something about last night? What did I say?"

"Last night? What happened last night?"

"Uh, nothing, nothing happened. I just wondered. You know I didn't come in until late. I was at work longer than I expected, which reminds me that I need to go get ready. I believe I've found a possible explanation for a client's complaint." Before Gabriel could ask any more questions, Elizabeth leaped out of her chair, made a comment about getting a quick shower, and was gone, leaving a bewildered Gabrielle staring after her.

After eating a bagel smothered in blueberry cream cheese, Gabrielle walked into Elizabeth's room. She thought, "Okay, little miss, what kind of secret are you harboring?" Gabrielle looked over at her friend's nightstand and wondered aloud, "When did she get rid of the picture?" Gabrielle was now concerned and curious. She had never known Elizabeth to remove the old picture frame. Gabrielle had once leaned over to dust it and Elizabeth had nearly gotten angry with her for it. Gabrielle had prayed that Elizabeth would one day let go of the embarrassing memory and was glad to see that the picture was gone.

The door opened and Elizabeth stepped from the room with a large burgundy towel wrapped around her damp head. "Gabby! What are you doing?"

Gabrielle shrugged her shoulders. "I'm standing here looking at a big mess. I was going to make your bed for you but I don't think I could untwist the covers in the amount of time I have before I'm supposed to meet Rebecca for some shopping."

Elizabeth sat down to comb her hair. "Gab, do you want to meet me for lunch today? We could go to Simon's Place. It will be my treat."

"Sure, what time?" Gabrielle sat down on the edge of the bed.

Discovering Elizabeth

"How about noon? It'll be busy then, but I think I'll have enough done to break away."

"Sounds fine. But, be forewarned, I'm in a steak kind of mood. You won't get off as cheap as you did taking me to Happy Land on my birthday!"

Elizabeth lightly punched her friend in the arm, and said, "Disrespect is all I get! I made sure that they put your present in your meal!" Elizabeth laughed and walked into the bathroom.

Gabrielle crossed her arms and yelled, "Yeah, and I didn't even get what I wanted. I told them I already had the girl toy. I wanted the boy one. Just because I'm a girl doesn't mean I don't like cars instead of those sissy baby dolls!"

"Quit sulking. I got her to exchange it. Now don't forget me, I don't want to dine by myself. I don't want to look like I'm dateless or anything." Elizabeth pulled her hair up into a wet ponytail, changed into a pair of casual shorts and a sleeveless shirt, slipped on her newest tennis shoes and headed for the door.

Elizabeth had just finished reviewing what she considered to be the last piece of the puzzle. It was 11:30AM and time had passed quickly. She didn't want to tell anyone but Ray about what she had found while reviewing the Peters' account. As she picked up her purse, she decided she'd enjoy part of her weekend. She made the decision to forget about her dilemma and just go have fun with her best buddy. Time for exchanging information with the client would come too soon, she reasoned. Why spend her private time dreading the inevitable? Elizabeth threw her purse strap over her shoulder and shut off her computer.

Gabrielle raised her hand, "Liz! Hey, Liz, we're over here!"

As Elizabeth's eyes focused in the new light, she saw her friend waving. As she approached the table, she was delighted to find Rebecca sitting at the table too. Rebecca got up and gave Elizabeth a quick hug. "How are you doing? Gabby says that you've been at work most of the day and most of last night. Do you need help with something?"

Lisa D. Piper

"Yes. I need help forgetting it. Let's not talk about work, okay?" Elizabeth smiled. The girls readily agreed that work would be a taboo subject during lunch.

After ordering from the unique menu, the three women began to talk about the current happenings in their lives.

Rebecca placed her napkin in her lap and said, "Guess what, ladies!"

"What?" came the reply in unison.

"I have a surprise for you both. We have to play a game in order for you to find out what it is!" Rebecca's eyes danced mischievously, as she seemed to glow with delight.

"Oh no, not a game. You know that we don't do well with games. We are too competitive, please don't make us do this!" Elizabeth pleaded.

"Come on, it's not that kind of a game." The two women couldn't resist the mounting curiosity of what could have possibly caused Rebecca so much excitement.

Rebecca continued, "Okay. I want to play a guessing game. I have something that I've never had before. It's new, and if you look closely you will be able to see that there is a change in my appearance."

Rebecca loved the attention she was getting while Gabby and Liz gave her a thorough eye sweep. "Come on, girls, you can guess!"

The waitress brought out the beverages. Rebecca reached for her glass as both Elizabeth and Gabrielle's eyes became fixed on her hand. Their eyes widened as they took in the significance of the beautiful diamond on the left hand of their childhood playmate.

Elizabeth and Gabrielle gasped. "So, what do you think?" Rebecca held up her hand high for them to take a closer look.

In the corner of the room, two men sat in silence. Both men were absorbed in thought as they watched two jubilant women congratulating their luncheon partner. Ray Morgan couldn't take his eyes off of the blonde-headed beauty whose smile seemed to light up the room. Ray was so engrossed with his own musings that he never noticed that his own luncheon partner had set his sights on one Gabrielle Foster. Ray didn't move as he said, "What do you think they're so excited about?"

Discovering Elizabeth

Eric Casey, still lost in the beauty of auburn hair, mused, "I think that Rebecca has gotten engaged. They're looking at her left hand."

The two men watched the women long after their waitress had served them. Unaware of their audience, Rebecca grimaced as Elizabeth and Gabrielle spread bleu cheese dressing over their salads. "How do you two eat that gross and repulsive dressing?" Rebecca dribbled red, runny liquid onto her own plate as Elizabeth and Gabrielle protested.

Gabrielle placed her fork on the table and pointedly looked at Liz while commenting to Rebecca, "Let's see, Liz, I take it that Ms. Married over here is now the expert on culinary combinations. Do you think she'll try to instruct us on laundry or perhaps child-rearing, next?"

Unmoved by Gabrielle's play, Rebecca retorted, "Oh, I might; however, if I were going to teach anyone anything about culinary arts, I would hope to begin with students who had a basic knowledge of the simplest things such as boiling water."

"My, my, my...touchy, touchy!" Elizabeth raised her cola in a toast. "To Rebecca: may her life be filled with the pleasures of marital bliss and may her kitchen knives be as sharp as her tongue!" The three women experienced difficulty in swallowing as their laughter continued with the friendly camaraderie.

Neither man spoke as they watched the three friends. The girls had their attention. A waiter walked up to the men to inquire about a dessert, momentarily distracting the two. When they looked back toward the table that had caught their attention, it was empty. Without one word, their eyes met and they stood in unison. Ray threw some bills down on the table and hurriedly made his way, with Eric by his side, to the restaurant exit.

After looking around the parking lot Ray stopped suddenly and pushed back on Eric. "Look." Ray pointed to a blue Camry with its hood up. "That's Rebecca's car, she's apparently having difficulty." All three girls were peering over the engine with what appeared to be sullen looks of confusion. Liz pointed to something under the hood while Rebecca shook her head. The threesome didn't see the men approach. All three of them jumped in alarm when Eric said in his naturally deep voice, "Do you need some help?"

Lisa D. Piper

Within seconds, all three whirled around at their would-be assailants. After a pause of shock, Rebecca was the first to speak, "Oh, hi, Eric. Hi, Ray. I'm so glad you guys are here. Do either of you have jumper cables?"

Ray wrinkled his brow as if he were thinking. "Umm, yes, I do. Let me go get them for you." Ray quickly walked to his car, drove it to where Rebecca was parked then, lifted his hood. "Eric, would you lend me a hand and place these on the... Eric?"

Eric hadn't taken his eyes off of Gabrielle. A display of interest like Eric was showing for Gabrielle would normally have caused her to lower her head in embarrassment. Gabrielle was mortified but she could not tear her eyes away from the loveliest man she had ever seen. When the man with the jumper cables interrupted her thoughts she was wondering how unfair it was to other men that this one man was blessed with every perfect feature. Yes, this man's name would have to be Absalom. His jet-black hair only enhanced his beautiful dark features. She had seen green eyes before, but not one pair that had looked into her very being so completely.

"Eric?" The unison of Ray and Rebecca calling his name brought him back to reality. Still, he had difficulty looking away.

"What." Came the monotone reply from the smitten man.

"Would you please give me a hand?"

"Yeah, sure." Eric finally turned and helped Ray with the task of getting the car started. His mind was racing and his heart was not far behind.

After Rebecca's car purred to life, she waved and said that she was late and needed to go. She smiled and waved at her good friends as she drove away.

Ray waved, then looked directly at Eric and Gabrielle. After noting that Elizabeth was also looking at them with disbelief, he made a gesture to her by lifting his shoulders and holding up his hands as if to say, "I give up." They both smiled. It seemed natural for Ray and Elizabeth to just walk toward her vehicle and leave the couple to their trance like state.

Ray decided to make the most of the time they had by discussing the only thing he knew they had in common, "So, how's the investigation

Discovering Elizabeth

going, and are you going to work today?" Ray placed his hands in his pockets and then, lifted his head.

The picture of Ray sleepily reaching up for her and calling her a pretty lady flashed in her mind. Elizabeth hesitated then answered, "I've actually been at work this morning and have made some progress. I think that I need to speak with you and Fred as soon as possible. I need to speak with Fred about some problems I had with some of my staff Friday, too." Elizabeth shifted her weight as she tried to think of something to say that didn't include work.

Ray leaned on the vehicle. Elizabeth stopped and turned toward this man whom she felt she knew so well as a businessman but knew nothing about the real man. "Elizabeth, you may as well know that Fred won't be working with the company any longer. This hasn't been announced yet, so please don't say anything to anyone about it. Since I know the basic details of what's going on, you'll just need to speak to me about any concerns or problems you have."

Elizabeth couldn't hide the shock of the news. She didn't want to pry. Actually, she wanted to pry, but she decided that Ray would not reveal to her what had happened, so she decided not to ask. He was impressed when Elizabeth didn't ask the circumstances of Fred's separation from the company. He didn't want to have to tell her that it was confidential. He was much relieved when Elizabeth just said, "Oh, okay. I hope he's okay. That is shocking news." After an appropriate pause, Elizabeth continued, "Will you have some time Monday morning to talk about this, I really need some advice."

"Advice?"

"Yes, but right now I've got to get back to the office and finish compiling the information on the investigation if I'm going to get to bed at a decent hour tonight. I really think that we have some, shall I say, challenges ahead that need to be handled with tact." Elizabeth glanced back at her friend who was talking with Eric. Before Ray could respond or ask questions about her comments on the challenges, Elizabeth wondered aloud, "What are they doing?" Ray looked at the spot where Eric was standing.

"It looks like they are introducing themselves." Ray watched as Gabrielle got into her own car while Eric walked towards what appeared to be his own transportation.

Lisa D. Piper

"Well, I think they've finished introducing themselves and seem to be leaving without even telling us good-bye. How do you like that?"

Elizabeth shrugged her shoulders. She wrinkled her nose as she did when she was perplexed. As Ray looked down at her and saw the wrinkle, he thought that he'd like to just playfully tap her on her cute little nose. Ray pushed unwanted thoughts out of his mind and addressed his company's accountant. "Elizabeth, I don't have any plans for the rest of the evening. I'll come to the office and we can work out the details of whatever is going on with the Peters' account." Before Elizabeth could protest, Ray walked over to Eric's car, conversed a few minutes and then slid into his own vehicle.

Elizabeth had enough time to have become engrossed in her work once again before Ray entered her office. "Hey! What've you been doing in here?" He pointed to the stacks of papers on Elizabeth's otherwise organized desk.

Elizabeth grinned mischievously. "I've been pretending like I'm Sherlock Holmes, my dear, Watson. Pull up a stack and have at it, Boss."

Ray wasn't sure what she had done with the starchy businesswoman, but he was glad that the only remnant of that woman was the proficient manner in which she worked toward her goal. Ray ran a hand through his wavy brown hair then pulled a comfortable looking chair to the desk where Elizabeth was working. "Yes, Holmes. Point me in the right direction and I shall do you the honor of assisting you in the case of the erroneous invoice! While I'm doing that, you can tell me what's on your mind, oh great detective."

Elizabeth sat back in her chair to release the tension of leaning over the documents. "This is going to take a few minutes. I don't think I can review these forms and chat at the same time though. I don't want to make a mistake."

Ray smiled. "We have all day. I don't have any plans if you don't."

Elizabeth returned his smile then began her explanation of what she believed to have happened. "As you know the Peters' have been clients for many years. Although most of the work we do is ordered by Mr. Peters, Mrs. Peters has access to the account and often calls to make changes to the account or to check on the status of job orders.

Discovering Elizabeth

Occasionally, Mr. Peters hires us for a job that is so small that he pays for it with cash and requests that an invoice not be sent."

"Really? I didn't know that." Ray interjected.

"Well, I didn't know it either. He has apparently done this through one of my employees. I can't prove it right now, but I believe that he gets Jillian to accept the cash. I think Jillian must give him a receipt when he pays. There would be no reason for any of us to question this since there wouldn't be an outstanding balance to draw the attention of any one else in the accounting department. Someone, presumably Jillian, would send the order to the upper offices. She would mark 'paid' on the invoice and then file it in Mr. Peters file."

"Okay. I can see that we have a breach of protocol, but I don't understand why this would be a problem." Ray shifted in his chair, placed his hands behind his head, and crossed his legs.

"I checked the invoice in question. It reflects the request for work to be done for a private home. Although a name isn't mentioned on the invoice, I was able to track the invoice number and compare it to a specific work order."

"You've lost me, Sherlock." Ray furrowed his brow in confusion.

"Mr. Peters requested some professional cleaning on a residential address. According to his file, he has done this periodically over the years. The invoices that were paid with cash all have one thing in common. They have nothing to do with Mr. Peters professional business because this work was done for a private home. I have checked the address, and it isn't where our client lives."

Ray asked, "Are you saying that work is being done and is then being disguised so that no one would know about it? I presume you're thinking that there could be an affair or something like that going on?"

"That is why you are the CEO! Sharp as a tack!" Elizabeth was afraid that she had overstepped her bounds and added, "I didn't mean that in a condescending manner. I realize that this is serious and I'm not meaning to belittle the circumstance by being sarcastic, Sir."

Ray grinned, "I understand, Ms. Pennington. You have worked a lot of stressful hours this week. Sometimes it's easier to poke fun at something in order to deal with it. If not, you might find yourself collapsed in a pile of carbons and paper."

Lisa D. Piper

Elizabeth was grateful for his calm manner. "I'm not sure how this certain invoice was sent to the client. I found a duplicate in their file that was marked paid. I have a theory though. Jillian's a perfectionist when it comes to her work. Every 'i' must be dotted and every 't' crossed. The invoice that was sent to the client has an error on it. When it was printed, the numbers at the bottom aren't aligned. Jillian would have never allowed this invoice to be sent to a client without correcting it first. I remember that a few weeks ago Jillian was looking for an invoice. She questioned everyone about it. I knew that she was pretty frantic so I asked her if she had ever found it the next time I saw her. She had said, "Well, I guess I shredded it as I had intended to do. It was an invoice with an error on it and I wanted to make sure that no one sent it." Elizabeth looked at Ray. "If this is the invoice, someone did see it and sent it. What do you think?"

"I'm not sure." Ray scratched his head and sighed. "Let me get this straight. You think that Jillian could have been taking money to cover up the fact that Mr. Peters is paying for invoices with cash. She probably hasn't been sending a copy of the bill to the Peters' address since Mr. Peters would have the copy when he paid it in cash. You're alluding to the fact that Mr. Peters is probably supporting...umm...another household and not wanting his wife to know about it. Do you mean to tell me that Mr. Peters has remained silent about the truth while his wife parades her arrogance in front of practically everyone in this building?"

Elizabeth paused before shaking her head in the affirmative. "Yes. I think that is what has happened."

"Let's collect all of this data and place it in a readable report. We may need to explain this to the board. We can do it together while you tell me of the other challenges you said you're having." Ray stood to help Elizabeth transfer all of the files and papers to a long conference table. It was going to be a long night. "Do you have a radio? Let's listen to some music. The absence of sound from the weekday traffic is beginning to get on my nerves."

"I have a CD player. You may not like my taste in music though." Elizabeth removed the CD from the plastic container then turned it on the random setting.

"Stephen Curtis Chapman." Ray looked very proud of himself as he recognized the singer.

Discovering Elizabeth

"Yes, it is. You know of him?"

Ray grinned, "But, of course, madam, and how fitting it is. This is a great adventure, we need some motivational music!"

Elizabeth smiled and was glad that Ray liked her selection. As they worked and listened, Elizabeth began to unfold her tale of what had been happening in the office, how she had handled it and how she wished she had handled it. Elizabeth asked what he thought she needed to do.

"Why didn't you tell me she's been doing these things?"

Elizabeth looked intently at him before looking down as she responded. "I thought I could handle it on my own, I guess. Okay, I have to be honest. I was guilty of listening to what she had to say for so long that I didn't feel as if I had a right to report it to anyone without being found guilty myself. After awhile, the frustration just built up and then I just had to do something about it. I felt pressured by the fact that she seems to be very proficient in what she does with her work. It would be hard to replace her." Elizabeth was tempted to cover her eyes with her hands. She knew that her reasons were all wrong.

"Elizabeth." Ray wanted to place his arm around her and hug the fear out of her. Ray become very still as his mind began to insist that he wanted to touch this woman. He wanted to put his arm around her and tell her everything would be okay. What had gotten in to him? He tried to remind himself that as an employee of the company, in which he was entrusted, he had no right to even imagine such a thing. Suddenly, Ray's thoughts became frantic. What would Homer think? How could he give Elizabeth the instruction she would need while he was having such personal thoughts about the blonde haired beauty? Elizabeth awaited a reprimand from Ray but was stunned when he merely stood up after several moments and said, "I'll be back in a minute."

Ray returned after twenty lonely minutes. She noticed that the easygoing mood that had accentuated most of the evening was gone. He spoke to her but seemed to be guarded. She never knew that he had just given himself the biggest pep talk about how he could work with her and not become involved emotionally. When he spoke, his voice was steady, "Elizabeth, what if I told you that my cousin has gangrene on his toe?"

Lisa D. Piper

Elizabeth giggled nervously. "What?"

Ray had intended to keep his reserve with the woman but he couldn't help but grin at her response to his unexpected question. "I know this is kind of a bad example, but I can't think of anything else. So, please play along. Now, what if I told you that my cousin has gangrene on his toe?"

"I guess I would say that he needs to see a doctor."

"Yes, that's correct. What would happen if he didn't?"

Elizabeth looked at him cautiously before answering, "I guess that the gangrene would spread to the other parts of his foot and more of his body would begin to die."

"Elizabeth, that's how it is when, as managers, we fail to take care of a little problem. It spreads, it damages, and it hurts. I fully realize that you know you were in error. We're going to have to deal with Jillian. I would have expected Fred to deal with you, but I'm going to have to do that. Do you know what our policy is on malicious gossip?"

She knew what was coming. "Yes, I do."

"Okay, then as a supervisor, I expect you to follow the policy. If you need help enforcing the policy, there is support available to you. The personnel department will give you feedback for clarification and help you in deciding what you need to do. This got out of hand before you knew what happened, didn't it?" Ray wanted to tell her that everything was okay and that it didn't matter; he had learned through Homer that if he were to candy-coat the problem, it would be unfair to Elizabeth and would rob her of a very important experience.

"Yes, I guess it did. I know what the policy says about gossip." Elizabeth groaned inwardly, "I also know the consequences for managers who do not follow the disciplinary guidelines outlined in the policy. You will give me a coaching session for not properly administering the policy in question and then I'll have to make sure to follow through from now on or face tougher consequences. Ray, if I may ask you this, I would prefer for you to do it right now if you're going to do it. I don't want to dread talking with you Monday when there is so much work to be done." Elizabeth thought about it and she knew she deserved at least a coaching on the matter. It would be

Discovering Elizabeth

embarrassing if Rebecca were to overhear the session so she hoped Ray would have mercy and just talk to her immediately.

Ray didn't want to admit it. He knew how Elizabeth felt. Just as Elizabeth had not wanted to correct Jillian, he didn't want to correct her. To break policy would be detrimental to his working relationship with her and he knew it. Somehow he also knew that she would expect him to follow protocol with her and not be more lenient than the guidelines allowed. There in the privacy of her office, Ray coached her on how to become a better leader and manager and taught her how to utilize the policies that were set in place to cause the organization to stay focused and run like a well oiled machine.

Although the session of coaching was as difficult as it was educational, Elizabeth would take the knowledge Ray shared with her and use it for almost all aspects of her life.

After talking about policies and procedures, Ray and Elizabeth began to focus on the task of finishing the paperwork for the Peters' inquiry. With the conversation about Jillian's escapades behind them, both of them relaxed and found that they worked incredibly well together.

Elizabeth had left the room to make copies when Ray shouted, "I can't believe it! It's nine o'clock."

"You're kidding me!" The phone rang as Elizabeth re-entered her office. Her hands were full of the copies she had just made, so she motioned for Ray to hit the intercom button. She began separating some of the copies as she said, "Hello?"

"Liz? Is that you? You sound like you're in a barrel!" Gabrielle remarked.

"I've got you on the intercom. My hands are full. What's up?"

"It's getting late. I just wanted to check on you. Are you still working? Don't forget that we have to be at church early in the morning. We promised Pastor that we wouldn't be late again. I have no intention of allowing you to embarrass me like you did last Sunday!"

Ray's eyebrow lifted in question at the accusation. If he wasn't mistaken, Elizabeth looked embarrassed. She turned her head where Ray could not see her and said, "I'll be home soon, and we won't be late. What've you been doing?"

Lisa D. Piper

"Nothing much. I've cleaned up the mess you left and started working on a list of people we should contact so that we can have a shower for Rebecca."

Elizabeth sighed, "Don't you think you're getting in a bit of a hurry. She didn't tell us whether or not they have set a date."

Gabrielle scoffed, "I know that. If you don't remember, I don't have a date again tonight. The house is clean, and I have nothing better to do, unless you have some better ideas. If you don't have any other ideas, leave me alone and let me plan someone else's life, okay!"

"Well of course I have some ideas. I just can't say right now." Elizabeth grinned mischievously at Ray.

"I know, I know, you're busy. Say, you wouldn't happen to know that man who was with your boss would you?"

"Uhhh...No, I don't know him." Elizabeth quickly picked up the phone and turned off the speaker. "Why do you ask?"

"Well because, oh never mind. I just thought you might know if he's single or not."

Elizabeth laughed, "You better hope he's single the way you two were looking at each other. What's up with you anyway? I've never seen you look at a man like that." Elizabeth had spoken before she remembered that Ray could still hear her side of the conversation.

Gabrielle couldn't explain what had made her act so blatantly interested in the stranger. She found him attractive, but it was something different. He'd been looking at her like no one had ever looked at her before.

"I expected you to be home several hours ago." Gabrielle waited for an explanation. Elizabeth reassured her that she hadn't been abducted by office bandits and hung up the phone before Gabrielle could ask any more questions.

Elizabeth turned to walk back to the copier. She glanced back to see if Ray looked as if he had been paying attention to what she'd been saying. He was grinning and his apparent amusement made her heart skip a beat

"Office bandits?" He mocked.

Discovering Elizabeth

Elizabeth knew that she was flirting with him. She'd never been able to openly flirt with any male, and she was quite pleased with herself for being able to do so finally. After all, it was harmless. Ray Morgan was off limits to her. His mannerisms were non-threatening and Elizabeth felt safe. She placed her hands on her hips, swished her hair with a jerk of her head and said, "Yeah, haven't you ever heard of them? Their trick is to find out when a girl is working on a lonely Saturday. The bandit follows the girl and then makes her work until she nearly faints from food deprivation!"

"Oh! Those bandits, I've heard of them. We probably need to send out a memo so that others will beware, just in case a bandit tries to hit these offices!" Elizabeth's heart fluttered as Ray grinned at her.

Ray began picking up the last forms to be reviewed. He picked up the nearly completed report and said, "Come on."

Elizabeth turned in time to see him pick up her shoes. He held them out to her while she stood gawking at him. She'd forgotten that she'd pulled them off before he had arrived. She took the shoes and finally asked, "What are we doing?"

"Ms. Pennington, I'll not be given a challenge and then back down from it. My honor is at stake here, Madam. I'll not be labeled a bandit. We're going to eat, and don't give me any excuses. We'll take some work so we can get it finished while we fill your deprived stomach." Ray guided her out the door and to his car in the parking garage.

Elizabeth quickly became uncomfortable as she slid into the leather interior of Ray's car. She was no longer in what felt like safe territory. She was in Ray Morgan's vehicle. Never had she dreamed that she would be riding with him alone. As Ray slid into the drivers seat, Elizabeth forced herself to breathe normally although she felt anything but normal.

Ray turned the key and was welcomed by a loud blast of acoustic guitar. Elizabeth grinned as a loud Steven Curtis Chapman blared out of the custom speakers before Ray sheepishly turned the volume down.

Several minutes passed and neither spoke. Ray didn't seem to want any conversation and for that she was glad. She began to think about all of the times that she had been with him. Her thoughts took her back to the staircase where they had collided. She began to snicker as she thought of his papers flying about wildly in the stairwell.

Lisa D. Piper

Ray glanced at her as she tried to stifle her amusement. He wasn't sure if he should ask what was causing her so much joy, but decided that she didn't have to tell him, but he would inquire. "What's so funny, may I ask?"

"I'm sorry about the black eye."

"Black eye? Oh...yeah. Well, it isn't colorful anymore. Did anyone ever tell you that you have a hard head?" Ray looked as if he was sixteen and grinning at his first date.

Elizabeth loved his teasing. She admitted, "Well, I'm not sure if it's the same, but I've been told that I'm hardheaded before."

Ray chuckled. "I'm not sure if it's the same thing or not, but I would say you have the potential to be both."

Elizabeth gave him what she hoped was a serious look, "Don't forget that you're not the easiest person to fall into. I really hurt my knee that time in your office. Maybe our height gives us that non-graceful edge or something. Maybe that's why we've had so many run-ins."

"Speak for yourself. I may be tall, but I'm graceful through and through. Did you see the way that I floated to the floor in my office? I may be a male, but clumsy I am not." Ray flipped on his blinker as he prepared to turn.

Elizabeth retorted, "Oh no, you floated all right, you floated with a thump and nearly broke my leg doing it. And if you want to talk about a hard head, you didn't do me any favors when we bumped heads. I didn't get a black eye, but I have a knot on my head. A lesser woman would've collapsed in tears." Elizabeth crossed her arms.

Ray turned into the nearest restaurant and then responded by saying that he had no intention of finding out whose head was the hardest again. Before getting out of the car he took off his seat belt, turned to look at Elizabeth and said, "I never thought about the fact that you didn't cry. I'm sorry that you were hurt." Ray opened his door then walked to the passenger door to open the door for a woman who thought that at any moment she would have to be carted away by an ambulance due to heart failure.

Elizabeth ignored the thumping coming from her chest and followed Ray into the restaurant. Finishing the details of the report didn't take as much time as they had anticipated. As Ray and Elizabeth discussed a

Discovering Elizabeth

possible selection from the dessert menu, both were delighted that they had found a common bond: a love for chocolate. When the waitress brought the huge bowl of fudge brownie with creamy white ice cream drizzled with fudge sauce, Ray became uncomfortable. Elizabeth stared at the large dish with two long spoons protruding from either side of the treat. Ray cleared his throat and apologized, "I guess I didn't think about how this would look or how we'd do this when we decided to share. I'm sorry, Liz. I'll order another one."

Elizabeth noticed that he had called her Liz instead of Elizabeth or Ms. Pennington. As she looked into his hazel eyes, she noticed that he looked warm and caring. How had she missed seeing it for three years? When had he become so sweet? Elizabeth waved her hand in the air, "No, don't worry about it. That is, if you don't mind. If you don't mind, I don't."

He didn't argue. "Okay, tell you what, I'll stick to my side; you stick to yours, and I'll meet you in the middle!"

Bystanders would have thought that the restaurant was hosting the most perfect couple for a very late dinner. Unknown to Elizabeth and Ray, their contrasting looks made them a very striking pair. They looked as if they could've walked out of a family sitcom and taken up residence in reality. More than one patron looked at the couple longer than necessary to appreciate the friendly chatter that was taking place between the two.

Elizabeth closed her eyes as she took her first bite of ice cream covered warm brownie. Her eyes remained closed as she whispered; "I am in paradise."

Ray caught his breath. The woman was absolutely the most beautiful woman he had ever seen. He couldn't lift his spoon to taste what Elizabeth seemed to be enjoying. Her long lashes remained closed long enough for him to take in every detail of her face. He hadn't wanted to look at her like this before, for fear that she would find him rude, but now he just couldn't seem to take his eyes off of her.

As Elizabeth opened her eyes, she saw that Ray was looking at her with that expression. He wasn't exactly smiling. His voice was soft and low as he breathed, "You are beautiful." Ray didn't know his thoughts had been spoken until he saw Elizabeth's eyes widen and turn into a

Lisa D. Piper

magnificent hue of blue. "Uhhhh...Elizabeth, I uh...I didn't mean... What I mean is that I didn't...."

Elizabeth forgot that she was sitting with a man for whom she worked. She forgot about Jillian, about the Peters, and about the challenges surrounding her occupation and concentrated fully on the man that sat opposite of her. Elizabeth smiled lightly and said, "Thank you." She lowered her eyes as the intimacy of the moment engulfed her.

Ray refused to listen to the voice that warned him of what he was doing. He didn't want to think of Elizabeth in a personal way. He didn't want to think of all of the reasons that he shouldn't do what he was about to do. He just wanted to know this complex but seemingly carefree woman. As the dessert was left mysteriously untouched, all common sense was abandoned. Ray lifted his hand and placed it on Elizabeth's and asked, "Would you like to take a drive?"

Elizabeth couldn't shake her shyness. She thought that she might lose her ability to hear him speak at any moment. The interference of the loud thumping sound coming from her chest was overbearing as she murmured, "Yes, Ray, I would."

Ray paid the bill, grabbed the finished work, and then led Elizabeth to his car. It seemed natural to walk hand in hand. Ray opened her door, dreading the moment he would have to let go of her hand for the time it would take him to walk around the car. He was afraid that if he let go of her hand, the demands of the real world would flood in and ruin everything. Once they were on the open road, he slowly took Elizabeth's hand and held it as if he were holding the most fragile porcelain. He knew he shouldn't be so presumptuous but his desire to hold her delicate hand overwhelmed him.

Ray couldn't see Elizabeth's expression as she looked at his strong hand gently holding hers. As she looked at his hand, it seemed as if she were watching something happen between two people that didn't look like or feel like Ray Morgan and Elizabeth Pennington. The warmth of his hand enveloped her. She felt something that she couldn't remember feeling before. She had never felt like this when she had been with Jonathan. At the thought of Jonathan, Elizabeth began to feel an ever-present dread. She wouldn't relent to the doubts and fears that seemed to want to overtake her. She squinted her eyes shut, determined not to allow her mind to be catapulted into the past. Her effort to concentrate

Discovering Elizabeth

on the present became easier as the smell of salt water teased her nostrils.

The soothing sound of a lapping wave found Elizabeth and Ray parked, overlooking the evening tide. She breathed in and let the sound of the waves comfort her pounding heart.

Long minutes passed before either one of them spoke. Ray was the first to make a sound. "Liz." He couldn't finish what he was going to say. The effect of the sound of her name on his lips was enough to warrant discretion.

While Ray fought within himself, Elizabeth squeezed his hand and whispered, "Ray, this is lovely. Thank you for bringing me here. I didn't know how tense I was until a few minutes ago when I began to look at this view." Elizabeth looked out at the creation of luminous salt water.

Ray looked at the view that had captured her attention. As he turned toward her to see at what part of the beach she was looking, the inevitable happened. Blue eyes met hazel. He didn't remember moving his aching arm. She leaned her head forward and allowed his arm behind her shoulders. Neither closed their eyes or blinked, as the distance between them became smaller. Elizabeth Pennington and Ray Morgan began a kiss that would haunt them for longer than they would imagine. It didn't matter that the kiss only lasted a moment; it wouldn't allow itself to be forgotten. Elizabeth willingly slid closer to the man sitting behind the wheel and placed her head on his shoulder. She knew that what was happening was impossible. A tear slid from the corner of her eye then rolled down her cheek as she leaned into the warmth of Ray's arms. Elizabeth breathed carefully. She knew that this wouldn't happen again and she wanted to remember the comfort. She wanted to remember his scent. She wanted to just remain parked in the moonlight in front of the span of moving water and not return to reality again.

For the hour that followed, the couple took in the moment and sat close enough to hear the nervous breaths being taken by the other. Content to sit in silence, Elizabeth and Ray let the sound of lapping waves permeate through the air. As he considered that he would need to take Elizabeth home, he placed his chin on the top of her head and combed through her blonde hair with his fingers. He had wondered what Elizabeth Anne Pennington's hair would feel like in his hand. Now, he knew, and would remember. His heart fought his mind.

Lisa D. Piper

Although he was truly content for the moment, there would be nights that the memory of the moment would prove to be his tormentor.

The time came for the evening to end. Elizabeth groaned within then forced herself to move. As she lifted her head, Elizabeth touched his face with a warm smile then kissed him on the cheek. There were volumes he wanted to say but he was reeling inside.

Ray fought the desire to drive as fast as he could in the opposite direction of the town he and Elizabeth called home. He backed out of the parking spot and placed the gearshift in the drive position. He found her soft hand and held it all the way back to the parking garage. As she pushed the button to release her seat belt she glanced at him one last time. He pulled her into his arms where she embraced him with everything that was within her. With much resignation, she groped for the door and exited the car. Ray watched Elizabeth as she unlocked her car. He didn't leave until he made sure that her vehicle started. Through the windshield, blue met hazel ones and if she wasn't mistaken, she wasn't the only one who looked sad.

Elizabeth felt numb as she drove home. Her mind raced over the events of the evening. Questions plagued her mind. Questions she desperately tried to push away. She could still feel the warmth of his arms. The memory of that place of safety and rest caused her heart to yearn to be there again.

As Elizabeth placed her key into the door, it swung open with one swift yank. "Where have you been? I've been so worried!" Gabrielle demanded frantically. Gabrielle's eyes bore into Elizabeth as Gabrielle began to cry. Elizabeth wasn't a fool, she knew that if Gabrielle was upset enough to cry, she was either so worried that she had feared for her friend's safety or she was truly angry. "You said you'd be home in a bit and that was several hours ago! I phoned the office. I called Rebecca. I drove to some of the local restaurants and you weren't there!"

Elizabeth would have loved to tell her worried friend that she was a big girl and could take care of herself and that Gabrielle was not her keeper or mother. She didn't. She knew that Gabrielle's concern for her was the motivating factor of the outburst of tears and not selfish control. Elizabeth reasoned that it was a good thing for both of them to know what the other one was up to, especially during night hours. Elizabeth knew that if something had gone wrong, Gabrielle would be

Discovering Elizabeth

the one who would begin looking for her before anyone else. This fact was proven as a car pulled up to the house. She turned to see a uniformed gentleman walking up the sidewalk. Elizabeth turned and gave Gabrielle a questioning look.

Gabrielle met the officer outside. Elizabeth could hear her friend apologize to the man and explain something. The man looked at Elizabeth then shook his head. He spoke with Gabrielle for a few more minutes then got back into his car. Gabrielle wiped at her tears and walked back toward the house. As she had talked with the man she had begun to cry even more profusely. It was probably the stress of the night that had caused her to weep in front of the officer, Elizabeth thought.

"What did the officer want?" Elizabeth questioned as she followed Gabrielle back into the house.

"He wanted to know about a person that may have been abducted." Gabrielle blew her nose. "Since he saw that the person has been found, he decided he wasn't needed."

"He was looking for me?"

"Elizabeth, Yes! He was looking for you! I've been looking for you; and Rebecca's been looking for you! Could you just tell me where you've been? Are you okay?"

Elizabeth stammered, "Yes, I'm okay. What did you tell the officer?"

"What could I tell him? You hadn't the time to answer any of my questions so I just gave him my assumptions." Gabrielle sat down and sprawled out on her favorite chair, avoiding Elizabeth's glare.

"What did you say? He looked at me as if I had committed a heinous crime?"

"I told him that you had just wandered in and weren't saying where you'd been. I told him that you were a bit confused and that I'd take you in, give you some coffee and maybe you'd talk to me then." Gabrielle covered her eyes.

"Gabrielle! That man probably thinks I'm drunk or something; I just bet he did! How could you!"

"Liz, I didn't mean to imply that you were intoxicated, but I guess he could've thought that." Gabrielle wanted to remain upset but began to snicker.

"Ms. Gabby, my reputation is now soiled. Thank you." She threw a hunter green plaid pillow at the fatigued redhead.

Gabrielle returned the pillow by tossing it back at her friend. As Gabrielle continued to laugh, Elizabeth hoped for too much because Gabby didn't forget her original question. After crossing her legs on the couch, Gabrielle became solemn and asked, "Okay, Ms. Party Girl, where've you been?"

Elizabeth fidgeted. "I don't want to tell you." Dark red washed over her neck and face. Gabby didn't miss the color

"Okay, with whom have you been? Let me guess! Have you been with Ray Morgan?"

"Rrrray Morgan? Wh-wh-what makes you ask that?" Elizabeth stuttered.

"It seems that Rebecca has been trying to reach her boss today and she had about as much success finding him as I had locating you. The last time I saw you, you were with him."

Elizabeth admitted, "Well, I have been with him most of the day. He came to work and we worked on the project I was telling you about."

Gabrielle retorted, "I know you haven't been at work all night. We checked and...Oh No!" Gabrielle covered her mouth with her hand.

"What?"

"He was there." Gabrielle gulped.

"What are you talking about?" Elizabeth questioned.

"He heard me on that confounded intercom. That's why you picked it up after I asked about his friend. Oh no!" Gabrielle covered her face with a pillow then sunk into the couch cushions.

Elizabeth grinned. It was time for Gabrielle to be sidetracked and now Elizabeth had the goods. She knew it would be a short-lived victory; nonetheless, it was a bit fun watching a flabbergasted Gabby.

"You are in big trouble! Did he say anything?" Gabrielle didn't remove her pillow as she asked her question.

Discovering Elizabeth

"No, he didn't." The phone rang, interrupting Elizabeth before she could say anything else.

Gabrielle picked up the telephone guessing that the late caller was Rebecca. Gabrielle answered, "Rebecca, don't worry. The lost sheep has been found! I'm giving her the third degree right now!"

"Hello?" questioned the male voice. "Is Elizabeth there?"

Silence.

Gabrielle looked at her friend then slowly handed the handset to Elizabeth. "It's not Rebecca."

"Hello?" Elizabeth answered.

"Hi. I just wanted to make sure you made it home okay." Ray's sweet voice sounded so wonderful. Elizabeth hoped she could steady her pounding heart.

"Thanks for checking up on me. I made it home just fine."

Ray was at a loss for words. He had just wanted to call and make sure that she had remembered the last few hours. He couldn't forget them. Finally he whispered, "I really had a nice time. I'm not sure what's happening, Liz. I just want you to know that, well, that I'm glad we spent the day together."

Elizabeth was delighted. "I am too. I won't forget it anytime soon."

Ray was secretly delirious. That was what he had wanted to know. "I'm glad. Well, get some sleep. I'll see you Monday." He hung up the phone, turned his nightstand lamp off and whispered, "Yes!" As Elizabeth hung up the phone she noticed that Gabrielle was gaping in disbelief.

"What are you doing?" Gabrielle had her hands on her hips.

"I'm thinking."

"You've been out with him. You were out with Ray on a date-like thing! I can't believe this! You were out with Ray Morgan and didn't breathe a word of it to me and don't deny it. It's written all over your face. Okay, I'm not going to ask any more questions. I'm going to bed. I know you're not going to affirm or deny it, so I'll just put the pieces together for myself." Elizabeth didn't stop her from going to her own room.

Lisa D. Piper

She was content to memorize the day's events without any interruption. Ray Morgan had had a good time with her and she was just going to bask in the memory of it.

"Gabrielle, wake up Gabrielle!" Elizabeth pushed her friend's shoulder back and forth frantically.

The worry of the evening before had caused Gabrielle to sleep fitfully. "What? Oh, go away, I'm awake."

"Gabrielle, shut-up and wake up. I know that you think you're awake, but you're not! We've got fifteen minutes to be out of the door or we'll be late for services. We've already missed half of Sunday School."

Gabrielle sat straight up in the bed. Her tousled auburn hair hung around her shoulders; covering the top of the picture on her nightshirt. Most of her peers wouldn't have guessed that the elegant Gabrielle would only sleep in HoneyBearWear. Gabrielle Storm was a faithful HoneyBearWear collector. She rubbed her eyes quickly and exclaimed, "Oh No! Why didn't my alarm wake me up?" Gabrielle looked for her clock, but it wasn't on the bedside table.

Elizabeth turned to go, obviously in a hurry to get ready while informing Gabby of where her beloved HoneyBear clock had gone. "Gabby, it looks like the alarm did go off, and you sent it soaring into next week."

Gabrielle looked around and shouted, "Oh no!" Her HoneyBear clock had been thrown across the room and was now upside-down in a clothesbasket. "Poor, HoneyBear. You don't deserve the on-the-job abuse you get." Gabrielle rushed to the basket, grabbed her clock and set him back in his spot. She wound him up, grabbed her clothes and headed for her bathroom.

Neither girl was sure of how she had done it, but they both were washed, dressed, primped and brushed and ready to go only a couple of minutes behind schedule. Elizabeth prayed while Gabrielle weaved in and out of traffic. "Oh, Lord, please turn all of the lights green, and keep us safe. You know we meant to be on time, it's just that this always seems to happen to us."

Discovering Elizabeth

Gabrielle shook her head at her friend. "Elizabeth, I don't think you should be praying for green lights. And, it isn't God's fault that this stuff happens to us on Sundays. If you'll remember, you didn't get home until this morning. Speaking of which: if you hadn't kept me up, I wouldn't have been in the frame of mind to toss an innocent bear across my room, now would I? No, I wouldn't." Gabrielle honked her horn at a slow moving vehicle.

"Okay, Little Miss Priss, are you saying that the reason we're late is because of me? Is that what you're saying! And don't you make fun of what I ask God. He knows why we're late, and I was just asking for favor, that's all. If He cares about whether or not a sparrow gets fed, or if He took such meticulous detail in every part of His creation, then He cares about whether I break my promise to one of His servants or not. And, for your information, I am a big, very big girl. I didn't ask you to stay up all night waiting for me. I didn't even ask you to call the cops. I didn't ask you to call Rebecca. I didn't ask you to call me at work and I didn't ask for all of this grief!" As Elizabeth finished the last word she looked out of the window determined not to cry. She knew she'd hurt Gabrielle's feelings, but she just didn't care. She was tired and embarrassed at the thought that they might walk into the services once more, late.

Gabrielle flinched. If they hadn't been entering the driveway of the church, she would've let Elizabeth have a piece of her mind. She wouldn't let Elizabeth Anne Pennington talk to her with such disrespect! Gabrielle grinned to herself as she thought, "Alright, Ms. Gabby, give her some of her own medicine."

Both women scrambled out of the car, grabbed their Bibles, and slammed their doors in unison. As they nearly stomped toward the church, they were relieved to find that they were just in time. An elder, Scott Riso, opened the door to welcome and usher the twosome into the sanctuary. Before they were in hearing range of the kind brother, Gabrielle turned to Elizabeth and said, "Excuse me for worrying about your sorry self. Don't worry about the future. I won't waste my Saturday night being concerned for the safety of a thankless female!" With that, Gabrielle marched into the church, leaving Elizabeth to her anger.

Brother Scott was not oblivious to the fact that Gabrielle and Elizabeth had come to church having had some kind of squabble. The elder looked to the sky with a grin and prayed, "Lord, they're in the right place. Work on them."

As Elizabeth entered the church, she thought that she would sit on the opposite side of the area where she knew Gabrielle would want to sit. Her second thought was that she would look guilty and cause more commotion if she didn't sit with her friend. Elizabeth surprised Gabrielle by walking right up to her and asking her to please allow her to sit down. Their eyes locked and Gabrielle gave a sweet smile and cooed, "Certainly. Here, you sit on the outside, just in case you need to go repent of something."

Elizabeth's mouth dropped open as Gabrielle hid her face. She couldn't believe what she'd just said. It was uncalled for and she knew it. A message that Gabrielle had heard as a child rushed into her mind. The minister had said, "When you come in here angry with your children or with your spouse, your hardened heart makes it difficult to worship the Lord. Take thought of the attitude with which you present yourself to God and to your church family." Gabrielle sank into her seat as low as she could without actually lying down. God began to deal with her and she instantly began to regret every harsh word she had dished out to her friend. At first, she rationalized with God by reminding him of what Elizabeth had said. In the end, all she could think of was that God would not forgive her if she didn't forgive her brother...or sister.

Elizabeth tried to convince herself that she didn't feel any conviction over her actions. She stood up from her pew to sing to the rhythm of the choir and began to sing:

> "Take this heart and the hardened parts.
> Make me like you, Lord, in every way.
> I want to be Pure and Holy, saturated solely, with
> the Glory of your presence, everyday[8]"

As the words of the song penetrated her heart, she stopped. She knew that what she was singing had nothing to do with the way she was acting. As she examined her actions, she stood with the awareness

---

[8] "Take This Heart" ©1994 Lisa Piper/BMI/All Rights Reserved

Discovering Elizabeth

that she had been inconsiderate to the only one who had noticed that she didn't come home at a decent hour the night before.

After the singing, Elizabeth sat down and looked to the front. The Lord that she had relied on had everything planned and had, without Elizabeth and Gabrielle knowing it, prepared them to receive the Word. Pastor Matthews couldn't have known what was going on, but the girls wondered about what God might have revealed to him when he stood up and began the service.

"Good morning. I'm so glad to see you here today. I woke up this morning so thankful for you." Pastor Matthews looked to each of the pews with gratitude. "You know that I don't have any family of my own, with the exception of my lovely wife. You must know that you've become my extended family; and I know that many of you feel the same way about each another. You know, Proverbs 18:24 says, "A man that hath friends must show himself to be friendly and there is a friend that sticketh closer than a brother." That's what you are. You're closer than a brother. Often, when I have gone through a great deal of trying times in my life, God has used one of you to lift me up in prayer or in some kind of kind deed. Chapter 4 of Ecclesiastes talks about two being better than one. It goes on to say that if there are two and one of them falls, there's still one left to pick the other one up. But, if one is alone and he falls, there's no one to pick him up. That's what we are church! We are boo-boo picker uppers." The congregation laughed as their beloved pastor continued, "I know you were waiting for the time when I would use the word boo-boo in the pulpit! I guess what I'm trying to say is that I feel so thankful for you. I also want to encourage you to build each other up and not to tear each other down. Give each other the same encouragement that you have given to me."

No one made a sound as their pastor continued; "I realize that in a small congregation like this, we all know one another by name. This closeness also allows us to know the weaknesses of each other… or some of them anyway. As a pastor, I stay in prayer because I know that we need each other. Church, hurt is the four-letter word that will divide us. Patching up the hurt is what will knit us together. I have one last scripture for you all to think about during this week that may help you during the times when you might be tempted to give up on one another. It's Proverbs 18:19, "A brother offended is harder to be won than a strong city: and their contentions are like the bars of a castle." The pastor paused to allow the scripture to sink in then continued, "Okay,

Lisa D. Piper

we're ready for the message today and I think that you're going to be able to bask in the scripture that I have for you. Get ready for some food for thought. The title of my message is "Pride Goes Before Destruction, and a Haughty Spirit Before a Fall." Please turn to Proverbs, chapter 16 and verse 18. Hold your Bibles and sit tight; I want to tell you a story about Nebuchadnezzar. You're going to love this."

Their pastor's opening words had already stung Gabrielle and Elizabeth. As he unfolded the story of Nebuchadnezzar and his pride, Elizabeth and Gabrielle sat near the edges of their seats. Old Nebuchadnezzar had not been prideful in the way that they had, but the end was still the same. As the pastor beckoned for those who needed prayer to come forward, the girls took each other's hand and walked the distance to the altar. Both women poured their hearts out to God and asked forgiveness of one another. By the time the service was over, mascara was all but a memory and an old friendship had been renewed with vitality and strength. Pastor Matthews shook each other's hands as the girls walked through the door to go to their car. "I'm so glad you all made it today. I don't know what God's doing in you, but it looks wonderful from where I'm standing."

The girls rode home in silence. When they entered their home, they changed clothes and headed for the kitchen to perform their Sunday afternoon ritual. Gabrielle unwrapped a head of lettuce and began the preliminary work on what would be a tasty salad. Elizabeth sliced up some lemon for tea and then toasted some bread for a light sandwich. "Gab, what about some strawberries with whipped topping for dessert? I bought some a couple of days ago."

"Sounds good."

Elizabeth looked into the refrigerator then frowned as she touched the container. "Gab, my couple of days ago must have been longer. The strawberries have company."

"How does that happen?" Gabrielle expounded upon the pitfalls of being a workingwoman. "Where does the time go and don't you feel guilty for letting this happen?"

"Yes, I do. I'm not going to think about it or I won't be able to purchase anything perishable again." Elizabeth offered grace over their food with heartfelt gratitude for all of God's blessings. As Elizabeth

Discovering Elizabeth

began to dig into her salad, Gabby began to eat her sandwich. Elizabeth poked at a piece of bleu cheese and then admitted, "Gabby, I was with him last night. I know that I don't owe you an explanation about Ray, but I'm sorry that I worried you so much. You're a good friend, and I'm thankful that you look out for me. You know that I'm time-challenged. I'm sorry."

Gabrielle looked at her friend and opted for a lighthearted approach to the subject. "Well, you taught me a lesson. The next time I call a cop to come out and look for you, I'll make sure that he knows to look for one Mr. Morgan right along with you."

Elizabeth began to blurt out the secret of her heart, "He's everything I would have asked for in a male friend, Gab."

"What?" Gabrielle dropped her sandwich and stammered in mid-chew.

"Ray. I am talking about Ray. We did work yesterday, but I got to know him a little better and he is so sweet. I think he may even be a Christian. I haven't asked but I'm pretty certain that he is. I've never been so, oh I don't know... I guess intrigued would be the word. I have never been so intrigued by another person."

"I have never heard you speak this way about another person, particularly a person of the male persuasion. Are you sure you know what you are doing?" Gabrielle's voice was cautious and motherly.

"No, I don't know what I'm doing. I have no idea. Don't you realize the problem this poses for me? Ray is wonderful and I'm crazy about him, but that's on an informal basis. Tomorrow, we both will be suits, and the rules will change. Our company has a policy against fraternization. That means that I can't become involved with the man that I think may be the one because it's unethical." Elizabeth let out a frustrated bellow. "Gabby, you don't know how I get. I'm like a different person when 8 A.M. arrives. I'm so afraid."

Gabrielle patted her friend on the hand and said, "Oh, Liz, I wish there were something that I could do. What are you going to do?"

"Pray. I will pray. I can't take on this worry now, Gab. I've prayed often enough for God to send me a mate. I know that I've told you that I want nothing to do with the opposite sex, but that's just an anti-rejection defense thing that I do."

Lisa D. Piper

Elizabeth and Gabrielle spent the rest of the afternoon napping. HoneyBear woke Gabrielle up in time so that they weren't late for evening services. Afterwards, Elizabeth and Gabrielle couldn't remember a service they had enjoyed more. Pastor Matthews spoke on Proverbs 21:9: "It is better to dwell in a corner of the housetop, than with a brawling woman in a wide house." Neither woman was sure how the good pastor made it out of the church without getting a book over the head by a disgruntled female. God was with him, of that they were sure, and the men were glad. The circumstances were unknown to the pastor, but on Saturday evening more than one woman had been angry with her husband and given her mate a verbal execution. The pastor had delivered the message with such love and anointing that each one of the women had snuggled a little closer to her husband instead of becoming defensive. For Elizabeth and Gabby, the sermon had a different meaning. With two females in one household they needed to be able to get along or living a life of peace would be difficult.

Monday morning found Elizabeth slipping into a smart pair of gray slacks and a double-breasted jacket. She seemed to lighten up when she replaced the white silk shirt she usually wore under the jacket with a magenta blouse. She pulled her hair up in her usual work hairstyle, but decided to make a bit of a change. She pulled out a couple of wispy strands, curled them, and let them fall around her face. She felt like she would need some extra courage and boldness so she decided on some deep lipstick and dark eyeliner. She normally wore the same perfume day after day; however, she decided to wear one that she normally saved for special occasions. After she slipped into a pair of leather flats, she said a prayer, grabbed a banana and stepped out the door into the world of business.

Chapter SEVEN

"Where there is no talebearer, the strife ceaseth.."
Proverbs 26:20

Monday proved to be a busy day for Jillian. Wanting to get to Fred before Elizabeth could, she clocked in fifteen minutes early, then went to his office. The only person that seemed to be in the building was the janitor and he was busy talking into a walkie-talkie. Jillian knocked on the door and called out, "Fred! Fred, this is Jillian, I need to see you right now if you're in there!" The janitor looked up at the commotion. Jillian glared at what she considered to be a busybody janitor and spewed venom at him, "What do you think you're looking at? Get out of my face you little toad, before I smash you. You wouldn't want me to tell Fred when he comes in that you were gawking at me, now would you?" Jillian smiled with contempt.

The janitor smiled and apologized, "I'm sorry. No, ma'am, I wouldn't want you to do that. Please don't tell him. I'll go on and won't say nothin' to nobody!"

Jillian sneered as she warned, "You better not! Now, go on before I change my mind."

Homer turned away and chuckled. He loved his job. As Homer was nearing the corner of the hall, he turned just in time to see Jillian opening Fred's door then walk inside. "What is that crazy woman up to?" he asked himself. He looked at his walkie-talkie and said, "Hey Goober 91, are you still there?"

The response came back immediately. "I am not going by Goober 91. I thought you understood that. Don't call me that again. It's embarrassing. Yes, I heard it."

"We've got a code thirteen-twenty up here in Fred's office." Homer waited for a response.

"Roger, be there in a second." Ray darted toward Fred's office. His adrenaline was pumping as he wondered what a thirteen-twenty would prove to be. His theory was that Homer didn't know either and that he was just making it up to sound like he did. No one else had access to the walkie-talkies that Homer and Ray used ...and that was a good thing. Homer must have held the send button while the woman was belittling him. There was one thing for certain. He didn't care who she was; he wasn't going to put up with her self-righteous arrogance.

Ray walked up to Fred's door and listened. He slowly opened the door only to find a bewildered Jillian feigning innocence. He heard her mumbling to herself, "What in the world happened?"

Ray cleared his throat as Jillian gaped at him. "H-hello Mr. Morgan. I, uh, was looking for Fred. Do you know where he is? I thought I heard him call out to me; so I stepped in, but neither he nor his things are here."

"He isn't here. Jillian, isn't it?" Ray crossed his arms and looked at the little bit of a woman.

"Yes, it is. I work with Elizabeth Pennington." Jillian held out her hand to shake his. "How do you do?"

"Is there something with which I can help you?" Ray was having a difficult time controlling himself. He was fighting the desire to kick her into no return. How dare she stand there acting as if she were the queen of hospitality? In one week she had managed to embarrass the company, enter into an executive office without permission and belittle Homer.

"Actually, perhaps there is something you can do. I do hate to be a bother but, oh, I just hate to say this. My supervisor would just kill me if she knew I was taking this to a higher level. Oh, never mind...I just can't." Jillian placed one hand on her stomach as if she were fretting. The other hand held her forehead.

Discovering Elizabeth

Ray was now amused. "This should be good," he thought. "Oh, no Jillian, please fill me in. What can I do to help you?" He uncrossed his arms in disbelief.

Jillian fluttered her eyelashes then whispered, "Okay, but please don't take this the wrong way. I just love working for Elizabeth. Even if she is a bit of an ogre, she just can't help it." Jillian noticed that he was standing at full attention and while she had his attention she decided to give him the full show. "Sir, you don't know how it's been. I do my best to keep our team working. Let me give you an example of what I'm put through." Jillian daubed at her eyes with her index finger. "I was working with Sophie Friday. Elizabeth saw that I was talking with her and just assumed we were talking about her. Mr. Morgan, sir, she is so paranoid. She pulled me to the side and cursed me to the top of her lungs…she…she…said things I can't repeat." Jillian began to weep and continued, "I just can't take it anymore. I'm afraid that Elizabeth is going to come in here and get me fired this morning. She said she would speak to Fred about what happened. I just know he'll believe every word she says without questioning me. All I want to do is reveal the truth. I can't keep this to myself any longer. What should I do?"

Ray had had enough. Jillian's eyelids blinked rapidly as he demanded, "Jillian, I've heard enough. Stop it."

Jillian sobered immediately. "What are you saying, Mr. Morgan? Oh please don't tell me she's gotten to you too?" Jillian covered her wet face with her little hands. Her breathing became labored and Ray became painfully aware that if he didn't know better, he would have been tempted to believe every tear and every accusation.

"Jillian, you're lying. Not only are you lying, but you have also just broken into an area for which you are not authorized. You belittled Homer and now you are trying to keep yourself from being dismissed, by telling me your version of what happened before Elizabeth has a chance to do it."

Jillian was dumbfounded. She couldn't think of a way to get out of the accusations he hurled at her. Everything he said was the truth.

"Jillian, do you have any comments about what I've just said? I'd love to hear why you would do such a thing."

Lisa D. Piper

Jillian stammered, "Why? Am I to understand that you believe that old janitor over me? I guess that I'm the underdog here. If you're going to believe him, I guess Elizabeth could spread lies and you'd believe her too. You may think you have one over on me, but I know the truth." Jillian tilted her head in defiance.

Ray was disappointed. He had the tiniest amount of hope that Jillian would confess to what she'd done. If she'd done that, he felt as if her position may have been salvageable. He had focused on the positive attributes of many persons in his company who began their career down the same path Jillian was traveling. The only difference was that those who proved to turn and be successful ultimately took responsibility for their own actions. Only a fool would respond the way Jillian had and he couldn't afford to have a fool on the payroll.

"Jillian, you could've saved your job with the truth. Come on out, Homer." Homer had been within earshot of the conversation. "I heard you speak to this janitor a few minutes ago. I heard it with my own ears, Jillian; I have documents that prove that you've been undermining Elizabeth. In addition, you've just told me several lies. I have no choice but to terminate your employment immediately. Please give me your keys and name badge. Security will be escorting you to your car. Do not return to these premises. Your personal belongings will be sent to you shortly. The personnel department will be contacting you concerning your insurance benefits and your last paycheck." Ray couldn't be too careful. He didn't want Jillian running around in the building unescorted.

Jillian was livid. She pursed her lips together as she fumbled for her keys. As Ray ended his speech, two security guards walked around the corner to escort her out. She threw the keys at Homer then stomped toward the elevator.

Homer asked how the guards had gotten there so quickly. Ray told him that he had called and told them where to meet him in ten minutes. He was very happy that he had thought of that. He didn't want to deal with the woman any longer.

Homer sighed, "What are you going to tell Elizabeth?"

"I guess I'll go meet her and tell her the truth. She may feel like I've overstepped my boundary by not getting her involved since she's

Discovering Elizabeth

Jillian's supervisor, but I don't think I would've wanted to let that loaded gun wander around the building.

Ray thanked Homer then walked the route that would lead to the office where Elizabeth would be arriving shortly. When he arrived, she was already working. Ray paused as he thought about how striking his accountant appeared. He interrupted her concentration as he casually greeted her. "Hi Liz."

Elizabeth looked up and smiled. "Hello, and how are you this morning?"

"I'm okay. I need to speak with you. I have some news." Ray sat down on the edge of her desk. With one look at her sweet face, his heart began to beat like a drum. He cleared his throat with the hope that she would never guess how she affected him.

"News? Okay, what is it?" Elizabeth looked up at him and tried to concentrate. She had thought about him since she had last seen him and now he was less than three feet away. He was in a black suit and looked like he had just walked off a business fashion magazine.

"It's about Jillian. Please hear me out before you say anything."

"What about Jillian? She isn't here yet. I've been looking for her."

"She isn't reporting for work. Jillian broke into Fred's office to inform him of what happened Friday before you had a chance to tell him. She spoke very inappropriately with Homer and then she had the nerve to lie to me. Elizabeth, I couldn't wait to contact you. I let her go.

Elizabeth's eyes did that chameleon thing and Ray could tell that she was immensely affected by what he had said. "She's gone?"

"Yes, Elizabeth, and she isn't coming back. She's not to even be in this building. I would've worked with her, Liz, but she just wouldn't own up to what she had done. This was a business decision, not a personal one. Do you understand?" Ray felt his heart breaking. Even though the decision was the best for all parties concerned, it sure felt personal.

Elizabeth squared her shoulders and sighed, "I understand."

Ray could tell that she was deep in thought. He decided that she would tell him if she wanted to. He said, "We need to meet in a little while before Mrs. Peters has a chance to call. We'll need to decide how to handle this now that Jillian isn't a factor. I want to give you support. I know that you relied on Jillian to do a lot of the important busy work that needed to be done. Think about what you want to do with her position and let me know, okay?"

"Okay. I will. Just let me know when you want to talk. I'll block off the morning for you." Elizabeth turned and looked at her computer screen. How could she tell him that she felt like the biggest failure? If she hadn't put up with the unprofessional behavior from Jillian in the first place, maybe this wouldn't have happened. As she watched Ray leave she prayed, "Oh God, not another Monday like this. I don't think I can take it today." She checked her email, then spent some time thinking about what Jillian would do with herself. Elizabeth thought about the newly vacant position. If she wanted to make some changes, now would be the time to do it.

Nothing seemed to be going like she planned. She expected to see Ray, look into his eyes, and just know he was thinking about her. She became irritated with herself at what she considered to be childish daydreams. She wasn't confident that she'd be able to make herself focus; nevertheless, she would work harder to prove to herself and to Ray that she was a good leader.

Throughout the day, Elizabeth continued to criticize herself for what had happened with Jillian and for being so infatuated with Ray. She hadn't asked God what she needed to do. She was keenly aware that the reason she was ignoring her prayer time was that she was afraid that if she prayed about the situation, God might reveal that dating Ray might be out of His will. She didn't want it to be out of His will and refused to think otherwise.

Before Elizabeth could retrieve her purse to go out to lunch the telephone rang and Ray asked her if she would please get the Peters file, and come to his office.

Elizabeth had everything together and took the files to him as quickly as she could. He'd sounded like he was in a hurry and she didn't want disappointment him. As soon as she stepped through the door into Rebecca's office, Rebecca rushed her into Ray's office. "She's here, Ray. I'll tell security to let me know when the client arrives."

Discovering Elizabeth

"What's going on?" Elizabeth questioned.

"Mrs. Peters called. She is on her way to the office right now. We need to decide what we're going to do. I've tried to think through the options. We could tell them out right what you found in the file of her husband's account. This will cause embarrassment to Mr. Peters and he may deny it. We would probably lose every account in the future if that happens. The only thing I know is that we will be honest no matter what. Another option might be to apologize for the invoice because it has been paid, and let them know that we regret the error. This might work, but it probably won't stop Mrs. Peters from telling all of her friends that we overcharged this account. If we do this, we may still lose any future business. Elizabeth, on a personal level, I don't care if we do business with a man who would do something like this. On a professional level, I'm responsible to the board and I need to protect the Interest of the company and its employees. What do you suggest? Veil it or reveal it?"

Elizabeth was amazed that he would ask her opinion. "I'm not sure what will work. I've been thinking through this as well. Do you think Mr. Peters would allow us to reveal the truth if he was positive that we've figured this thing out?"

Ray stood up, "I don't know what he'll do."

There was no more time for thinking. Mrs. Peters burst through the door unannounced. "Hello, I need to speak with someone." The sour woman didn't wait for a response. She flitted toward the chair near the desk and waved her hand in the air. "Mr. Morgan, can this woman be trusted? I have something to tell you."

Ray watched Elizabeth as her smile turned into a neutral facade. His heart almost sank. He missed the smile. He then looked at Mrs. Peters and said finally, "Yes, Mrs. Peters, she can be trusted."

"Well then, I have to tell you that I'm here to pay that invoice and I want to apologize for being such a nuisance. My husband and I have talked and I understand that he had some work done, about which, I was never told. He is so absent minded, poor thing. Okay, here's the check. Do accept my apologies." Mrs. Peters held out the check to the CEO of Wright and Wingold.

Lisa D. Piper

"Mrs. Peters, I cannot take this check. Elizabeth here has found the error and we have the receipt; it was paid in full." Ray motioned for her to keep the check.

Mrs. Peters seemed slightly annoyed. "Oh, good then. Another oversight I guess. Mr. Morgan, does anyone else know about this little...miscommunication?"

Ray almost felt sorry for the woman. She knew what kind of business her husband had been supporting; of this he was certain. He shook his head, "No one knows that there has been a question about the invoice. There have been others who have seen the invoice while processing, but only Elizabeth and I have worked on the investigation."

"Good. Thank you, I appreciate your help." Mrs. Peters didn't acknowledge Elizabeth anymore. She got up and left the office without another word.

After the door closed, Ray sat down and exhaled. "Whew, this seems to have taken an unexpected turn."

Elizabeth agreed. "Poor lady. I can't imagine the hurt of knowing your mate was unfaithful. To top it off, she knows that others know about the situation. I'll have to remember to pray for Mrs. Peters."

Ray stared blankly at the unopened file.

Elizabeth looked over at Ray. He was uncomfortably silent. She suddenly felt self-conscious so she stood up to go. She was disappointed when he didn't stop her. Elizabeth reasoned that he was probably still upset over her managerial capabilities. The thought never crossed her mind that she had just said the words that took Ray back to a time that he would have rather forgotten. He had been young when his father left his mother. If he'd been older, he would've gone after him and tried to make him apologize to his wife. The man had cheated and made the error of not keeping it a secret. If Ray could have saved his mother from the public embarrassment, he would have. Instead, he was stuck in a situation that was out of his control.

When Ray had faced his own heartache as a college student, he had begun to believe that a relationship with any woman couldn't work. He had opted to dedicate his life to his God while operating Wright and Wingold. Until he'd bumped into the lovely Elizabeth, he had been somewhat lonely for human companionship, but had been content.

Discovering Elizabeth

"What have I been thinking?" Ray admonished himself for being selfish. He couldn't see how he could offer Elizabeth anything. He wasn't a man who could trust easily. He was the CEO and he had been willing to break company policy without as much as a word to his partner. Ray shook his head as if he couldn't believe what he had allowed himself to do.

He noticed that while he had been reminiscing, Elizabeth stood looking at him with those curious wide eyes. He thanked her for her work and led her quietly to the door. For a moment, Ray thought of just opening up to her, but thought better of it as he realized that he needed to seek wise counsel from an old friend.

Ray picked up the phone and dialed the number that gave him comfort.

"Hello?" Annie Mae Foster answered.

"Hi, Annie. How are you?" Ray closed his eyes as he listened to her voice.

"I'm fine, young'un. What's up with you, Dear? You sound downhearted." Annie wiped her hands on her apron as she listened.

"Awww, nothing really. I just wanted to hear your voice."

Annie smiled. "You sound like you did when you were ten and couldn't go out to play because it was raining, Darlin'."

"Do I?" A smile played on his lips. "Awww, Annie, don't go a sayin' that."

Annie's smile widened, "Yep, that's what I'm talking about...does my heart good to hear you talk like that. It makes me remember back when..."

"When Mama was alive?"

"Yes, I guess it makes me remember her. Is that what's wrong with you, boy? Are you missing your mother?"

He ran his hand through his hair. "Well not really...and kind of. I just wish she were here right now so I could talk to her. He lowered his voice, "Annie, what kind of a wife did she want for me?"

Annie cleared her throat, "Well, you're not going to believe this but she did tell me she was praying for your future wife. She wanted her to love you and be faithful to you Ray, that's all."

Ray folded his arms. "Annie, how am I going to know the right one…if there is a right one. I've sort of found somebody that is like no other woman I've met before, but…"

"But what?"

"But I don't know for sure if she'd be faithful and the situation is just impossible. Truthfully, we just can't be together and I know that. I'm just so sorry about the whole thing. I don't know how this happened. I'm so confused."

Annie said a quick prayer before responding. "Ray, I can't say that I know exactly what you're talking about. I expect that you just needed to get your thoughts out in the open. I'll tell you one thing though. The Lord is faithful and He will work it out. If you are following Him and it's meant for the two of you to be together then it will happen, Son."

"I guess that's what's bothering me. I don't think it's going to happen and I want it to. I wish I could just stop thinking about it." He picked up a pen and began to doodle while he finished his conversation with Annie Mae.

By the time he hung up the phone, he looked down to see that he had doodled EP+RM all over his calendar. He tossed his pen up in the air and threw the paper into the trash.

Chapter EIGHT

"To Everything There is A Season." Ecclesiastes 3:1aNKJV

The phone rang. Ray waited for Rebecca to get it. After three rings, he picked it up. "Hello, this is Ray Morgan. How may I help you?"

"Hi, Ray, this is Eric. I was wondering if I might come up and talk to you just a minute. I'm down in the lobby and wanted to make sure you weren't busy before I intruded."

"Come on up, Eric. I think Rebecca has left her desk for a minute."

It didn't take Eric long to find the familiar office. Ray shook Eric's hand. "To what do I owe the honor?"

Eric took the seat offered to him and said, "I've been thinking about that job offer. It's been awhile since I worked for this company but I think I'd be willing to come back on the terms that we discussed the other night. Are you still interested?"

"Sure, I'm interested. I'd be crazy not to be. You have a brilliant mind and excellent leadership skills. I think that you're exactly what Wright and Wingold is looking for. I'll need to go over this with my partner and the board, but I don't think it'll be a problem. I've tried to keep him abreast of what we've discussed." Ray was relieved that Eric decided to take the position. He couldn't think of anyone he'd rather have working on his team.

Eric was tempted to question the identity of the silent partner. Everyone at Wright and Wingold knew that Ray didn't "run the show" by himself, but apparently, his partner was content to allow others to think that he did. He also knew that the board had been given the authority over the business, but Ray and his partner were the backbone of its success. Eric decided that if Ray trusted him enough to elaborate at some point about the secret, he would do so without Eric having to ask him to.

The two men talked for a while about the plans for the company. Ray gave Eric an update on changes that had been made since he'd worked for them more than five years earlier. Ray asked Eric when he would be able to begin working full time. Eric admitted that two weeks would give him adequate time to get everything he needed in order. Eric knew that once he began working, he would be spending most of his time there and he wouldn't have time for himself until he was operating efficiently in his new role. Eric was a perfectionist and wouldn't stop working until he felt as if he had earned his wages. Ray asked, "Can you start in three weeks...maybe four?"

"Three weeks? I guess so. Actually, that would be great, but..." Eric looked puzzled. He had thought that Ray needed him sooner.

Ray smiled as he extended his hand to Eric. "I know, I know...I was thinking that I would love to have you sooner, but I'm kind of wanting you to go with me on a trip of a personal nature. I have a speaking engagement in a few weeks. If you want, you can go with me. We'll spend some time getting re-acquainted in an informal atmosphere. Maybe we can spend a day playing some golf and see how competitive we are five years after the great tournament. After that, we'll come back and be all business. What do you think?" Ray hoped Eric wanted to go. He wanted to get to know Eric again and make sure he wasn't making the same mistake as he had made with Fred. The trip would include some comprehensive brainstorming about the current status of the company.

Eric squinted and purposely withdrew his hand. "Don't remind me of that tournament. Why did you have to do that? Sure, I'll go with you, as long as we don't golf on opposite teams."

Ray laughed then agreed. He needed the time away from work as much as he hated to admit it. Maybe the thing he needed most was a little time with a fellow bachelor to get his mind off of the fair Elizabeth.

Elizabeth looked at the clock over the office door. The day was over and she wondered where the time had gone. The rumor mill, as

Discovering Elizabeth

productive as ever, broadcast the news that Jillian and Fred were no longer employed. Most had assumed that one absence had something to do with the other.

At the end of the day, Elizabeth gathered her things to prepare to leave. She had hoped Ray would stop by to see her, but he didn't. She was weary of analyzing the possible reasons why he hadn't made any more attempts to talk with her. By the time she was sitting in her car to leave, she had decided that she didn't have the time or strength to deal with what seemed to be an emotional roller coaster. Perhaps she was infatuated and perhaps this relationship thing wasn't a good idea.

Gabrielle's vehicle was nowhere in sight when Elizabeth drove into the driveway. She remembered that Gabrielle had been called away to New York. The note Gabrielle had left on the table said that she hoped to return by the week's end. Elizabeth kicked off her shoes while throwing her briefcase down on the floor by the couch. She wanted to run to her room and throw herself over the bed. She decided instead, to take a long bath and put on her thickest flannel nightgown. In her opinion, there was nothing more wonderful to make her feel warm and snuggly than a granny gown. After bathing, she lotioned her tired feet then slipped into a pair of fuzzy slippers. Elizabeth grabbed a pillow and blanket then padded to the living room.

She rummaged through the video cabinet until she became frustrated. "Scarlet O'Hara, where are you, Darlin'?" Elizabeth was still talking to herself when she heard a knock on the door. As she straightened the towel on her head, the knock became more persistent. She frowned, picked up her movie and headed for the entrance to her home. She was in no mood for any type of salesman. She made sure the chain was on the door then pulled the door open enough to see who was interrupting her planned evening of self-pity.

"Hello, Liz, can we talk?" Ray Morgan stood less than two feet from her toweled head. He didn't seem to notice that she wasn't dressed for visitors as he awaited her response.

"How did you know where I live?" As Elizabeth anticipated an explanation she touched her towel in one self-conscious movement. "I'm not really..." Liz paused, then swallowed every ounce of pride as she reluctantly murmured, "Well, come on in." Elizabeth stepped back to allow him room for entrance.

Lisa D. Piper

He stepped through the door and suppressed the desire to put his arms around one well-worn flannel granny gown. The reason for his visit caused his heart to lurch in a tangible way. He wasn't sure what a heart attack felt like, but it couldn't have been a lot different than what he was feeling, he reasoned. As he looked at her, he envisioned walking through the door to a home they would call their own and seeing her dressed just as she was now. He would say, "Liz, I'm home." He would then shower kisses on his lovely bride. The thought of what could never happen began to torment him.

"Liz, I know this is unexpected, but I needed to talk and I need to be away from work when I do. I hate to bother you but I just can't wait." He followed her lead and sat on the couch next to her. He looked at the tape she still held in her hand and then read it aloud, "Gone with the Wind?"

Elizabeth smiled and said, "Yes, Sir. My plans for tonight consist of being cuddled up with Gabby's HoneyBear cover, and losing myself in Tara."

"Bad day, huh? I know what you mean." Ray smiled kindly then paused. "I guess I had better get to what I came here to discuss with you. I'm so sorry about barging in here...is this okay?" He looked at the floor as if he were looking for something.

Elizabeth nervously pulled at an unraveled thread from her robe as she waited for what must be bad news. She prayed she would not do as she felt she was about to do and throw up. She forced herself to speak, "What is it, Ray?"

Every fiber of his being wanted to back out of what he was about to say; yet he wouldn't allow himself to do the thing he wanted most. "Elizabeth, I don't think that I've made it a secret that I'm interested in you. Well, I guess I'm more than interested." He held up his hand as if to stop himself from continuing on that thought. Out of breath, he continued, "Elizabeth, I'm inappropriately interested in you. I've worked hard to make sure and follow the rules and do what I expect of others. I guess I shouldn't really even be here alone with you. Even so, I wouldn't want anyone else around to overhear, so this is as good a place as any other." Ray resisted the urge to take her hand. "I have been out of line. My position at Wright and Wingold has certain responsibilities, as you know, and I can't place my own desires in front of the company's best interests. I'm afraid that my interest in you

Discovering Elizabeth

breaches any confidence you may have had in me as a leader. A relationship between us would also place you in a very difficult situation. Liz, I couldn't stand to hear rumors about you or our relationship circulating the corridors of work. I know that there would be those who would talk about you and insinuate that you have gotten where you are now by becoming involved with me. I have seen it happen before and when that happens, it places so much stress on a relationship that the relationship is torn apart. I know that we shouldn't worry about idle talk, but Liz, I just can't justify supplying the wood and matches to the gossips that exist at Wright and Wingold. I know that you're aware that, as the CEO, I shouldn't date anyone in the company. Liz, this is killing me; but unless God provides a way, I can't continue to do what I want to do in this situation." When he finished his drawn out speech, Elizabeth could see the indecision and conflict that was tearing him apart.

Elizabeth touched his arm and forced herself to say, "I understand." She didn't understand. She didn't like what he was saying; and she definitely was not happy about it, but she knew that to say so would be futile.

Ray looked more torn than he had when he first began as he said, "Elizabeth, I don't know why you aren't just plain upset with me."

She didn't remove her hand from his arm; she just couldn't. "Ray, I can't be upset with you. You wouldn't be so frustrated by all of this if you weren't truly interested in me, and because of that I don't feel so rejected." Elizabeth sat for a moment and decided to make a request of the man whom she wanted to be with so desperately. She wasn't a brassy, forward type of woman. However, as she sat there thinking of the unfairness of the situation, she decided to be a little selfish. She just had to ask him. She knew that granting her request would mean future torment, but she didn't care.

"Ray, I'm trying to understand, and you don't owe me anything. I do have one request". Elizabeth stammered, "I've one last request from you of a personal nature."

Ray's throat began to contract. How could he deny her anything? "What is it?" His question was softer than a whisper.

"I'm a Christian woman and I want you to remember that so you don't think I'm asking you for a fling." Elizabeth started to retract her question, but didn't think she would breathe the next breath if she didn't ask. "Ray, you're here this evening. This is the last time I'll see you in this kind of setting. Would you prolong this decision just a little longer? We can go back to work tomorrow as the CEO and Accounting Manager, but let's make that tomorrow. Ray, I have never asked any man to stay longer with me when he wanted to leave. I don't want you to go." Elizabeth could see that Ray's eyes were revealing the inner turmoil her question evoked. "Listen, you don't have to stay late. We can fix some munchies and watch Scarlet. Just this once, Ray, let's forget our titles and just have a couple of hours together." Elizabeth wouldn't reveal it to him, but she needed him. She felt so safe when he was near her, and she became sick in the depth of her stomach at the very thought that this night would end all too soon. "Ray?" Elizabeth called his name as if asking one more time for the favor. Her eyes were passionate, and her request was urgent.

Ray's mind raced. Sanity bellowed that he should get up and leave immediately; however, his feelings for Elizabeth wouldn't allow him to run. He was sure he wanted more time with her than she did with him.

Tuesday morning found Elizabeth in an emotional mess. She couldn't figure out what was wrong with her. The evening before had been so wonderful. Elizabeth had made her famous chip dip with Ray's help. Together they had watched her favorite movie. It was the first time Elizabeth had ever been so thankful that the movie was the length of a double feature. At some point during the show, her head found Ray's shoulder and it didn't move after it discovered this marvelous resting-place. They enjoyed the movie, but relished the company. After the long movie ended, Elizabeth and Ray took turns giving their version of how they thought the movie should have ended.

Ray wanted to kiss her but decided that it would be one memory he didn't want haunting him for eternity. The two talked about their own lives and dreams for about an hour after show time. Although they enjoyed one another's company, the fact it wouldn't be the same again hung between them. Elizabeth hesitated before asking him the question she should have asked at work. "Ray, I know this isn't a good time, but I need some time off. I'm going to need some time to think about what I want to do." She wanted to add, "without you," but decided that she shouldn't. "Gabby wants us to go on a vacation. Gabby was so sure that I could go and so excited about it that she has already made all of

Discovering Elizabeth

the arrangements. Do you foresee a problem with me going if I can get an assistant hired before then?"

Ray looked at her for a while. She was hurting and he knew it. Time away would do her some good and might cause the rumor mill to work a little slower. "Sure, no problem."

When he stood to leave, Elizabeth had wanted to scream for him not to go. She wanted to find a reason for him to stay but she knew that she would be stalling the inevitable. As she opened the door to allow him to exit she breathed, "Good-bye Ray." He wanted to pick her up and hold her tightly to himself. He didn't.

He waved at her and said, "Good-bye, Liz." She watched the most incredible man she had ever known walk toward his car, and leave her alone. She had crawled to her kneeling place beside her bed and called out to the all-knowing God whom she knew loved her. She went to sleep hiccupping from the aftermath of the onslaught of a torrential rainstorm right there in her little bedroom.

Elizabeth had trouble believing that the night before had happened. She reassured herself that it was real so she wouldn't forget. She prayed that God would give her the guidance she needed to face the office on what turned out to be a drizzly Tuesday morning.

Lisa D. Piper

Chapter NINE

"He has made everything beautiful in its time." Ecclesiastes 3:11 NKJV

Elizabeth was never happier to see four o'clock on a Friday. The week had been more than trying. She was looking forward to Sunday morning services where she would just soak in the presence of the One who knew what the future would provide for her. She'd done preliminary interviews for those interested in the vacant assistant position. She thought that she would spend the last few minutes of work organizing for the next week.

She picked up her purse and briefcase while allowing her shoulders to sag. She was relieved to be going home. Gabby would be returning soon. Her need to pour her heart out to her friend was overwhelming.

Elizabeth heard a door open as a female voice called, "Ms. Pennington?" She spun around to see a timid Sophie. "May I speak with you? I know that it's late. It's taken me all week to get the courage to come and see you. May I have a minute of your time?"

Elizabeth hadn't seen Sophie since the day of the Jillian fiasco. She made a point to place her purse on her desk and smile a welcoming smile to the distressed woman. "Hi Sophie, how may I help you?"

Thankful for the way in which Elizabeth was addressing her, Sophie said, "I want to tell you that I'm so sorry about what happened downstairs the other day. I have thought about what you said, and realize that I never gave you an opportunity as a professional woman before that day. I listened to anything that was said to me and accepted it as truth. I was so foolish. I was doing something to you I wouldn't have wanted done to me. I'll admit that my first reaction to you was mistrust. It's taken some time for me to see that my attitude toward you and what I was participating in was affecting my performance. I guess I just want to let you know that I'm thankful for your patience with me and that I'm trying to change as you suggested."

Elizabeth sat quietly until Sophie had finished. "What did I suggest?"

Sophie looked at her shyly and said, "You gave me an example of a child who was tortured by some bullies." Sophie paused and then added, "I used to be that kid. I guess I forgot what it felt like when I became the one who was watching the slaughter of someone who was ignorant of what was going on. I assisted in making a victim of the defenseless."

Elizabeth could tell that Sophie was sincere. She extended her hand to Sophie. "All is forgiven. Thank you for sharing that with me. I guess we all need confirmation of what we do that affects others in a positive way. Thank you, Sophie."

Sophie glowed with pleasure at the manner in which Elizabeth accepted her apology. "Thank you! I almost didn't come here, but I'm so glad I did. Please let me know if I can do anything for you." Once again Sophie looked uncomfortable as she acknowledged the fact that she knew Jillian was no longer with the company. Elizabeth didn't know that Jillian had phoned Sophie only hours before Sophie's visit to Elizabeth to try to spread lies about Elizabeth and Ray Morgan. Sophie had done what she had promised she would do. She had told Jillian that she was sorry that she was upset, but that she wouldn't sit and listen to gossip from her or anyone any longer. Sophie opted to not share this conversation with Elizabeth for the very reason she had ended the conversation with Jillian. She didn't want to gossip or even appear to be a gossip ever again.

Sophie clarified her statement to Elizabeth. "I mean, I know you're short staffed. I saw the posting at the beginning of the week for Jillian's job. I'm not here to discuss that. I just want you to know that if you need any additional help, let me know and I'd be happy to do whatever I can."

Discovering Elizabeth

Elizabeth thanked Sophie and tried to end the conversation with humor by saying, "Unless you know something about the calculations set up by the new company we signed on last week to do a custom billing, I don't need anything right now. I may take you up on the offer in the near future, however." Elizabeth gave a small laugh at her own lighthearted, flippant remark, hoping that Sophie wouldn't think that she didn't want her help. Elizabeth just didn't have the time to explain what she needed to have done. By the time it would take her to explain, she would be well on her way to discovering whatever she had needed to know for herself.

Sophie thought for a moment and said, "Are you talking about the Smithton account and the 40 day rotating cycle?"

Elizabeth was shocked. "How do you know about that?"

Sophie could have told Elizabeth that Jillian hadn't been the efficient assistant she had portrayed and professed to be. She decided not to mention how she knew the account so well. Jillian couldn't juggle all of the activities that she had needed to do. Her solution to this challenge was to gather all of the work, tote it to Sophie, and leave it for Sophie to sort through. An organizing genius with the creative skills of an architect, Sophie was able to manipulate her own work to help the troubled Jillian. At the time, Jillian had explained that she couldn't complete all of her work because Elizabeth was so demanding. Sophie had believed the lies without question. The positive result was that maybe she could make up for what she had allowed to happen with Elizabeth by providing help to the woman who had begun to win her confidence. "I've worked with Jillian to get work done and most of the time all of the forms pass by my desk either for filing or follow-up. What is it that's giving you difficulty?"

Elizabeth explained the predicament and within minutes Sophie had turned on the computer, accessed the correct file, inserted an equation and fixed what could have been an accounting disaster.

Elizabeth wanted to hug the woman. Sophie was more than pleased with Elizabeth's personal reaction. She glowed with the sensation that could only come from truly being appreciated. There would be a time to come in the future when Elizabeth's investment of time and appreciation would build a loyalty from Sophie that could not be manufactured nor purchased. Sophie had felt that no one had ever noticed her contributions to the company; much like what she felt during her years of growing up.

Elizabeth and Sophie walked to the parking garage together and discussed other problems that had arisen since the absence of Jillian. Elizabeth was relieved to know that she wasn't completely at a loss since Sophie seemed to know the routine pretty well.

Gabby wasn't home when Elizabeth drove into the quaint driveway. Elizabeth sighed with disappointment. After shedding her business wear, she decided to check the phone messages just in case Gabby had called. She would then make something special for her buddy's coming home surprise. There were two messages on the machine. The first one was Rebecca needing some information on a cruise line that Elizabeth had traveled a few years ago. The second one was Gabby's friendly voice saying that she would not be home until Saturday morning.

Frustrated and emotional, Elizabeth decided that she just wanted to be around other people. She brushed her hair, then French braided the golden strands into a long rope. She inserted fun looking earrings, pulled out her tennis shoes and found an old denim purse to carry as a useful accessory. She didn't feel like doting over her looks, but figured that the better she looked, the better she would feel. Her theory was correct. She was confident in her looks and that knowledge seemed to give her the nerve to do what she normally would not do; eat alone.

As Elizabeth was driving through the downtown traffic, she looked for a place to waste some time. Her church was supposed to have had a singles night out, but she couldn't remember where the designated meeting place was to be. She and Gab didn't usually attend the functions. They didn't avoid them on purpose; it just seemed as if they never had the time to join in on the activities. As Elizabeth saw the sign advertising, "Yancey's Family Comedy Barn and Grill", she called out, "That's the place!" Elizabeth pulled into the parking lot then checked her watch. Anyone planning to meet from church should have already been seated by now. Elizabeth made sure that her hair was still hanging in a neat braid then slowly walked toward the restaurant.

Moments went by before Elizabeth's eyes adjusted to the darkness. She looked around and immediately saw some faces she recognized. Joe Mason, the group leader, saw her and motioned for her to join them. The excited group sat near the front of the stage. Heads turned as Joe motioned for Elizabeth to join them. A patron sitting in the balcony

Discovering Elizabeth

was particularly interested in the commotion as Elizabeth made her way to the table where her friends were happily munching on peanuts.

"Hey, Liz, glad to see you!" Joe gave her a quick, brotherly hug. Elizabeth was grateful for their kindness. She was greeted by Mary Stelp, the pianist; Josie Burnard, the Youth Sunday School teacher; Kenny Lillian, who helped do whatever needed to be done; and Jay Armstrong, who led the children's choir.

Elizabeth was glad to be among friends, as she knew it would bring comfort to her in a time of emotional upheaval. These men and women had spent time in prayer for her many, many times.

The first act came on as Elizabeth was eating her favorite appetizer: cheese sticks with marinara sauce. The man was too funny. His act was based upon the irony that most men and woman marry opposites. As he unfolded the humorous tale of his inability to understand the "woman blessing", the crowd cackled. Elizabeth had to hold her sides. Jay began sticking her in the ribs with the end of his fork. Mary slapped him on the arm for his efforts and reminded him that he wasn't the stage act. As the man continued with his stories Joe leaned over to Elizabeth and said, "He's revealing the reasons why I haven't been married."

Elizabeth laughed at his self-imposed teasing. Joe gave her a friendly shoulder slap and said, "I've been seeking only the attentions of those females who are exactly like me. If only opposites attract then that's why I can't attract a mate."

Elizabeth bit the bait. "What do you mean?"

Joe's eyes twinkled. "Well, if I've been doing it the wrong way to attract, then I've been successful in doing the opposite. Which is subtract, right?"

Elizabeth looked at the man with disbelief and hooted with laughter. "Joe, if anyone could cause a girl to subtract, it would be you!"

Joe enjoyed the teasing. He had been a teacher for eight years and was liked by everyone Elizabeth knew. He was a tall, thin, intelligent sort of gentleman. Joe looked as if he could've been Elizabeth's natural born brother. He picked at her enough for him to qualify as a blood brother, and he loved to remind her of that very thing.

Lisa D. Piper

Everyone was having a good time. Everyone that is, except a man in the balcony, who didn't find anything he was looking at amusing.

Homer and Annie had been worried about Ray. Homer had noticed that Ray seemed to be distressed over something. Annie had urged Ray to accompany the elderly couple to the Comedy Barn, which was Homer's favorite hangout-outside of Annie's kitchen. Ray seethed as he saw the man touch his accounting manager. For all he knew, Elizabeth had just treated him as she would any other male. His first thoughts were to go down to the floor and make her face him while sitting with her little boyfriend. After thinking about it, he decided that there was no reason for him to do such a thing. He had already told her that they couldn't become involved. He had no intention of ever becoming involved with the woman. He berated himself for being bothered with any jealousy. He couldn't face her when he had no right to demand anything personally. He was thankful that he had driven his own car to meet his friends. As soon as he could leave without appearing to be rude, he would do it. The display was making him nauseated. He tried not to look at her. She looked as if she didn't have a care in the world and it sickened him. While he was sick to be with her, she was unaffected. He willed himself to not look at her. He couldn't stand to see her smiling so beautifully in the direction of another man.

As Ray purposely avoided the view, Annie looked toward Homer. Homer acknowledged the worried expression that lined his wife's astute face.

Ray wanted to leave the building. The reality of his decision to not pursue a relationship with the woman who sat laughing at a table of strangers seemed to escalate his pain. He had to have known that if he didn't want her or couldn't have her then some man would ultimately make her his own. He began to think about the past. "Perhaps this is the best. I wouldn't have wanted to become involved with a woman like Felicia," he thought. Deception was something that he just couldn't tolerate. As Ray looked on, the oxygen he had just breathed in turned into a suffocating element. He had to leave. He couldn't tolerate his thoughts or her display any longer.

Elizabeth found that she had more fun at the Barn than she ever thought she could have after mourning for Ray. The camaraderie of the group helped to loosen the tension she had felt mounting since the Monday before. The group was in such a good mood, she wasn't sure

Discovering Elizabeth

if the comedians were as funny as they thought they were, or if the crowd was just happy and joyful. The only regret she had was that Gabby wasn't with her to experience the fun.

After the last act, the group decided to go visit the beach for a moonlit walk. Elizabeth didn't want to go near the beach. She had lost her heart there and didn't think she could stand the collage of memories the sparkling sand would generate.

As the singles left the food area, Elizabeth thought she saw a familiar face. She told the group to go on to the beach and that she would see them on Sunday. She made her way to the side of the building where she met a smiling Homer who was waiting for the crowd to clear out before trying to exit from the building.

"Hello, Mr. and Mrs. Foster, I'm so glad to see you. Did you enjoy the show?" Elizabeth extended her hand to Homer.

Annie held out her delicate hand to Elizabeth and continued to hold it as she said, "Hello, my dear, we did enjoy the show, did you?"

"Oh, yes I did. I really needed a good laugh tonight." Elizabeth felt as if she were talking to close family. She wasn't certain what had given her the right to feel this way about two persons she hardly knew but she couldn't seem to keep from it.

Homer watched as his wife spoke to Elizabeth. All Homer could think of was that the girl was absolutely beautiful. This would be the kind of woman that could break through the layers of invisible armor that Ray had kept around him since his college days with Felicia. Homer could see the genuine caring personality in Elizabeth. It seemed to declare itself through the way she talked, looked, and responded to those around her. He wasn't sure but something about the young lady reminded him of Annie Mae Wright more than a few decades earlier.

Annie asked Elizabeth if she and Homer were keeping her from joining her friends. Annie had figured out what had been disturbing Ray all evening and was relieved as Elizabeth unknowingly explained her relationship with those around her. Annie smiled as she realized that Elizabeth wasn't involved with any of the men who had been seated with her.

Elizabeth explained, "They're going for a walk. The singles group from my church meets once a month to support each other and have some clean fun. I have had a really difficult week." Elizabeth lost her smile for a moment but recovered quickly. "My roommate is out of town until tomorrow morning and I was…I was tired of basking in my sorrows. I didn't want to spend the entire evening at home without my roommate so I decided to do something. I was thrilled to see my friends here, and I think it was good for me. I feel so much better."

"I'm glad. Dear. Say, would you like to go to the Frozen Blizzard and get a double dipper with us? We'd love for you to come along!" Annie looked so excited about the possibility that she might join them that Elizabeth just couldn't say no.

Homer smiled in agreement with his wife, so Elizabeth told them that she wouldn't resist the temptation of the treat of spending time with the loving couple. Elizabeth consented to meet them at the snack shop in ten minutes.

"Homer! You look like a ten-year-old little boy. Get back from that glass so we can all see the flavors!" Annie fussed at her husband and then teased him while talking to Elizabeth. "Homer here has more than an obsession with ice cream. He has a love affair with pecan praline."

"Now, my sweets, don't go getting yourself into a tizzy. I've got a decision to be makin' and an important one at that. I'll not have you rushing me." Homer looked back at the ice cream display after winking at his wife while rubbing his tummy.

Annie rolled her eyes and placed her hands on her hips. "Homer, quit your confounded childishness! You always get the same thing so order it and be done with it! Elizabeth and I want to get our order in before closing time!" Homer turned and swiftly gave his wife a quick peck on the cheek. Annie blushed and tried her best to keep the grin that was developing around her mouth from forming.

Homer put up his hand to place his order and said, "One double-dipper praline pecan and heavy on the praline, Miss!"

Elizabeth hadn't expected to have such pleasure in the company of the couple. Before she parted from the Foster's company, she decided that she wanted a marriage just like the one that Homer and Annie had built. Elizabeth shared this with Annie while Annie beamed with pride. A certain businessman had also made Annie swell with joy when he had shared his feelings with her and told her the exact same desire.

Discovering Elizabeth

After the mini ice cream social, Elizabeth went home. While getting dressed for bed she examined the strange emotions she was feeling. She still felt lonely but a new numbness seemed to well up inside of her.

As she thought over the surprise about Sophie and the evening with Homer and Annie, she decided that she felt like she was on a runaway train. She figured that she would sleep for a full eight hours, unlike the previous Friday night, so she didn't even turn the alarm clock on before snuggling into her covers.

With the realization that there was a noise in the house, Elizabeth rolled over and tried to concentrate. Even her breathing was too loud for her, so she lifted her head from the bed to be able to listen intently. After listening for a moment, Elizabeth recognized the rattle of Gabrielle's keys as she opened up the junk drawer then threw her things into the unorganized collage of miscellaneous debris. Elizabeth ran to the kitchen and shouted, "Gabby, I'm so glad that you're home!"

Gabrielle didn't remember ever having such a grand reception from her friend. Gabrielle turned and tried to smile; however, Elizabeth wasn't prepared for the haggard look on her roommate's face. "Oh, Gab, what's the matter?" Elizabeth drew her friend to her as Gabrielle burst into tears. Elizabeth patted Gabrielle on the back of the head while allowing her friend to cry on her shoulder.

Elizabeth led Gabby to the living room where she collapsed on the couch. Elizabeth retrieved a box of tissues. She had avoided the living room since the first night of Gabby's absence. Elizabeth pushed her own pain to the back of her mind as she sought to comfort her lifelong friend.

"What's the matter?"

Gabrielle covered her face. "I don't know what to say. I'm so embarrassed."

Elizabeth couldn't think of one thing that would have made her friend so upset. "Okay, you don't have to tell me. Just let me know what you need."

Gabby began sobbing deeply. "But, I want to tell you. You look away from me. I don't want to see your face when you hear what I have to say. This is going to affect you too."

Lisa D. Piper

"Affect me? What are you talking about, Gabrielle?"

Gabrielle hiccupped, "Don't look at me. It will affect you; it will affect us! I don't want your pity Liz, so don't look at me when I tell you."

"Disease!" Elizabeth thought. Elizabeth's mind began reeling. "She is sick! Oh Lord, please don't let it be." As she finished her silent prayer, she closed her eyes and said, "Go ahead. I can take whatever it is."

Gabby stopped sniffling then looked at her friend. Elizabeth truly looked concerned, but how would she take the news? "Elizabeth, I've been fired."

"Oh, Thank the Lord!" Elizabeth sighed.

"What? Excuse me?" Gabrielle sat back in shock.

"No, no, no, I mean I'm shocked at the news but I thought you were going to tell me that you were dying or something. Never mind. Gab, what happened?" Gabrielle knew that Elizabeth's exceptional imagination probably did have her dying the moment Gabrielle said she had bad news. The effort to explain was exhausting.

Gabby began wringing her hands. "Well, you know how I can react sometimes? Well, I went to New York to audit a firm that wasn't doing well in a part of an audit. One of the managers asked me out shortly after I got there. I told him that I could not, of course." Elizabeth sat quietly. "I noticed that he kept staring at me but I ignored him until he walked up behind me and grabbed me."

Elizabeth gasped. "Oh my! What did you do."

"Well, as you can imagine, it took me by surprise. I turned around and elbowed him in the face. He's just a bit shorter than I am. I was so upset by what he had done that before he could recover from the blow to the nose, I pounded on him." The hilarity of the facial expressions that Elizabeth began exhibiting caused Gabrielle to lighten the news. Gabby smiled through her tears. "Let's put it this way; I am positive that he will not look like his old self for quite some time. That isn't necessarily a bad thing. I think everyone is tired of looking at his old self."

"What do you mean?"

Discovering Elizabeth

Gabby played with the fringe on the pillow by her side then said under her breath, "I broke his nose."

"What?" Elizabeth looked confused.

"I broke his nose and he has two black eyes. He also has no job, but neither do I." Gabby held up her hand to keep Elizabeth from protesting. "Liz, we have a policy about how to handle these types of situations. I didn't follow it. If I were treated in a manner that is inappropriate, then I should have notified my supervisor and reported what had happened. That is what I should have done, but something happened to me and I just went off on him. I take responsibility for what I did. You know the old saying: two wrongs do not make a right. It makes sense that my company couldn't possibly sit back and do nothing to me when the CEO's son is no longer climbing the corporate ladder. Yes, it's political to a degree."

"It's your career!" Elizabeth couldn't believe what she was hearing.

Strength that Gabby hadn't felt until she told Liz everything brought her hope. "Liz, I'm upset and still bewildered by what has happened. I can't help but know that this isn't a surprise to God. The Bible says that the Lord orders the steps of the righteous[9]. I don't know what I will do, but I will trust in His ability to take care of me." Gabby looked very determined to do what she had said she would do even if it didn't feel like everything was going to be okay at that moment.

Gabrielle began to weep again. Elizabeth looked at her and tried to comfort her with friendship while she allowed her own tears to flood from deep inside. "Here you are with your life turned upside down and you're declaring that you trust in God. I have a little problem and I have a difficult time just giving it to Him. Thank you, Gab, for being such a faithful woman of our Lord. I don't know what I'm going to do but I will trust in Him too, right beside you."

While Gabby napped from her long trip, Elizabeth cleaned the house. She took care of Gabby's luggage and did her laundry. Liz retrieved the only crock-pot they owned and began adding the ingredients to make Gabby's favorite dish: chicken and dumplings.

After completing her chores she sat down and looked over the Pensacola Convention Brochure. Elizabeth sighed, "Yes, this is exactly

---

[9] Psalm 37:23

what we need to do. This is an excellent idea, Gabby." Elizabeth thought about a week without having to go to work or see anything that reminded her of Ray Morgan. "Yes, this is what I need." Elizabeth turned her thoughts to what they would do without the extra income that Gabby brought into their home. She decided that she wouldn't mention the finances to her friend. They would just get caught up on the week's happenings and relax.

"Lord prepare me, to be a sanctuary; pure and Holy, tried and true..."[10] "The chorus played over and over again inside of Elizabeth through the night and into the morning. Elizabeth awoke on Monday morning to the tune of her own singing. She stretched and said, "Good morning, my Lord. Thank you for this day. It is Monday again and I don't think I can get out of this bed without you."

Elizabeth could hear Gabby rummaging in the kitchen and decided to get up and check on her instead of going back to sleep until her alarm went off. She steadied her tired body as she stood to her feet. She found Gabby sitting in the floor surrounded by pots and pans. Gabby looked up and smiled. "Hey Liz, don't worry! I'm cleaning out the cabinets. I'm going to clean this place from top to bottom while I figure out what I'm going to do with myself."

Elizabeth wiped her eyes and looked down at her friend. "Oh! Well, since you're at it, don't forget to clean out my closet, will you!"

Elizabeth turned to walk to the bathroom while Gabrielle yelled after her. "Don't count your chickens! I'm not as brave as to venture where no cleaning lady has gone before!"

Elizabeth giggled and proceeded to begin her morning routine. She was glad to see that Gabrielle was keeping busy and not moping around the house.

Half way through the busy Monday morning, Elizabeth remembered that she was supposed to present a new budget proposal to all of the department heads on Tuesday morning. She began to gather all of the information. Normally, Jillian would have been responsible for logging in the information daily so it would be easy to transfer the logs into a report format. Elizabeth went to Jillian's old desk and tried to get into the appropriate program, but a password prompt stopped her from

---

[10] Sanctuary/John W Thompson/Randy Scruggs

Discovering Elizabeth

proceeding. Elizabeth became frustrated. As she tried to think of a quick resolution, the notion occurred to her that Sophie just might know the password.

Elizabeth picked up the phone and dialed Sophie's extension. Elizabeth was surprised to learn that Sophie indeed knew the password. Apparently Sophie had been the one to keep the log instead of Jillian. Elizabeth thought that was odd but didn't dwell on the fact.

After writing down the password, "Sophie", and gathering the data, Elizabeth made a phone call to Rebecca. "Rebecca, would you try to make an appointment with Mr. Morgan for me today? I really need to speak with him about Jillian's old position. It'll only take a few minutes." Elizabeth waited in dread.

Rebecca asked Elizabeth to hold then said, "Elizabeth, he doesn't have any openings today.... But hold on a moment."

Ray had been standing beside the desk as he was leaving for lunch. He took the phone from Rebecca and said, "Elizabeth, my schedule is packed today. I have a few minutes to run and get a bite to eat at that place where they make the homemade bread. If you want to walk over there, I'll lend an ear."

Elizabeth swallowed. She didn't want to spend time with him outside of the office. Ray was thinking the same thing, but he was trying to place the business's needs before the relief of his own misery. Elizabeth thought about it and decided she really needed to talk with him. "Okay, I'll be over in a few minutes. Ray, I wouldn't have bothered you, but with Fred gone, I..."

Ray reassured her, "I understand. We're all being spread thinly. I'll see you in a few minutes."

Ray was smothering a piece of bread with a glob of honey butter by the time Elizabeth arrived. She stiffened her back, then slid into the seat across from him.

He passed the basket of breads toward her and then took a bite of the tasty roll. He didn't give her any indication that he remembered holding her in his arms. It didn't seem to Elizabeth that he was even affected by the decision not to pursue a relationship with her. She was relieved yet hurt, then berated herself silently, "What did I expect?"

Lisa D. Piper

Elizabeth repositioned herself in her chair then proceeded to fill Ray in on her thoughts about Sophie. Ray raised an eyebrow and asked, "Didn't you say that Sophie was the one who was in the desk huddle with Jillian?"

"Yes, she's the one. Ray, uh, Mr. Morgan, you said...."

Ray interrupted, "Ray will do."

Elizabeth became visibly uncomfortable with Ray's directness. She wouldn't show him that he made her feel vulnerable. She purposely smiled at him and said coolly, "Ray it is." Ray's breathing stopped momentarily at the sound of his name.

"Ray, you told me to address situations as they arise. I've been doing that. I corrected, or coached rather, what I thought needed to be addressed with Sophie. She received the coaching well and has put forth an effort to do better. She knows how to do Jillian's job because she had been deceived into doing it all along. I do want to talk with her about how to challenge a decision or directive in an appropriate manner, but I really would like to work with her. If you had told me that I would've been inquiring about this even one week ago, I wouldn't have believed it. I have had misconceptions about the woman because of one circumstance, just as she had about me."

Ray sat for a moment then consented with more than one reservation. "Liz...Elizabeth, you do what you think is appropriate. I have to be open with you and tell you that you are and will be held accountable for your department. Treat it like it's your own business. I'll give you support if and when you need it, but it's your decision."

Elizabeth smiled at the man who had earned her respect. "I would've been surprised if you had said anything else. I'll remember my responsibility." Elizabeth hesitated then pointedly added, "...and I do take it seriously." After a few serious moments, she decided to let him off the hook and smiled at him.

The smile that had haunted him was again branded in his memory. His arms ached to wrap around her and carry her away from all that they knew. He decided to not respond to her remark about taking her job seriously. He knew what she had meant and knew she probably needed to say it to him.

Discovering Elizabeth

After finishing their meal, the silence became uncomfortable. Elizabeth glanced up to look at her lunch partner one last time before excusing herself.

Midnight blue met blazing hazel eyes; two wounded hearts felt the sear of fresh pain.

Simultaneously, the two leaped from their chairs to declare their need to leave. The joint decision to flee brought wry smiles to the ashen faces. Neither wanted to walk side by side. Elizabeth was the first to think of a plan. She fumbled with a tip then said, "Ray, I need to go powder my nose. I'll see you at the meeting in the morning."

He was relieved, "Okay. See you then."

As Elizabeth turned to go, he remembered the email she had sent. She was quickly making her way to the ladies room when he called out, "Elizabeth! I almost forgot...I received your email reminding me of your vacation. I'm relieved to know that you'll have someone to work in the office while you're gone. I know that you need the time off, so forget work and have some fun." He hoped the fun didn't include any portion of time spent with the man at the Comedy Barn.

Elizabeth turned towards him but didn't walk back to the table. "I saw the memo that you'll be out part of that week too." Elizabeth decided to add some light humor to the conversation. "Do you think the company will be able to survive without us?"

He smiled, "Sure, between Homer and Sophie it should run well. Let's hope that we're missed a little so that we still have jobs when we return. Homer's been itching to try his hand at operating the entire company."

The two waved good-bye. Elizabeth walked toward the restroom mumbling, "Powder my nose? Surely I could have thought of something a little less stupid to say."

Once inside the quaint little room, she looked into the mirror. She saw a businesswoman. She had worn a navy skirt with a while blouse. She had decided on a matching navy blazer, and had placed a small golden broach on her lapel that looked like a little lamb. Her blond hair was pulled back into a neat, sleek twist. No strands were out of place. Her post earrings were no-nonsense and the shoes of choice had been slightly uncomfortable but classic looking in the leather pump fashion.

Lisa D. Piper

As she looked at herself she felt as if she were looking at one of the pictures she had been given in grade school. The picture would depict a scene of a busy street or city. Her task as a child was to look at the picture and circle the objects in the picture that didn't belong. As she stood in front of the mirror, something didn't seem right. She looked okay but what she was feeling on the inside didn't quite match what was being mirrored. Elizabeth suppressed the desire to take her finger and draw an outline on the mirror of herself. She no longer felt like she belonged.

She breathed in the fresh air as she walked back to the building. On her way back she decided to see if Sophie would even be interested in becoming her assistant. Any doubt she had about the decision to offer the job to Sophie was obliterated when she entered Sophie's work area. Elizabeth overheard the gossip coming from Sophie's cubicle as Elizabeth approached.

They hadn't seen her coming. A plump young lady was standing over Sophie while Sophie was apparently trying to work. Her voice was animated as she said, "Sophie, listen to me! This is juicy news! I have it on good authority that it's true!" The woman hurriedly blurted out, "Ray Morgan, our lovely president, is leaving for a week to seek out a replacement for his position! He's being given an ultimatum by Wright and Wingold's silent partner to..."

Sophie swiveled around to look the woman in the face. She looked kind but firm as she said, "Veronica, I have told you that I don't want to hear this. I've tried to be nice, but I'll not sit here and listen to gossip! I know that you have said it isn't gossip, but I have it on good authority that it is. Please do not continue with your story." As Veronica tried to protest, Sophie held out her hand to stop her as she repeated, "I said, I don't want to hear it. If you need anything else relevant to our work, I would love to help."

Veronica sighed deeply as if she had been deflated. "Okay, Sophie. I won't come near you. I want you to know that I'm not gossiping. You'll see what I'm saying is true. Then, you'll wish you still had me to fill you in on what is going on with the "higher ups," but I'm not going to be so willing to share confidential information with someone who considers me to be a talebearer. I'll see you later!" With a defiant look of frustration Veronica finally left Sophie to her work.

Discovering Elizabeth

Elizabeth watched as Sophie rubbed her temples and arched her back as if she had been sitting too long in one position. As Sophie leaned over to pick up the ink pen she had dropped as she was shifting her weight, Sophie saw navy shoes. Her heart seemed to stop and without looking at the owner of the footwear she asked, "How much did you hear?"

Elizabeth calmly responded, "Most of it."

Sophie's shoulders drooped lower. "I'm sorry, Elizabeth, I..."

Elizabeth interrupted, "I know, Sophie. I'm so proud of you."

"You are?" Sophie was still embarrassed by what Elizabeth had obviously heard but responded to the praise by blushing.

"Sophie, I am here because I need to speak with you. Do you have a few minutes?"

Sophie gulped. "Sure, what do you need?"

Elizabeth smiled and proceeded, "Sophie, I need for you to consider a change in your occupation."

Sophie opened her mouth to protest. "What?"

"I'd like for you to become my new assistant."

Sophie was speechless. "What?" Sophie realized that her high pitched voice didn't communicate effectively what she had intended to say. "I can't believe that you would even offer it to me. You've got to know that I haven't the qualifications yet to be able to do the job to your expectations."

Elizabeth thought for a moment and then asked. "What part of the job would you not be able to perform?"

It was Sophie's turn to think. She tried but couldn't think of one aspect of the job she could not do. Sophie grinned and said, "There's nothing that I can't do for you. I'd be more than happy to work beside you, Elizabeth."

"I'm pleased, Sophie. I want you to make the transition quickly. Have you any idea of who could replace you? I need you like yesterday!" Elizabeth smiled kindly.

Sophie was quick to respond. "Actually, we've been using a temp service for coverage when one of us down here has to be gone. There's

Lisa D. Piper

a girl by the name of Susan who has done an excellent job when I've needed her. She is efficient and could step into my shoes with little difficulty since she has been trained for all of the secretarial positions."

Sophie and Elizabeth shook hands and a partnership was formed.

The human resource department contacted Susan. To Elizabeth's delight, Susan accepted the position. Sophie was so organized and efficient that Susan had little trouble taking over Sophie's responsibilities.

Because Susan learned the tasks so quickly, Friday found Elizabeth and Sophie working together to get caught up on the work that had been mounting since Jillian's departure. Both women found that they worked easily as a team. Elizabeth had a suspicion that they were going to make an impressive pair. She had thought that she was satisfied with Jillian until she worked with the incredible Sophie.

Elizabeth knew there were times when Jillian would roll her eyes as Elizabeth walked away. She had ignored the behavior. Elizabeth knew that if she suggested to Jillian that she might need to perform some additional tasks other than those she was used to, Jillian would become silent for the rest of the day. She had no idea that Jillian would pile all of her work onto the secretarial pool downstairs while complaining to the unsuspecting about what kind of load was upon her.

As Elizabeth thought about Jillian, she decided that she needed to have a talk with Sophie. She didn't want to make the mistake of not telling Sophie the expectations for her job. She decided that she would like to be in a more comfortable setting where Sophie would likely consider Elizabeth to be a peer instead of the boss. She dialed Sophie's extension and said, "Sophie, I'm glad that I caught you. You're doing an excellent job and you have made this week bearable! I have something that I need to ask you. You can say no for today, if you want to, but I do want to do this sometime soon."

Sophie continued to look for the error in one of the billings as she responded, "I'm enjoying myself. I'm feeling the strain of new surroundings, but thanks. As for your question, ask away, what is it that you need?"

Elizabeth knew that Sophie was still working as she was talking to her and smiled. Elizabeth often did the same thing when talking on the phone even though it wasn't always a good idea. Elizabeth really had

Discovering Elizabeth

to work to concentrate on one thing at a time, and by the sound of it, Sophie would need the same focus. "Sophie, do you have plans for this evening?"

Sophie stopped what she was doing. "No, I don't, why?"

Elizabeth hurriedly finished the question so that Sophie wouldn't think her to be nosey. "Sophie, I'd like to talk to you about the office and how we will work together, but I'd like to do it in a different setting. I would like to be somewhere where we're not being interrupted, and where we can get to know one another. Would you want to meet for dinner this evening?"

Sophie was surprised. She couldn't believe that Elizabeth Pennington was asking her to dinner. Sophie had been overlooked in every social affair. She was never asked to go places with the girls downstairs when they went out on the weekend. She had never even been asked to stay all night with a friend one time in her life. The invitation from a woman whom Sophie believed to be too classy to associate with her was unbelievable. She knew that the dinner would be a business affair, but just going out was a temptation.

"Sophie? Hello? Please don't say no! Let's go somewhere fun. If we meet at the Comedy Barn before six o'clock, it'll be quiet, so that we can talk. I'm more comfortable in a casual setting, and we can have some fun while the comedians are entertaining us!"

Sophie was even more stunned. She thought that Elizabeth would have only gone to the country club or to a private restaurant. Sophie was about to find out that she had taken the little bit of information that she knew about Elizabeth Pennington and created someone who didn't exist. She was intrigued by the invitation and eventually relented. "That sounds like fun. I'll meet you at six. Do I need to take anything from the office?"

"No. We won't need anything like that. I basically just want to talk. Six it is. I'll be the one who's happy that it's Friday!"

Sophie laughed and hung up the phone as she began to dread the meeting. She just couldn't figure her boss out. Elizabeth had just made a joke about Friday. The only time that Sophie had seen Elizabeth was when she was concentrating on a task. Jillian had said her boss was incapable of making a joke. Before Sophie could stifle the memory of Jillian's words, she began remembering the sneers from some of the girls downstairs. Elizabeth had been the target of more than one joke. Sophie squinted as she remembered what they had called her. Victoria had said that she was the "Queen of Bore!" Veronica had said, "She wouldn't know how to smile if you drew a smiley face on her..." Jillian had always laughed at the remarks but nodded while adding, "Let me tell you girls... She is just plain old personality-challenged."

Sophie sat in disbelief as she recalled past conversations. She had been unaware of the mental garbage she had retained as a result of working around habitual verbal trashing. When the taunts circulated, she had grinned and silently agreed. Something in her had changed. Now she wished that she hadn't even heard the jibes. Sophie determined that she would give Elizabeth a chance. For some reason, the teaching of her grandmother sprang from the past. Sophie would have said that she didn't know any Scripture, but somehow she suddenly remembered something her grandmother had said one day after Sophie came home with tears dried on her face, "Sophie, the Good Book says, 'A man's belly shall be satisfied with the fruit of his mouth; and with the increase of his lips shall he be filled.[11]'" Sophie hadn't known what the verse meant. Once again she was very sorry for what she had heard and said. The thought occurred to her to pray, but she had no idea how to do such a thing.

Elizabeth walked in the door to her home and found Gabrielle putting on her make-up and wearing something she wasn't accustomed to seeing. Gabrielle was wearing jeans and a t-shirt. "What in the world are you doing and where are you going?"

Gabby stood up and put her thumbs in her belt loops then tipped an invisible hat. "Howdy ma'am. I'm a goin' to the rodeo that's in town. Me and the gals at the singles group have challenged the boys to a ropin' contest. Do ya wanna come little missy?"

Elizabeth was so happy to be home. Life was never dull around Gabrielle Storm. "Well, little filly, I don't guess I rightly will. I've got plans of my own. I'm a goin' to Yancey's with Sophie. Tell the guys and gals that I said they better take plenty of pictures." Elizabeth stood back and whistled, "I haven't seen you dressed in jeans in forever. I'm almost jealous. You look so petite and sweet. How do you do it?"

---

[11] Pro. 18:20

Discovering Elizabeth

Gabby wasn't ready to give up her cowgirl character, "Petite? That's stretchin' it pretty fer ma'am. Well, ma'am it's like this. If you got it, you got it. If'n you ain't, wear somethin' that makes ya look like ya do!"

Elizabeth rolled her eyes at Gabrielle's sad attempt at a cowboy drawl. She was very happy to see Gabby looking forward to being with the group. She walked into her own room and found a pair of jeans. The comedy barn didn't require dressing up, and she was very glad. Elizabeth hadn't worn the shirt that Gabby had bought her for her birthday so she decided to make use of it. She wasn't sure what Gabby was thinking when she had picked it out, but after looking in the mirror, she was glad she had it. It may have been a practical joke, but it was perfect for tonight's environment. The smiley face pattern would be perfect for the light atmosphere of her dinner destination. "Hey, Gabby, can I borrow your smiley socks?"

"Not my smiley's, Liz, anything but that! That's my signature pair." Gabby giggled as she went to her room to retrieve her favorite socks. She handed them to Elizabeth and said, "Here is the test of our friendship. If I like someone enough to let them sport my footwear, you can say that we have bonded or something."

Elizabeth muttered, "Or something...what has gotten into you tonight?"

Gabby shrugged her shoulders. "I have no idea. I feel as free as a bird. I don't know where my life is going or what I'm doing and for some reason, I'm at peace. This has got to be the peace that passes understanding that Pastor Matthews spoke about last Sunday."

Elizabeth was left to think over Gabby's last statement. "Why don't I feel like I have that peace? Why do I feel as if I'm in a deep well, just living day by day to survive?" Elizabeth's thoughts were followed by a deep conviction. She knew that she had not truly given Ray to God. She wanted Ray Morgan in her life, and if she were truthful she would have to admit that she didn't really care what God wanted. Her desire was hindering her from discovering the peace Gabby spoke of so often. The fact that God was completely aware of her true feelings made Elizabeth frustrated. No matter what she did, she knew she could hide nothing from her creator.

Lisa D. Piper

Chapter TEN

"The Peace that Passes Understanding." Phil 4:7

Ray Morgan had spent an hour fiddling with his favorite mechanical pencil. He knew that he should be going home. For some reason, he just didn't want to face his quiet house any time soon. Without a reason to stay, he finally got up and walked out if the door. As he was driving through town, he saw a friendly face and without thinking twice he pulled into the gas station where she was standing.

Her back was turned away from him, but he would recognize her anywhere. Her chestnut brown hair hung in a long ponytail and she wore her usual overalls. He walked up to her and said, "Hello, Jessica, what is a nice girl like you doing at a place like this on a Friday evening?"

Jessica Montana whirled around to see what she thought was one of the finest men in the world. "Oh, Ray! How are you doing?" She walked over to him and gave him a brief hug. "How dare you sneak up on me you scalawag!" She pulled at his tie while teasing, "My, my, my, don't we clean up nicely."

Ray laughed aloud, "What did you expect? I'm no longer feeding pigs and carousing with you through the woods, little Jessie."

Jessica snickered. "Don't call me that! By the way, I still have some pictures of you on my dad's farm. I was looking at them just last week. Do you recall the one where you were the recipient of my famous mud pies?"

Lisa D. Piper

Ray placed his finger on his lips as if to quiet her. "Don't remind me. I'm about to go out for dinner; I may not be able to eat if I think about your pies." Ray resisted the desire to ruffle her hair like he did as a boy. "Don't you dare show those pictures to anyone. I happen to be a corporate executive now!" He took his hand and straightened his tie and smoothed down his shirt.

"Yeah right! You need to face the truth, old pal!"

Ray looked puzzled. "And, what truth would that be my old friend?"

Jessica loved every minute of teasing the pal of her youth. "The truth is that you look like a big ole successful businessman and even act like one. But, underneath that pomp and circumstance there's a boy who would still love to walk around in ripped jeans and pretend like he was relishing my fancy mud pies. You can fool the corporate world, but I know how ornery you are."

Ray reared back his head and let out a deep laugh. "Why, I ought to remind you of what I used to do to persnickety, loud mouth females when I didn't like to be teased."

Jessica backed up and picked up the windshield squeegee. "Oh no you don't, Harold Ray Morgan, I've never been afraid to clobber you before, and I'm not afraid to do it now!"

The public display had little effect on Ray. He stood up straight and said, "I won't tickle you until you cry uncle if you don't call me by my first name and if you allow me the privilege of taking my favorite softball pitcher in the world to dinner."

Jessica didn't move. She knew not to trust him too quickly or she might be screaming for mercy. She peered into his eyes and finally said, "Well, I'm not doing anything particular this evening so I will make the deal with you. However, if at any time you decide to tickle me in any fashion, it will be the last thing you do. Also, I don't want to go to some fancy place where I can't wear what I've got on. Do you understand?"

Ray smiled and said, "Perfectly. My car or yours?"

Jessica grinned mischievously, "Ray Morgan, I quit riding around with you after that little run-in with the police. I shall drive."

Discovering Elizabeth

As Ray climbed into her vehicle, he put on his seat belt and said, "That was years ago Jessica, and I was only squealing the tires because you and your sister told me to! No more talk about that, let's go."

For effect, Jessica squealed her tires as they left the gas station. Ray slithered down into his seat as far as he could and Jessica loved every minute of it.

Elizabeth and Sophie pulled into the restaurant simultaneously. Sophie hadn't been sure what she should wear. She had seen patrons coming out of the comedy barn and decided to wear what she saw almost everyone else wear: good old-fashioned jeans and a t-shirt. She had a difficult time hiding the shock of seeing Elizabeth out of work clothes and in smiley face attire. Sophie thought about the remark the girls had made. Elizabeth was smiling as she motioned for the shy Sophie to walk with her to the entrance.

As Sophie tried to decide what she would like to eat, she peered over her menu to look at her dining partner. Elizabeth felt the stare and looked up in time to see Sophie disappear once more behind her menu.

Elizabeth ordered her usual cheese sticks while Sophie decided to try the flowered onion. It was apparent to Elizabeth that Sophie wasn't used to going out so Elizabeth tried to make her comfortable. She learned that Sophie was from a small town in Ohio called Newcomerstown. She had been the eldest of five children and was the only one to move away from home and had never married. Unlike her siblings who had married early, she had elected to get her high school diploma and begin working in an office. Sophie explained that she was taking night classes at a nearby college, but didn't allude to what she was studying. Elizabeth began to find the woman fascinating. Sophie was overwhelmed by the genuine concern Elizabeth seemed to have about her.

Sophie tasted her onion after dipping it in a horseradish sauce. As they chatted about trivial matters, Sophie relaxed. Elizabeth had never considered it before, but Sophie was actually a lovely young woman. She seemed to hide behind a pair of glasses that were too large for her face. Her eyes were the palest hue of blue. Not many people noticed her eyes since Sophie made it a practice to continually look down as if she were too ashamed to look up. Elizabeth decided that Sophie had seen enough of her own shoes and would soon lift her head high when she walked into a room.

Lisa D. Piper

Sophie stirred her cola with her straw then plunged into the question she had been keeping to herself since her arrival. "What is it that you needed to speak to me about, if I may ask?"

Elizabeth took a drink of her own cola and said, "Why, yes, you may ask." Elizabeth positioned her hands on the table where Sophie could see them. She let her relaxed to either side of her as a gesture that she was being open with Sophie. Elizabeth swallowed and smiled as she began to do what she should've done with Jillian.

"Sophie, I'm afraid that I've made some great supervisory errors in the past. I'm trying to continually improve in every way possible. I want to start out our professional relationship by taking some time to tell you what I expect out of our newly formed team. Then, I want to know what you expect."

Sophie's eyes widened. "You want me to tell you what I expect?"

"Sure I do. We all have expectations, and if I don't know what yours are, I won't be able to meet them. And, it may be that one of us or both have unrealistic expectations. I think now is the time to let each other know if our expectations are unreal, so that we won't be disappointed in the long run."

Sophie nodded as Elizabeth continued, "Sophie, I expect for you to treat this department as if it is yours and to do what is best at all times for the company, employees, and our clients. I expect you to be honest, dependable, and friendly. I expect your speech, dress, and attitude to be no less than professional. If you ever have any questions as to what is appropriate, please let me know and we will work it out." Sophie didn't have a problem with any of the expectations until she heard the ones that followed. "I expect you to express your disagreements. If you think I've made a bad decision, then I expect you to tell me and to tell me why you think so. If possible, I would like for you to disagree with me in private and I will do the same with you. If your expectations change in the future, I expect you to let me know. And lastly, I expect you to treat me like you want to be treated and I shall do the same. Does this sound fair to you?"

Sophie didn't want to disagree; she wanted to say it sounded fair. Her first thought was to just agree, but if she did that then she had already begun to not meet Elizabeth's expectations. Sophie was self-

Discovering Elizabeth

conscious as she met Elizabeth's sincere gaze. "Umm-okay-well, I don't know if it is fair or not. May I ask you to clarify something?"

Sophie had just stepped out on a limb and Elizabeth knew it. She knew that if she answered with anything but a true appreciation for her inquiry, Sophie would probably not open up to her about anything that concerned her again. Elizabeth shook her head and said, "Please do."

Sophie took a breath and explained, "You have said that you expect me to tell you when I disagree, if I understand correctly. It's been my experience with other supervisors that disagreeing or pointing out an error has gotten me into more trouble than I wanted. I'm not comfortable with having to disagree with you on any matter. You're the boss. You're the one who's responsible and I don't think that I could make myself interfere where I have no business to do so. I'd be more comfortable if you will just give the orders and I'll do my best to follow them to the best of my ability. I'll not speak of you in a derogatory manner behind your back, on this I give my word."

Elizabeth was momentarily distracted as Sophie finished her speech. She had thought she had seen Ray out of the corner of her eye. The fact that she was still thinking of him no matter what she was doing began to irritate her. Focusing on the conversation at hand would be difficult, but she determined she would do it. Sophie sat in her seat waiting for a response as Elizabeth hurriedly tried to regain control of her thoughts.

Elizabeth began slowly. "Sophie, I think I understand your reservations about what I've asked of you, and I'm so glad that you trusted me enough to share them with me. I want to share some of the reasons that I have asked what I have of you. First of all, we're a team. The accounting department isn't my department; it's ours. It includes every person who works in it and who is affected by it. For example, if Susan saw that you had made an error on an invoice should she tell you or not?"

Sophie was quick to respond. "She should tell me immediately. I think Susan would tell me. She wouldn't want us to look as if we don't know what we're doing." Sophie hated the thought that she might make an error.

Elizabeth calmly stated, "That's exactly correct. If Susan didn't tell you, but told someone downstairs that you had made an error, or kept it to herself I doubt you'd be too happy with her. It's only fair that I'm

Lisa D. Piper

given the same courtesy. Just because my title states that I'm the manager, that doesn't mean that I can't make a mistake. I have to depend on you to be my eyes." Elizabeth knew that she had Sophie's attention so she continued. "Here's an example of what I'm talking about." Elizabeth clasped her hands together in an effort to focus. "If you heard me give information on the telephone to Mr. Morgan that you knew to be incorrect, I would expect you to correct me on it. Just think what might happen if I did that and someone were to find that I made an error that could have been prevented. I wouldn't be happy about it to say the least. If we're afraid to communicate with one another openly, then we'll not function as a team. We've got to take all kinds of feedback from each other. Now, I'm not saying that I would want you making a big deal out of telling me something I could do better...but I would want to know."

Sophie continued to look down and said, "Okay, I see what you mean. But, surely you wouldn't expect me to tell you if I had a personal problem with you."

Elizabeth was direct. "I certainly would. Do you know why partnerships, marriages, teams and families fail? They fail by not communicating. If I hurt your feelings, I want you to tell me. I can assure you that I wouldn't do such a thing on purpose, but things like that can happen, and can affect the development and success of our team. If I pile so much on you that you can't get it done, tell me or I am positive that the pile will just get higher. We can work through anything together if we'll just be open with each other. Now, there will be times that we won't have the same viewpoint, but we can make that an asset too. Sophie, I cannot succeed without your succeeding first. Mr. Morgan can't even succeed if we don't succeed. We're in this thing together."

The couple that had been seated behind Elizabeth had been silent for most of Elizabeth's speech. Sophie had been so engrossed in what Elizabeth was saying that she hadn't even paid any attention until now. Sophie stammered as she commented on what Elizabeth had just told her. "Okay, Elizabeth I understand what I must do. Be assured that it won't be easy for me, but I'll try to do as you ask. And, Elizabeth, there is something you must know right now. I don't want to tell you; however, I think you might want to know." Sophie leaned toward Elizabeth so that no one else could hear.

Discovering Elizabeth

Elizabeth lowered her tone to match Sophie's. "What is it Sophie?"

The hair stood up on Elizabeth's neck when Sophie whispered, "Mr. Morgan is behind you and he's close enough to have heard everything you just said. I'm sorry...I just noticed him."

Elizabeth was more than speechless as she hoped Sophie was joking. As she debated whether to turn around or not, she became aware of his presence behind her. Something similar to panic began to course through her body. She couldn't stay in the same building with him, but how could she flee without looking as if she were hysterical. As Elizabeth tried to breathe normally, she thought of Gabrielle. She thought, "Okay, in times like these Gab would say to do the Barney Fife. Come on Elizabeth, you have the courage to do the Barney Fife." The ridiculous thought of Gabrielle's advice was enough to help her relax.

As Elizabeth thought of how to "Nip it in the Bud," Sophie watched her carefully. Within seconds, Elizabeth smiled a winning smile at Sophie to assure her that everything was okay. "Sophie, is he by himself and are you sure that he heard me saying his name?"

Sophie smiled and whispered, "No, he's with a lady. And, yes, they were listening. You were pretty animated and didn't speak softly. I'm sorry." Sophie sat back to prepare for Elizabeth's response.

Elizabeth turned to say hello to Ray and to greet his friend. She wasn't, however, prepared for her business-suited boss to be sitting with a woman in bibbed overalls. Elizabeth thought her to be beautiful and thought she looked so youthful and fun in her relaxed attire. As Elizabeth turned, she prayed she would be able to speak to the man and his guest without looking like a fool. She smiled at the woman who saw Elizabeth turn first. "Hello. Hello, Mr. Morgan, I'm beginning to think that this town isn't big enough for the both of us." Elizabeth smiled at Ray as she teased him.

Ray was uncomfortable. Didn't Elizabeth even care that he was with another woman? Was everything a joke and fun to her? Then he thought, "Wait a minute. She has the posture like she had when she dealt with Mrs. Peters. Her eyes are that stormy color, and...oh, yes, Ms. Elizabeth Pennington, you are having a bit of difficulty with this situation, aren't you? What would it take to break that icy barrier that you put up when things get difficult?" Ray didn't want to be the one to hurt her or cause her to lose control, but she had caused his curiosity to be piqued. Ray smiled back at Sophie then looked at Elizabeth as he answered. "Why hello, Ms. Pennington." Ray used the same formal address she had used for him. "I'm beginning to wonder if you are following me, or could it be that I'm somehow following you? You were here first." Ray made a hand gesture toward Jessica and said, "Elizabeth, Sophie, this is Jessica Montana. Jessica, I work with these ladies at Wright and Wingold."

After exchanging the greeting, Elizabeth turned back in her seat and looked up at Sophie. Although she was looking ahead, she was very aware of the man sitting behind her.

It was Sophie's turn to make Elizabeth feel comfortable. Sophie decided that she would bring the work topic up again so that Elizabeth could focus on something other than the fact that she had spoken about her boss within his hearing. Sophie didn't understand why Elizabeth seemed so distressed over seeing Ray, but Elizabeth was definitely bothered by it. Sophie decided to keep this observation to herself. "Elizabeth, I will try to meet your expectations and I think I have mine ready for you. Do you want to hear them now?"

Elizabeth looked up at the waiter as he set two large plates of Grilled Chicken Artichoke Salad dripping with Blue cheese dressing in front of them. "I'm more than ready to hear it now, if you don't mind my eating while you talk. I love their salads, and this one is my favorite!"

Sophie took a bite of her salad and had to agree with Elizabeth. After taking a drink of her soda she proceeded. "First of all, I expect you to be truthful and honest with me. If I'm not meeting your expectations, I want to know immediately. I don't want you to tell me in front of anyone, but please talk to me privately when you speak with me about matters that concern you. I've had my share of public humiliation." Elizabeth listened intently as Sophie continued. "I have the expectation that you will understand that I'm going to make mistakes. I want you to know that I'll try to not do anything in error twice. However, if I am going to be accountable for what's going on in the operations, then I want to be able to make informed decisions without the fearing your anger. If I make a mistake, I want to know about it, but I don't want to be considered with less respect if and when I do make a bad choice. I know this may seem unimportant, but I have worked with a supervisor who asked me to do a task without giving me the details. When the

Discovering Elizabeth

result did not meet her expectations, the supervisor pounced on me and embarrassed me. And if I'm going to have to tell you when I disagree or have a different opinion, then I expect for you to listen to me." Sophie's courage was teetering as she continued. "I want to know for sure that you won't get angry at my opinion. If you can assure me that you won't get angry with me, then I'll give you all the feedback you want. I want you to know that if you don't take any advice I give, I will be okay with it, but I want to know that my opinion matters." Sophie shifted in her seat as she added quietly. "I want to be a valuable team member. For once in my life, I want to count."

Sophie looked down at her plate. Elizabeth couldn't have known, but Sophie had never been so open with anyone else for as long as she could remember. Sophie squirmed as she realized how vulnerable she felt. She lowered her fork to the table, as the desire to run out the door became stronger. Sophie was relieved when Elizabeth simply said, "Done deal. I will try to meet those expectations." A wide smile spread over Sophie's face as her efforts to communicate with her new boss paid off.

From the table behind Elizabeth, Jessica picked up on Ray's interest in Elizabeth. Jessica giggled, as she had no success in stifling her desire to tease her friend. "So, Mr. Morgan," Jessica cooed, "What is being said at the table behind you that you would find it so fascinating as to ignore your dinner guest? If you lean back any farther, I'm afraid that you might tip over."

Ray leaned forward, afraid that Jessica might be correct. He had no desire to fall in front of Elizabeth ever again. "Jessica," Ray denied, "I don't know what you're talking about. Why would I be eavesdropping when I'm sitting with one of the most gorgeous and available women in Georgia?"

Jessica kicked him under the table. "Now, Ray Morgan, don't play games with me. Have you not given her your Solomon speech yet? No woman would be able to resist that!" Jessica began to laugh at her mischievous antics.

As Ray reached under the table to rub his leg he asked, "Solomon? You are making no sense, woman!" He had only temporarily forgotten until Jessica gently reminded him of his most embarrassing moment. Ray groaned, "Oh, Jessica, I wish you hadn't reminded me of that. I was doing well at suppressing that awful memory. It's been so long ago that I don't even remember the details."

Jessica was delighted to relive the Solomon moment. "Sure you remember! Okay, okay, as I recall, we were in the fifth grade. Does the name Denita Moss mean anything to you?"

Ray glared at his friend. "Don't say another word! I don't want to hear that name. So maybe I do remember, but I don't want to think about it." As Jessica tried to re-ignite the conversation about Denita Moss, Ray smiled and covered his ears. "I'm not listening to you." As Jessica continued, he spoke at the same time saying, "You are not telling it like it was, I didn't do it like that!" Although Ray knew he looked ridiculous, he didn't care. He felt like a teenager arguing with his spitfire best friend.

Jessica would not be thwarted. "Oh, yes, you did. You quoted Solomon to her in front of half the class. I have witnesses!"

As Ray feared, Jessica had gotten loud enough for others to hear her. He knew that Elizabeth had turned around again and was looking at them because Jessica lit up as if she were now ready to rehearse the entire story to a willing audience.

Ray gave her a stern look. "Jessica, don't do this! I'm serious."

Elizabeth started to turn back around. She had tried not to look at the couple, but what she was hearing was too baffling so she turned around to make sure she wasn't imagining things. As she turned, Jessica called out to her and said, "You guys have to hear this."

Ray leaned back in defeat. "Jessica, every time I see you I seem to end up either embarrassed or feeling as if I'm a kid again in the grips of your scheming mind. We're not ten anymore!"

Sophie and Elizabeth were curious at what Jessica had to say. Finally, Jessica poked at Ray and said, "Oh, you are a big guy. A little bit of reality as to what the boss is like would be good for you. Oh please, Ray, can I tell it?"

Ray laughed, "So you are asking now, are you?"

"Yes."

Ray rolled his eyes and sighed. "You are asking to appear to be kind, aren't you? You'll go ahead and tell the story even if I say you can't.

Discovering Elizabeth

You first want to see if you can do it without having to take a chance that I'll never speak to you again, right, Jessica?"

Jessica grinned. "You know me."

Ray squinted. "Then be my guest. I may as well go down as a willing subject than to lose the friendship of a woman I should've left at the gas station. Just be easy on me, don't tell the whole thing." Ray loved Jessica. He couldn't have loved a blood born sister any more than he loved the woman who was about to embarrass him. Ray added, "Jess, you know that I can't say no to you. If I did say no, I have no doubt you would tell it anyway. Have at it. Tarnish my reputation as a lady's man!"

Elizabeth was startled. She had no idea that Ray knew that his reputation wasn't a desirable one when it came to the opposite sex. Jessica challenged the reputation, "If you're a wild lady's man, I'm a sumo wrestler." Ray rolled his eyes and threw up his hands as if all of his secrets were about to be revealed. Jessica looked at the girls to make sure she had the attention of her audience. "Okay, now remember this was the fifth grade and Ray over there wasn't the man you see before you today. He was shy and very polite, most of the time." Jessica gave Ray a winning smile that spoke volumes. "He always tried to be a good boy. He read his Bible faithfully and probably thought everyone else read the Bible too. And while I agree that every answer one may need is in the Word, there are those who use it, shall I say, without wisdom."

Ray remained quiet as Jessica continued her story. "Anyway, there was a girl in our class who sat in front of him. Her name was Denita and Ray was totally smitten with her. He was fascinated with her because she wasn't afraid to pick up bugs and little creatures like the other girls. Denita had long blonde hair and Ray spent the better part of the fifth grade just staring at the back of her golden head. Girls, he was so infatuated with this gal that he was willing to make a fool of himself for the cause of love. Ray's challenge was that Denita was a tomboy until we were freshmen in high school. I have to tell you that she would've loved to have had Ray on her arm by then, but by that time the damage had been done."

"Damage?" Elizabeth worried. She and Sophie had been listening intently to the most animated woman Elizabeth had ever seen. She couldn't wait to hear whatever it was that Jessica was telling on her beloved boss.

Jessica continued, "Yes, damage. After much thought and little prayer, Ray thought that the time had arrived for him to declare his faithfulness to little Ms. Tomboy Moss. Like I said, Ray was an avid reader of the Word. He had read and reread the scriptures to come up with the right wording. To Ray's embarrassment, he picked the wrong passages to quote to the young girl." Jessica had difficulty keeping her composure as she continued. She could still see him kneeling down at recess in front of their classmates. Ray had thought that he was showing his devotion by the public display, but his devotion had not yet been tried through the fire.

Elizabeth was grinning as she asked, "What did he do?"

Jessica enlightened her listeners. "Have you ever read 'The Song of Solomon'?"

Elizabeth shook her head. "Yes, but it's been a while. I don't read there often, why?"

Jessica grinned while Ray allowed the corners of his mouth to turn upward. Jessica said, "You'll have to read chapter four, verses one through three. That's what Ray here recited to the unsuspecting Denita. You would've thought she could have felt his gaze on the back of her head, but she had no idea. Ray knelt as he held out his arms like a Shakespearean actor and quoted, 'Behold, thou are fair, my love; behold, thou art fair; thou hast doves' eyes within thy locks, thy hair is as a flock of goats, that appear from mount Gilead. Thy teeth are like a flock of sheep that are even shorn, which came up from the washing; whereof every one bare twins, and none is barren among them. Thy lips are like a thread of scarlet, and thy speech is comely: thy temples are like a piece of a pomegranate within thy locks.' Ray sat there expecting a grand reception from his beloved but that's not what he got." Jessica had graciously acted out the speech as she quoted the scripture without difficulty. Elizabeth, Sophie and Ray were unable to keep from laughing. Several other customers smiled in their direction.

Ray interjected, "Okay, Jess, I'm going to tell them what happened from that point. It doesn't seem as bad as I remember it, but it has been years ago."

Elizabeth teased, "Okay, Casanova, what happened?"

Discovering Elizabeth

Ray winked at her. "You've got that right. I wooed her until she began to cry. She was so upset. She thought I was making fun of her so told the teacher on me."

The story was sad but amusing. Sophie quietly asked, "What did the teacher do to you?"

Ray grimaced, "That's the part that I will never forget. I received a paddling for my efforts and was moved to a seat far from my little Shulamite girl."

The two tables shook for a moment as the occupants laughed together. After the laughter died down, Elizabeth asked Jessica, "How did you remember all of that scripture?"

Ray spoke before Jessica could respond, "Liz, Jessica has a photographic memory and was just sweet enough to remember my speech."

Jessica poked at her date, "Now, don't downplay my intelligence. You could have made her believe that I was super-intelligent but, no, you had to spoil it…"

Ray grinned and apologized.

Elizabeth and Sophie turned around to work on their meal. Elizabeth had thought that Jessica and Ray were just friends but they kept laughing long after she and Sophie had turned around. The handsome couple sounded as if they were having a lovely time. Elizabeth was having a good time talking with Sophie, but the feeling that she was about to burst into tears began to escalate. She began thinking that she might be having some kind of hormonal imbalance. She kept thinking about how beautiful and at ease Jessica was with Ray. The woman was probably so intelligent that Elizabeth probably seemed stupid in comparison. Right before the comedy acts began, Elizabeth had what she considered to be a great idea.

"Sophie, do you like rodeos?"

Sophie hadn't expected such an unlikely question. "I guess, I don't know. I've never been to one. Why do you ask?"

Elizabeth explained, "I was wondering if you would like to go to one right now. My roommate gave me a couple of tickets before she left to go tonight. A group from our church met there to have some fun.

Would you want to run up there with me?" Sophie looked uncomfortable so Elizabeth added, "I know that you probably don't want to be around people you don't know, but I promise you that you will love them...if we even see them. What do you say? Do you have anything better to do?"

Sophie thought for a moment then decided that it was an honor for Elizabeth to even ask her to go, "Sure, I'll go."

"Great! Let's go then. I can drive if you don't mind and I'll just drop you back off here in a little while. How does that sound?"

"That's fine." Sophie grinned. She cringed at the thought of meeting new people but decided to make herself go. Many times she almost backed out of going before she ever left the Comedy Barn.

As the two women stood to leave, the first act appeared on the stage. Elizabeth was glad. She wouldn't have to actually say good-bye to Ray and his...whatever. She could act like she didn't want to block anyone's view and just scurry out.

Ray didn't miss the fact that Elizabeth and Sophie skipped out on the show. Even though he had his opinion about Elizabeth that stemmed from seeing her the night before with another man, he had still wanted to be around her even if it meant only being seated behind her. He pondered the current circumstance. He sighed as he realized that he and Jessica probably looked like a couple. The thought gave him some hope. Perhaps Elizabeth felt lonely and had been with friends. He hoped that was true but became discouraged with himself for even thinking about it. "It's none of your business," Ray reminded himself.

The ground was dusty and Elizabeth was glad she and Sophie both had on jeans. As they made their way to their seats, Elizabeth saw her church family. Gabrielle was standing up waving a white cowboy hat and looked to be having a wonderful time. As Elizabeth and Sophie took their seats, the rowdy Christians hollered a welcome and motioned for Elizabeth and Sophie to join in on the fun.

Elizabeth looked at Sophie for approval and when Sophie smiled, Elizabeth took the lead to maneuver through the crowd. Sophie was understandably nervous, but kept telling herself that she would survive.

Discovering Elizabeth

Joe was the first, as usual, to welcome them. "Hello, ladies! Here are two seats between this ole cowpoke, Jay and me. Have at them if you think you can keep Jay from spitting that ole backy juice on your feet!"

Jay wasn't as extroverted as Joe and reddened with the play. Jay wouldn't have been bashful around his friends but immediately became silent in the presence of an unfamiliar face.

Gabrielle introduced herself to Sophie then shouted at Elizabeth, "Where's your hat, young lady? Don't you know that you can't be a real cowgirl without a hat?"

Elizabeth looked at Gabby. "And where did you get that hat? I know for a fact that when you left home earlier, the only hat you had was the invisible one you kept tipping at me."

Gabrielle giggled, "That's for me to know and for you to mind your own business!"

Elizabeth loved to tease her friend and the more spectators the better. "Oh, Gabrielle, you didn't snatch a hat off of the head of some little old lady or child did you?"

Joe chimed in, "Yeah, it was the little lady that was sitting by Jay. Jay spit on her shoe and Gabby grabbed her hat. The lady left after she gave them a piece of her mind."

They all began to laugh, but Gabby had the last word. "Oh what a tangled web we weave..." Elizabeth and Joe stopped smiling, Gabrielle giggled with delight.

As Elizabeth became involved in the events of the evening, she tried to forget the fact that Ray was with another woman. She cheered, she laughed and she cherished the time spent with her friends-but she didn't forget.

"The weekend has gone by too quickly," Gabrielle protested as she and Elizabeth entered the church for Sunday evening services. Elizabeth agreed and revealed to her friend that she felt no desire for the restful weekend to end. As the girls shook hands with those around them, a woman sitting in the corner of the church caught Elizabeth's eye. She smiled and walked toward the visitor.

"Sophie, I'm so glad to see you!" Elizabeth hugged Sophie as she stood to greet her.

Sophie returned to her seat, and sat down with her hands folded in her lap. "Thanks, Elizabeth. I hope you don't mind me coming here with us working together and all. I liked the people we were around Friday and just thought…"

Elizabeth wanted to hug her assistant again. "Sophie, they liked you too. I don't mind one bit, as a matter of fact, I couldn't be happier that you're here. Has anyone introduced you to Pastor?"

As Sophie shook her head no, Pastor Matthews approached the pew where Sophie and Elizabeth were talking. He held out his hand to give Sophie a warm welcome. She seemed shy but pleased with the pastor introducing himself to her. Elizabeth explained that Sophie worked at Wright and Wingold. Pastor Matthews smiled and said, "Well, I know you have your work cut out for you. I understand you're working with Elizabeth. I've been trying to set her straight for years." He had a wonderful time teasing Elizabeth until he heard who was behind him. Sophie loved the bantering but was overwhelmed by this strange yet wonderful environment.

Pastor Matthews stood straight as the female voice behind him said, "Now, don't be telling the girl things like that. Why, you know you're not the one who has worked so hard on Liz." Elizabeth looked confidently at her pastor until Pastor Matthew's wife declared, "It has been me! I've worked to keep her on the straight and narrow." As she laughed at Elizabeth's friendly scowl, Pastor Matthews placed his arm around his wife and gave her an affectionate squeeze.

Elizabeth took a step back and said, "Now, listen you two! If you're ever going to see me get married, you'd better start making it look just a little bit more attractive!"

The couple snickered and looked at one another as if they were sharing something secret. The pastor and his wife loved to tease and pick on each other, but their love was unmistakable. Sophie looked at the couple with a new look of hunger in her eyes. She wondered if that kind of special love was reserved for a small few or if she would one day attain such a passion for another human being. Sophie giggled nervously at her strange thoughts.

Joe interrupted the foursome when he walked up to greet the giggling Sophie. He noticed how innocent she looked as she sat with

Discovering Elizabeth

her hand over her mouth to veil a sheepish grin. Joe looked directly into her eyes as he asked, "May I sit down?"

Sophie looked up at him then glanced to see to whom he could be talking. She was startled to realize that Joe was talking to her. Sophie pointed at herself as if he were sure he meant her.

Joe put both hands in his pockets. "Yes, Ma'am. I'm asking to sit beside you. Is it okay?" Joe was never unsure of himself but he was keenly aware that he may have just overstepped his boundaries to be so forward with a woman he barely knew.

Sophie stuttered, "Sure, sure, go ahead." Sophie looked at the seat next to her as Joe sat down at an appropriate distance from where she sat fidgeting.

As Pastor Matthews began the evening service, he announced that several young adults were going to a retreat in Pensacola, Florida. The zealous pastor told the ones going that he would expect them to come back with testimonies to share with the congregation. He asked for the church to pray for those who were attending the conference. The announcement made Elizabeth more than a little nervous. She hadn't known that others from the congregation were going to the same event as she and Gabrielle. Pastor Matthews asked everyone going on the trip to stand. As Elizabeth and Gabrielle stood, so did most of the singles group. She whispered to Gabrielle, "Did you know that everyone was attending this? Where did you get that brochure anyway?"

Gabrielle smiled. "No, I never thought to ask anyone else if they were going. I received the invitation in the mail."

Pastor Matthews was visibly excited for the group. "Okay, I expect you to come back fired up for what God is and will be doing in your lives. Watch out for each other will you?" The pastor decided to add some humor to the expectations as he added, "Someone needs to watch out for Joe particularly and make sure he behaves himself. I'd hate to have a report that someone from my congregation was being ornery."

Joe raised his hand and asked, "May I comment on that, Brother?"

Pastor Matthews smiled patiently as he answered, "Certainly."

Joe stood and faced the audience as he said, "I make a vow to you right here and now that I shall do my best not to let you folks down. I'll not behave any differently than I do right here in our own hometown."

Lisa D. Piper

Joe sat down and adjusted his shirt as if he were being totally serious about his declaration.

Pastor Matthews wiped his brow with the back of his hand. "Joe, that's what we're afraid of." The congregation cackled as their beloved pastor teased the famous prankster.

Joe sat back as if he'd been given the Pulitzer Prize. He was proud of his mischief and loved the way he got back what he gave, usually. As he looked at the audience as if he were offended, he looked at the pretty lady sitting beside him. Joe smiled and waved his hand at Sophie. Being unused to any attention, Sophie grinned then looked down at her hands. Although she was embarrassed since everyone still had their eyes on Joe, she was delighted that she wasn't a wallflower and finally someone was noticing her. Sophie was elated.

After the service, the group of singles congregated in the back of the church. They were all ecstatic about finding out that there were others attending the retreat and commented on how coincidental it was. As Pastor Matthews approached the animated group, someone asked how he knew they were going. He grinned and said, "Well, I didn't know for sure. I received an invitation to speak at the conference and had been told that several of my members were attending. I wasn't sure who was going, so I thought I would find out and make sure you all know that you're going with my prayers and blessing. I won't be able to go speak on behalf of our little church, but I know you all will be blessed."

Pastor Matthews suggested that since there were enough persons attending from the church, perhaps they should drive the activity van to Florida. The lively singles decided to accept the offer to drive the church van. Jay would drive and Gabrielle would take over when he became fatigued.

Chapter ELEVEN

"The Lord is near to those who have a broken heart..."Psalm 34:18a NKJV

Monday came and Elizabeth was thankful for an uneventful day. She reviewed the task list with Sophie and made certain she would know how to address any possible challenge that might arise in Elizabeth's absence. She and Sophie went to lunch and Sophie seemed to be more at ease with her boss than ever.

Elizabeth had only spoken briefly to Ray. He had nodded but hadn't acted as if she were any different from any of the other department heads. She scolded herself for even thinking that she should be treated any differently. Elizabeth berated herself, "That's the reason he doesn't want to have a relationship with you, Liz. He knows it would be too difficult. Keep that in mind when you daydream about him and it won't be so bad." She decided she would just make herself treat him as if nothing had happened between them.

A special meeting had been planned for team building on Wednesday for all leadership personnel. Elizabeth felt as if she were too busy to attend but made time to go anyway. Ray introduced Eric and informally announced that he would be coming aboard as the Senior Vice President in two weeks. Eric was included on the team building exercise.

The facilitator began the workshop by placing the group into teams. In order to evaluate how they would work together, he gave them a special puzzle. Each participant was given ten pieces to the puzzle and instructed to put his puzzle together. What the teams did not know was that the puzzles were designed so that the pieces weren't workable unless the team worked together.

Lisa D. Piper

Elizabeth was trying to figure out what to do with the task that had been assigned for her to do as a part of the team building exercise when she felt as if someone were watching her. She was correct. As she turned, she saw the new vice president looking in her direction. He wasn't smiling or frowning. Eric looked as if he were formulating a question. Elizabeth turned around and began working on her puzzle with apprehension.

From across the room, Ray misinterpreted the look that Eric was giving Elizabeth. He was silently thrilled that Elizabeth had noticed him but had completely ignored the stare. He was pleased that she could ignore Eric when he knew for a fact that Eric was used to getting attention from females. Ray liked for everyone to be treated with respect and he couldn't help being ticked off at his new team member. Ray tried to control the emotions that were gaining momentum as he stood watching the entire group.

Eric had just glanced back up at Elizabeth when Ray asked to see him outside. Eric was shocked to hear the counsel of the man with whom he would work. "Eric, I don't know what you think this is, but I'm surprised by your actions. In your position, you can't stare at a woman in any way. Elizabeth doesn't deserve to be ogled at and it's unprofessional for you to be doing it. I think it might make anyone in her position uncomfortable."

Eric was unsure of how to respond to Ray. He couldn't deny that she had captured his attention. "Ray, I guess it did look like I was staring at her. I wasn't meaning to make her feel uncomfortable. Your advice, however, is valuable and I'll make sure to check myself from now on out. I don't want to do anything that others would perceive as being inappropriate. I hate to admit this but I was thinking that was the girl who was with that red headed beauty that day we went to lunch. I haven't been able to get her out of my mind. You have no idea how disturbing it has been." Eric shrugged. "I guess that I was shocked to see Elizabeth again and my mind took off with me. I apologize. I'll apologize to the woman. I know this isn't a good excuse and I wasn't professional. I'm sorry."

Ray thought for a moment and said, "Well maybe you need to tell her at an appropriate time. You'll want to make sure that you don't say anything to make it worse."

Discovering Elizabeth

Eric agreed and thanked Ray. Eric was disappointed and felt as if he'd let Ray down. He made a commitment to not let his personal interests interfere with work again.

As Eric pondered the conversation he came to the conclusion that Ray must have had a special reason for noticing the glances he had made toward the blonde headed woman. The blonde was beautiful, there was no doubt about it, and Eric had recognized her from the parking lot the day that he had met the woman of his dreams. He hated that he'd been staring at her. He'd been trying to figure out a way to ask her about her friend without looking like a clumsy teenager. Eric didn't have a photographic memory, but he had no difficulty remembering the memory of the auburn haired beauty. He couldn't figure out why his heart had begun to beat so erratically when he first looked at her. He remembered her wonderful voice. It sounded to him like something from the movies: sensual and feminine. He became frustrated with himself for looking at Elizabeth while he had been thinking of her friend. He wasn't sure how he was going to do it or when it would happen but he knew he must see the beautiful red head again. When he did, he wouldn't walk away as quickly as he had the last time.

The Friday came for Elizabeth to turn the reign of the office over to the capable Sophie. Sophie was nervous and fidgeted most of the day. At last, she spoke about her worries to Elizabeth. "What if I make a wrong decision and everything blows up in my face? What if..."

Elizabeth interrupted, "Sophie, I've told you that it's likely that you will make mistakes at some point. I won't become upset with you while you're trying to do your best and while you're doing exactly as I've asked you to do. Go by the book and don't break the rules. Use your common sense and think about what I might do if I were here, if you think that'll help. If you make a mistake, then you'll learn from it and everything will be okay. I trust you Sophie." Elizabeth smiled at the woman who had won her respect as a truly dedicated and caring person. As Elizabeth watched her, she thought that she would never have guessed after the incident with Jillian downstairs that she would have enjoyed working with Sophie, let alone trust her with the department. Sophie had moved into the role with ease. When Elizabeth offered suggestions on how she could improve, Sophie took the suggestions and constantly became better and better. Elizabeth knew that Sophie was finishing up her degree in the evening. With the knowledge she was gaining there, plus her on the job experience in a renowned company, Sophie would be able to pick whatever job she wanted not too far down the road.

Sophie seemed to relax as Elizabeth went over the tasks and meetings scheduled for the following week for the final time. By the end of the day Elizabeth was confident that Sophie would be fine. She phoned the CEO's office to let him know what she was doing. After several rings, Elizabeth started to return the telephone to its cradle when she heard a voice say, "Hello, Ray Morgan, here."

"Oh, hi, Ray." Elizabeth quickly put the phone up to her ear. "I thought no one was going to answer. This is Elizabeth and as you know I'm going to be out of town next week. I wanted to give you an update on the department before I leave." She held her breath while awaiting his response.

"Hello, Liz. I've got a few minutes, update away." He sat down to rest his back. He'd been trying to go faster than normal to get more accomplished because of the few days he'd be gone the following week.

"Sophie is aware of the financial planning meeting on Tuesday, which is the most important one next week. She knows what to take to it and is aware of the goals for the meeting. She has my calendar of other events and is ready to handle whatever happens, short of a natural disaster. I'll be gone from Monday until late Saturday evening. I've left the numbers of the hotel with Sophie in case there's a real emergency. Is there anything else I need to do?" Elizabeth asked.

Ray paused. "Yes, I guess you can have fun and get your mind off of work. That's what I'm going to do."

Elizabeth had forgotten about Ray's planned absence. "What are you going to do?"

Ray sighed, "Well, believe it or not, I'm speaking for a friend. I have to come up with about an hour's worth of important information and present it to an audience of about five thousand. I'm looking forward to getting the speech over with. Eric will be going with me and he and I'll be spending some time planning for the future and doing a little fishing on the side. If I can coax him into it, we may knock around a few balls on a golf course if we can find one that'll put up with us.

Discovering Elizabeth

"That sounds like fun. Are you leaving today?

Ray tapped his chair with his pencil. "No, I'm not speaking until the middle of the week. I guess I'll finish getting things wrapped up here then leave whenever I can. I'm not in a big hurry and neither is Eric." Ray couldn't resist the temptation to ask Elizabeth about Eric. "What do you think of our new vice president, Elizabeth?"

She nodded as if he could see her. "I guess he's okay. I haven't had an opportunity to speak with him."

Ray was somehow relieved. "There'll be a formal announcement after we return next week. I decided to make the announcement with the department heads early. I should've waited, I guess." He paused before continuing, "You'll be reporting directly to Eric as you did Fred. Do you foresee any problems with that?"

Elizabeth wasn't sure why he was asking her but decided to be truthful. "Ray, I can't think of any. Fred wasn't, well, he wasn't exactly the greatest support that ever existed. I guess I'm hoping that the new SVP will be more like you." She clapped her hand over her mouth and hoped that he hadn't heard her latter statement.

Ray didn't know how to respond to what Elizabeth had said. He could tell that she wished she hadn't said it by the lingering silence. He heard her inhale sharply after the mention that she wanted Eric to be like him. The comment pleased Ray so he decided to ignore the remark. "Well, I think that you'll like him. We've selected him with a lot of forethought. I'm sorry that you've had bad experiences in the past. Let's hope you have no more of them. Oh, and, uh...Elizabeth."

"Yes?"

"Have a good time next week." Ray paused as he heard her say good-bye. He was in misery. Pure, plain old misery seemed to be his lot. The woman he wanted to be with would be away for a week, with who knows who, doing who knows what, at who knew where. Ray threw his pencil down then began what Annie Mae called, "The Ray Pace." While pacing and thinking, he decided that it was time for a visit to the woman who was as dear to him as his own mother had been.

Lisa D. Piper

Chapter TWELVE

"Commit your works to the Lord, And your thoughts
will be established." Proverbs 16:3"NKJV

Ray had never been what one would call a sentimental kind of man. As he drove up the driveway of the woman who loved him as a mother would have, he became a little uncomfortable. He stretched his legs as he got out of his car. He breathed in the oceanic air. He leaned over and retrieved a vase that held twelve multi-colored roses. While knocking, Ray began to wonder if his favorite couple was home. Homer finally answered the door and as he surveyed the contents of Ray's hand, Homer held out his hands and said, "You old softy! You shouldn't have!"

Ray stepped back and pulled his gift away from Homer. "Oh no you don't! There's no way you're touching these. I wouldn't doubt that you'd take off with my gift and go present them to that pretty lady of yours. You'd probably announce that you were the thoughtful, sweet gentleman who had thought of her."

Homer grinned. "You little whippersnapper! Bring your dandelions to my woman and then accuse me of interfering with your capers!"

Ray tried to look severe but couldn't. "Capers? Dandelions? Little? Why, I do believe you are in error. Are you going to let me in or do I have to climb the rose trellis?" By now, Ray's grin was barely concealed.

Lisa D. Piper

Homer stepped back and opened his hand to usher Ray inside. "Enter young man. Were you to climb that trellis and break it, I wouldn't want to be the one living with the queen of this house. If she discovered that I made you climb it, I'd be toast."

As Ray entered the door, Homer surprised him by screaming toward the kitchen. "Annie, darling, take heed! There's a scalawag coming toward the kitchen to entice you!"

Ray had almost made it to the kitchen door when he turned around and laughed as he repeated, "Scalawag? Okay, I'm calling a truce, Homer. I didn't come to heckle with you, you know."

Homer looked satisfied. "I know why you came here. You came to siphon a meal out of the chef."

Ray grinned, "You know it! I'll be right back to beat you in a game of chess as soon as I give your lovely wife a quick kiss on the cheek and some dandelions for her trouble."

Annie glowed as she took the roses from her favorite bachelor. She patted him on the head and insisted that he stay for dinner. Ray didn't refuse. Annie was in the middle of her preparations so she pointed to the door and said, "You boys stay in there and leave me here in the kitchen. I'll have none of your picking on one another. Do you hear me? Let's keep the peace in here tonight."

Ray shrugged his shoulders quickly then grabbed a warm chocolate chip cookie as he chuckled, "Too late!" Ray was in the process of grabbing another cookie for Homer when Annie's spatula found the back of his hand.

"Ouch!" Ray let go of the cookie.

"Now git outta my kitchen before this spatula finds your behind, young man!" Annie feigned anger as she pointed him out of the kitchen. This familiar scene had happened hundreds of times over the years.

Ray was still grinning while rubbing his hand when he handed Homer half of his morsel. Homer looked at it and said, "What happened to it?"

"Don't complain. The one I grabbed for you is still in there." Ray shuddered and pointed toward the kitchen. "I'm not about to enter that

Discovering Elizabeth

kitchen again. The last time I entered after being told not to was about twenty-five years ago. I still have difficulty sitting sometimes over that one." Ray grimaced as he remembered his misfortune of personally meeting Annie Mae's wrath.

Homer slapped his knee and chuckled. "She hit you with the spatula, huh?"

"I'm glad it was the spatula. You married an excitable woman, Mr. Foster." Ray sat down, picked up the pieces to the game, and challenged Homer to a duel.

"You're not kidding! Why do you think I bought the plastic type of utensils and tossed out the metal! I'm no fool, boss!"

After a round of chess where more talking transpired than actual playing, the two men enjoyed a delicious meal followed by Annie's key lime pie. As the three sat around their empty plates, Ray finally spoke of the reason he needed to visit the Fosters. Ray cleared his throat, "I want to apologize to you both for running out on you the other night at the comedy barn. Annie looked at Ray with pride and said, "Oh, Son, don't worry about it. We hated to see you go. However, we weren't alone for the rest of the evening. You know the girl who was the queen at the beach? Well, she went with us for ice cream after the show. We had a wonderful time. She's just delightful."

Ray was stunned. "Do you mean Elizabeth Pennington?"

Annie was convinced that her assumption as to why Ray had left their company that night was correct from the way he responded to her news. Annie Mae decided to have a little fun with Ray. "I think it was Elizabeth. She has blonde hair and a stunning smile. She was sitting down there on the floor area while you were there. Did you notice her?"

Homer knew what Annie was doing and poked at Ray. "Watch it boy! The question's loaded."

His first thought was to hide his interest; however, he could use some advice from the couple who had been faithful to one another so long. Ray unfolded the story about Elizabeth and told them how stupid he felt when he saw her with another man just hours after he had broken off something with her that had never been fixed in the first place.

Lisa D. Piper

Annie was compassionate. "Ray, she wasn't with one of those men as a date. They go to her church and the entire singles group met there that night. She went with us when all of them decided to go to the beach. She told them she just couldn't go there with them. She went with Homer and me to eat some ice cream."

Ray was trying to take it all in. "What did you say? What did you say about the beach? Why wouldn't she go to the beach?"

She wasn't sure she was following him. Ray had only given them an overview of what had transpired and not details. "Well, let me think. She said she just couldn't go there right now and declined gracefully. When she came with us, I suspected she didn't want to be alone, but didn't want to go either. I don't know what to think of it really."

Ray knew he didn't have the right to hope Elizabeth was thinking of him at the very moment that she declined the beach invitation. He felt very foolish as he recalled that at about that time he was probably sitting in his car stewing over the fact that Elizabeth was already out with another man and not even considering him. He decided to ask Annie her expert opinion. "What do you guys think of her?"

Homer answered, "I think she's pretty, smart and sweet. She seems to be genuine and cares for others. You're right about one thing though. She does work for the company which does pose a problem."

Annie thought about the question and said, "Ray, I have to say that I really like her. I may be partial to her, but you do have one thing in common. You're looking for the same thing in a mate as she is."

Homer interrupted, "What're you talking about? Marriage? A mate? There are some distinct problems with this relationship right now!"

Annie ignored Homer. "Ray, she told me that she wants a marriage like ours. She wants a Christian who will be faithful to her and to whom she can be faithful. She wants to grow old with a man of integrity, who is confident in himself and the love his wife has for him. Should your circumstances change she may be the one. Only God knows so pray carefully."

Ray was full of questions that neither Foster could answer. He didn't want to mention what he'd been thinking to Homer. He wouldn't want to prematurely upset the man; however, he'd begun thinking that he would rather be happily married to Elizabeth than work at the company

Discovering Elizabeth

that had been entrusted to him. He sat and talked for a couple of hours then decided to go home. He needed to get packed for the following week or he would find himself rushing around when the time to leave arrived.

The group of men and women met Friday evening to discuss their travel itinerary. The decision to leave immediately following Sunday Morning's service was made. Everyone seemed to be alive with the anticipation of the trip, with the exception of one sad face. Gabrielle sat listening while nodding her head in agreement with the others. She seemed distant to Elizabeth. Elizabeth knew that Gabrielle would be okay, and if she thought about it, she wasn't sure what she would do, but if she were in Gabrielle's predicament. One thing she knew undoubtedly was that she would stay beside Gabrielle through whatever lay ahead of her. Elizabeth decided to spend more time with her to try and make her friend feel better.

Saturday proved to be a busy day for the entire traveling group. Elizabeth awoke to a ringing telephone. She rolled over, reached past her alarm clock, and sleepily lifted the receiver. "Hello."

"Good morning, sleepy head!" The vibrant greeting blared in Elizabeth's ear.

"Josie, is that you?"

Josie squealed, "It certainly is! I've got Florida on my mind, Baby, and knew you'd want to have it on your mind too!"

Elizabeth tried to open one tired eyelid. "You did, did you? And just what part of Florida are you thinking about?"

"I wanted to know if you are taking a hair dryer or does the hotel have one available in the room? I don't think we should over pack... Who has the directions and who's responsible for bringing the snacks?" Josie rambled incessantly with excitement.

"Whoa now! One question at a time, Josie! I think Gab said that the hotel does have hair dryers in each room. I don't want to over pack either. I usually take one bag no matter where I go. I'm a semiprofessional packer; I don't need a lot of room. It's not you and I who need to worry about over packing."

Gabrielle had picked up the phone at the same time as Elizabeth and had started to hang up until she realized it was Josie. Gabrielle chimed in. "Liz, pray tell, about whom would you be speaking, my dear?"

Elizabeth answered sweetly, "Good morning, Gab. Say, I haven't been in your room yet; so tell me, how many suit cases do you have open and packed full of almost everything you own?"

Josie giggled causing Gabrielle to dismiss the idea of hanging up on Elizabeth. Gabrielle looked around her room. She had three large suitcases, an overnight bag, and a garment bag prepared for filling. "Liz, I can't believe you'd say such a thing. I don't have one full and I have only a few bags lying out."

"A few? I would guess at least four suitcases, Gab. Confess now! We'll all know the truth tomorrow." Elizabeth wiped her eyes and sat up on the side of the bed.

"That shows how much you know. I have five, so there!" Before Elizabeth could respond, Gabrielle addressed Josie. "Josie, Jay has the directions and Mary is getting the snacks together. We thought we'd just split the snack cost before we leave."

Josie was agreeable. "Oh, yes! You know, Mary is a fellow chocolate lover, and I'm sure whatever she gets will be great."

Gabrielle and Elizabeth chimed in at the same time. "Oh, yes! Chocolate is a definite."

The three women made plans to collaborate on supplies to keep the luggage bulk down. Gabrielle promised to keep her luggage to a limit of two suitcases and an overnight bag.

Sunday morning was a happy time for the travelers. They all arrived at the little church with great expectations. None knew what the week would hold but all had the same expectations: to get there alive since Joe was driving, and to seek God. Pastor Matthew's message was uplifting and exhilarating. He preached about how God chooses people whom man despises. The pastor's voice became animated as he told how the Hebrew boys went from a slave status to ruling Hebron. He told them the story of Esther, a Jewish orphan, who became the queen. She eventually saved her people from a wicked man who wanted all of

Discovering Elizabeth

her people to die. He explained that Esther's playmates, while growing up, would probably not have ever believed she would be the queen. God, however, had a glorious plan. As the man spoke, Elizabeth, Gabrielle, Joe, Mary, Jay, Kenny, Josie and Sophie began to believe that God would do great things through them, if they just yielded to His plan.

The service ended and the singles gathered to move their luggage into the church van. "Pastor Matthews," Kenny asked, "do we have to ride with Joe?" Kenny grinned at Joe.

Pastor Matthews looked sternly at the men. "Now fellows, mind your manners. Don't be fussing all the way there. Look after one another." Pastor Matthews turned to Elizabeth and said, "Liz, I have a request. Do you have a minute?"

Elizabeth looked confused as she said, "Sure." She walked to the side of the vehicle out of the hearing range of the group.

"I received a phone call from the coordinators of the retreat. Their singer for Tuesday has become ill. Would you consider doing a solo performance in her place? I know that you have some sound tracks you could use in the church." Pastor Matthews knew Elizabeth was contemplating the request. "I think you should do it. Don't be shy. You need to share your gift with as many people as possible. Be a blessing and share it."

She couldn't and wouldn't say no to the respected man of God. "Sure. I need to go back in the church and get a couple of soundtracks so that I can pick whichever song I want when the time comes. Let them know that I'll do it. Would you also let them know where we'll be staying just in case they get someone else or change the plans?"

"Great! Thank you, Liz. I'll be praying for you." The pastor shook her hand before she walked into the church to get her CD's.

Everyone was sitting in the van patiently waiting for Elizabeth to come back. Joe was in the driver's seat with Jay sitting to his right as his co-pilot. Mary and Josie occupied the second seat in front of Gabrielle and Elizabeth. Kenny had reserved the entire fourth seat for his laptop computer and briefcase. The side door opened revealing an elated pastor and his wife. Sister Matthews looked in the back and teased, "Kenny, did you bring the portable desk and telephone?"

Kenny lifted his cellular phone and said, "I forgot the desk. I do look the executive part, don't I?" Kenny's dimpled relaxed his features as he smiled.

The pastor told him that he should be on vacation and needed to leave his work at home, knowing all the while that Kenny wouldn't take his advice. After the final good-byes, the pastor asked, "Is everyone ready to pray?"

A shout of affirmation came and Pastor Matthews asked his charming wife to lead the prayer. "Dearest Lord, I thank you for these fine young men and women. We pray that they find your perfect will in all areas of their lives. I know that your thoughts toward them are good and how much you want them to fulfill the awesome plans you have made for them. I ask that you protect them as they travel. May they be a blessing to all those they meet. In Jesus name I pray, Amen."

"Amen!" They all sang out.

As Pastor Matthews was about to close the door, Joe said, "Thanks for not praying that I'll behave! I know it was an effort for you, mam!"

Sister Matthews stuck her head back in the door and said, "Joe, I'm saving the most important prayer for my prayer closet. Now, behave yourself and do us proud!"

"Yes ma'am." Joe winked at the couple as he fastened his seat belt and shouted, "All aboard that's going aboard!" As He shoved the gearshift into drive, the trip that would prove to be an unforgettable journey began.

Sophie waved good-bye from her car in the parking lot. Joe honked at her and waved in her direction. Jay noticed the smile that played on Sophie's lips and sighed.

Pastor and Sister Matthews walked over to say good-bye to Sophie. Sophie turned to the pastor and said, "That was a wonderful sermon. I really am enjoying my visits here."

Her new pastor thanked her and pointed toward the heavens, mentioning that any good preaching came from the result of an Almighty God being merciful to him and those listening. Sophie smiled and decided that she had never met anyone quite like these people. She wanted to come back to this place again and again.

Discovering Elizabeth

She was unsure how it had happened, but she'd never felt so much hope inside of her before. She'd been experiencing some strange sensations since she had been attending the loving church. When the heart palpitations began during the singing, she thought she would need some medical attention. The strangest thing was that Sophie only felt unnerved when she was at the church. She didn't know what was going on with her. She did know that Elizabeth and Gabrielle had something she lacked and she determined she was going to get whatever it was for herself.

"Joe, please stop!" Mary was holding her sides as she begged the driver.

"What? Am I to stop stopping or stop something else?" He acted as if he wouldn't turn onto the exit that would take them to the much-anticipated rest area.

"You know what I mean!" Mary's sides hurt from laughing. "If you don't stop running your mouth and stop at this rest area, there'll be consequences to pay. I'm too much of a lady to tell you what they are right now."

Kenny yelled from the back seat. "Joe, give them what they want. Haven't you read Proverbs 21:9?"

Joe laughed aloud. "Hasn't every man read it and known it to be true!" Joe pulled to a stop at the rest area while continuing to laugh at his own statement.

Josie looked perplexed and asked, "What does it say?"

Kenny had been waiting for one of the women to ask. "Well, do you want the Biblical version or the version suitable for today?"

Josie looked at the other women and carefully insisted, "Give me the Biblical version."

Kenny looked disappointed. "Okay, I'll give you the Biblical version and then I'll give you my translation so that you can get the full effect of Solomon's wisdom."

Lisa D. Piper

As he began to explain, Mary was hurrying out the van door. "Now, Mary, you'll want to hear this. It's short and if you'll remember, the pastor spoke on it not long ago. It says, 'It is better to dwell in a corner of the housetop than with a brawling woman in a wide house.' I could loosely translate that to say, It is better to leave the woman alone in the wide van so that we do not have to dwell on the corner of the van roof." Kenny broke out into a hardy chuckle while the women took turns belting him with whatever they could find.

Mary exited the van then scurried into the building. The other women followed. They walked into the building with their heads held high. An air of defiance marked the women as they strode stiffly into the building. Within fifteen minutes, all of the travelers were buckled back into their seatbelts. The women had agreed to be silent and not speak to the men. After only two miles of travel, Joe was the first to speak.

"Okay, Ladies, we're sorry. We were just playing around."

Silence.

Kenny shifted in his seat and agreed with Joe. "Oh, come on, you know we were just joking. What did you all do in there, agree to a conspiracy? There are scriptures about forgiveness you know!"

Josie didn't look at any of the men as she said flatly, "Proverbs 18:19."

Jay and Kenny looked at one another then shrugged their shoulders. Jay picked up his Bible to search for the mysterious scripture. He read, "A brother offended is harder to be won than a strong city; and their contentions are like the bars of a castle."

Joe slapped his forehead with his palm and said, "Oh brother! This is going to be a long trip."

Elizabeth looked at Gabrielle and replied, "Loosely translated, that means you have your work cut out for you if you think you can tease us all of the way to Florida and get away with it."

The women began giving each other high fives to the muffled grunts of the males.

After a couple more minutes of silence, Jay, the quiet one of the bunch, lifted a bag filled with orange wrappers and asked, "If a sister

Discovering Elizabeth

offended is harder to win than a strong city, could she be won over with a combination of peanut butter and chocolate?" Jay jiggled the bag and sniffed the air.

The four women quickly looked at one another. Gabrielle turned to look at Jay then declared, "Blessed are the peacemakers. Now, hand over the chocolate!"

Jay gave the bag to Mary to distribute the prize evenly. It wasn't long before the happy chattering that had been so prominent since the trip began was again in full swing. The trip to Pensacola seemed to go by quickly. They had decided to pick a hotel on Pensacola Beach where they could hear the tantalizing sounds of the gulf from the balconies of their hotel rooms.

As they drove a three-mile bridge over salt waters, Joe pointed at a little girl pulling her prize fish out of the water while an elderly man hurried to her side. While the van made its way to the island, happy faces were plastered to the windows. Josie pointed to a pelican perched on a rail as if he owned the entire bridge. Seagulls circled above the fisherman on the side of the bridge as if they were interested in the activities of the humans.

Elizabeth could feel the stress leave her body. She felt like a teenager again. "Joe, roll down your window! I want to breathe in the air! Jay, are you getting this?"

Jay didn't move the camera from his eye as he murmured, "Yes, I'm getting it. I'm also recording your questions and demands about the window, Elizabeth Anne Pennington! Don't forget the church will be watching this tape!" Jay chuckled softly. He turned in his seat to capture the exuberant faces of his friends as the reality of the wonderful majesty of the land left them mesmerized. As the Ooh's and Ahh's continued, Jay teased his friends, "It isn't like we don't live near the beach ourselves."

Gabrielle continued to look as she said, "Yeah, I know, but this is a beach we've never seen before!"

Jay rolled his eyes but the travelers agreed that the land was incredible and continued to look at the wonder of creation until they finally arrived at their destination.

Lisa D. Piper

Getting the suitcases out of the vehicle proved to be an unwanted ordeal. The men and women were in a hurry to get their week started. Each rushed out of the van to grab his own bags. Kenny, the planner and problem solver, held up his hand. "Now wait just a minute!" He motioned to the bellboy and asked for his help in getting their things from the van to their rooms. "Now, stand back and this man and I will make sure you don't hurt yourselves in a suitcase avalanche! Go check in and we will join you in a moment. Your tips and gratitude will be much appreciated."

No one cared that Kenny was giving the orders. No one even argued with the man. He was a natural born leader. No one was offended when he spoke. His deep voice was unassuming and polite. Kenny had been a college basketball player. If he stood up straight, he could be measured at six feet, five inches tall. He reached into the van with his long arms and began handing the cases to the bellhop as the others walked into the hotel to check in.

Elizabeth and Gabrielle squealed as they walked into their room. Gabrielle rushed over to the balcony door and threw it open. "Liz! We are in paradise!"

Elizabeth stood beside her friend, basking in happiness.

Someone began knocking on the door that adjoined the women's room. Gabrielle walked over and opened it to reveal a jubilant Josie and Mary. "Hey, you guys, isn't this the greatest!"

Mary stretched lazily and sighed, "I think I could live here."

Gabrielle invited them in and said, "Okay, once we get settled in, what are we going to do next?"

Mary wondered, "I don't know. Did you hear the men say what they were going to do?"

Elizabeth laughed. "I'd say it has something to do with ordering a pizza and flipping channels. There's some kind of game on tonight that they've been waiting to see. I heard them talking about it and I heard Kenny say that he had to make some phone calls."

Josie rolled her eyes. "I say we tell them that if they're staying here, we're going to be gone with the wind. I don't want to waste one minute. A week is too short to spend it cooped up in a hotel room."

Discovering Elizabeth

Elizabeth hadn't heard the phrase derived from her favorite movie since the last evening she had spent with Ray. Gabrielle noticed that her friend seem to sway a little. "Are you okay, Liz?"

"Sure." Elizabeth smiled. "I must be suffering from van lag. I'm ready to go feel the white sand beneath my feet. What about you guys?"

Josie thought about it then said, "I have an idea! Let's go get some dinner in that restaurant downstairs and then step out onto the beach. We can roll up our jeans and take a moonlit stroll."

They all agreed that Josie had a marvelous idea. Josie and Mary went back into their room to freshen up. Gabrielle and Elizabeth began to scurry about their lovely room to prepare for some girl time.

Heads turned as the four beauties entered the hotel restaurant. The hostess led them to a table beside a window where they could look down and see the waves rolling onto the sparkling white sand. Their waiter introduced himself as Alfred. He was neatly groomed and quite the service professional. He was dressed in a black pair of trousers and white shirt. His black tie was neat and he had a smart black apron wrapped around his waste.

Elizabeth ordered a spinach and cheese appetizer while Josie ordered the shrimp cocktail. Gabrielle and Mary shared nachos and cheese. By the time they were finished, none of them were sure they could walk back to their rooms. Gabrielle urged them onto the beach where they collapsed in some vacant beach chairs. They were all leaning back and relaxing when someone decided to spray them with a mist of water.

Josie jumped up to address the perpetrator. Joe, Kenny, and Jay were standing over the sleepy women. "What are you doing out here?" Josie asked.

Kenny muttered, "We've been worried about you all. We called your rooms to no avail. We waited for you to call us but you didn't. You can't be too careful, girls."

Elizabeth looked up at Kenny. "We appreciate your concern fellows but we are adults. We should've called, and meant to, but just kind of got caught up in our plans. We knew that you had your own agenda, so we didn't think anything about just doing our own thing. I'm sorry we worried you."

Lisa D. Piper

Joe placed his hands on his hips. "And what do you know about our agenda? Perhaps we were counting on going to dinner with four ladies and then channel surfing later. Channel surfing is what you thought we were going to do isn't it? Isn't it? Stereotyping us again is what you were doing. I, for one, am wounded."

Gabrielle squinted up at the man. "The game's been canceled?"

Joe looked down at her and sighed, "Yeah."

Gabrielle snickered. "I have just one question. Did you all start checking on us before or after you found out the game was canceled?"

All three men looked unbelievably guilty. Joe grinned, "I can't believe you would ask such a thing. By the way, it sure is pretty out here, isn't it?"

Josie looked at the girls and rolled her eyes. "After the cancellation. Definitely after."

The men didn't deny the accusation but found enough seats for them to join their friends. Kenny looked out at the water while placing his hands behind his head. "You know, this is the life." Kenny hadn't felt this relaxed in years. "Anybody up for a stroll?"

The women shouted, "Yes, we are!" None of the women had wanted to admit their reluctance to comb the beach without escorts. With the arrival of the confident men, they felt safe enough to walk across the tide-covered beach.

No one wanted to talk as they quietly walked along the shore side. The setting provided a tranquil peace that no one wanted to disturb. They had slowly walked about fifteen minutes when they decided to sit down and just take in the scene that engulfed them. No one mentioned the white grit that clung to his clothes. The moment was too special to complain about anything.

Hearts were touched as Jay began to praise the One who had made the very thing they were so very much enjoying. "Thank you, God, for all you've done to give us pleasure. Your beauty is revealed in your creation. I can think of no other thing as lovely as you." Jay's voice trembled with emotion as he unashamedly called out to his God there on the secluded beach with some of the best friends he had ever had.

Discovering Elizabeth

"Amen." was the sole reply of those around him. Their hearts were elated. Jay had spoken the truth in each of their hearts. It would be an hour before anyone even felt compelled to move. Perhaps they wouldn't have moved until daybreak if they hadn't been so fatigued from the long day of travel.

When Gabrielle and Elizabeth arrived back at their room, they were quick to shower and prepare for a night of wonderful rest. They agreed to leave the seventh floor balcony door open to allow the soothing sounds of the gulf to permeate through their room throughout the night.

Elizabeth awoke to the smell of perking coffee. "Gab?" Elizabeth had difficulty adjusting her eyes to the sun soaked room.

"Wake up sleepy buddy! We've got to get to the church where the classes are starting in just two hours. We'll need to get there early to register. I went down to the café and got us some doughnuts, milk and coffee so that we can just sit out here and chill out before our day begins. Good idea?"

"Great idea! There's nothing like climbing out of a warm bed and sitting in my PJ's to eat my favorite breakfast while admiring a lovely view. You, my friend, are a near genius"

"Near?"

"Don't press it! Near is good. What kind of doughnuts did you get?"

Gabrielle held up the plate as she walked onto the balcony. "What do you take me for? They're chocolate of course!"

Gabrielle and Elizabeth had been sitting on their balcony for a couple of minutes when the adjacent balcony's occupants hollered in their direction. "Hey you guys! Great idea, huh?"

Mary and Josie were beaming as they raised their coffee cups for a mock toast. Elizabeth and Gabrielle raised their milk mugs and yelled, "Great minds think alike, yes they do! We're all geniuses."

A booming voice from another balcony bellowed, "Make that three sets of geniuses!" Kenny was standing on his balcony lifting a cup with the logo of the hotel emblazoned on the side. "Can you meet us at the van in an hour?"

"Absolutely!" All four women agreed.

Lisa D. Piper

Joe peaked over the balcony to sarcastically say, "You can? I've never seen you guys look like this before. Are you saying it only takes an hour for you to look the way we usually see you? Now that is genius!"

The women scowled then stood to their feet. Mary hollered out as she reentered her room. "Tell Jay to get the chocolate ready, Joe!"

Kenny glared at the man who hadn't thought before he'd spoken. "Joe, now look what you did! I think they should've offered a class on male and female communication. Although, now that I think about it, you would've failed the class." Kenny went back into the room.

Joe followed Kenny while flippantly demanding to know what he meant by the remark. Kenny picked out what he would wear then headed for the shower. "Joe, if there were something you shouldn't have said, it was about their looks. Women are touchy when it comes to their looks. Don't you know that?"

Joe grinned mischievously, "Yeah, I know it. But, those aren't women are they? They're comrades, buddies, you know... fellow folk!"

Kenny raised an eyebrow. "Yes, they were that when we were adolescents. Let me enlighten you on something, my friend. Just in case you've missed it or haven't been paying close enough attention. Those comrades are women." Kenny smiled. "As a matter of fact, they are attractive, intelligent women." Kenny concluded his speech by walking into the restroom to leave Joe alone and full of questions about Kenny's declaration.

Joe sat down and thought over what he'd said. He was still sitting in dumbfounded silence when Kenny returned. "Joe, are you going to get ready?"

Joe looked up. "Uh, yeah, let me get my clothes. I'll go on in and begin the old grooming process." Joe paused then said, "Kenny, you know, I really hadn't noticed that they had somehow turned into women at the same time we became men. I wonder how I missed that?"

Kenny smiled. "I've caught myself thinking that in the past too. I guess we still think of each other as the brats running around in Sunday school, pulling on the braids of any one who dared to wear them. I only

Discovering Elizabeth

realized that they had grown up quite gracefully the other day when we were at the rodeo. We need to pray for them, you know. It would hurt me to see any of them end up alone or, worse than that, with the wrong man. I'm glad they're here but I feel a little overprotective. I'm positive there isn't a fellow in the world worthy of any of those ladies. I'm trying hard not to let my over protectiveness come out and I'm sure they wouldn't appreciate it anyway."

Joe agreed. "Guess you're right. Say, you aren't interested in one of them are you?"

Kenny became serious. "It wouldn't matter if I were, would it? I'm still little Kenny the girls." When Joe smiled, Kenny warned him. "Joe, if you say a word of this, I'll thump you; and you know I can."

Joe protested, "I don't know anything of the sort. Out of respect for you, little Kenny, I won't say a word. I would never have guessed you were interested at all. Don't tell me which one interests you. I say I won't tell, but you know my mouth, so don't trust me with such delicate information, just in case." Joe grinned.

Kenny went back to the balcony while Joe finished getting ready. He was glad he hadn't told Joe all of his personal thoughts.

As he stood on the balcony to allow the wind to blow his wavy chestnut hair, he turned toward the place where the women had been earlier. His brown eyes were met by what he thought was the most beautiful pair of blues ones. She had never caught him off-guard before. The woman didn't turn away as he looked at her as he had only done in his dreams. He'd never seen her look lovelier. Without forethought, his lips formed the sweetest smile. When she returned his smile, his first instinct was to just walk across each balcony that had been placed between them until he captured the woman who had somehow, somewhere, captured the mighty businessman's heart.

After moussing, gelling, spraying, and ironing, the troops were ready to attend the first day of Godly education. Everyone had gotten to the van on time. No one mentioned it, but there was a different feel to the atmosphere. It was almost electric. Joe drove while the others commented on the different sights. Once they arrived, they waited in line for nearly an hour to register at the large church that was hosting the event that would change the rest of their lives.

Lisa D. Piper

The first class was a general session for everyone. Afterwards, they took a small break and chose what they would like to take for the next class. The second class would take them up to lunchtime. Jay, Joe and Mary decided to take the class entitled, "Will You Go Where I Send Thee?" Elizabeth and Gabrielle chose the, "You Have A Future, and He Knows What It Is," class. Josie and Kenny opted to attend the class entitled, "Making Important Decisions With Godly Wisdom."

Josie had the forethought to organize a picnic by filling a large cooler with colas, sandwiches and snacks to avoid leaving the church area during their lunch break. All agreed to meet back at the van before the evening's general session. Josie and Kenny were the first ones in the group to be dismissed from their class and decided to return to the van and begin getting the meal prepared for the others. It wasn't long before a teary-eyed Gabrielle and Elizabeth joined them. Elizabeth asked, "How did like your classes, you two?" Elizabeth picked up a bag of chips to open while she waited for the details of what her friends had thought of, "Making Important Decisions With Godly Wisdom."

"If the rest of the classes are like what we heard today, I believe that this is going to be a great week." Kenny looked at Josie. "What did you think, Josie?"

Josie looked back at Kenny with a tear in her eye. She wiped at her eyes as she looked at her two friends. "I liked it. It was what I needed to hear, I guess."

Kenny stopped trying to get the pickle jar open when he realized Josie was crying. "What's wrong Josie? Are you okay?"

Elizabeth and Gabrielle looked concerned as Josie replied, "I'm okay. I was thinking that I haven't made the wisest decisions in my life. There are things I shouldn't have done and things I wish I'd done a long time ago. I've become one of the most successful women in my line of business, but I don't remember asking God for wisdom more than three times." Josie sobbed. "I only did that when I was in trouble and thought I couldn't pull it off on my own. If you had asked me when I came here yesterday if I were serving God one hundred percent, I would've told you an absolute yes. And now," Josie took the tissue Gabrielle offered and blew her nose. "And now, I can see where I've just been going after everything I want without even thinking about what God thinks, or even giving him an opportunity to have his perfect will in my life."

Discovering Elizabeth

Kenny couldn't say anything that would comfort her. He had heard the anointed speaker present the Word. He'd been uncomfortable as the speaker had unveiled truths that seemed to have been pulled out of the secret places of his soul. Josie was only vocalizing what Kenny felt.

Elizabeth wrapped her arm around her friend. "Josie, I'm not going to say anything to hinder what God is apparently trying to do in you. Just make sure that if you've done something you shouldn't have done, repent of it. But, don't beat yourself up for your mistakes. Keep yourself open to whatever God wants to do. I've a feeling that we're all going to be finding that God has sent us here for some fine tuning for spiritual reformation."

Josie hugged her friend and thanked her. She hadn't noticed before but Gabrielle and Elizabeth were no longer wearing make-up. In fact, a tiny smear of mascara still marked the spot where Gabrielle had apparently wiped her eyes at some time during the day.

As Elizabeth and Gabrielle lay awake in their hotel room on Monday evening, Elizabeth looked at Gabrielle who was sprawled out on her bed in her HoneyBear p.j.'s. "Gab, have you ever had the feeling that you were about to meet up with a plan God had for your life? I'm feeling really, really strange. If I could describe what I feel, I think I would call it a giddy apprehension. I know that makes absolutely no sense."

Gabrielle rolled over to look at Elizabeth. "I sure have. I'm also feeling strange now. Liz, I've never heard the gospel taught as it was today. I have to tell you that I'm feeling compelled to just give up on my own agenda and let God do whatever He wants to do. There's still a part of me that wants to do whatever I want to do though. By the way, did I tell you I dreamed that you and I moved out of our house last night? I always figured we'd be really sad but in my dream we were both excited. I dreamed it over and over."

"Who got the couch?" Elizabeth smiled.

"Very funny. Good night!"

After a restful night of sleep, Tuesday morning came finding Elizabeth and Gabrielle resting on their balcony with chocolate doughnuts and milk. Elizabeth had been the first one to wake, so she took her turn at getting their breakfast up to the room. As they sat sipping their drinks and devouring their doughnuts, Gabrielle asked, "Liz, aren't you supposed to sing today before the general session?"

"Yes, I am. I've not forgotten by a long shot. I'm nervous about it now that we're here."

"What are you going to wear and how are you going to wear your hair, Liz?"

Gabrielle began fumbling with her long hair as if to get ideas on a suitable style.

Elizabeth shrugged, "I thought about wearing that black dress. I guess I'll wear my hair in a clip."

"Oh no you will not!" Gabrielle was aghast.

Elizabeth winced at the passion of Gabrielle's statement. "What do you mean that I'm not? I most certainly am!"

Gabrielle gave Elizabeth a motherly look and said, "Liz, don't go up there looking like some kind of executive yuppie." Gabrielle saw that she might have offended her friend when Elizabeth's eyes widened then darkened. Gabrielle hurriedly rushed on, "Liz, you're so beautiful. Why don't you wear my navy and magenta outfit? It has the dark colors that you like but it has enough color to bring out your best features. Wear your hair down so that you look friendly and approachable. You aren't just going to be singing; you'll be ministering in song."

Elizabeth wanted to argue but found that there was nothing she could say that would be as strong as Gabrielle's argument. "Okay, I'll try."

Gabrielle was elated. "Great! What are you going to sing?"

Elizabeth asked mischievously, "Why don't you tell me? You're planning everything else."

Gabrielle sulked, "Don't be unkind."

"Okay, I think I'll sing Steven Curtis Chapman's, His Strength Is Perfect."

"Oh, Liz, I do love that song. I can't wait!" Gabrielle picked up the empty breakfast plates then left the balcony to get ready for the day that would change the direction of her future."

Chapter THIRTEEN

Proverbs 17:22 "A merry heart doeth good like a medicine: but a broken spirit drieth the bones."

He had thought during the night that he might have imagined that Josie was interested in him. As he stood and looked at the woman he wanted to spend the rest of his life with, he became fearful. Even though his blood ran cold, he couldn't look away from her balcony. He watched, as she looked torn between the choice of continuing their silent communication or going back in to get ready. Finally, Mary came out and told her something. Josie turned to follow Mary back into the room. Before stepping onto the carpet, Josie turned and was relieved to see that Kenny hadn't moved and was still standing only a few yards away. She blushed with a slow spontaneous smile.

Kenny walked back into the room. If he could've leaped into the air and shouted, "Yes!" he would've done it. Instead, he bottled up the emotions and told Joe he was going for a quiet walk.

As the church van pulled into the parking lot where the activities were being held, Elizabeth noticed that there were several persons in the van who were trying to completely avoid any eye-to-eye contact. Elizabeth thought about the atmosphere change then put it out of her mind.

After finding where she would sit when she came off the stage, Elizabeth went to the front of the church where she found the minister of music. The minister of music briefed her on the plans for the morning then showed her where to sit until it was her time to sing.

Lisa D. Piper

From the stage, she had an excellent view. She watched the excited participants pour into the auditorium. While she didn't usually suffer from performance anxiety, her stomach clenched as if to remind her that something strange was going on within her. She had to pray, "Oh Lord, please help me. I don't want to throw up in front of all these people. Please, oh please, hear this prayer."

She was looking at the crowd when an usher walked up behind her and said, "Ms. Pennington, I would like to introduce you to our morning speaker. He'll be speaking immediately following your song. Ray Morgan, this is Elizabeth Pennington. Ms. Pennington has come to us with glowing references. I'm looking forward to hearing her sing."

Ray looked at Elizabeth intently as he watched the shock of seeing him register on her face. "Liz, I had no idea that this is where you planned to vacation. I wouldn't have sprung this on you, I promise. I'm just as surprised as you are."

She didn't have time to respond to the speaker of the hour. She heard her name announced over the monitor in front of her. Elizabeth swallowed, then mechanically walked to where she would sing in front of over five thousand hungry souls. As the music began, she decided that she was about to put the song she was singing to the test. She raised her microphone to her lips as she looked over the crowd until she saw Gabby. "Oh God," she prayed silently, "I need you now. Be my strength."

Just as He had done in times past, God heard His little girl. Renewed strength flowed through her being as she began to sing. There was something about her voice that caused the crowd to allow a sweet hush to spread over them. Some began to weep while others lifted their hands into the air to worship. Elizabeth became lost in the One the song was written about as she closed her eyes. When the song ended, she opened her eyes to find that, throughout the building, hands and hearts were raised to heaven.

Elizabeth turned to be seated. She had almost forgotten that Ray was sitting behind her. As she walked to the back of the stage then headed toward the area where she knew Gabrielle was sitting. As Ray Morgan's name was announced, she heard applause. Gabrielle's mouth opened as she looked at Elizabeth.

Discovering Elizabeth

Elizabeth couldn't speak so she answered the unspoken question her friend had by moving her mouth to form the words, "I didn't know."

When Elizabeth sat down, Joe leaned over and whispered, "Hey, I think I recognize that guy."

Elizabeth didn't respond as she watched the man from whom she was running prepare to speak.

Ray began his speech by praying. Elizabeth thought that she had never heard a more lovely prayer. "Father, you are my strength. Please use my words to convey what you would like to say to your people. Thank you for perfecting your strength in me; I'm not worthy nor am I able to understand what you see in me, but I love you for looking past my own blunders and instilling your own personality in me. Make me more like you, Father. May we use this forum to lift up your name and draw close to you. I love you, my God, in the name of my Lord Jesus, Amen."

Elizabeth could not tear her eyes from the man who had no difficulty holding the attention of thousands of listeners. Even though she knew she had seen a side of him that no one in the audience could say they had seen, she seemed to be learning more about him as he spoke with love, compassion and humility to the crowd of interested listeners. He was talking about praying to God for the will of one's life. He spoke about the decisions he had made without prayer. Inevitably, those decisions became stumbling blocks to his walk with Christ. He explained by telling stories of how he had gone after his own desires before making sure that the One who knows everything gave his final stamp of approval. As Elizabeth sat drinking in the wisdom of her boss, Ray suddenly began to say something that interested Elizabeth greatly. She sat quietly as he unfolded a part of his life that she hadn't known.

Ray had decided while sitting beside Elizabeth that he wouldn't share his private testimony with the crowd. During his prayer; however, Ray felt compelled to tell a part of his past that was still painful. He believed God was leading him to share his pain this with others as instruction for them and for healing for himself. Before arriving at the convention, he had no qualms about speaking about his private life, but that was before he saw someone he knew personally.

As Ray began to speak about his past, he could feel her eyes upon him. He wasn't sure where she was seated, but he could feel her

Lisa D. Piper

looking at him. As he spoke, his spirit prayed for help. As he called out to God, he was given peace to speak as God had ordained. He would share his most painful secrets. Only the Fosters knew of the horrible loss Ray had after graduating from college. Ray would tell those gathered that Tuesday morning about the effects of ignoring the convictions of the God he had served most of his life.

Ray inhaled and began to reminisce, "I know that you have heard of have read the scripture that says that if we'll draw nigh to God, He will draw nigh to us[12]. There is also a scripture that states, 'Seek ye first the Kingdom of Heaven, and these things shall be added unto you[13].' God doesn't want us to put Him first to cause us pain or trials. He knows that it's good for us to obey him and to have him lead us. He tries to show us that we are blessed greatly when we trust in Him. If you think about it, you can see that we'll never be blessed in ourselves or by our own motives. The Old Testament reveals the fact that God is faithful and those who trust Him are blessed."

Ray paused before continuing, "I've made my own bad choices. Ray smiled and Elizabeth's heart melted. "I was in my sophomore year of college when I took a psychology class. As a part of an experiment, I went to the park every day to watch the children interact. I also would take notes on how each adult reacted to the different escapades of the unruly tykes. I had a lot of fun and could probably write a book on the orneriness of some of the little boys I watched. One day, I noticed the cutest little girl playing by herself. She seemed to be in a world all pf her own. I noticed that she arrived at the park with a group of children every other day right before lunchtime. It wasn't long before I was fascinated with the way the other children treated her. They weren't mean to her; yet, they didn't pay much attention to her either. She looked to be about four years old. Curly black hair framed chubby pink cheeks. One day, she saw me watching her. She lifted her chubby little hand and waved shyly. Her glistening hair was pulled back with a bright pink bow. She was always dressed as if she were going somewhere that would require lace and frills. After that day, she waved at me every time she saw me."

Ray took a sip of water that had been left for him by the minister of music then continued, "Eventually, I walked over to the lady whom I

---

[12] James 4:8
[13] Matt. 6:33

Discovering Elizabeth

assumed to be her caregiver. Her name was Nancy. Nancy was friendly and had been observing me. I guess she didn't think I was a threat because she spoke openly to me about the children. Two days later I saw them again. I asked Nancy if I could play with the little girl and she said that I could. Nancy watched me carefully and I was glad that she was so careful. The little girl told me that her name was Shelley.

Shelley stole my heart with the first question she ever asked me. She looked up at me with those coal black eyes, tugged on my pant leg and said, "Hey man, are you as tall as a tree?"

I laughed. She and I walked over to the nearest tree where she could measure me. To her amazement, I wasn't as tall as that scarred oak tree." The audience laughed as Ray continued.

"During that semester I pushed swings, slid down slides, made castles in the sand and loved every minute of it. I eventually became Shelley's sole playmate. She thought there was nothing I couldn't do. I would find her watching for me when I would be a few minutes late. Her smile was payment enough for the enjoyment I got from being with her."

"One day, Shelley's mother drove to the park to pick her up early. I was pushing Shelley on a swing and singing some silly song to her when her mother approached me from behind. As I turned, I came face to face with a woman who was unmistakable to me. I knew that she belonged to Shelley. Her hair was as curly and as black as her daughter's. Shelley's mom was very pretty. I sensed that there was something not right about her, but I ignored it. After meeting Shelly's mother several more times in the park, I learned that Shelley's dad had died when she was three. I felt so sorry for the father-deprived child. Having grown up without a father myself, I just wanted to be her dad. By the time I entered my junior year of college, I had asked Shelley's mother, Felicia, to marry me."

"Felicia accepted my proposal. She wasn't a Christian and I should've known better. If I could speak anything to you that would make a difference in whom you choose to spend the rest of your life with, it would be that you date only those who have made a commitment to Jesus Christ. If you fool yourself into believing that you can change a person, or that it doesn't matter whether they believe in Christ or not, you're probably setting yourself up for disappointment."

Lisa D. Piper

"Pray about your decisions. I've heard that God is mute, but I tell you He is not. He wants to share His idea for your future with you more than you want to hear it." Ray paused and snickered. "Okay, okay, I'll stop preaching for a moment and finish the story. I guess you can tell I'm really sure about what I'm saying." Ray smiled.

The audience had warmed up to him and didn't seem to mind his preaching, as he called it. Ray smiled at his captivated audience.

He surveyed the room as he addressed the crowd. "It's possible to fool yourself into thinking that you can change another person. I made the decision to become one with someone who was not a Christian with the hope that she would one day follow Jesus. I wish I hadn't played around with my future. I wish I'd left it in God's capable hands. I knew that I shouldn't have even considered marrying Felicia, but her daughter won my heart. I cared for Shelley's mother, but not in the way that a man should love a wife. However, if I had been passionately in love with her, she was still not even a candidate for marriage because she wasn't a Christian."

"Two months before we were to be married, Felicia was in a terrible accident. She didn't survive the car crash caused by her drunken state. Shelley was alone and I was the only one that I knew of who truly loved the child. My desire to become her father came in a way that I hadn't expected."

"Felicia had shared with me that her parents had died when she was small so I didn't even know of anyone who could be contacted about the care Shelly. I vividly remember the day that I picked Shelley up from her caregiver and told her that her mother had been in a car wreck." Ray held back the emotions that were exploding inside him. "I was so angry at Felicia for dying and leaving my little girl alone."

Ray cleared his throat then continued. "I spoke to a lawyer and explained the Shelly's situation with him. We made preparations for me to adopt Shelley. I was still attending college and was balancing my work responsibilities while trying to care for the five-year-old. I didn't mind the sacrifices of being a father. I loved reading bedtime stories to her. I loved brushing her hair and my heart melted when she called me Daddy.

"Three months after Felicia's death, I was frazzled and tired but still happy to have Shelley near me. One Sunday while we were getting

Discovering Elizabeth

ready for church, there was a knock on the door. I opened the door to a familiar looking, well-dressed man. He told me that he had come to get his daughter. I threatened to throw him out of the house if he didn't leave immediately. To sum up the situation, Felicia had been married to a wealthy businessman. She had taken off with their daughter when Shelley was two. The worried man had spent a lot of time and money looking for his beloved child. I won't go into all of the details, but the worst pain I've ever had was watching that man take my sweet girl away. Shelley didn't really remember him and was afraid. I felt so helpless. I cannot express the emotional despair I felt the moment that I hugged her for the last time. I can still remember the smell of her blankets and the sound of her little voice." Ray paused as if he were trying to keep the memory from enveloping him. "Ladies and gentleman, I didn't follow God's direction for my life, and I've eaten the fruit of my waywardness."

As Ray began to expound upon the different ways to know the will of God, Elizabeth became overwrought with emotion. She didn't know the man whom she thought she cared for so deeply. She began to think of why she would've even thought she knew Ray Morgan. The things Ray had said made sense to her. He had apparently prayed about a life with her, but Elizabeth now feared that Ray wasn't the one that God had intended for her life. As Elizabeth began to meditate she heard a familiar voice within her say, "When are you going to ask me?" Elizabeth became still. She knew that God was trying to get her attention. The fear that He would not allow her to have Ray caused her to hesitate before responding to her Creator. Elizabeth's heart pounded as the voice rang out inside of her, "When are you going to ask me?" Finally, Elizabeth began to weep. She hadn't cared what God's plan for her life was. She whispered, "Oh Lord, You know my heart. You know that I want to be with this man." Something similar to pain or regret found its way into her throat as she finished her prayer. "Lord, this is difficult but I know Your way is the best way. I ask you to give me Ray as a mate providing that my being with him is in your will. I haven't cared what You think, but I want to know now. I love You, Lord. Thank you for taking an interest in me." She knew that her surrender could mean losing Ray forever.

Elizabeth didn't receive an immediate response from the One who knew what was in her heart. She leaned over to Gabrielle and asked, "Would you go to the ladies room with me, Gab?"

Lisa D. Piper

Gabrielle touched her on the arm as she replied softly, "Sure, I'm ready whenever you are."

Ray noticed the two women walk out of the sanctuary. He didn't hesitate as he proceeded with his lecture, but his heart lurched. He continued to speak until time for the first break. He received a standing ovation from the tearful yet hopeful crowd; Ray smiled through his pain. What he wanted to do was to grab Eric and to fly as fast as he could straight back to Wright and Wingold. He would engross himself in his work until he forgot Elizabeth Anne Pennington. While some of the people gathered around him to let him know how helpful his comments were, the woman he loved was in the restroom hyperventilating.

Gabrielle held the bag to Elizabeth's mouth. "Come on, Liz, just breathe in, girlfriend!" Gabrielle was frantic as she watched her friend lose control of herself.

After breathing in and out of the little paper bag, Elizabeth was finally able to breathe normally. Tears streamed down her face as Gabrielle wiped her the eyes of her lifelong friend. "I don't know what's wrong with me, Gab. I just don't know! I'm so sorry."

Gabrielle brushed her friend's hair out of her face and comforted her. "Don't worry about it, my friend. I'm not going anywhere without you, so don't even start feeling guilty, alright?"

At first, Elizabeth had wanted Gabby to be with her, but now she felt embarrassed. "Gabby, you're a good friend. If you don't mind, I want to sit in here for a little while by myself and just spend some time thinking. I'm glad you came in here with me. You're the best. I just stood before this congregation a little while ago and proclaimed that His strength is perfect and now look at me. Please go on and meet up with the guys and I'll meet you in a little while. Please?"

Gabrielle didn't want to move, but she also knew that her friend could be stubborn and that eventually Elizabeth would have her own way. "Okay, I'll go, but I don't want to go. If you're not out there in a few minutes, I'll come looking for you, young lady."

Elizabeth sniffed, "Thanks, Gab. I don't know what I would do without you."

Discovering Elizabeth

Gabrielle grinned. "You'd do just fine old buddy of mine. I'll be saving your seat so don't get all caught up in thinking in here and forget about me."

Elizabeth tried to smile as Gabrielle reluctantly stood up to go back into the auditorium. She had wanted her to go, but now she wanted her to stay. With the turmoil of her emotional roller coaster, Elizabeth began to cry again. "What's wrong with me?" Elizabeth asked herself aloud.

As she made her way back to her seat, a dark hand reached out and caught her arm. Gabrielle turned quickly. She was ready to give someone more than they bargained for if she were indeed in danger. Gabrielle was aware that she was in a church, but she could be jumpy when she was emotionally charged. As Gabrielle whirled around, she was stunned to come face to face with the man who had managed to keep her awake at night even though she didn't know him. Gabrielle looked at his hand that still touched her arm then stammered, "Hello there."

The man smiled as he let his arm drop to his side. "Hello. I'm sorry about startling you. I guess I was just so amazed to see you here that I kind of overreacted. I do apologize."

Gabrielle couldn't hide her smile. "Not a problem. I'm surprised to see you again, especially in the Sunshine State. I hope you're having a good time."

Eric leaned toward her and whispered. "I just arrived here today. However, I think my chances of having a good time are improving by with every passing moment."

Gabrielle was embarrassed by his forward remark. She wasn't sure how to respond to his flirting so she hurriedly said, "I, I guess I'll sit down now. I'm waiting for a friend. Bye."

Eric frowned as she hurried away. "Okay, see you later."

Eric could not pay attention to the speaker. He continued to glance to where Gabrielle was sitting in order to see who the friend would be. The lecture was halfway over when he saw Elizabeth Pennington walk up to Gabrielle and sit in the empty chair beside her. Relief flooded his being as he made plans to draw the attention of one lovely redheaded lady to himself before he got back onto his plane.

Lisa D. Piper

As soon as the speaker finished the his last sentence, Eric leaped from his seat so that he could get to Gabrielle before she became lost in the sea of people. Eric called to her, "Gabrielle!"

Gabrielle turned toward the man who was briskly walking toward her, "Yes?"

He hadn't thought of what he would say once he won her attention. His goal had been to not lose her. As she stood waiting for him to tell her what he wanted, his mind raced.

Elizabeth walked to the end of the row of chairs to give them privacy, but she wasn't so far from them that she couldn't hear Eric ask, "Would you like to have dinner tonight? Please don't say no."

Gabrielle's heart fluttered as her head argued with her desire. Gabrielle was surprised to hear herself accept the invitation.

Eric smiled. "Wonderful!"

"Where are you staying?" Eric took a pen from his Bible then wrote down the directions to her hotel. As Gabrielle finished giving him the instructions, Eric looked into her eyes and said softly. "Thank you, Gabrielle. I'm so glad you said yes."

Chapter FOURTEEN

"He has made everything beautiful in its time." Ecclesiastes 3:11a NKJV

The day progressed quickly. Gabrielle's attention span was greatly affected by the fact that she would only have a few minutes to pick out something fabulous to wear, change and freshen up before Eric arrived for their first date. Elizabeth was a little perturbed at Gabrielle's spontaneous decision to accept Eric's invitation, but to admit her concern to Gabrielle would be futile.

The telephone was ringing when the girls reentered their hotel room. Gabrielle nearly tripped over the corner of a bed trying to get to it before it ceased its ringing. "Hello?"

"Hello Gabrielle, this is Eric."

Gabrielle happily looked up at Elizabeth while she pointed excitedly at the receiver. She cooed, "Hello, Eric."

"Gabrielle, I need to ask you a question. Would it be a problem if I brought a friend along? He's not feeling like his happy self and I don't want to leave him."

Gabrielle thought about it. There was no way she was going anywhere with two men. She had been quietly apprehensive about going somewhere alone with a man she hardly knew. Gabrielle held her hand over the phone, "Elizabeth, I need to ask a favor of you."

Elizabeth looked up at the ceiling. "What, Gab?"

Lisa D. Piper

"I want you to come with us. Please?" Gabrielle lowered her voice. "Come on, Elizabeth, I know you don't want me going out alone with a man we hardly know. Please, oh please? I think this could be the real thing, Liz. How am I going to know if he's the one? I would do it for you." Gabrielle grinned, "The alternative is for you to stay here while I go out. I know you'll worry about whether or not I'm out with an ax murderer. Please say you'll go, best buddy?"

Elizabeth threw up her hands. "Gabby, I don't know why I'm letting you talk me into this, but I will go on one condition."

Gabrielle was hopeful, "What condition?"

Elizabeth couldn't keep from giggling as she tried to sound motherly. "If you smooch him, you had better do it in private; and if you do it in private, you had better expect a lecture when we get back here about first date etiquette! And, that man is going to be my boss so please don't embarrass me!"

Gabrielle stuck her tongue out at her friend. She spoke into the phone, "Eric, would you mind if Elizabeth came with us? I'd be uncomfortable otherwise." Gabrielle felt a little deceptive as she purposely avoided the fact that she was kind of arranging a blind date for Elizabeth. Gabrielle grinned as she thought of how Elizabeth would react when she found out. She knew that her friend would go along with the plan and be kind. She also knew that once the men left, it wouldn't be long before Elizabeth gave her the third degree.

Eric was glad that Elizabeth would be coming along. He had decided to not tell Ray that they were picking up two women. He had let Ray believe that they were going to Pensacola Beach to eat a nice dinner. Eric decided to not think about Ray's reaction to the set up, as he finished his first telephone conversation with the woman he decided he would one day marry. "Gabrielle, I'm so glad that you still want to go. We'll be there in about an hour." Gabrielle was about to hang up the phone when Eric continued, "Oh, and tell your friend that I do not smooch on the first date." Eric hung up with a chuckle as Gabrielle's mouth hung open in warm embarrassment.

Gabrielle turned to scowl at her friend. Elizabeth questioned, "What did I do? What?"

Discovering Elizabeth

"He heard what you said about smooching. He'll be here in one hour and I am so embarrassed that I don't think I can do this now." Gabrielle quickly recovered as she squealed. "Help me to get dressed!"

Elizabeth laughed. "You're too funny. That was the shortest bout of humiliation I've ever seen. You recovered nicely." Elizabeth helped Gabrielle fix her hair.

After they had finished with Gabrielle, she turned to Elizabeth and said, "Okay, now let's get you fixed up a bit. What are you going to wear?"

Elizabeth grimaced. "I'm not going out on a date-you are. I will go as is. I can't believe I'm even going."

Gabrielle shouted, "Oh no you will not!" She then lowered her voice and said, "You can't do that. This is special and you don't know where we'll be going. You've got to look nice."

Gabrielle coaxed Elizabeth into wearing a flowing hairstyle and helped her to put her make-up on to perfection. Mary knocked on the door and began to whistle when Gabrielle opened the door. "Where are you girls going?"

"Out! Do we look okay? We have a date!" Gabrielle stated excitedly.

Elizabeth corrected her. "No, Gabrielle has a date. I'm a chaperone; I'm a tag-a-long actually."

Mary commented, "Well, you both look lovely. You look wonderful!"

Elizabeth asked, "What are you and Josie doing tonight?"

Josie heard her name and walked up behind Mary. Josie said, "We're going to an aerial museum and Civil War fort or something like that with the guys. It sounded fun, so we conceded."

The telephone began to ring. Elizabeth answered it. She quickly put the phone down and told Gabrielle that a visitor was waiting for them downstairs. Gabrielle rolled her eyes when Elizabeth added, "You owe me big time, Gab, and I mean big time."

Josie and Mary asked to walk them down so that they could get a look at Gabrielle's date, but she wouldn't allow them the privilege.

"Just pray for us. We're both nervous and hoping he's not an ax murderer."

Josie and Mary assured them that they would pray but that they were leaving in a few minutes themselves.

Gabrielle fidgeted with her purse as they waited for the elevator to descend to the first floor. The door opened and there standing in front of the baby grand piano was the most handsome man Gabrielle had ever seen. Eric ceremoniously bowed to his date then held out his hand inviting her to take his offered arm. Gabrielle smiled sheepishly as she locked her arm in his, completely forgetting about Elizabeth.

Elizabeth's breath caught in her throat as she saw the tall man standing behind Eric. Ray looked as surprised as she did, but quickly recovered as Eric and Gabrielle walked away. He decided to do as his friend had done and held out his arm to the lovely lady. "Madam, may I escort you to an evening of chaperoning pleasure?"

Elizabeth was too overwhelmed to refuse. She took his arm. Ray whispered, "I see that you are shocked. Elizabeth, Eric just told me about his scheme when we entered the hotel. I wouldn't have done this to you."

Even though Elizabeth was thinking of the things she'd tell Gabrielle once they were back in the room, she was slightly disappointed that Ray hadn't searched high and low for her and found out where she was staying as she had first thought he had done when she saw him in the foyer.

Ray stopped her and turned her toward him. "Liz, I didn't mean that I wouldn't want to go out with you. I just wish Eric would've thought about the consequences before he and your friend arranged this blind date. Eric, after all, has no idea how I feel about you."

"How he feels about me?" Elizabeth's mind raced as she turned his statement over and over in her mind.

Ray drove to a restaurant specializing in fresh seafood. The foursome were seated at a table with a dynamic view of the land's exquisite splendor. Eric and Gabrielle found that they had no difficulty finding common interests to create their own conversation. They seemed not to notice the two that had come along with them. Elizabeth and Ray sat in silence; both were afraid to look at each other. After

Discovering Elizabeth

dinner, Eric explained that there was a pier behind some of the shops that would be an ideal spot to take an evening stroll. By the time they had finished paying for their meal and walking to the pier, the moon shone brightly, sparkling on the water like moon glow glitter. There were no clouds to obstruct the awesome view of the heavens.

As the two couples walked to the pier, Eric and Gabrielle walked over to where a huge pink faux shell had been erected with a wooden platform around it. As they sat down on the platform, they both began to remove their shoes before their stroll. It was obvious that they wanted time to themselves as they walked along the beach hand in hand-without inviting their two friends to come along with them. Elizabeth and Ray were left sitting in front of the huge shell.

Ray lost some of the confidence he had felt earlier. He smoothed out his pant legs while trying to get the courage to ask the lovely woman next to him if she wanted to walk down the pier with him.

Elizabeth was grateful when he broke the silence by asking her to walk. Elizabeth stood to her feet. "Sure, why not?"

He wanted to hold her hand as Eric had done with Gabrielle, but decided that he wouldn't be able to continue with the night if she refused. Ray looked like a little boy as he peered over the edge of the wooden planks. He glanced at Elizabeth and asked, "Do you want to dangle your feet? You aren't afraid of sharks are you?"

Elizabeth grimaced, "I would have if you hadn't mentioned sharks!"

"Oh come on, Liz. We can dip our toes where the water is shallow. If a whale tries to swallow you, it will have to fight me first." Ray began to walk to an area where he thought it would be shallow enough to dip their toes in the cool water.

Elizabeth followed him while looking wryly at the unknown waters. "If you're sure you can protect me, I'll do it. If a shark bites your toes, don't hold me responsible! I'll be running away very fast if I see just one!"

As Elizabeth tested the water with her bare feet, she hesitated. "Ray, do you see fins anywhere?" She looked at him as if he had the ability to see what she could not.

He was nervous but courageously put his feet in the dark water. "Uh, well, I don't see or feel anything. Just relax, we aren't going to get our toes eaten off."

Elizabeth looked to the area where she had last seen her friend. "Ray, do you think they're okay? They've been gone for longer than a normal walk would take. Eric is an okay guy, isn't he? I don't want to see Gabrielle get hurt. I'm afraid for them. They seem to be moving so quickly and..."

Ray lifted her hand and put it into his. He squeezed it gently as if to loan her some much needed comfort. "I think he's okay. Elizabeth, we can't run their lives for them and protect them by judging their actions by our own fears. What we can do is pray for them."

Elizabeth wanted to lean against his shoulder while she looked at the breathtaking view before them. The memory of her head resting on his shoulder made her shudder. Ray turned toward her then gave in to the desire to pick up a strand of her hair just to remember how it felt. He whispered, "Elizabeth."

She felt as if someone had dropped a bolt of electricity into the waters. "Yes?"

"I will resign."

"You'll do what?" Elizabeth pulled her feet from the water and turned to look him in the eye as she awaited an explanation.

Ray held her hand securely. "I will resign my position. I don't know what you think about me after listening to what I said today about Felicia. You may not even be interested in me, but I can't help but tell you how I feel." Ray rushed on, "I will resign as CEO of Wright and Wingold to have a lifetime with you, to love you until the day that I die. I want you to be my family." Ray stopped speaking when he realized that Elizabeth had begun to weep. "I'm sorry, Liz, I didn't mean to upset you."

She had difficulty speaking. "Ray, I couldn't ask you to do that. You've worked too hard to be where you are. I'm glad I heard about your life today; it kind of makes sense. Ray, I have my own secrets you know. You wouldn't want to resign your position if you knew everything about me. You are so sweet." Elizabeth began to sob. She

Discovering Elizabeth

knew that he had a lot invested in Wright and Wingold and that it was rumored that he owned most of it.

Ray was sorry that he had said anything so abruptly. After fighting the urge to just let her cry on his shoulder, he finally gave in and pulled her into his arms. He could feel her hot tears roll down the back of his shirt. He stroked the back of her head as he pleaded with her, "Liz, tell me why you are crying. You can trust me, sweetheart, you really can. Have I hurt you so badly? I'm sorry."

Elizabeth felt a need to share what had happened to her early in life that had caused her to be the woman she had become. "Ray, you need to know something but I'm too embarrassed. Could you just not look at me while I try to tell you? Only Gabrielle knows about this."

He tried to comfort her. "Liz, you can tell me anything. I'll not judge you and I won't I tell anyone else. I won't look at you, if that's what you want."

"Okay." Elizabeth paused for several minutes before gaining the courage to tell him. "Ray, I was married before, or I kind of was anyway."

He wanted to look at her but remained silent and still. He wasn't sure how one could be "kind of" married but was interested in finding out.

Elizabeth rushed on with the admission. "As you know, I'm very serious when I'm at work and kind of a goof off when I'm not." Elizabeth smiled at the analogy Gabrielle frequently used of her dual personality. "I was immature when I graduated from high school. What I'm about to tell you is incredulous, I know. I made so many mistakes due to my immaturity that since my "eye-opening moment" I've tried very hard to be mature or appear mature... particularly in public."

Ray smiled and held on to the troubled lady who was once more dangling all ten polished toenails in the gulf.

"First, I want to give you an explanation so that you don't think I'm completely ridiculous. Now, let me finish." Elizabeth poked him in the ribs and Ray became quiet. "I dated a boy named Jonathon my senior year of high school. I was infatuated with Jonathon to the point that I spent all of my waking moments dreaming of the day we would marry. It didn't help that neither of our parents wanted us to date. We disobeyed our parents and began to see each other in secret. That made it much more tempting somehow." Elizabeth swished her feet in the water while silently praying that her toes didn't look like shark bait.

She continued, "He wasn't a Christian. He came from a well-to-do family who had never gone to church. At the time, I was the only Christian in my family. I grew up in an upper middle class family with all of the perks of having extra money, but I was given no structure, so to speak. I basically did what I wanted to do, when I wanted and with whom I wanted with the exception that my parents disliked Jonathon and his parents." Elizabeth looked up at Ray who was trying not to look at her. "Are you with me so far?"

"Yes. But...please get to the part about being married."

"Okay. Right after graduation, Jonathon and I secretly met at the home of a friend of ours. We began talking about our future. We talked about the concerns we had about never settling down." Elizabeth laughed. "We were naïve and thought that life decisions had to be made right then before we were too old."

Ray laughed, "I can relate to that mind set, believe me. I was once eighteen. I recall thinking that whatever I wanted to do with my life, I had to do it right then."

Elizabeth nodded. "Exactly. We began to map out a strategy to do what we wanted to do despite the advice and warning of our parents. Rebellion is a horrible thing. Jonathon and I thought that if we sneaked away and married, our parents would have no other choice but to accept us as a couple, and then we could live happily ever after. I'm not sure how we outlined how the plan would work, but in our minds the world had just inherited two geniuses for the adult population. Neither of us had jobs and we both had plans to attend different colleges. We had no place to live and no money other than our allowances. Like myself, Jonathon wasn't thrifty with the money he was given by his doting parents. For some reason, marriage sounded so romantic and appealing that we finalized the plans to accomplish the task. We didn't think about what would happen afterwards. Our thoughts were purely on how we would accomplish the task of sealing our future with blissful matrimony."

Elizabeth chuckled. "Ray, do you remember when you complimented me after we finished the last hospital account? You were amazed that I was able to foresee every probable challenge that might

Discovering Elizabeth

occur-before we agreed to give them the details of what we could do for them as a service."

Ray looked down at Elizabeth, "Yes, I do. You were able to see things in the future that others didn't pick up. Actually, your intuitiveness has kept us from losing a lot of money."

Elizabeth grinned. "You didn't think I obtained all of that wisdom without having been burned before did you?"

Ray laughed. "I never thought about it! I was just glad that you had the ability to see the consequences of bad decisions."

Elizabeth nodded. "Yeah, I was the queen of bad decisions for awhile. Jonathon and I chose to do the deed on my birthday. I sneaked out early that Saturday morning before my parents awoke. I drove my car to Gabrielle's house where Jonathon was nervously waiting. Gab's mom watched us outside her bedroom window. Being a parent of my best friend, her mom decided to call my parents and inquire as to what I was doing. My mother panicked. She went up to my room and found my diary where I had detailed the entire plan for future generations to read. My mom called Jonathon's parents. His parents blamed mine, and mine blasted his parents for allowing their son...I think they called him their filthy son... to talk their daughter into ruining her life. In the end, our parents joined together to find us and save us from matrimony."

Ray patted her on the back while smoothing down her wind blown hair. "So, what happened?"

Elizabeth lifted her head to peek up at him and smiled. "Our parents found us as we were walking out of the tiny wedding chapel as Mr. and Mrs. Jonathon Hartenknocker."

"Elizabeth Hartenknocker?"

"I know, the name sounds horrible doesn't it?" Elizabeth laughed.

Ray squeezed her to him. "Don't leave me in suspense; what happened?"

Elizabeth covered her face with her hands, "We ran back into the chapel with our parents in hot pursuit. We had parked his car in the back, so we ran out of the back door, jumped into the car and tried to drive off like we were wanted criminals."

Ray grinned. He couldn't imagine Elizabeth in such a predicament.

Elizabeth again covered her eyes with embarrassment. "Ray, we were scared; I mean terrified. Our parents were irate and we knew we were in trouble." Elizabeth began to laugh.

"What's so funny, Ms. Pennington?" Ray chuckled.

"I've never found this part of my life to be humorous. I've considered that time in my life to be dismal failure. Now as I talk to you, I can see that it has helped make me who I am."

Ray agreed. "The Bible says not to despise your youth[14]. We all do things we wish we hadn't done."

Elizabeth snickered. "Yes, that's something I know about. Jonathan's dad raced to the car before we could get away and that's the end of the story."

Ray laughed with Elizabeth. "Liz, you're telling me a tall tale, aren't you?"

She denied it. "I'm not telling you a falsehood. Listen, this has been a very painful and embarrassing part of my life!" To prove a point, Elizabeth expounded on the result of her folly. "I've been so embarrassed by what we did that I have refused to talk about marriage. I've avoided any serious relationships with men because of the shame. I never wanted to answer the question, 'Have you ever been married?' Any man would find the whole thing ridiculous."

Ray comforted her. "I don't find you ridiculous. I find the situation a unique one. How did it end?"

"My parents have never pretended to forget about what I put them through. I still can't mention Jonathon's name today without hearing about how dumb the ordeal was."

"I'm sorry, Liz. You never did say how the marriage ended and I'm really waiting to hear that part of the story." Ray looked at her expectantly.

Elizabeth smiled, "I was eighteen, but boy was I ever grounded. I was married and eighteen, yet grounded to my room for what Dad said was eternity. Later that day, I heard a car drive up. Within minutes I

---

[14] 1 Tim 4:12

Discovering Elizabeth

heard arguing coming up the stairs. My in-laws were screaming at my parents and vice versa. As you would suppose, I didn't get the "Welcome to the family" speech that I had expected. I would've called Jonathon, my husband, but I was grounded from the phone and so was he." Elizabeth didn't mind as Ray began to chuckle. Elizabeth teased him. "Don't you laugh! How would you like to be held hostage after you had just become a full-fledged, 100% legal adult?"

Ray grinned. "I'm not sure how I would like it, but at this point, I'm glad that they locked you away!"

Elizabeth shook her head defiantly. "Thank you very much, you have no idea of the pressure of being locked away while others are deciding your future." Elizabeth turned to Ray, "I am now thankful, but I wasn't happy back then. Let me finish this horrible story." Elizabeth grinned. "Our parents decided that we should've the marriage annulled."

Ray asked, "How did they decide that they would convince you to agree to end your marriage before it even started?"

"They told us that the only way we were going to be ungrounded and live was to annul our marriage. I pictured growing old in my room with no education, no life and no Gabrielle. It didn't take long to convince us to call it off. I only saw Jonathon once more after that. I guess we were both so humiliated that we couldn't look each other in the eye again…so much for love and devotion, I guess. I used to keep his picture in my room as a final sign of mourning. I don't even have that anymore. I just did that to irritate my mother and remind myself not to do anything like that again." Elizabeth became somber. "Ray, it really was a humiliating experience."

He looked at her and said softly, "I'm sure it was, sweetheart. I think I love you even the more for it."

Elizabeth sat back, relieved to have spilled out what she had thought was a horrid secret. Several seconds passed before she caught what he had said. "Ray, do you love me?" Elizabeth wanted to avoid his stare as she became uncomfortable.

He swallowed then said a silent prayer, hoping he was doing the right thing by admitting his feelings for her. "Elizabeth Pennington, yes I do. I can change my position at the company, but there is no other woman for me but you."

Lisa D. Piper

Elizabeth was shaken by his admission. She could no longer sit beside of him and breathe normally. She stood and walked to the other side of the pier. She had left Ray feeling rejected until she began walking back to him slowly. He stood up as she looked at him with those dark eyes. "Ray," she began, "I can't ask you to separate yourself from your company or to step down from its leadership. I want to be with you but I can't ask you to give up a lead role in your company. I don't think I could stand the guilt that would arise from asking you to change your entire life."

Ray began to interrupt but Elizabeth wouldn't allow it. "Ray, I will resign."

Ray stood back, "You? I don't think…"

Elizabeth interrupted, "Ray, I have a favor to ask of you."

"What is it? Name it."

"I don't want to talk about our jobs. One of us will resign or we'll arrange something different later. I don't want to argue with you under the moon and stars. I want to take this time to just be with you without worrying about anything. Can we do that?"

Ray wrapped his tanned arms around her. "My lovely lady, I wholeheartedly agree. Let's do that." He heard Eric call out his name. Ray yelled, "We're over here!" He looked at Elizabeth with regret that their private time had just ended. Elizabeth smiled at the man whom she now knew God would let her have.

As Elizabeth said a quiet prayer, a very merry couple joined them on the pier. Ray didn't want to give any explanation as to what he and Elizabeth had been doing. He quickly asked, "Is anyone in the mood for ice cream?"

Everyone agreed that Ray had a great idea. The truth was that no one wanted the night to end. When Ray stopped his car in front of the hotel, no one said a word. Meaningful looks were exchanged from the front and back seats. Ray walked around the car and opened Elizabeth's door. He whispered, "I'll call you later. I've signed up for the session tomorrow. May I have the pleasure of accompanying you?" Elizabeth shook her head yes, then joined a beaming Gabrielle to walk back to their room.

Discovering Elizabeth

Elizabeth wasn't sure if she and Gabrielle were walking on the floor or if their feet were somehow walking on air as they glided into the hotel. Elizabeth snickered and looked at her friend. "Gab, I don't know about you but I can't seem to wipe this silly grin off of my face. You don't look much better than I do."

Gabrielle's grin widened. "Elizabeth, this is it. This is the man I've been waiting for all my life. I think you're going to have to find a new roommate soon. If he had asked me to be his wife tonight, I would have said yes."

Elizabeth stopped smiling. "Gabby, you've only just met the man. You haven't even had time to pray about it!"

Gabrielle turned swiftly, "Elizabeth, do not ruin this for me. This is it; I just know it. Eric thinks so too; please, just be happy for us."

Elizabeth did as Gabrielle wished her to do although she definitely wanted to say more. Gabrielle was so caught up in her evening with Eric that she never seemed to notice that Elizabeth and Ray had made some kind of resolution to their differences.

As soon as the two women entered their rooms, pounding sounds came from the adjoining door. Elizabeth opened the door and said, "What are you two doing? People are trying to sleep you know!"

Josie looked indignant. "Well, Ms. Pennington, one of those people trying to sleep would be yours truly. How could we sleep when you could have been out with an ax murderer?"

Elizabeth pulled off her shoes as the two women followed her into the room. "They weren't strange men and we're sorry if we kept you awake. What really kept you awake, ladies? Was it that we were out with a stranger, or did you want to know how it went once we returned?"

Josie slapped Mary softly on the back. "Now that's the way to be discreet."

Mary agreed, "Liz, I can't believe you would ask such a question. Now, tell all! I thought you were going out with only one man."

Elizabeth sat on her bed. "There was supposed to be only one man, but that man and this shyster of a friend that I have, set us up! Do you remember the man who spoke today about staying in the will of God while seeking a mate?" Mary shook her head emphatically. "Well, that's who came with Eric, while I went along to chaperone Gab. Ray Morgan, the man who spoke, is also my boss. Eric is going to be my new boss, so everything went well and the subject of axes never came up."

Although Josie and Mary wanted details about the evening, neither Elizabeth nor Gabrielle could part with the private information of her date. Gabrielle mentioned the place where they ate minus any romantic information. Gabrielle ended the chat session by adding, "Of course, you can look at us and tell that we weren't harmed in any way, but we had an excellent time, thank you very much. What did you ladies do tonight?"

Josie glanced at Mary. Mary sounded mysterious as she spoke. "We went to the aerial thing with the guys. There's a neat looking lighthouse right next to it, so we walked around that area. We came back here before dark. We then went for a romantical stroll on the beach."

"Romantical?" Elizabeth rolled her eyes. "When is a walk with Josie romantical and where in the world did you get such a word?"

Josie smiled mischievously, "Don't ask any more questions because we aren't telling. I wasn't walking with Mary nor was she walking with me, and that's all we have to say about it."

With that said, Josie and Mary marched off into their own room leaving Gabrielle and Elizabeth gaping behind them.

The group decided to leave early on Friday. Elizabeth hated to leave Florida and all of her wonderful new memories. She'd spent all of Wednesday with Ray. They attended the same classes and the evening service together. They were only apart for one hour when Elizabeth and Gabrielle attended a class reserved for women while the men went to a leadership class.

A banquet was held on Thursday for all of the attendees. The event was informal but gave the students time to speak one on one with the speakers of the week. Ray was approached by several attendees who made comments about how his speech had affected them or caused them to think about their current situations. Elizabeth and Ray purposely sought out the speaker who had spoken about ethical issues concerning Christian dating. Both Elizabeth and Ray knew that there

Discovering Elizabeth

were issues that would need to be resolved in order for their relationship to work.

The elderly man who had loaned his wisdom to the singles during the week was empathetic and helpful to the new couple. He had a great understanding of the moral issues and temptations involved in any adult relationship. The couple knew that it would be difficult to discuss their private situation with a stranger but felt led by the Holy Spirit to do so. Elizabeth and Ray agreed to take the man's advice. Ray pulled Elizabeth into a room where only strangers remained. "Elizabeth, what this man says is wise. For one thing, I think that we need to make sure to not place ourselves into a compromising situation. I don't want to spend time alone with you. Let me correct that. I do want to spend time alone with you and that's why I think we should limit our personal encounters to public places."

Elizabeth agreed. "I think that's best, even though I don't want to be without you. I love you, Ray Morgan."

Ray touched Elizabeth on the nose. "And that, my dear, is exactly why I'm going to visit Annie Mae some time in the near future."

Elizabeth was confused. "Annie Mae?"

Ray grinned slyly. "I can't tell you why. I've just have to see her."

Lisa D. Piper

Chapter FIFTEEN

Proverbs 18:21 "Death and life are in the power of the tongue: and they that love it shall eat the fruit thereof."

The drive back home was nothing like the drive to Florida. Elizabeth and Gabrielle were sullen after being torn from the men they adored. Elizabeth had enjoyed the training and instruction she had received while at the retreat. She'd use the information over and over again during her lifetime. Both women felt as if they were closer to God than they had ever been. They had made a decision to take the classes seriously and found the challenges that were given to them by their instructors to be timely and beneficial. Elizabeth and Gabrielle vowed to make some much-needed changes in their prayer lives as well as in their Bible reading time.

As the van neared their hometown, Elizabeth could tell that Gabrielle was getting anxious. Elizabeth knew that she had to be thinking of her current jobless state and financial circumstance. Elizabeth was concerned that so many changes were happening in Gabrielle's life at one time and she couldn't believe that Gabrielle would entertain the idea to marry a man so soon after meeting him.

Gabrielle had remained silent for the final twenty miles that lead to the church where they would wearily unload their baggage. Elizabeth wanted to talk to someone; the silence was getting on her nerves. She looked around the van and realized that the seating arrangements seemed to be quite different than when they had traveled to Florida. Elizabeth called out to Joe, "Hey Joe, are we there yet?"

Joe was thankful for some conversation. "For the hundredth time, we will be there when we get there and not a minute sooner, young lady!"

"I thought as much!" Elizabeth complained as he turned on his blinker to pass the slow moving traffic. She looked at her friends. Interestingly, Jay was no longer in the co-pilot seat. A pile of what looked to be Kenny's laptop, briefcase and business paraphernalia had replaced Jay. Jay was now sitting in the seat in front of Gabrielle. Josie was quietly sitting in the fourth seat beside Kenny. Elizabeth nodded her head and decided to take a quick nap.

The energy that had been exuded the first time they had tried to unpack their luggage was absent in the second deploying of baggage. The seven adults were in no hurry to unpack anything. Pastor Matthews walked from his parsonage and met them in the parking lot with a big smile plastered on to his loving face. "How did it go, kids?"

Kenny was noncommittal as he looked at his pastor with a blank stare and said, "Pastor, the trip wasn't what I expected it would be."

Pastor Matthews looked disappointed until Kenny added, "That isn't a bad thing, Pastor." Kenny smiled sheepishly but didn't elaborate.

Pastor Matthews turned to the flamboyant Joe and asked, "How was the conference for you, Joe?"

"It was educational and wonderful. I learned some things at the church that I needed to learn. I also learned something about this bunch that I should've learned long ago." Joe stopped talking abruptly then walked to the back of the van to help with the luggage.

Their confused pastor wasn't sure he wanted to understand what Joe and Kenny had just said, so he turned to the women. "Okay, Elizabeth, what about you?"

"Overall, it was very wonderful. I think we have all grown in one-way or another. Thank you for supporting us in going."

"You are most welcome. I'm glad to see that you are home safely." The pastor began to help remove their luggage from the van and tote it to the awaiting vehicles. He didn't miss the fact that the group was paired up entirely differently than it was when they had left. He made a

Discovering Elizabeth

mental note to pray about the situation and hoped that everyone had acted according to his faith. He was almost sure they had, but refused to be ignorant to the temptations of the flesh.

Upon arriving home, Gabrielle threw open the door and greeted her things. "Hello, house!" Both of the women put their suitcases in their rooms, grabbed a cola and planted themselves on the empty couch. Gabrielle glanced toward Elizabeth before asking, "Do you think they're home yet?"

Elizabeth retrieved the mail while answering her roommate. "Probably. Unless their flight was delayed, they were home several hours ago. Maybe we need to check the answering machine."

Gabrielle looked at the phone to see if there were any blinking lights. "Well, it looks like there are fifteen messages." Gabrielle pressed the button to begin listening to their callers.

The first message was from Gabrielle's former employer. The message said, "Gabrielle, Hello, this is John. I sent you a letter and have not yet received a response from you. I need your answer on the proposal by Monday at the close of office hours. Please don't be difficult about this. I've tried to be as fair as possible. Have a good weekend."

Gabrielle grimaced. "What in the world is he talking about?"

Elizabeth held up a legal envelope. "Here it is, this envelope is postmarked from New York. It looks like the postman had to bend it to get it into the box." Elizabeth gave the envelope to her friend and waited to see what its contents would be. She placed the rest of the mail on the table while Gabrielle sat quietly reading the letter. Finally, Gabrielle sat back and closed her eyes. A tiny tear slid down her cheek.

Elizabeth's imagination went into overdrive. "What is wrong, Gabby? What's the matter? What else can that company do to you after firing you?"

Gabrielle handed her letter to Elizabeth then leaned back on the couch. Elizabeth hurriedly glanced over the letter and attached forms. "Does this mean what I think it means, Gab?" Elizabeth eagerly waited for Gabrielle's response.

"I think so. It means that John is afraid I'm going to get a lawyer. You see, I complained about that client the last time I was at the firm.

Lisa D. Piper

John knew that that junior executive had tried to manhandle me before. Apparently nothing was done about it. My guess is that, while they don't want to lose the business with that client, they don't want me taking legal action against them. I'm glad that I'm not working for them now. They have a lot to lose if I don't agree to what John is asking." Gabrielle stared in disbelief at the ceiling while she thought about John's motivation to send her the letter.

Elizabeth wasn't satisfied with Gabrielle's explanation. "Are you telling me that they're offering you a big whopping severance pay package for silence?"

Gabrielle glanced toward the paper that Elizabeth still held in her hands. "Elizabeth, I was a good employee. I never complained and I did whatever asked to do. I always tried to exceed their expectations and succeeded most of the time. There are absolutely no negative complaints about me in my personnel file. The company has been good to me and I'm sure that John hates the way it ended. I've earned the respect of the company and my peers. I've known that I have a viable lawsuit against them, but I decided not to take legal action. I'll sign the papers they want me to sign and I'll do what I've been praying about all week."

"What is that?" Elizabeth had no idea what her friend would say.

"I am going to open my own business. I want to open a Christian bookstore and gift shop. There is a real need for something like that here and why shouldn't I... or we, be the ones to offer this service to our hometown?" Gabrielle let the thought sink in for a few minutes before giving Elizabeth her greatest sales pitch. "Liz, we could be entrepreneurs. We both have a little money saved. We could put the severance pay with it and open up our own business. I know we could do this."

Elizabeth made a time-out hand signal. "Hold on a minute there, lassie. You're going too fast. Have you checked out the market for a bookstore? Do you even know the possible revenue for such a venture? I can't believe you are actually considering this."

Gabrielle looked guilty as she answered. "I've actually been thinking about becoming self-employed for a long time. I couldn't make my dream come true by myself, and didn't want to ask you to give up your job at Wright and Wingold. I think that things have changed though. I

Discovering Elizabeth

have actually done some preliminary work, including a business plan draft. Those long airport delays came in handy for planning. If you want me to do so, I'll get in the filing cabinets and pull out the information so that you can look through it and see what you think after reviewing the facts."

Elizabeth felt as if she were in a whirlwind. "I can look at the plan. This is news to me, Gabrielle, I had no idea you'd even been thinking about becoming an entrepreneur."

Gabrielle retrieved the research she had done months earlier and placed the folders on the living room credenza. Elizabeth looked at the neat folders. Elizabeth was puzzled as she asked, "Gab, why didn't you ever tell me about your idea?"

"I told you why I didn't tell you. I don't even know why I kept this stuff as long as I did. Some of it will need updating; but I've saved my resource numbers, so it shouldn't be that difficult to update it."

Elizabeth looked over the plans until the words and graphs blurred together. As she went to sleep that evening she began to feel hopeful that the business really might work.

Gabrielle and Elizabeth rested from their journey most of Saturday. Both were disappointed when they didn't hear from Eric and Ray. When the telephone rang Saturday evening, both women sprinted toward it. Elizabeth grabbed the phone and smiled as Ray said hello and explained that he had talked Eric into participating in a double date.

Ray's voice was sweet. "Liz, I'm glad to hear your voice. I'm guessing that you made it home without any difficulty?"

Elizabeth willed her voice to sound sure and calm. "Yes, we made it home just fine. It was a strange trip; we're in the middle of recuperating now though."

Elizabeth could tell that Ray was smiling by the sound of his voice. "Elizabeth, what are you and Gabby doing this evening?"

She looked at Gabrielle while covering the mouthpiece of the telephone. "Gab, are you doing anything special tonight?" Elizabeth snickered because she knew the answer. Gabrielle didn't say a word but gave Elizabeth an unkind look. She removed her hand to answer Ray's question. "No, we're not doing anything too special."

"Good. Eric and I are prepared to help you recuperate from your trip. Are you two up for some possible pampering?" Elizabeth gave her friend a 'thumbs-up' sign and bounced up and down on her toes as she anticipated seeing Ray again. Gabrielle smiled and giggled nervously as she waited to hear the details about the call.

Elizabeth decided that the question was loaded, so she opted to sound non-committal as she replied, "That depends, Mr. Morgan. What do you have in mind?"

"What I have in mind, Ms. Pennington, is an evening of the most informal kind. Eric and I are prepared to foot the bill for two scrumptious pizzas and as many sodas as you can hold. We'll also watch the chick flick of your choice; and to show you that we are the noblest of gentleman, we'll clean up any mess as well." Ray chuckled.

Elizabeth was quite amused. "And what, may I ask, is a chick flick, kind sir?"

"That's Eric's term, my sweet." Elizabeth could hear Eric protest in the background. "It means that we'll not watch anything that you ladies don't want to watch. We won't insist on ESPN if you don't want to watch it. A chick flick is really something that only chicks or girls like to watch. I apologize for the offending word, ma'am. Please say you'll come."

Elizabeth feigned her best French imitation. "Where and when is the chick flick to commence, monsieur?"

"Well, if you ladies would be so kind as to travel with us to the video store to help us pick out a movie, we'll bring you to my house then take you back home when you want to go." Ray waited for her response. He realized he had also spoken to her with a French accent. He turned and Eric was looking at him with a lopsided grin. Ray straightened his shoulders then turned away from Eric's mocking gaze.

Elizabeth became apprehensive at the thought of being in Ray's house. She decided that if she were to Ray's home, it might be best if Gabrielle was with her. "That sounds okay! I'd love to, but let me ask Gab." Elizabeth became tickled when Gabrielle gave her response. "Ray, Gabby says that she would consent as long as we don't have to watch whatever you guys want to watch next Saturday." Elizabeth giggled. "She also says that we are not sports chicks and we detest channel flickers."

Discovering Elizabeth

"Channel flickers?" Ray tried to sound disappointed. "Rob a man of his power and control, and what do you have? Okay, we'll not make you watch what we want to watch next Saturday, and we'll turn the channel flicker over to you so that we aren't even remotely tempted to channel surf." Elizabeth could now hear Eric laughing at the loose pun.

"Very funny." Elizabeth asked, "Now that we all know the rules, what time will you be here, Mr. Morgan?"

"Five minutes."

"What?"

"I'm just kidding. How about no later than six o'clock? Can you both be ready by then?"

"Yes we can." Elizabeth began to hang up the telephone when she decided to whisper a message to her caller. "Ray, are you still there?"

"Yes, I almost wasn't though. What is it?"

Elizabeth quietly whispered so that Gabrielle wouldn't hear her message, "Ray, if you want me to, I'd watch sports with you." Elizabeth told him good-bye then hung up the phone.

Gabrielle was glaring at Elizabeth. "What did you just whisper to him?"

Elizabeth looked at her friend defiantly, "That would be none of your business!"

"None of my business? Did you just tell him that you would watch sports with him! Since when?" Gabrielle put her hands on her hips then added, "Now I look like the stuffy old maid and you look like Ms. Can I Watch Some Boring Ole Man Show Pennington. That's not fair!"

Elizabeth humored her friend, "He's not going to tell Eric what I said. And for your information, I would watch sports with Ray Morgan! What do you think about that?"

"I'm thinking that I left the real Elizabeth in Florida." Gabrielle changed the subject. "When are they coming and what are we going to wear?"

"I think it sounded like a blue jean kind of affair. The real problem to solve is how I'm going to wear my hair." Elizabeth posed with her hair pulled into a ponytail at the top of her head.

Lisa D. Piper

Gabrielle interjected. "You look like a floozy with your hair like that! Let me French braid it. I'll pull some tresses down around your face; then you can do my hair." Elizabeth agreed. "What about that rope thing you do, Liz? How would that look tonight?" Gabrielle studied her own reflection in the mirror in the hall.

Elizabeth studied her friend. "That sounds like a winner. I'm beginning to get nervous. How are you remaining so calm about tonight? I am about to break into pieces. I have one half of a nerve left."

Gabrielle put her hands out for Elizabeth to see. "Looks can be deceiving, old friend. I couldn't paint a picture of a stick man right now." Gabrielle's hands were trembling.

Elizabeth felt sorry for her. "Gab, we can manage going out with Eric and Ray. We're just suffering from some kind of date deprivation disorder; that's all."

"Is that our problem? I thought we were in love or something."

Elizabeth sat still. "Are you in love, Gab?"

"Whatever I am, I haven't been here before; so how would I know? I do know that there's something either very right about what I feel or there's something very wrong with me." Gabrielle became quiet.

Elizabeth turned to her friend, "What do you mean?"

Gabrielle bit her lip. "You may not have noticed it, but I've devoured every piece of chocolate in this house today. I had fingernails yesterday and now I'm sporting lonely nail beds. Let us hope that I don't make us both look like women who are suffering date deprivation disorder. I'm so worried that I'm going to trip up in front of those bachelor men tonight. Either this is love or I'm having a breakdown of some kind."

Elizabeth rose to her feet. "Gabby, I think we need to work on our outward appearance right now. If we're to look the part of two chicks worthy of picking a flick, we need to get busy."

Gabrielle shook her head. "That was bad, Elizabeth. That was really, really lame."

Discovering Elizabeth

Elizabeth grinned. "I know. My nerves are affecting my sense of humor. They'll be here by six so let's get busy, and I'll won't entertain you with any more creative comedy."

Gabrielle followed Elizabeth to her closet to help Elizabeth pick out something to wear as she said, "Thank you very much. I don't know how much of that kind of humor I could take in one night."

Ray and Eric showed up at exactly six o'clock. The women were very glad that they had chosen jeans and button up shirts. The men were dressed in the same manner, with the exception that they were both wearing baseball caps. Gabrielle stood back to look at them. "Are you sure we're not being tricked into watching some type of a game? You guys sure look like you're about to enjoy some kind of a sporty male bonding ritual."

Eric looked at Ray and frowned. "Ray, our honor has been questioned. What do we do now?"

Ray ignored the two stunning females. "Eric, I would say that we either rescind our invitation or just prove them wrong. I'm willing to put out a wager. Should we turn out to be men of honor, then I think these lovely ladies should have to agree to go to the next baseball game we go to. What do you think?"

Eric stroked his chin as if it sounded like a good idea. Gabrielle broke his concentration as she quickly retracted her statement. "Actually, I think that you both are very honorable. Why would you think I was questioning you? You silly men!" Gabrielle quickly ushered the men and Elizabeth out of the house and locked the door.

Ray leaned over to Eric and whispered, "You've got your hands full, sir."

Eric smiled. "Yes, sir, I'm fully aware of what I have in my hands. I may need your advice some time in the near future. I've never met anyone quite like her."

Ray walked toward the passenger side of the car to open the door. He winked at Eric and said, "I know the feeling."

Both Eric and Ray proved to be perfect gentleman. Eric served the cheesy, gooey pizza as Ray put the movie in the DVD player and forwarded it past the commercials. Elizabeth regretted their selection once the movie began. Elizabeth was sure that the men would never let

Lisa D. Piper

them pick again. She and Gabrielle hadn't seen Little Women in a long while and wanted to see if the men would like it. Ray and Eric were patient with the women as they began the emotional roller coaster of laughing and then dabbing tears from their eyes. As Elizabeth became self-conscious of her emotional state, she decided she needed to compose herself so she asked Ray for the directions to the rest room. Within minutes, Gabrielle stood up to follow her friend's lead.

Ray nervously glanced at Eric as Gabrielle stood up to check on Elizabeth. Eric whispered, "What do you think they're doing anyway? I don't understand women, do you?"

Ray chuckled as he picked up the last slice of pizza. "No I don't, but I don't want to take a chance on them hearing us talk about them. I hereby refuse to verbally contemplate the ways of a female. I think they may be doing that thing they do with powder and their noses. I have no idea and I'm not sure I want to know."

Eric looked at Ray inquisitively, "What's up with that nose thing anyway? And, why did they leave at almost the same time? I hate to ask, but I just have to ask."

Ray cocked his head to the side. "What do you want to ask?"

"Umm, did I hear you sniffling when that sister died in the movie?"

Ray picked a piece of lint off of his shirt and answered the question with a question, "Were you?"

"Was I what?"

"Were you crying?"

"Now what kind of a question is that, Ray Morgan!"

"You asked me first!"

"I'll admit nothing."

Ray crossed his arms. "Nor will I."

Elizabeth was relieved to hear Gabrielle knock on the bathroom door. "Come in here! We're making royal fools out of ourselves. Did you bring any extra mascara?"

"No I didn't. Why did you insist on that movie?"

Discovering Elizabeth

"Me? Ms. Gabrielle, you were the one who was reminiscing about watching your favorite show when I simply asked you if you wanted to watch it again."

Gabrielle pursed her lips. "Never mind whose fault it is. The damage has been done. What kind of fools do you think those men out there think we are? It was all I could do to keep from blowing my nose."

"Gab, they know that we're women. What I hate is trying to eat that sloppy pizza while trying to appear graceful and dignified. I have used five napkins and have a sauce stain on my shirt." Elizabeth checked her hair to make sure it was in place. "About the crying, surely they've been around crying women before tonight. Besides, I have an idea to help us. Let's just go out there in a really good mood and finish watching the movie. If we try hard enough, we can keep ourselves from being so emotional about the entire thing. You do know what part is coming up though, don't you?"

Gabrielle was mortified. "I forgot about that part! Frederick is about to think that Jo is married to Amy's husband. I always tear up on that one. I tell you what, let's go tell them to turn the movie back on because they paused the movie when you left. As it nears the Frederick scene, we can go into the kitchen and get cola refills for everyone. Are you with me?"

Elizabeth was with her. Both women walked out of the restroom as if nothing had happened. Both men smiled as their dates walked toward the living room where they were ready to get the movie playing once more. Ray asked, "Is everything okay, ladies?"

Both women shook their heads yes. They were trying to avoid looking too obvious when Gabrielle said, "You go ahead and turn on the movie. We'll go and get drink refills for everyone.

Without hesitation both men grabbed the girl of their dreams by the hand and shouted, "Oh no you don't!"

Elizabeth and Gabrielle weren't happy about their plans being thwarted but decided to sit down to avoid a scene. Ray had grabbed Elizabeth's hand to keep her from scurrying to the kitchen. He continued to hold her hand as she sat next to him.

Eric glanced at the couple and whispered, "Twitterpated."

Lisa D. Piper

Gabrielle giggled as Eric teased the other couple. "What is twitterpated?"

"It's from the movie Bambi. I don't know if you and Elizabeth should rent that movie or not. Some of the scenes are kind of heart wrenching." Gabrielle and Elizabeth glanced at each other while Ray gave Eric a look of warning. "The owl looked at the love birds and called them twitterpated; that's where I got it." As Eric finished his explanation, he tapped Gabrielle on her tiny nose.

Ray squeezed Elizabeth's hand then winked at her. "Did you hear what he said? I just hired a corporate executive who uses the word twitterpated."

Eric boasted, "I don't want you going into this business venture with your eyes closed, Ray. I also have in my vocabulary, words from Bugs Bunny, and on occasion I've been known to quote Mr. Rogers."

Ray protested. "That's all well and good. I can't, however, work with a man who watches the roadrunner. I'm a Bugs man myself, but if you tell me you like that awful coyote and boring roadrunner, I'll be forced to believe that I have teamed up with the wrong man."

Eric gave Ray a thumbs up. "I'm with you one hundred percent. I'm a Bugs man myself and uh, I like that little martian too. He cracks me up."

Gabrielle nudged Eric in the rib with her fingernail. "Lay off of the roadrunner!"

Elizabeth sided with the men. "Oh, Gabby, you're the only one in the world that likes that silly bird and numbskull wolf."

Gabrielle corrected her friend. "He is not a wolf; he is a coyote. There is a difference."

Ray clapped his hands to interrupt the friendly feud. "Okay, you guys! Let's not get too deep into cartoon politics. Are we going to watch the rest of the show or what?"

Gabrielle began to reinitiate the plan once more. "Sure, go ahead. Liz and I'll just go and get a refill. Do you want something?"

Eric wouldn't let her go. "I'm not going to sit and watch this movie without you right here!"

Discovering Elizabeth

Elizabeth said what she thought would help. "Why don't we just forget the rest of the movie and uh, just uh, go do something else."

Eric and Ray looked at each another as if searching for an answer. One of them would have to admit it the truth. Ray decided that he would do the confessing. "Ladies, we want to see the end. We can't watch ninety-five percent of a movie then forsake it. Sit down here and let's finish this torture."

Elizabeth tilted her head to look at her date. Gabrielle said, "Okay, I know what's going on here. You want to know if Jo ends up with Laurie or not, don't you?"

"Certainly," came the reply.

The foursome watched the rest of the movie. Elizabeth and Gabrielle sobbed, then rejoiced at the ending. Eric and Ray rolled their eyes as Frederick declared his love for Jo. Elizabeth was the first to begin yawning. Ray pecked Eric on the shoulder and said, "Fellow, I think we need to get these two lovely ladies home if they're to be at church on time in the morning."

Gabrielle protested, "You haven't been talking to Pastor Matthews have you? Why would you think we might be late?"

Ray grinned. "Gabby, Have you read the scripture that reads that even a child is known by what he does?[15]"

Gabrielle yawned. "Then get us home. I don't want to be known as the sleeping pew warmer in the morning."

Ray turned out the lights then drove all three of his passengers home. As he returned to his lovely yet lonely home, he missed Elizabeth. He stepped inside of his door then turned on the light. As he shut the door and locked it, he felt as if something were missing. He wanted Elizabeth to be with him. He decided in that moment that he never wanted to drop her off at someone else's home again. He wanted his home to be her home. He even wanted his towels, his church, his things, to be her towels, her church and her things. As he sat in the place where Elizabeth was sitting an hour earlier, he decided that he wanted his future to be her future. Ray decided once and for all that he would visit Annie Mae Foster after Sunday morning services."

---

[15] Pro. 20:11

Lisa D. Piper

Chapter SIXTEEN

"Whoso findeth a wife findeth a good thing, and obtaineth favour of the Lord." Proverbs 18:22

Ray sat through Sunday morning services with a lopsided grin on his face. He tried to stop grinning but could not. Pastor Hill didn't miss the fact that one of his most faithful parishioners was full of joy. Several of those from Ray's Sunday School class at Victory and Life Tabernacle glanced at one another as it became apparent that Ray, or God, or both of them were up to something. At the end of the service, Ray leapt to his feet to retreat out of the back door when Pastor Hill stopped him.

"My, my, Ray, don't you look like you ate a bowl of Happy Wheaties this morning." As the pastor greeted him, he fervently shook Ray's hand. "It's good to have you back. I hope your trip went well."

Ray still smiled from ear to ear as he answered. "Yes, sir, I had a wonderful trip."

Pastor Hill leaned forward and stated candidly: "You are in love, my boy, aren't you? Don't deny it."

Ray stepped back and laughed. "I guess I am. That obvious, huh?"

Pastor Hill chuckled. "Actually, Sister Hill and I have been praying for this day. We knew it would happen." His pastor hesitated. "She is a Christian, isn't she, Son?"

Ray nodded. "Of course she is. I feel kind of silly after all of the fussing I've done over the years about remaining a bachelor for the rest of my days."

Pastor Hill shook his head. "I'm sure you'll get some much deserved teasing, but I think everyone will be glad God has answered our prayers."

Ray looked at his pastor reflectively. "He's sent me someone who surpasses every expectation I ever had. I just hope she'll agree to put up with me for the rest of her life."

Pastor Hill placed his hand on Ray's shoulder and said, "Only God knows her patience level...I'm kidding, Son." Several of those standing close by turned around to see what their jolly pastor was doing as they heard him laugh heartily at his own humor. Ray shook his hand once more. On the way to his car, he pointedly dodged some curious churchgoers.

As Ray drove the road that would lead him to what he considered to be his only family, he looked into the mirror. His eyes looked as if they were dancing, and he noticed that he still wore the goofy looking grin. He wasn't sure what it was like to be in a total state of nervous shock but he was almost positive he was experiencing something quite like it.

Homer met Ray at the door. "Is everything okay, Ray?"

Ray grinned at his friend. "I am about to blow into a million pieces if I don't talk to you about something. I want to talk right now!"

Wiping her hands on her apron, Annie stepped through the kitchen door before Homer could inquire about what Ray was saying. "Hello, Ray, I thought I heard your voice. Why didn't you call and let us know you were coming and I would have fixed something special. I've just put some frozen pizzas into the oven. You're welcome to a slice, but if I had known, I would've made something to put some meat on to your bones."

Ray walked over to Annie Mae and hugged her. "I didn't want you to make a fuss, so don't. Pizza will be just fine. I have to talk to you."

Homer had endured enough suspense. "What have you come to talk to us about, Son?" Homer grinned. "What kind of a feller barges into another man's home, dumps a mystery in his lap, and then doesn't spill his guts?" Homer patted the seat next to the one he had taken. "Now,

Discovering Elizabeth

sit down here and tell us what has stymied you so that you can't quit that confounded grinning."

As Ray sat down, he suddenly had difficulty putting what he had come to say into words. He cleared his throat then tried to relay what he had to say. "I have something to say to you. I've been thinking... What I mean is that... What I mean to say is that I've been thinking." Ray shifted in his seat while smoothing down his pant legs with his palms. "I'm pretty sure that I want to move forward. I think..." He looked at Annie for help.

Ray jumped in his seat as Homer pounded his fist on the side of his chair. "What is it, boy? What in tarnation are you talking about?"

Annie shook her finger at her husband. "Now quiet down, Homer. There was a time when you stammered just like this. I remember only one time when you lost your words; you didn't know what to say or how to say it."

Homer looked offended. "I'll not have you saying such things. I've never been lost for a word in my life." Suddenly a faint memory came to him. His eyes studied Ray as he recoiled, "I did once become fidgety and goofy looking with a grin about as crooked as yours when I..."

"When you what?" Ray was hopeful.

Annie finished it for him. "When he asked my father if he could have my hand in marriage. He acted as you are acting now."

The couple was silent as they waited for Ray to confirm their suspicion.

Ray gulped then shook his head while stammering, "C-Can I have the ring?"

Annie folded her hands, while Homer sat back in shock. It was Annie's turn to stammer. "Sure, Ray, the ring is yours after all." Annie stood to her feet then walked to the bedroom. Several minutes later, Annie produced an old worn royal blue crushed velvet box. Ray held out his hand nervously as Annie gently placed the tiny box into his large palm.

Ray was motionless. Trembling, he looked at the box without moving his hand. "When I thought about coming to get Mama's ring, I didn't think about the fact that I would be holding it again. I almost

Lisa D. Piper

feel like I will find my mother in here when I open it. I guess that's silly." The emotion of the moment caught in Ray's throat and a solitary tear streamed down his face. "Thank you, Ms. Annie, for keeping the ring for me. You are a true friend to me and to my mother."

Annie looked at the box. "Oh, Ray, I loved your mother, you know. There have been many times that I've opened that box with the hope that I see in your eyes. She made me promise to keep it for you. I'd begun to give up hope that you would ever ask for the little box." Annie had offered the treasure to Ray when he had proposed to Felicia, but he had said did not want to see the ring again. Annie had just assumed that the ring brought back too many painful memories.

Ray turned the box in his hand as he felt the velvet brush across his skin. Finally feeling courage rise within him, he quickly opened the box. His memory did not do the jewel justice. Ray picked the ring up from its cushion to place it on his fingertip. "Oh Annie, it's so beautiful."

A tear found its way down a withered cheek as she watched the man, whom she thought of as an only son, appreciate the beauty of the only remaining link he had to his beloved mother. Annie could tell that Ray was remembering or trying to remember what the hand of his mother looked like when it was decorated with the most brilliant combination of sapphires, diamonds and gold.

Homer squinted as he looked at the ring. "Son, no woman would be able to turn you, or that ring down."

Annie patted her pocket as she watched Ray and waited for more information about the woman he had chosen to be his wife. Ray didn't know it, but his mother had written two letters to be presented to him the day of his wedding. One letter was addressed to, "My Son," and the other simply said, "My Daughter."

Ray smiled and said, "Homer, I hope she doesn't turn me down. This is it for me; it is this woman or no woman."

Homer arched his bushy gray brow. "Who is the woman anyway? Is it who I think it is?"

Ray sobered and pronounced matter-of-factly, "Elizabeth Pennington."

Discovering Elizabeth

Homer became quiet as Annie smiled, "Oh Ray, she is a lovely young woman!"

Ray smiled, "Yes Annie, yes she is."

Ray looked over at his long time friend. His worst fears were displayed on the man's face. "Oh please, Homer, please don't do this. I know what you're thinking."

Ray put up his hand. He was normally amused when Homer shed his country boy slang to become the epitome of a grammatical genius. This time, Ray wasn't amused as Homer shared his concerns with him. "Ray, I do not have a problem with the fact that you are in love or that you are getting married. I have waited patiently for this day, but there is a good possibility that the board will not look kindly upon what you have done. What were you thinking? You cannot fraternize with any of the employees. In order to get close enough to someone to want to marry them, you have had to break the rules. Ray, there is a time and place for all things and work is not the place to get romantic notions."

Ray wasn't happy; yet, he wasn't surprised by Homer's predictable comments. "Homer, I tried to stay away from her; I really did. I can't deny that I have spent some personal time with her. As a matter of fact, she attended the same Florida meeting I went to last week. It was purely coincidental. No, I think it was something God orchestrated. I did spend a lot of time with her there." Ray was exasperated and torn between the lines of right and wrong. "I know that I shouldn't have become involved, but I did. Homer, I have no intention of hurting you, or the board, or anyone else. However, I'm willing to resign to be with Elizabeth." Ray looked down at the ring as he said softly, "I'm would be willing to give up my share of the company, if necessary. Please don't make me choose." Ray looked Homer in the eye as he continued, "Now, I will tell you that Elizabeth has expressed to me that she will resign if need be. I respect your wisdom…"

Ray looked at the floor until his curiosity got the better of him. When he looked up, Homer was in deep thought. Without warning, Homer made his last comment. "Ray, right is right and wrong is wrong. I have no doubt that you'll do the right thing. I assume that you have prayed about what you are doing. If a relationship with Elizabeth is of God then He will make a way. Son, don't get in a big hurry to seal your future. I have to remind you not to do anything you might regret later." Ray didn't want to listen, but knew that to not listen would be foolish. Being able to take correction or instruction was what had caused Ray to be able to grow and learn faster than others who had wanted to do what Ray had done with his career. He had learned, from Homer, to be wise and to use discretion. He wouldn't stop listening to the man who taught him more than any college professor could have.

Homer continued, "I know that you are on an emotional, love-hungry high. That's not the best description, I know, but I'm going to call it as I see it. Marry the girl, but don't date or marry her while both of you are an employee of the company. Neither of you are above the policies and standards of Wright and Wingold. To handle this matter with little to no regard for future consequences would be foolish as well as ignorant." Homer wanted to deliver his unwanted message with hope. He looked at the man whom he admired, loved and cherished. Ray was his best friend next to Annie. "Son, Annie Mae and I are happier than larks that you've found someone. We've prayed for this more than you'll ever know. Remember this; whatever you do; do it as unto the Lord."

Ray couldn't be angry with Homer. He looked down at the glistening stones as he shut the case with the same hand that held it. "Homer, I know that you're right." Ray's smile was gone, but he looked hopeful. "Would you please pray that God answers my prayers about this quickly. I know that it's His will for Liz and I to be together. I don't want to do anything unethical where the company is concerned. You don't have to remind me that my job doesn't only affect me." Ray placed it in his pocket then ran his right hand through his hair. Regret that his new SVP had seen him fraternizing began to sweep over him.

Ray would have been pleased to know that at that very moment God began to work on his behalf. The lovely lady who held the key to his heart was about to experience a miracle.

Gabrielle and Elizabeth arrived for services on time. Pastor Matthews was very excited as he spoke to each of the singles who had traveled to the convention. He and his wife smiled at each other when Kenny walked into the church and sat down by a beaming Josie. The pastor winked at his wife when Mary and Jay walked down the aisle totally engrossed in their own conversation. Sister Matthews approached Elizabeth and said, "Hello my dear. How are you this morning? Have you rested from your trip?"

Discovering Elizabeth

"We have rested some. The trip was a lot of fun and very wonderful in many different ways. And don't worry, we were all on our best behavior." Elizabeth said that last part louder than normal as her peripheral vision caught the pastor approaching.

Gabrielle didn't miss the opportunity to tease him. "Yes, Liz is exactly right. We were on our best behavior because we didn't know who knew your husband, Sister Grace. We wouldn't have wanted a negative report of hoodlum activity to get back to you from the Sunshine State."

Pastor Matthews played along, "That's right! You never know who's watching!"

As the bell began to ring signifying that services were about to convene, the group of singles greeted one another as if they hadn't seen each other in weeks. The church was glad to see the group home and were eager to find out what they had done while away. As their pastor graced the pulpit, he picked up a microphone and said, "I'd like to have some of you who went on the trip come up and tell us what God has done in your life since you last left us." Each one who had attended the meetings stood to give an account of what God had done during the retreat. Joe had the crowd mesmerized as he recounted what he had learned about his Creator on the trip. Jay, Elizabeth, Gabrielle, Kenny, Josie and Mary hadn't paid a lot of attention to Joe. Somewhere between his talk with Kenny in the hotel room that first morning and crossing the state line, Joe met with God in a real way.

After morning services, animated chatter filled the halls. The Florida trip seemed to be the topic of most conversations. Elizabeth and Gabrielle accepted an invitation for lunch with an elderly couple from the congregation. Aubrey Heimlin and his wife Thelma drove the two girls to their home on the other side of town. Thelma prepared lunch while Mr. Heimlin showed the ladies his antique toy collection.

Lunch turned out to be a wonderful affair. Elizabeth wasn't sure she had ever had a better sandwich. Both women became totally engrossed with Thelma's homemade root beer.

After the host and hostess took a vow of secrecy, Elizabeth and Gabrielle told the two about the business plan. Gabrielle's enthusiasm encouraged Elizabeth to spill all of her ideas. By the time Thelma served her award winning chocolate chip cookies, the elderly couple was just as excited as the soon to be entrepreneurs.

As the ladies munched happily, Aubrey and Thelma began to share meaningful glances. They were up to something; Elizabeth was sure of it. Gabrielle was noticeably uncomfortable with the sudden silence of their lunch partners. Gabrielle asked, "Did we say something wrong?"

Aubrey shook his head. "No, you didn't." Aubrey turned to his wife and asked, "What do you think; is this it?"

Thelma grinned as Aubrey leaned forward and said, "Ladies, my wife and I have been praying about our future. Every time we begin talking about it, your names seem to come up in the conversation. We aren't sure what you will think of our proposition, but we would like to offer it to you with hope that you will accept."

Elizabeth and Gabrielle looked blankly at their hosts. Gabrielle asked, "What are you talking about? What proposition?"

Gabrielle and Elizabeth hadn't paid attention when the couple had excused themselves to go to change clothes shortly after they had begun talking about their plans. Thelma and Aubrey had taken the time while changing to thank God that their prayers were answered. They had both agreed privately that they had been correct in thinking that Elizabeth and Gabrielle were the ones God intended to use in their behalf.

Aubrey grinned and sat back in his chair. "Girls, what do you want your business to look like? What do you have in mind exactly, and do you have any idea where you would open your shop?"

Elizabeth and Gabrielle shared the rest of the information that they had left out earlier. Aubrey and Thelma seemed to be impressed with the work Gabrielle had done with the business plan. The excitement was contagious, as Aubrey and Thelma offered their own ideas about how to operate a successful business.

Aubrey winked at his bride as he took a drink of frothy root beer. He purposely looked at Gabrielle and Elizabeth and said, "You know, I was quite the businessman in my day. Thelma here was not so shabby herself. We've been talking about opening up a business; and, after speaking with you, we're interested in a joint business."

Discovering Elizabeth

"You want to partner in a Christian Bookstore?" Elizabeth asked incredulously.

Thelma laughed, "Not really, but sort of. We've always dreamed of opening a little snack shop or a bakery. Actually, we also have a business plan, but have been waiting on the okay from the heavenly instructor. Now do you get it?"

Gabrielle and Elizabeth shook their heads up and down but then said in unison, "No."

Laughter broke out as Aubrey offered to clarify the proposal. "We own a large building downtown. Thelma inherited it from her aunt about five years ago. It's about fifty years old but has a lot of character. Her aunt had remodeled it, so it's in excellent shape. Her aunt was eccentric so it's a little odd, but it would provide a wonderful atmosphere for what we want to do. It needs some cleaning since we haven't had it open for a while. What if we offer to allow you to use the majority of the building for your business? We could open a bakery in a section on one side of the building. We would be helping each other. We could use the fresh aroma of baking to tantalize your customers into coming into our shop, while our customers might venture into your store."

Elizabeth and Gabrielle didn't move or blink. Elizabeth questioned, "You want to lease your building to us?"

Thelma replied, "No, honey, not lease it, don't you understand? You can use the building. We expect you to pay the utilities and pay for any changes you might want to make to it."

Gabrielle raised her naturally arched eyebrow as she asked, "Why would you want to do that? I mean, I don't want to sound ungrateful, but I don't understand." Gabrielle looked at Elizabeth as if she'd be able to help her comprehend what was happening.

Aubrey picked up his wife's hand and held it while he answered. "Ladies, we're not getting any younger. We're bored for one thing. Secondly, we have no heir. This is something we have prayed about for a long time. We have every intention of giving you the building with the stipulation that we can operate our bakery until we can no longer do so. When we can no longer operate the business, we would want you to hire someone who could do it for as long as it was profitable. All of the proceeds from the bakery must go to support the church."

Lisa D. Piper

Elizabeth touched her heart with her hand. "I don't know what to say."

Gabrielle added, "This is such a generous offer; are you sure? I'm overwhelmed."

Aubrey lifted his glass. "Don't be. We would like for this conversation to be kept between us four. No one else is to know about the details of our arrangement or the idea about how to get extra funds for the church. We know that you both will want to pray before making a final decision. We don't want to rush you into something that you're neither ready for nor want. Please take your time in giving us an answer."

Elizabeth smiled and Gabrielle joined her. Gabrielle shook her head and said, "This is too awesome. God is just so good."

Aubrey stood to his feet and said, "I am honored to be in the house with three lovely ladies. Is anyone up for a walk in the garden? I could use the fresh air." Aubrey held out his hand. Thelma placed her hand in his and allowed him to help her to her feet. Thelma and Aubrey led the way through the beautiful garden that had been a praying place for them during the years they had lived there.

During the evening service, Pastor Matthews preached on the sovereignty and absolute perfection of their God. Elizabeth and Gabrielle found confirmation, regarding what they were about to do in the timely sermon.

Sophie seemed to enjoy the sermon as much as anyone else did. Elizabeth was glad to see her new friend and co-worker. She had been disappointed when Sophie had missed the morning service. As she shook Sophie's hand, Sophie expressed how much she had missed Elizabeth the last week. Elizabeth wondered about what would happen to Sophie when her successor took over the accounting manager position.

Neither Gabrielle nor Elizabeth said anything on the drive back to their home. It has been a long, but exiting day. Elizabeth fumbled with the keys until she found the correct match for their lock. She allowed Gabrielle to pass through the door and then followed her. Elizabeth closed the door and stood still. Gabrielle turned to look at her friend. Tiny grins began to form on their faces. Elizabeth yelled, "Hallelujah! We're in business, Gab!" Elizabeth shook her purse off her shoulder

Discovering Elizabeth

and began to jump around the room. Gabrielle lifted her hands to the heavens in an effort to thank the Lord for answering her prayers in such a marvelous way. Elizabeth was grateful that they didn't have close neighbors. She and Gabrielle ran around the house for nearly ten minutes trying to release the excitement that had been building all day. After shouting and leaping, they both collapsed on the couch in a tired heap.

Elizabeth looked at Gabrielle and said, "Call them."

Gabrielle didn't have to ask who she meant. Gabrielle picked up the telephone then smiled at whatever was said to her. "Yes, sure, no problem, that's a good idea. Okay, we'll see you then." Gabrielle leaned her head to the right as she normally did when she was about to end a telephone conversation. "Thank you both. Thank God for you. See you tomorrow. Bye."

Gabrielle looked at Elizabeth and squealed. "We have an appointment with our partners to see the building tomorrow at six. That's not a problem is it?"

Elizabeth rolled her eyes. "If it were, it isn't anymore. I'm so excited, Gabrielle. There's no way I'm going to miss seeing my future. I have to ask you a quick question. What kind of a time frame do we have? If the building is suitable, what kind of a time frame until the business is underway, or until I'll be needed full time to get it ready?"

Gabrielle thought quickly. "I'm not sure. I'll tell you one thing though. I don't mind working on the building arrangements, advertising, supplier information and whatever else needs to be done until you can leave Wright and Wingold on a good note. I would say that I could go at it alone for six weeks before absolutely needing you full time.

The accountant emerged from Elizabeth. "What about the financial end of the business? I want to look at the figures you have and get an idea of what we'll need to do about putting a workable budget together."

Gabrielle walked into her bedroom to retrieve a manila folder. "This is what I have on a budget. I think you'll find it very detailed and pretty accurate. See what you think about it and let me know. I hope you get a chance to look at it before we go to see the building tomorrow. After surveying the place, we should know more about what we'll need financially. We may need to get some estimates on any repair work that needs to be done if it surpasses our own fix-up capabilities."

Elizabeth took the folder and said with a tinge of regret, "We've already told our new partners that we would take the building and have not looked at it or covered the details of the financial responsibility with them. This would have unnerved me just two weeks ago."

Gabrielle laughed. "True. I have never known my number driven buddy to forget to add every plus and to subtract every minus before making a decision as important as this one."

Elizabeth gave her friend a worried look. "Gab, do you think we are rushing things a little? I'm thinking of giving up the best job I have ever had. If you had told me that I would be doing what I am about to do this time last year, I would have told you that you were mad."

Gabrielle nodded in agreement. "I know it. I would have said the same thing about myself. I never intended to leave my company or to get the official boot from them. There is an explanation for all of this and God knows what it is. I can say that I'm more excited than I have been in a long while. Don't worry, Liz. If this is God's will; and I know it is, we will have a successful business. You'll be able to see your sweetheart with no guilt and I'll no longer be unemployed!"

Gabrielle and Elizabeth went to bed late because neither one felt as if she could go to sleep. Six o'clock was the last thing Elizabeth wanted to see on a Monday morning but it came quickly. Gabrielle's bedroom door was closed; Elizabeth didn't want to bother her, so she crept around quietly. Elizabeth decided that she needed some extra lift for her tired eyes so she selected a blue pants suit with white accessories. The cut of the outfit would've looked odd on anyone else, but Elizabeth pulled it off well. At first, she thought she would leave her long hair down then thought better of it. She didn't want to look too drastically different for work, even though she felt like a brand new woman.

Sophie had been hard at work for thirty minutes when Elizabeth arrived. She was elated when she saw that Sophie had surpassed her expectations while she'd been gone. Sophie had left a detailed list of what had been accomplished, as well as, what contacts had been made for a new client. She had drafted a checklist of what needed to be done and had noted the meetings that had been scheduled for Elizabeth in

Discovering Elizabeth

her absence. After Elizabeth reviewed all of the information and opened her mail, she picked up the telephone and called Sophie's extension to tell her how happy she was with what appeared to be the proof of a very productive week. Sophie was overjoyed with the compliments her boss showered on her.

Elizabeth was so caught up in her work that she almost forgot to attend the scheduled department head meeting. Elizabeth was the last person to arrive, as evidenced by the seating arrangement. The only vacant chair was the one opposite of the CEO. Eric was seated to the right of Ray and Homer was on the left. Elizabeth purposely didn't look up while she arranged her planner and took her seat. She was glad to find that Homer was looking at her with a friendly smile. No one, including Elizabeth, saw Homer look at Ray and wink.

The meeting took less than an hour. Afterwards, Elizabeth rushed back to her office to meet with a new client. Ray was speaking with the sales manager, when from the corner of his eye, he saw Elizabeth leaving hastily. He had wanted to talk to her but thought it best to conduct business as usual. If she wanted to talk to him, she would call. Homer approved of the way Elizabeth and Ray handled the meeting, considering the fact that he didn't want anyone to know that his CEO and lovely accountant had spent last week professing their undying love to each other.

By the end of the day, Elizabeth was exhausted from playing catch up. She looked forward to meeting Gabrielle for the tour of what would probably be their new business. Elizabeth turned off her computer and grabbed her purse as the telephone began to ring. She thought it might be Gabrielle calling to make sure she would make the meeting. She placed her purse strap on her shoulder and answered the ringing telephone. "Good afternoon, this is Elizabeth, may I help you?"

A deep voice said, "Hello. I'm glad I caught you."

Elizabeth smiled. "Hello, I'm glad you did too. Has your day been as busy as mine? I'm still not caught up at all, are you?"

Ray chuckled, "Oh no, it'll take the better part of next week before I find myself. I called to see if you would have time to talk for a few minutes."

Elizabeth groaned inwardly. "Actually, I was just heading out of the door. I can make time if you like though."

Lisa D. Piper

"No, don't worry about it. I, uh, we just need to talk. That is, I want to run some things by you." Ray couldn't believe he was stammering. Somehow she made him feel like an inexperienced teenager.

Elizabeth wasn't sure how to interpret Ray's explanation for wanting to meet. "Could we talk tomorrow? You could call me at home if you like."

Ray hesitated. "Elizabeth, I want to see you in person. I can't call tonight but perhaps we can meet up at the end of the week. I'll be out of the office tomorrow. Check with Rebecca, if you don't mind, she should know what times I have available. I hate for it to come down to that, but, as you know I am fitting two weeks into one."

Elizabeth looked down at her watch and became anxious. "Listen, if I don't leave now, Gabby will be furious. We can't be late. I will see you this week, Ray." Elizabeth hung up the phone and darted out of the office. It would be Friday before they would have an opportunity to speak again.

Gabrielle was waiting at the door when Elizabeth pulled into the driveway. She unlocked the passenger door for her friend as Gabrielle sprinted to the car. "Hello, Gab, have you had a good day?" Gabrielle hopped into the car and smiled at her new business partner.

"Yes, ma'am, I have. It's been a glorious day, and you?"

"Busy, very busy. What's been so glorious?"

Gabrielle clasped her hands together. "Everything, just everything has been wonderful! I woke up this morning doing what you have told me you do sometimes. I woke up singing, 'He's got the Whole World in His Hands.[16]'" Gabrielle laughed. "I had the desire to read the Bible as soon as I woke up and guess what I found first thing!"

"What?"

"I found a scripture that helps me to see my situation for what it is. I wrote it down to read to you." Gabrielle reached into the pocket of her jeans and produced a piece of her favorite stationary. "I found it in chapter sixty-one of Isaiah. It says, 'The Spirit of the Lord is upon me; because the Lord hath anointed me to preach good tidings unto the meek; he hath sent me to bind up the brokenhearted, to proclaim liberty

---

[16] Author Unknown/Job 12:10

Discovering Elizabeth

to the captives, and the opening of the prison to them that are bound; to comfort all that mourn; to appoint unto them that morn in Zion, to give unto them beauty for ashes, the oil of joy for mourning, the garment of praise for the spirit of heaviness; that they might be called trees of righteousness, the planting of the Lord, that he might be glorified.' Elizabeth, I am living that scripture!"

Elizabeth turned on her blinker to pass a car and said, "That's beautiful, Gab."

"Beautiful? It's downright glorious! I was heavy with a burden and He caused me to praise. I was brokenhearted and He fixed it. All that was left in my life seemed to be ashes and look what has happened. I shall forever be amazed at God's handiwork!"

Elizabeth glanced at her friend. "You really did have a glorious day I see. I'm so glad for you."

"I don't know if you knew this or not, but I was so depressed and kind of angry at God. I thought He didn't care that I had lost my job, my pride and my entire career. Guess what though?"

Elizabeth frowned. "You didn't tell me you were feeling that, Gab."

"I know I didn't. I was too ashamed to say it but God knew I felt it. I guess I didn't realize how bitter I was becoming inside until He showed me. He also showed me that my job wasn't my means of living. He's my provider and I'll never forget that again." Gabrielle quickly sat back in her chair, closed her eyes and breathed in a slow breath of air as if relishing the moment.

Elizabeth asked Gabrielle to read the directions to the building. Gabrielle was looking at the instructions she had written down when Elizabeth turned the corner where the building was supposed to be. Elizabeth gasped. The quick response caused fear to run up and down Gabrielle's spine. Elizabeth glanced at her friend. "I'm sorry, Gab." She pointed toward the building, "I didn't mean to startle you, but that can't be what I think it is."

Gabrielle looked to the place where Elizabeth was pointing. "That building can't be it, Liz."

Elizabeth pointed to the parking lot in front of the building. There, standing by their vehicle, were Aubrey and Thelma. "Yes, it is Gabrielle, this is it."

Lisa D. Piper

As the girls approached, Thelma motioned toward the building and shouted, "What do you think?"

Gabrielle stammered, "It...it's perfect."

Elizabeth wanted to run up to the building, throw open the door and explore the inside of what she knew would be a place where any business could thrive. "It's amazing. I can't believe it!" Elizabeth almost shouted. She had passed the building a few times and appreciated its unique architecture. She never dreamed she'd get to view the inside.

Aubrey and Thelma were delighted with the response of their new business partners. "We knew you'd like it." Thelma chattered as she whisked the women to the front door. "Did I tell you that my aunt was an artist and interior decorator? She was eccentric but very talented. She clung to the belief that everything worth having had to be the biggest...or at least the greatest."

Elizabeth ran her hand over the large marble columns at the entrance. Thelma explained, "Those white masterpiece columns are not an original part of the building. She had those made with the intricate designs she created herself." Thelma pointed at the bottom and top of the exquisite marble. "She said that these would make her feel like she was walking into a place of importance. She was right." Thelma noticed Gabrielle staring at the entrance doors. "I know that the doors look overbearing, but I think there will come a time when we shall be thankful for them. My Aunt Joline loved the large airy look. The doors are solid cherry as is all of the trim inside of the building."

Gabrielle ran her hand over the wood grain as she peered through the windowpane. She had never seen anything more intriguing. A long solid brass doorknob complemented the dark wood. The etched glass added an ambiance to the large entrance. Neither Gabrielle nor Elizabeth could have prepared each other for what awaited them behind the magnificent door. Thelma unlocked it and motioned for the ladies to enter.

Both Elizabeth and Gabrielle wanted to remove their shoes as they stepped onto a floor made out of what appeared to be black marble. Golden chandeliers hung from the vaulted ceiling. Crystal glistened in a breathtaking cascade from each chandelier. A loft had been built into the room, which explained the magnificent shape of the building from

Discovering Elizabeth

the exterior. Breathtaking marble steps spiraled to the loft and tapered off in front of an exquisite stained glass window.

Elizabeth was in awe. "This is more than beautiful." She looked at Aubrey and Thelma who were enjoying their reaction to their gift. "Are you two sure you want to do this? I mean, you could sell this for a mint!"

Thelma was quick to respond. "Let's get one thing straight right now. We are sure we want to do this. We have had offers from others that want to do no telling what with this building. I know it seems like it might be a bit much for a bakery and bookstore. We'll probably have to give it a more comfortable feel by putting the right furniture in it, but I know this is what we want to do. Who says that a Christian bookstore can't look like this? I would say that beauty such as this would be better served for use in the Kingdom of our Lord Jesus than for use in the world."

The place was dusty but was in much better shape than they would've ever thought. It only needed some housekeeping work done to it. Both women were startled when they were asked by Aubrey, "Do you want to see the bakery?"

Gabrielle turned around to see what she had missed. "Where is the bakery?"

"I'm glad you asked; come this way!" Aubrey led them through a couple of French doors with the same etching as the entrance door. "Now, we can leave these doors open if we want so that your place smells like fresh baked goodies or we can close them." Aubrey opened the doors and waited for a response.

Gabrielle exclaimed, "The bakery is ready?"

Aubrey grinned, "Almost. We told you that we've been planning on doing this for a while. We've worked on it as we had the time and somehow we just worked on it until we got it like we wanted. We need to add a few things. We've been waiting on God to give us the go ahead to open it. What do you think?"

Elizabeth walked into the bakery and decided that Aubrey and Thelma had created the most wonderful atmosphere she had ever experienced for a bakery with a bookstore and gift shop. The glass display case was obviously new. Elizabeth could envision baked breads and sweets lined up in it. Small tables, each with two chairs, were meticulously placed in the small dining area. The round table tops were made of what looked like solid cherry wood. The tables' legs gleamed like polished brass. The chairs were made of cherry and the seats were covered with a paisley print of emerald green, cream and navy blue. In the center of each table was a small bouquet of magnolias arranged in a brass pot. The kitchen area looked functional and immaculate. Aubrey explained that a consultant had helped them organize the kitchen and the floor plan.

Thelma looked sheepish. "It doesn't always look like this. We wanted to impress you, so we arranged the flowers and dusted the place. I'm glad you like it."

Elizabeth shook her head. "I am absolutely blown away by you. I can't believe that this is happening."

Thelma's eyes misted. "I'm so glad. You don't know how I had hoped you'd like it. We knew this was in God's will, but I had begun to think that we'd acted out of our own desires and not the will of God when He didn't put everything together for us at once. I now know why." Aubrey hugged his wife.

Gabrielle walked over to Thelma and gave her a gentle hug. "Listen, we should be the ones thanking you. If you weren't willing to give us this opportunity, I don't know what we would've done."

Elizabeth's mind was calculating and planning. The fact that she was about to step out on a financial limb was absolutely overwhelming. They wouldn't have to go into debt to operate their business if they managed their budget wisely, but it was still a large endeavor. Elizabeth turned to Aubrey, "Would you mind talking to us more about this tomorrow to finalize some plans and discuss any legal issues that might arise? Could we meet at your house tomorrow evening? We have a lot of things to discuss so name the time and we can be there."

Aubrey ushered the three women out of the bakery. "Same time tomorrow is fine with us."

By the time Friday arrived, Gabrielle and Elizabeth were exhausted and elated with the developments of their business. They had made plans and talked until they thought they couldn't find one more thing to discuss or to plan. Both Aubrey and Thelma turned out to be adept businesspersons. Their ingenuity and creativity were second to none.

Discovering Elizabeth

Elizabeth and Gabrielle were thankful that God had paired them up with a couple who had retail experience and who were very wise in the ways of business and finance. Aubrey and Thelma's lawyer explained to Gabrielle and Elizabeth that all four of their names would be on the deed to the property. Should the original owners decease or become unable to care for themselves then Elizabeth and Gabrielle would become the sole proprietors of the building and businesses. An agreement was made that if the building were ever sold, all moneys made from the transaction would be donated to the church. The lawyer was confused when he was told that there was no purchase price.

Elizabeth and Gabrielle had kept their promise not to tell anyone of the arrangement. Elizabeth had spoken to her partners about the fact that she would need to give a month's notice to Wright and Wingold. Things were transpiring so quickly that Elizabeth felt as if she were being catapulted into each day. Elizabeth had entrusted Aubrey and Thelma with the fact that she was interested in someone with whom she worked, but couldn't date him with a good conscience until their professional relationship was severed.

Gabrielle helped Elizabeth draft her resignation letter. Both were nervous about the last act of cutting Elizabeth's ties to work. Gabrielle read the final copy then asked her friend, "Are you sure you want to do this? I'm getting apprehensive, Liz. If you think I've pushed you into something you're not sure you want to do, I need to know. I mean-I know you're actually investing more than I am. You're about to give up your career and your life savings. I never want you to look back and think I was pushing you into it. Is this what you want?"

Elizabeth was surprised by Gabrielle's concerns. "Gab, I'm a big girl. I'd be lying if I said this doesn't scare me a little. My sensible self is telling me to run away from this and to do it quickly but I like the idea of being in a business with you. Not only do I think I'll like it, but this is my chance to be with Ray. It's also an excellent financial opportunity. Anything worth having does seem to require some risk." Elizabeth's eyes widened as she realized she hadn't spoken to Ray all week. "Ray! Oh no!"

"What? What about him?"

"Oh, Gabby, I've been so busy with work and getting this store thing straightened out that I haven't gotten to talk with him or to get with Rebecca to see when I can talk to him. He left a message with Sophie on Tuesday for me to call him but I just plain forgot! There's no telling what he's thinking..."

"Why don't you call him?"

"I guess I could, but I don't think he wants us to contact each other outside of work anymore."

"Why not? You saw him last Saturday night."

Elizabeth sighed. "I know, I know, and that wasn't such a good idea you know."

"No, I do not know! We had fun didn't we? What could've been wrong with that? You saw each other in Florida."

"Gab, you don't understand. We were wrong. We were so caught up with each other in Florida that we just gave into it. Ray is a man of integrity. It may seem like a small thing to everyone else, but I understand that he's struggling with this simply because of his professional responsibilities. I can't ask him to do something with me that he'll regret later. We've broken the rules and I'll not be the cause of him breaking them again. It's tough, but that's the way it is." Elizabeth clasped her hands. "I don't know how I'm going to stay away from him, but I'm going to do it. I'm not going to call him at home. It'll have to wait until Monday."

Gabrielle whispered, "You're so strong, my friend. I'm proud of you."

Elizabeth began to cry. "No, I'm not. I don't want to do anything I just said to you. Will you please help me to keep from contacting him, please?" Elizabeth smiled weakly through her tears.

Gabrielle rubbed her temples. "Okay, whatever you say. I'm confused but I'll rip the telephone from the wall if that is what it takes, old pal. Now, where do you want to go to eat?"

Elizabeth mused, "I thought you were going out with Eric tonight?"

"I was, but I haven't had the time to call him either. I was supposed to call him back yesterday to tell him if I were going to go with him. I tried to call him today but he wasn't available. Rebecca said that he was out on business and wouldn't be back in until later. I've an idea. Why don't we call Rebecca and see if she wants to go with us?"

Discovering Elizabeth

Elizabeth stood up and stretched. "That sounds good to me. Why don't I give Sophie a call and make this thing a foursome." Elizabeth didn't wait for an answer as she picked up the telephone to call the two women. Both women were more than happy to fill their Friday evening with some "girl fun."

When they arrived at the restaurant, Gabrielle spotted Sophie who was already seated with Rebecca. More than one head turned to watch them as they sat down with their friends. Sophie looked up from her menu and greeted them. Elizabeth gasped when she looked at Sophie to say hello.

Sophie glanced down then made herself look into the eyes of her supervisor as she explained, "I went to the beauty shop after work and got the works. Do you like it?"

Elizabeth smiled with such genuine approval that Sophie sat up straighter in her seat. "You look absolutely stunning, Sophie. I'm flabbergasted, my dear. The change is drastic for sure but very, very nice."

"Thank you." Sophie smiled. Her newly cut and styled hair replaced what had looked like a hairdo resurrected from the 1930's. Sophie had added some make-up. Elizabeth would've said that Sophie was a plain looking woman, but not anymore. Now, she was absolutely striking.

Elizabeth teased her. "Wait until Joe sees you. He's going to have a fainting spell for sure."

After stuffing themselves with an entrée and desert, the four decided to go to the mall to comb through the clearance racks. By the time Elizabeth and Gabrielle returned home, they were exhausted but had had a lot of fun. The light mood of the evening ended once the messages on the answering machine were played. Eric had called and left a message asking why he had been stood up. Gabrielle placed her hands on her hips. "I didn't tell him that I would meet him; he assumed it! Men!"

Elizabeth moaned. "Don't worry about it, Gab. You can explain it to him later. You did what you could to call him today, so don't fret about it." Although Elizabeth sounded confident, she noticed that Gabrielle was deeply disturbed by the message from Eric. The fact that the man sounded perturbed didn't escape Elizabeth. Something bothered her about the fact that Eric seemed so possessive of Gabrielle when they had only known each other for a few days. Elizabeth knew that Gabrielle wouldn't listen to her concerns about it. He had called earlier in the week and left a message on the machine while Elizabeth and Gabrielle had been with Aubrey and Thelma. Gabrielle had never said so, but Elizabeth was sure that Eric had accused Gabrielle of being out with another man. She had heard Gabrielle's voice from behind her closed bedroom door as Gabrielle assured him that she'd been out with Elizabeth and that she was sorry she'd missed the call.

Gabrielle fidgeted with the telephone cord before deciding to shower and get ready for bed. "It's too late to call him now," she reasoned. "I'll try to call him in the morning first thing. I'm tired, Liz, I'll see you in the morning. Good night."

Elizabeth watched her deflated friend walk into the bathroom. "Oh, God," Elizabeth prayed, "watch over her and share your perfect will with her. I pray she listens." Elizabeth picked up the Bible from where she had been reading earlier and walked to her room. Elizabeth was sure that Gabrielle had already gotten into the shower when the telephone rang. Elizabeth picked up the receiver. "Hello."

"Elizabeth? Where is Gabrielle?" Eric's terse voice rang out.

"Hi, Eric. She's in the shower. How are you?"

"I'm fine, but I've been worried out of my mind. Do you know what happened to her tonight? She was supposed to meet me for dinner but she never arrived." Unfamiliar music played in the background as Eric spoke.

"I sort of know what happened. I heard your message when we came home. She apparently tried to call you today to confirm this evening but couldn't reach you. She had said that you had agreed that if you were going to go out tonight that you would touch base. When that didn't happen, we decided to go out to get a bite to eat. She hated it that she either misunderstood you or didn't reach you. Do you want me to have her call you when she gets out of the shower?"

Eric laughed. "She was disappointed, was she? I'm not at home, so no, she doesn't need to call me when she gets finished doing whatever."

Elizabeth noticed the slur in Eric's words as he pronounced his s's. "Sure she was disappointed. Are you okay?"

Discovering Elizabeth

Eric laughed once more. "I'm fine. I was just worried. Tell her I will call her some other time. You can tell her I'm a little disappointed too, but then again, she apparently knows how that feels."

Elizabeth was definitely worried. A feeling of foreboding came over Elizabeth as she began to pray fervently for her friend. "Oh, God, keep your hand on Gab and don't let her go for even a second."

Elizabeth waited for Gabrielle to finish showering. When her friend emerged from the steamy room, Elizabeth tried to explain the conversation she had just had with Eric and share her fears with Gabrielle. Gabrielle wouldn't listen. She made excuses for Eric then went to bed without saying another word.

Lisa D. Piper

Chapter SEVENTEEN

"Psalms 5:12 For thou, Lord, wilt bless the righteous: with favour wilt thou compass him as with a shield."

Elizabeth felt dread as she walked into the office the following Monday morning. The sealed letter she had prepared for Ray had been carefully placed in the side pocket of her briefcase. She avoided going in his office for about ten minutes before she decided that she couldn't take the suspense any longer. Elizabeth grabbed the letter and headed for the elevator. Rebecca was busy filing some forms when Elizabeth entered the office and asked, "Rebecca, is Ray in?"

Rebecca smiled a welcoming smile to her friend. "No, he isn't. Eric is covering for him today. He won't be back until Thursday." As if on cue, Eric walked into the office.

"May I help you, Elizabeth?" Elizabeth feared that her imagination had run away with her as she looked at the man. He looked like his normal friendly self. There was no way that he could be the man who had been rude and condescending to her on the telephone only a few of days earlier. Eric placed his hands in his pockets and waited for Elizabeth's response.

Elizabeth decided that she would need to turn the letter in to Eric. "Yes, you may. I need to speak with you about something." Elizabeth followed Eric to his office without explaining what she wanted until they had reached their destination. Elizabeth hadn't been in Fred's old office since Eric's arrival. As she turned around to observe the changes, Eric smiled.

Lisa D. Piper

"It looks different, doesn't it? I'm a man of different tastes than my predecessor, as you can clearly see." As Eric walked around his desk, he motioned for Elizabeth to sit down.

"Yes, your taste is drastically different than Fred's. That's a compliment, I might add. This office is lovely and has a very comfortable feel to it. It was kind of cold and starchy in here before." Fred had been a no-nonsense kind of man who had no concept of personalization. Elizabeth was genuinely impressed as she commented, "I take it that you're interested in art?"

"Yes, I am, but not just any art. This painter is called the "Painter of Light." I began collecting his work a couple of years ago and I'm just plain addicted to it now. Do you see how he uses light to make the work come alive? Let me show you what happens when I dim the lights." Eric reached over and turned the lights down.

Elizabeth inhaled quickly. "That lighthouse looks like it's literally lit up, and that old building looks like someone just turned the lights on inside! Eric, this is so pretty."

Eric smiled then turned the lights back to the normal setting. "Thank you very much. I must say that your taste is impeccable." He smiled.

They both laughed at his humor. Elizabeth paused then placed the letter on the desk in front of him. As he read the letter, a crease formed on his forehead. Eric looked up. "You are resigning? Elizabeth, Ray isn't going to like this." Elizabeth looked up in surprise at Eric's response.

Eric apologized. "I'm sorry, Elizabeth. I shouldn't have said that. Ray has told me his thoughts about keeping your relationship out of the business. I don't understand it, but I don't run any life but my own. Are you sure you want to do resign? You know, according to our policy, you cannot rescind your resignation once I accept it, right?"

Elizabeth shook her head. "I know. I really wanted to see Ray and tell him myself. I guess I should've brought this to you in the first place, since you're my immediate supervisor. I hope that a month's notice is acceptable. I'm going to personnel later today to find out how to withdraw my retirement savings."

Eric stamped the date on the letter then folded it. "Okay. I wish you the best, Elizabeth. I hate to lose you."

Discovering Elizabeth

She stood to her feet. "Thank you, Eric. I appreciate that."

Elizabeth felt as if she were walking ten feet above the ground as she walked back to her office. She had thought she would be depressed after turning in the notice but she was not. With only a month left of employment, she dove into her work. She wouldn't have anyone say that she had left the office in disarray. Sophie was disappointed with Elizabeth's decision to leave but didn't try what would be a futile attempt to talk her out of it. Elizabeth could tell that Sophie was upset, but didn't know how to comfort her. Sophie had been working with Elizabeth for only a few weeks, but Elizabeth knew that Sophie could hold her own when it came to the demands of the accounting department.

Elizabeth had just finished a purchase order when the telephone rang. Ray's voice sounded from the receiver. "What are you doing, Liz?"

Elizabeth was startled by his tone. "I'm looking at a purchase order."

"You know what I mean. I just talked with Eric and he says that you have turned in your letter of resignation. I would've thought that you would have talked with me about this before going through with it. When you didn't call me back last week I thought something was wrong, but not this!"

"Ray, I just got preoccupied with some things. I wasn't purposely avoiding you last week. I'm sorry for the way that I had to resign; but, then again, Eric is my direct supervisor. I wanted to give a month's notice, but could only do that if I gave the notice today. I have some vacation time left, so I want to take Thursday and Friday off. I'm working hard to make sure everything here is finished before I leave."

Ray lowered his voice. "Liz, I hope I didn't do anything to offend you. I know I should've kept my word to you about keeping things platonic between us and there's no excuse for my behavior."

Elizabeth wanted to cry. "Ray, are you saying that you're sorry that we became involved? Is that it? You haven't offended me until now. I haven't wanted to do the honorable thing and abide by the company policy, but have gone along with it for you and for my own conscience sake. Are you now telling me that you're sorry that you don't want to see me?" Elizabeth became angry.

Lisa D. Piper

Ray sighed, "No, I'm not. How could you think that, Liz? I do wish we'd met with different circumstances; I can't deny that. I've never wanted to break a rule so much in my life. I actually did break the rule, I guess. Oh, never mind that...I just thought we would talk about it as a couple before one of us turned in our notice."

Elizabeth spoke softly. "Ray, we're not a couple right now and can't be. You're probably right in thinking that I should've discussed it with you; but, at this moment, I do not owe that to you. I am sorry if it hurts you to hear this, but I've got to be straight with you. You've done what you thought was necessary for your career and for those things that you are responsible. I've prayed about it and I'm making a career decision. I can tell you that the thought of resigning might not have been so appealing if I didn't have motives where you are concerned. However, this is a move that I would've considered anyway. I can't tell you about it right now, but I'll tell you when I can."

Ray wanted to demand to know what Elizabeth was doing, He knew, however, that she spoke the truth in that he had no right to demand anything of her. "Okay, Liz. Do what you need to do and I'll try to not interfere. I ask you for one thing."

Ray could tell that Elizabeth smiled as she said, "Okay, what?"

Ray leaned into the telephone and said, "I want to see you in thirty-one days. I want to take you out on a formal date. Does the queen consent, or do I have to stoop to sending flowers every day until the end of my time of personal exile?"

Elizabeth blushed at the reference to her sand title. "The queen consents but holds you to the flower shower after the thirty days."

Ray wanted to call off the waiting period since she was leaving, but decided to do what he had said he would do. His life for the next month was sure to be tumultuous. He laughed within himself as he realized he wouldn't be able to stop thinking about the woman who had captured his heart.

Elizabeth's position was posted and resumes were solicited for the job. Gabrielle and Elizabeth spent all of their free time with Thelma and Aubrey. The plans for a quick opening took more time than expected. Vendors were chosen and distributors were contacted.

Discovering Elizabeth

Two weeks prior to Elizabeth's date of departure, she sat in the last scheduled department head meeting. Homer smiled at her with respect as he shook her hand for the last time as a Wright and Wingold employee. Elizabeth and Ray were careful not to look at each other squarely in the eyes for fear that the others would guess that they were counting down the minutes until they could be a real couple. When Ray saw her in the hallway, he would smile then dart away quickly. Elizabeth would grin at his apparent attempt to avoid her while her heart somersaulted at the thought of being with him without the constraints of work.

The thirty days passed swiftly and a surprise going-away party was given to Wright and Wingold's favorite accountant. Rumors about who would take Elizabeth's place seemed to be a hot topic of the party conversation. Ray attended the event but didn't approach Elizabeth except to present her with a plaque that had been signed by all of the department heads. As Elizabeth walked out of the building for the last time, her stomach somersaulted while her lips prayed, "Dear Lord, lead the way because I have no idea what I'm doing."

Night after night, Elizabeth had gone to bed with a throbbing headache. The thirty days following her resignation were filled with activity. Only at night did her mind become overwhelmed with thoughts of Ray. Some of the thoughts were fearful.

Elizabeth's first day of not working at Wright and Wingold was spent at the new building. There were more preparations to be made than she would have ever guessed. Although her tasks kept her mind from being idle, she couldn't help but wonder if Ray would remember his promise. She decided to leave early just in case he didn't forget.

She smiled as she pulled into her driveway. A van was pulling out of the driveway as she drove into it. Elizabeth lifted her hand to cover her mouth as she looked at the front of her home. To her delight, a bouquet of red roses was waiting for her on the doorstep. Elizabeth ran to the vase and plucked the card from the plastic holder and read,

"I'm finished waiting, period. I'll be here at six sharp. I will be in a black suit, please dress accordingly. Yours, Ray."

Elizabeth hugged the card to her as she lifted the vase to inhale the fragrance of thirty red roses. As she breathed in the fragrant scent, Elizabeth felt the sensation of excitement. After placing the flowers in her room, she sifted through her closet to search for an appropriate outfit.

Elizabeth didn't know Gabrielle had walked into the room until she exclaimed, "What are you doing?"

Elizabeth was startled. "You scared me, Gab! I'm hunting for an evening dress. I need a good one!"

"A dress? You aren't going to help move furniture in a dress are you?" Gabrielle looked from the closet to the table where a bundle of roses drew her attention.

"I'm no longer planning to move furniture tonight. I'm wearing a dress, if I can find one."

"Are you going out on a date with…what's his name?" Gabrielle teased.

"Yes, I am. I don't have a choice. Read the card!" Elizabeth continued to look through her closet as Gabrielle sniffed her flowers.

Gabrielle suggested, "Why don't you wear the midnight blue one? It matches your eyes."

Elizabeth clapped her hands together. "That's it! But, where is it?"

Gabrielle glanced up then down. "I used it for a dinner party. I have it. It's clean; I just never gave it back."

Elizabeth followed Gabrielle to her closet to retrieve her favorite dress.

Gabrielle curled, styled and coaxed Elizabeth's hair into a masterpiece. Soft, curly tresses framed her face. Gabrielle, a make-up expert, worked to create a flawless finish and succeeded. When Gabrielle stood back to look at her own handiwork, she was more than satisfied. "Look in the mirror, Liz. You are quite the catch! Ray Morgan won't know what hit him!"

Elizabeth looked at herself for longer than necessary. "Gab, I'm not sure what you've done or how you did it, but I love it!" Elizabeth hugged her friend.

Gabrielle commanded, "Don't cry! The mascara won't take it and you will ruin the effect. You just go out there and win that man. He's the one, Liz; I just know it!"

Discovering Elizabeth

"You're right, Gab. He's the one." As Elizabeth finished thanking her friend, she could hear the familiar sound of tires in their driveway. Elizabeth's stomach clenched as her teeth chattered involuntarily. "Oh no! He's here, Gabby. I just can't do it. I can't do it! I'm a mess inside."

Gabrielle giggled. "You're a mess; Yes, you are. You'll be fine, but, whatever you do, don't order pasta tonight!"

Elizabeth gasped. "You're right! What am I going to do! I don't want to go out to eat. I don't..." The dreaded knock on the door sounded.

Gabrielle clicked her tongue and said, "I'm letting him in if you don't. Get out there and greet the man. You'll be fine; just act normal. I spent a lot of time creating the new you tonight. You aren't staying home, and that's final!"

With trembling hands, Elizabeth turned the doorknob. A slow, dreamy smile formed on her lips as she took in the picture of her date, who looked more handsome than a groom on his wedding day. Elizabeth had no idea that while Gabrielle was prepping her for the evening, Eric had given Ray the biggest pep talk ever and helped him arrange the evening. Elizabeth spoke softly as she looked into rich hazel eyes. "Hello, Mr. Morgan."

"Hello, Ms. Pennington. You are absolutely breathtaking and I'm so blessed to have you by my side." Ray bowed to his date and kissed the palm of her hand. "Please get a wrap or whatever you will need to stay warm. He looked up to find Gabrielle peeking around the corner at the couple. "Hello, Gabrielle. Please don't wait up for this lovely lady. I'll have her home to you no later than is necessary."

Gabrielle consented and smiled at her friend. "Okay." Gabrielle then looked at Elizabeth and chided her, "I expect you to be on your best behavior or I'll be calling Pastor Matthews and tattling on you."

Ray offered his arm to Elizabeth as he said, "I've heard about that preacher. I shall do my best to be the gentleman I know I can be if I try hard enough. Now, Ms. Pennington, will you do me the greatest pleasure of allowing me to escort you to my stage coach?"

Elizabeth took his offered arm then waved to her friend. As the couple made their way to the parked car, She felt all of the tension that had plagued her leave. Ray opened the door for her and as she bent to get into the passenger seat Ray whispered, "You look absolutely perfect for this night." Elizabeth blushed.

As Ray drove through the downtown district, Elizabeth decided to inquire about where they were going. Ray grinned with the boyish grin that made Elizabeth want to hug him. "Liz, I'm taking you out to eat; don't worry. I have everything planned."

Within a few minutes Elizabeth and Ray pulled into a restaurant known for its exotic delicacies and impeccable service. He had apparently made reservations, as the couple didn't have to wait but was directed to a secluded table in a corner. Their table was slightly different from the others. A vase of deep red roses had been placed in the middle of the table. Two long gold taper candles burned, casting a romantic glow around the centerpiece. Elizabeth felt all eyes on her as she was seated. More than one diner had wondered who would eventually sit at the special table.

Ray seated himself beside Elizabeth then winked at her. She couldn't believe it, but he actually looked a little embarrassed by all of the attention. "Thank you, Ray. I don't know what to say."

The waiter approached the table. Elizabeth was surprised that he carried the first course of the evening.

Ray whispered, "I didn't want to waste a minute. I ordered for us tonight after conferring with Gabrielle. I have so much to put in this one evening that I've tried to remove all unnecessary things, such as ordering. I hope this is okay."

Elizabeth fell in love with Ray all over again. "Ray, I can't believe the time you must have spent preparing for this time with me." Elizabeth smiled then added, "Unless you've ordered something with green peppers or turnips, I'll eat it."

Ray grimaced. "Oh no! The stuffed green peppers and turnips looked too good to pass up. What's a guy to do?"

Elizabeth took his hand. "The guy is to get some taste buds and learn the difference between what tastes good and what's only good for furry little animals."

Discovering Elizabeth

Ray laughed. "Okay, okay, I didn't do that. How does artichoke salad with blue cheese dressing sound, followed by a piece of grilled chicken smothered in Monterey Jack and mushrooms?"

Elizabeth adjusted the napkin she had placed in her lap. "I think I take back what I said about you and your taste buds. If nothing else proves it, your ordering capabilities prove that you are the man for me."

Elizabeth thought she would melt into her shoes when Ray picked up her hand to press his lips to her soft palm. "Yes I am, Liz, and there is no one for me but you."

The elegant couple ate their meal in silence. A violinist approached the table and played a flowing melody as Ray watched his date try to keep her emotions in tact. After the last song, He escorted Elizabeth back to the place where the valet had just returned his car. Elizabeth knew that they were going somewhere other than home, but had no idea of the exact destination.

As he drove, Elizabeth became suspicious. She wasn't disappointed when Ray drove to the spot where they had kept one another company in the moonlight not so long ago. To Elizabeth's amazement and delight, a gazebo had been erected in the spot where they had parked. Ray escorted her to the gazebo where a dozen more deep red roses were waiting for her. The sound of rushing water soothed her soul.

Ray became nervous as Elizabeth surveyed his work. "Is this okay?"

Elizabeth looked at him. "Gabrielle told me that I can't cry, but I can't help it. I can't believe you did this."

"Don't cry, sweetheart; I don't think I can take it. Please sit down. I have something I want to discuss with you."

As she gently dabbed her eyes with the tissue Ray offered to her, she did as she was told, while Ray motioned for her to take the only chair that had been placed in the gazebo. He knelt down on one knee and took her hand. Elizabeth's mind raced as she listened to what he said.

"Liz, I'm a man whose faith is in the Lord Jesus Christ. Because of this, there are some things you need to know. I want you to be my wife, but will not ask you to do so until you know what to expect..." Elizabeth remained silent as she listened. "I've always said I would never marry, but God knew my heart. He always knows what I need and that's why He sent you. Elizabeth, the house we would have would be a Godly one. I would expect us to serve God as one. I want to be a Biblical husband and I want a Biblical wife. The Bible says that I would have to love and cherish you as myself and I'm willing and want to do that. I would expect you to love me, to pray for me, and to raise any children we might have in a Godly manner. Although you would be free to work as you please, I have no qualms with being the provider for our family. I would take my responsibility as the head of the household seriously. I would never leave you nor forsake you. I would expect the same faithfulness from you. Also, I promise to be honest with you and never forget that you are a gift from God. I want you by my side. I promise to cherish you, Liz." Ray paused long enough to retrieve a tattered velvety blue box from his pocket. As he placed the box in her hand, he asked the woman he loved, "Elizabeth Anne Pennington, would you consider becoming Elizabeth Anne Morgan?"

Elizabeth began to tremble. She looked down at the man whom she wanted to marry while Ray requested, "Please open the box before you answer. Liz, this was my mother's and I want you to have it as a token of my promise to you and my commitment to our love."

She carefully lifted the lid to the little box. The moonlight danced off of the jewel while Elizabeth's hands shook. She stared at the polished ring.

Ray couldn't tell if she liked it or not. "As I said, it was my mother's ring. It isn't new, but it would mean more to me than you would know if you would wear it. No one else has worn it since the day she took it from her finger and asked Annie to keep it for me."

Elizabeth whispered. "I'm afraid to touch it. It's exquisite." Ray took the ring from its cushion as Elizabeth watched his large hands work so diligently to place the ring on her finger. Elizabeth looked into Ray's eyes. "Ray, I would be honored to marry you. I understand and desire for you to be all of those things you said about a husband. I also agree to what you said about a faithful wife. I want you, Ray Morgan."

The sound of the tide lapping the shore accentuated every other sound. Ray held out his arms for his fiancé as he rejoiced. "Thank you, Sweetheart! You've just made me the most blessed man alive. I love you."

Discovering Elizabeth

Elizabeth held onto the man that she loved until the cool wind became unbearable. Neither wanted the night to end, but it inevitably did.

Winter came quickly and found the CEO of Wright and Wingold married to the Co-Owner of the newest Christian Gift Shop and Bookstore. Homer Foster gave the bride away while Annie Mae played the organ. Gabrielle and Eric were more than happy to stand up with their friends and to walk down the aisle side by side.

After the services, Homer and Annie Mae met the new bride and groom before the reception began. Annie Mae tried to hold back all of the emotions she was feeling as she relayed a very old message. "Ray, I have something for you, Sweetheart. Annie winked at Elizabeth. "I have something for you too, Dear."

As Annie Mae produced two yellowed envelopes, Ray's curiosity caught in his throat. At the sight of his mother's penmanship he asked, "What is this?"

Annie wiped away a tear. "Before your mother died, she wrote two letters. I was given instructions that they were to be presented to you on your wedding day. One letter is for you and one of is for Elizabeth." Annie held out the envelopes to the couple.

Ray hugged his wife to him as he read the words of his beloved mother.

> Dearest Son,
>
> How I wish I could be with you my darling. I have prayed fervently that you will marry the Christian woman God has designed for you. Be good to her Son, and pray over her daily. She is a gift from God. Since your birth, I've asked the Lord to keep a watch over your wife and to protect her from every harm. I have prayed for a faithful wife and am assured that she will be.
>
> I am so sorry that I have missed out on the important things of your adulthood. As I lay here in the hospital with thoughts of what I will miss, I rejoice in the fact that I have such a wonderful son who will, I know, make this world a better place. I cherish you my son and am so proud of you.

Lisa D. Piper

I assume that you've gotten my ring from Annie Mae. I am so glad. You know, my own mother wore that ring and when I didn't have a ring for my wedding, my father gave it to me. Be blessed my son. Never doubt that I love you, my sweetheart. God be with you and keep you.

−Your proud and blessed mother.

Elizabeth's hands trembled as she opened her letter to read:

My Sweet Daughter,

You have gained a treasure in my son. As I lay here on my deathbed, I can't think of another way to influence my son's life better than to speak to the woman who will spend her life beside of him.

How I wish I could place my arms around you and hug you. I have prayed for you often and know that you are a Godly woman. My son will be kind to you and I think he will make a wonderful husband. Remember my dear, that your marriage is a gift and never take it for granted. My own mama used to say that the secret to a successful marriage has to be prayer and I believe it.

If he gets on your nerves, pray. If you think he doesn't love you any longer, pray. I'm not speaking out of experience as much as I am of regret. Without a doubt, God placed you two together and there he will keep you.

Tell my grandchildren that their Granny loves them.

One last thing, Annie has a quilt for you that was handmade by my mother. My intent was to present it to my daughter-in-law myself, but all I can do now is pray that you will enjoy it. Please do that, Love. God bless you -Mother

Discovering Elizabeth

Lisa D. Piper resides in Kentucky with her husband of nineteen years, two children and a toy poodle. She has a heart for family, women's ministries, and enjoys sharing the gospel of Jesus through sharing the Word, through music and through creative story telling.

Lisa traveled with the trio, NewGrace, for over fourteen years. Her current focus is her family, church ministry and writing. Lisa accepts a limited number of speaking engagements for women's meetings and events. Send inquiries to the contact information listed on the following website:

For ministry information contact:

www.praisehimpublishing.com

Rescuing Gabrielle

(The Sequel to *Discovering Elizabeth*)

Rescuing Gabrielle is scheduled for release in 2007. When the mysterious partner of Wright and Wingold is forced to come out of hiding, Gabrielle faces the possibility that the secret she protects with her life may ruin her friendships and business.

Promoting Sophie

(The Sequel to *Rescuing Gabrielle*)

Promoting Sophie is scheduled for release in the fall of 2007. Sophie is living the American Dream as one of the most sought after executives in the nation. The introverted woman transforms into a woman of fortune, fame and passion. This final book in the Wright & Wingold series reveals the devastating past and the exciting future of Sophie McKlaun.

PraiseHim Publishing
PO Box 853
Nortonville, KY 42442
www.praisehimpublishing.com